ten y

"You know you're staring, right?"

I didn't, actually.

Thank God for sisters.

I leaned in to whisper back. "If I stare hard enough, do you think she'll disappear?"

Janie snorted as she picked at a piece of pepperoni. It was pizza night, and all six Briggs siblings sat around the table.

Six Briggs siblings.

And then one Juniper St. James.

"She's not going anywhere, Julian."

To all the night owls and midnight lovers who chase their dreams when the sun goes down.

This is mine.

CHAPTER ONE

THE WOMAN IN FRONT of me at my bustling neighborhood cafe made at least six modifications to her vanilla latte.

Six.

I'd thought she was done after four, but then she reared up from looking at her phone, almost swiping me with that larger-than-life bow on top of her head, and tweaked her order twice more. I couldn't actually hear what she was saying, but for every addition, she put a finger up, counting them so she wouldn't accidentally leave one out. Or two, apparently.

After the woman paid an ungodly amount for a cup of coffee—if it could even be called that—she swung her heart-shaped purse over her shoulder and cheerily thanked the barista. As she walked to the end of the counter in a whirlwind of bouncy fabrics, an entire goddamn bouquet of floral scents overtook the lingering smell of coffee beans in the air.

Fleetingly, it reminded me of childhood summers on the Cape.

It also reminded me of—no, that couldn't be.

"Sir?"

"Sorry," I rasped, stepping up to order my coffee. My plain, black coffee.

Coffee was one of those things in life that was supposed to be simplistic. I liked my coffee black, my beer cold, and my whiskey neat. Beyond that? It could be from the bottom of the barrel, and I wouldn't give a damn. Life ain't cheap, and after putting myself through years of law school, I'd learned that a hit of caffeine or a shot of booze did the same trick, no matter the quality.

My drink was ready when I reached the other end of the counter. But when I went to grab it, manicured fingers simultaneously wrapped around the cup.

"Oh!"

The woman, still armed with her heart-shaped purse, jumped back like the thought of touching a stranger disgusted her, and I took advantage of that by sweeping my coffee from her claws. Despite her initial surprise, she didn't give up easily.

"I think—I think that might—"

One of her peachy fingernails began tapping my coffee cup. I might have paid attention to what she was pointing at if I weren't distracted by how familiar her voice sounded.

I followed that fingertip to her hand and the delicate dangling bracelets on her wrist before finally locking my eyes on her face.

I was wrong. It *could* be her.

It *was* her.

Just my luck.

"Trying to steal my drink, Daisy?" I rocked back on my heels and watched with satisfaction as her eyes snapped up, too. And instantly, all that stumbling innocence drained from her voice.

"Julian?" Her nose scrunched as she processed whose coffee she was trying to steal. "You're not supposed to be here."

I raised a brow. She was so shocked she hadn't even argued about being called Daisy. And now we were both shocked.

"You're right. I'm *supposed* to be on my way to my first day of work. But I had to wait while you created a whole new drink with your order."

If there was one constant in my life, it was that Juniper St. James would always be the pain in my ass. The thorn in my side.

The gatecrasher of every childhood birthday party I ever had. The person holding up the line at the coffee shop.

She was only one year younger than me but somehow always seemed to be one step ahead of me. All the damn time. And God, wasn't that annoying.

"A drink which you are withholding from me." She pointed again to the cup in my hands.

I didn't give it up. "This is mine," I said flatly.

"Move your thumb," she said, mimicking my tone.

With a sigh, I slid my thumb down an inch to reveal—*shit.*

I'd seen the *Ju* on the cup and assumed—wrongly— that it was the beginning of a hastily scribbled *Julian*.

Juniper snatched the cup out of my hand, and I conceded.

"That's probably going to give you gut rot," I grumbled. "In fact, I hope it does."

"Oh, Julian." Her glossy lips spread wide with a smug grin. "Don't be one of those pretentious black-coffee drinkers. It isn't a cute look."

"Neither is you holding up the coffee line."

Juniper pursed her lips as she assessed me, and she did such a thorough job that I annoyingly felt a bit of heat on the back of my neck.

"You might be wearing a suit, Julian, but you haven't changed. Have you?"

Princess Peach here had always loved to imply things about me, and this time, it was that I was unpolished. That beneath my spotless dress slacks, I was unprofessional. Not that she'd ever gotten into my pants. Never would, either. Juniper thought I was better suited for getting rough on the football field or sliding beneath a car in a mechanic shop than in the Financial District in Boston.

But did I give a damn what Juniper St. James thought she knew about me? Absolutely fuckin' not.

I returned her look, dropping a slow perusal over her black

dress, which was cinched with a perfect bow around her waist. All perfect, pretty, and over-the-top, as usual.

"Seems like you haven't changed, either," I drawled.

Infuriatingly, Juniper only shrugged before bouncing away. I watched her with a scowl until a yelp directed my attention to my right, where a woman spilled her fresh cup of coffee across the tiled floor.

Wasted black coffee.

I spotted my cup—my actual cup—and handed it over to her. "Here, have mine."

The cafe likely would have replaced her drink, but I was going to need something a lot stronger than coffee to recover from running into Juniper St. James when I least expected to.

ACQUIRING MY NEW POSITION AS AN ASSOCIATE ATTORNEY AT GARDNER Law was admittedly easy, and that was only because of one thing. Well, person.

Cameron Bryant was one year ahead of me in law school. He'd had an in at Gardner Law through his advisor and landed a job by the time he woke up hungover after graduation. I remembered thinking he was a lucky little shit because everyone knew that the legal job market was a total wash at the moment, but now here I was. *Also* a lucky little shit. Neither of us expected to find jobs just a few minutes from where we'd studied our asses off for three years, but here we were.

The world of practicing law was entirely different from the world of practicing touchdown passes. Playing Division I football as an undergrad and being captain taught me that success hinged on perseverance, grit, and sweat. And while all of that had been important in law school, connections were the name of the game in this world. Work ethic only took you so far, and the people you knew took you the rest of the way.

So I supposed you could say I owed Cameron Bryant a round of drinks. Or two.

All the shits I gave about running into a certain brunette in my new neighborhood vanished as I refocused. My sister told me that Juniper had moved to Boston after she finished law school in New York, so it made sense to find her in the Financial District on a Monday morning; practicing law in the city had always been her goal. And *she* never hit any roadblocks. *She* hadn't needed to take a year off before law school to help back home. *She* didn't have five sisters to worry about putting through college.

Of course Juniper would be here.

And so what if we were living in the same city again?

I'd survived it before, and I'd survive it again.

Gardner Law was housed in Dewey Square, and though I'd pick a landscape over a cityscape any day, there was a certain satisfaction in seeing the sun bounce off shiny windows on the high-rise as I walked into it. An overly enthusiastic man named Tyler met me at the front desk before walking me through a set of glass double doors and into a large space divided into smaller work areas. There was a set of doors on the far wall, and Tyler brought me to the furthest one. Which, as a pleasant surprise, had my name on it.

But it also had another name.

And that was a hell of a lot less pleasant to see.

I choked down a surge of temper before logic quickly did its work to reassure me. Because there was absolutely no way. No goddamn way.

"Cameron put you up to this, didn't he?" I forced a laugh, pointing to the names on the office door.

My name.

And *her* name.

Like I said...no goddamn way.

Tyler responded by blankly staring at me, his enthusiasm wavering. "Put me up to what?"

Something turned in my stomach.

And then, a familiar voice barged into my ears for the second time that day. Sharp and irritated but also haughty. Smug.

"Believe it or not, I'm not a practical joke."

There was absolutely no goddamn way. Never, not once in my twenty-seven years, had life played such a cruel joke on me. I turned on my heel to find myself at eye level with that larger-than-life bow again.

"I would prefer to not," I said dryly, wishing I hadn't given up my coffee. I needed something to wash the sudden bad taste down.

My eyes lowered to find Juniper cocking her head to the side. And then I couldn't help my attention from dropping even further as she rubbed her lips together, almost absently. When she finally relaxed her grimace, they were puffy and plump.

"What?"

"Believe it." I tried clearing my throat with very little success before forcing my eyes up to meet her gaze. "I'd prefer not to believe it."

I wasn't a huge fan of practical jokes, but I'd happily accept one right now if it meant I didn't have to work with the one person who'd perfected how to drive me up a wall.

Silence greeted my retort, but a tick in Juniper's jaw gave her away. I was impressed with how well she was holding her tongue in front of Tyler, but I knew. I knew what she was thinking.

Stuck at a stalemate, I crossed my arms over my chest. Tyler didn't appear to know what to do, so he clapped his hands together and flashed an uncomfortable smile. "Well, I'll leave you both to get settled in. Arlo from IT will visit shortly to set you up and ensure you have access to our systems."

Without another word, Tyler hurried back to his post in reception. Despite the awkwardness, I was sad to see him go. Because now that he was gone, I was left with—

"You're not supposed to be here," Juniper said, repeating the exact words she'd said at the cafe.

I ignored her—because yes, I was absolutely supposed to be

Don't Blame Me – Taylor Swift
Kill My Time – 5 Seconds of Summer
My Home – AWIN
Teenage Dream – Stephen Dawes
Moonlight – Chase Atlantic
Late Night Talking – Harry Styles
Best – Gracie Abrams
Daylight – Taylor Swift
Universe – Kelsea Ballerini
Jealous – Nick Jonas
Shameless – Camila Cabello
Your Needs, My Needs – Noah Kahan
Books of Fantasy – Mark Diamond
Wildflowers – Ed Sheeran

ALIVE AT Night

alive at night

WILDFLOWER SERIES
BOOK 1

AMELIE RHYS

Published by R. H. Publishing

Cover Design: Caitlin Russell

Character Art: Alie Reighard at alies_artwork

Editing: Sandra Dee at One Love Editing

This book is intended for an 18+ audience. For further content warnings, please check out:

www.amelierhys.com

here—and rounded the corner into my office, striding past Juniper. Which I assumed was *our* office. Seriously fuck that, though.

The small space was bright. Clean lines and high-end, modern furniture. The kind that looked like it would likely send me to the chiropractor after one week of sitting in it. A beautiful city view spread out before one of the desks, and I watched Juniper drop into the chair in front of it. She leaned back, propping both her heeled feet on the desk as if to make a point. But that point was lost on me as her dress rode up, revealing lots of bare skin. Too much.

Juniper immediately grabbed her dress to keep it from riding up further before sitting straight again. Feet on the floor. Elbow leaning on the desktop with fake nonchalance.

I shifted on my feet, clearing my throat. "That's my desk."

"No, it's—"

"Move your elbow."

She looked over her shoulder at the nameplate. And then swore beneath her breath before rounding on me.

"How are you even here right now?"

"I imagine the same way you are, Daisy. I went to law school. I graduated law school. I applied for a job. And then I—"

"Do *not* start with the names, Julian. People will get—"

"Just wanted to drop in to welcome our newest associate attorneys!" A woman with one of those classic corporate bobs strode confidently into the office, demanding our attention. "I know you're meeting with IT this morning, but let's connect later this afternoon after you visit HR so we can review other aspects of your onboarding."

"Excellent," I cut in smoothly before Juniper could open her big mouth. "Thank you so much, Daphne. I'm thrilled to be here."

"And we're thrilled to have you." Daphne, one of the firm's partners, gave a succinct nod that was genuine but final. She didn't have time to sit around all day and exchange niceties. It was nice enough that she even stopped to check in with us, but I wasn't surprised. One of the reasons I was so eager to work at Gardner was because Cameron assured me its smaller size meant that the firm had a flat culture with partners who involved themselves in the development of associate attorneys. So far, Daphne was proving him right.

Her gaze settled on Juni. "Juniper, thank you again for the coffee. I can't believe you remembered our conversation after your interview."

I narrowed my eyes on the cup in Daphne's hand.

A vanilla latte with six different modifications, huh?

I should have listened closer this morning in line. What were the chances that Juniper would spill the secrets of Daphne's drink order? Zero to none, probably. *Fuck it all.*

Daphne disappeared down the hallway, the echoing of her heels fading the further she got. Before I could turn to Juniper and call her out for being a goddamn suck-up, another face appeared in the office's doorway.

Our office.

Hated that, by the way.

I didn't mind sharing. In undergrad, I lived with five dudes, and several of them had live-in girlfriends who didn't pay rent but also didn't fucking leave. Hell, I grew up dividing shower time with my five sisters. Sharing wasn't a problem for me.

But sharing with Juniper St. James?

"There he is!"

"Hey, man." Stepping forward, I slapped my hand into Cameron's outstretched one. Finally, someone who wasn't going to say something that would irritate the shit out of me.

"I have a client meeting in a few, but I just wanted to pop by." Cameron flashed a grin as he moved from me to Juniper, and I stiffened. "Cameron Bryant," he introduced.

Juniper's hand slipped into his, and a heavy blush spread over her cheeks as Cam gave it a firm shake.

"Juni—Juniper St. James."

Was that a *stutter?* Juniper smiled. I frowned. And when she still hadn't dropped his hand, I cleared my throat. Really, what was this?

"Juniper St. James," Cam repeated, his eyes growing wide with laughter and flicking meaningfully to me. He'd heard my complaints about my sister's best friend on more than one occasion.

"Who's the client?" I asked Cameron through gritted teeth.

Finally releasing Juniper, Cam waved the question away. "I'll fill you in later. Celebratory first-day drinks after work?"

"I'm in."

Wouldn't mind a drink right now, actually.

"You should join, too, St. James!" Cameron called over his shoulder as he hurried away, adjusting his suit jacket as he fell in with another guy walking in the same direction.

I could kick Cam's ass for that. And here I'd thought I could count on him not to piss me off.

"You should definitely not join, *St. James*," I said, turning to glare at Juniper.

"At least St. James is one of my actual names," she huffed, walking to my appointed desk and collecting her things to move them to hers. I raised a brow, surprised that she was conceding that easily, but she continued before I could say anything. "And it would seem that we actually *didn't* get here the same way."

The frown I'd been wearing since the embarrassingly awkward Juni-Cameron exchange deepened. "What's that supposed to mean?"

"It means *I* got here by working my ass off and making a good impression. *You* got here because of your connection with Mr. Bryant."

I didn't take the bait. Networking was nothing to be ashamed of. And sure, maybe connecting with a law school bud wasn't exactly networking, but it got me a job. I wasn't pretentious enough to care about anything else. "You could have connections, too," I said. "You know, if you didn't try to bite the head off of everyone you talk to."

"I have plenty of connections," she sniffed as she began setting out little decor pieces on her desk.

Amused at her immediate switch-up, I leaned against my desk and watched her. "Oh, yeah?"

Juniper's brow arched as she busied herself, and I took that to mean yes.

"I don't think bribing people with gut-rot coffee counts," I added.

"It wasn't a bribe." She set a lamp down on the corner of her desk with unnecessary force. "It's called being *nice.* Because I do not, in fact, bite people's heads off when I talk to them."

A forbidden smile lingered on my lips. "If you're so *nice*, why have you never brought me coffee?"

She glanced at me over her shoulder, her brows drawing together. "Where *is* your coffee?"

A shrug. "I gave it to a woman who spilled hers."

"Oh."

"No comeback?"

Well, well. Today was just full of surprises, wasn't it? Hopefully, this was the last of them.

Juniper answered with a flick of her eyes, but that was all. The office fell quiet as Juniper continued to unpack. Since I didn't have anything other than the one framed picture of my family to set on my desk, Arlo helped me set up my laptop first when he swung by. Juniper didn't speak to me again until after he left, and I nearly choked on my own tongue when she did.

"So, where are we getting drinks after work?"

Dear God. She was serious, wasn't she? While there might have been a bit of familiar mischief dancing in her expression, there was also earnestness.

Ignoring her, I grabbed my phone and typed a short message to Cameron.

I hate you.

CHAPTER TWO

juniper

I'D ALWAYS HATED THE feeling of sweat. I hated the stickiness, the sensation of wet clothes clinging to an even wetter body. There wasn't anything more uncomfortable.

This meant that tanning sessions, any sort of exercise, and tropical vacations were typically things I happily passed on. Air-conditioning was a must-have, and I preferred a heavy winter storm to a heat wave any day. My dislike for sweat wasn't good for my weight or wallet, but sacrifices occasionally had to be made in life.

It was a mild fall day today; it wasn't very warm.

But my blood was running hot.

I'd take anything, *anything* over this. I would sprint across a tropical beach in the middle of a July heat wave if it meant I could snap my fingers and magically make Julian Briggs disappear from my office.

Our office.

I wrinkled my nose and resisted the urge to do a pit sniff.

I was stress-sweating. I had been for hours, but it had only gotten worse since I'd declared I would be joining for celebratory drinks after work. Was I interested in getting drinks with Julian and some law school bro of his? Hell no. Even if Cameron was easy on the eyes and made my legs feel a little bit like jelly when he'd flashed those dimples at me.

But I'd grown up with a terrible habit: committing to any and all things that were a surefire way to piss Julian Briggs off.

I glanced at my watch. Five o'clock.

Julian had already left, and the last thing I wanted was to be alone at the bar with him, allowing the opportunity to pick apart and replay everything I'd said today. But enough time had passed that Cameron's four o'clock meeting must be done. He'd likely be there by the time I packed my things and managed to find the Bellflower Bar.

I unplugged my laptop, stashing it in my bag next to that stupid envelope I'd found in my mailbox this morning, which reminded me that I needed to call Gemma ASAP. Firstly, to tell her that her irritating brother had ruined my first day of work, and secondly, to ask for her help in figuring out what to do about this damn wedding invitation.

After waving to Daphne on my way out the door, who flashed a friendly smile, I checked my phone for directions. Only a five-minute walk, which meant it wasn't worth pulling out my earbuds. Unfortunately, my audiobook would have to wait until after I made it through a round of drinks with Mr. Buzzkill.

The Bellflower Bar was charming. It was the type of place I would have picked myself—exposed brick walls with eclectic framed pictures, a modern flair with a nod to the classics, warm but not stuffy. A local pub that wasn't afraid to redecorate every now and again. And it was clearly well-loved, considering how busy it was for a Monday afternoon.

"St. James!"

Cameron's head popped up over the row of patrons lining the bar as he waved to get my attention. Hoisting my bag higher on my shoulder, I pushed through the suits and slacks until I reached an empty chair on the corner of the bar top. It wasn't until I was settled in my spot that I glanced up to see Julian staring at me, his light blue eyes nearly translucent, even in the darkened bar lighting.

Their entire family had eyes like that. Not to mention the auburn hair and fair skin with a slight dusting of freckles.

Somehow, Julian always managed to tan more than the rest of the family, and his face had an irritating golden glow to it. Damn him for looking like that when I was definitely bright red and brushing sweat off my brow. He'd shed his suit jacket, but beyond that, he didn't look even a bit flushed. His dress shirt was unbuttoned at the collar, and his exposed chest looked dusted by the sun. Not blasted with it, like I felt. *Ugh.*

"So nice of you to join us, Lily," he drawled before tipping his beer bottle back for a swig.

Cameron's brows drew together, so I interrupted his thoughts before he could ask.

"Ignore him." I cleared my throat. "He thinks it's cute to forget my name, even though it makes him seem incompetent."

I shot a glare at Julian. He took another pointed drink of his beer.

It was hard enough to be named after a freaking plant without having someone constantly remind me about it.

"*Cute* is not usually the vibe I'm after," Julian muttered.

"Oh?" I cocked a brow. "Then what precisely are you going for?"

"Precisely?" His beer bottle clinked loudly against the bar top as he set it down. "A certified pain in the ass that you just can't *help* but find endearing."

I snorted. "You had me until the end."

Julian's lips spread slowly, cockily, as though he didn't believe I thought he lacked any endearing qualities.

He sure as hell couldn't be more wrong about that.

"Come now, Willow. You know *exactly* the vibe. You've been practicing it for the last fifteen years or so. I'm just following your example."

"You always have been unoriginal." I rubbed my dry lips

together, wishing someone would swing by so I could order a drink. "Is this how you spend your free time, Julian? Jotting down plant names in a little journal you keep next to your bed so you're ready to antagonize me?"

"The things I keep next to my bed have nothing to do with you. Trust me." Julian's eyes met mine, a dare of sorts, and I felt more sweat tickle the back of my neck before he kept talking. "Besides, that would imply that I had some sort of intention of seeing you, which couldn't be further from the truth."

"Well." Cameron clapped his hands together, clearly wanting to interrupt us. "This is going to be fun, isn't it?"

Cameron and I had different definitions of the word *fun.*

I turned toward him while jerking a finger at Julian. "Did you know that when he saw my name outside our office, he actually asked Tyler if you'd put him up to it?"

Cameron threw his head back and laughed. "I can only imagine Tyler's reaction to that. Poor guy."

"Tyler's not the one we should be feeling bad for in this situation," Julian snapped.

He always did have a short temper.

"You're right," I interjected. "It's me, isn't it?"

My temper had never been much better.

Stuck between us, Cameron didn't seem to know what to do. Or say. His mouth opened and closed twice before he figured it out.

"I knew we were onboarding more than one new associate attorney, but I was gone last week, so I didn't catch all the details." He gave Julian an apologetic glance as though he was sorry for not warning him. About me. But he was also struggling not to keep a smile off his face, seemingly amused by our far-from-ideal situation and how his friend was suffering from it.

I resisted the urge to roll my eyes. Was I happy to see Julian Briggs on my first day as an attorney? Absolutely not. But at least *I* wasn't acting like a little drama king about it and guilt-tripping my friends.

I hated the phrase *drama queen.* It implied that women were more sensitive and driven by feelings than men, which couldn't be further from being true. Case in point: Julian Briggs.

I caught a bartender's attention while Julian asked Cameron about his recent trip—the reason he was out of office. Soon, an Aperol Spritz appeared in front of me, and I sipped on it while listening to Cameron's account of visiting his sister in California.

"Collins is mad at me."

Out of the corner of my eye, I saw Julian frown with concern. Genuine, actual concern.

"Why?"

Cameron shook his head with a laugh. "I said something about how they should move to the East Coast, and now Beau's throwing out house offers left and right."

Julian perked up. "They're actually coming?"

"No." Cameron's dimples appeared as he smiled into his drink. "But he wants to buy property so they can spend more time visiting."

"Damn, that's too bad. Would love to have them move here."

Julian's disappointment was evident. Maybe his range of emotions was broader than I thought.

The pieces slowly came together as they talked; Cameron's sister, Collins, and her husband, Beau, were Julian's friends from undergrad, which explained how Cameron and Julian connected in law school even though they weren't in the same year.

I leaned back, listening to them go on about all of Julian's hotshot friends from his early college days. A billionaire, a few pro football players, an upcoming singer-songwriter. Apparently, playing Division I football at a California university also meant collecting famous people as friends along the way. It was hard to wrap my head around, but then again, Julian was always that golden boy, the fan favorite at every school he went to. For some goddamn reason, he attracted people everywhere he went.

Meanwhile, I struggled even making one new friend as an adult. I'd had the same singular best friend since childhood.

"You remember meeting them, right?"

Julian directed the question at me, and I was so taken aback that he deliberately included me in the conversation that it took me a second to figure out what he was talking about.

"Who?"

"My friends from college. You must have met them when you and Gemma came to visit."

Oh yeah. *That.*

I'd blocked out most of the memories from that night in California. After Julian found me on the floor by the toilet at the end of it, there weren't any other options except to forget it ever happened. But if I skipped through my recollections to the earlier part of the evening, I *could* recall being introduced to a handful of nice couples and having a tipsy conversation with one of Julian's hot roommates.

"That was years ago," I said, deciding Julian didn't need to know that I understood exactly who, what, and where he was talking about. "Their names ring a bell, though."

"They're all great," Cameron said warmly. I could tell he was someone who always gave his undivided attention. And I couldn't help but melt a bit at being on the receiving end of it. "Honestly, I was concerned when Collins wanted to live across the country from my mom and me, but she made friends with the right people."

He said it so sincerely that I bit down on a teasing retort about Julian being considered one of *the right people* and smiled back at him. "It sure sounds like it. I'd love to meet her again sometime. Maybe when I'm sober enough to remember it."

Cameron laughed, his deep brown eyes twinkling. He ran a hand over his black, buzzed hair, smoothing an already perfect style, and it occurred to me that maybe *he* could solve all my problems. Well, not all of them. That was probably impossible. But at least the one involving needing a date to my sister's wedding. My only sister. The one I'd never met and felt the innate need to impress.

Cameron was *very* impressive.

"I don't blame you for being too drunk to remember," he said. "I've heard about the parties Julian used to throw."

He shot a look at the party-thrower himself, who I expected to smirk. But Julian had his eyes narrowed on me instead. He even went as far as to tip his head slightly to the side, studying me, and I resisted the urge to look down at my dress to make sure nothing had spilled on it.

Distracted by Julian's sudden stare-down, I jumped a little when Cameron pushed back from the bar and excused himself to go to the bathroom.

Great. Alone with Mr. Killjoy again.

Julian silently took another drink of his beer, holding the stem of the bottle with two fingers lazily. Finding my mouth suddenly dry, I also threw back some of my Spritz.

"For the love of God, don't go trying to get into Cameron's pants," he said abruptly after a few seconds of only the chatter from nearby drinkers to keep us company. He didn't bother looking at me, keeping his gaze on the bottles that lined the mirror behind the bar.

I took another sip of my drink to buy myself time on how to respond.

Finally, I decided, "Why not?"

That seemed to annoy Julian—which had definitely been the point. His jaw ticked twice before he took another drink and then pushed his empty bottle away. Blue eyes darted around, likely searching for a bartender before they came to rest on me again.

"I'm just saying..." He leaned back, slinging an arm over the back of Cameron's empty chair. "You've got double the competition. So good luck."

"Oh, so that's it," I said, catching his meaning. "You want him for yourself, then?"

The question was a little snarky on my lips, which always seemed to happen when Julian Briggs was involved. But it was genuine. I would immediately let go of my wedding date idea if it got between some friends-to-lovers destiny these two had going on.

"No." Julian shook his head. His answer was as genuine as my question. "I'm just protective of my friends like I'm protective of everyone in my life."

"Everyone in your life, huh? Does that include me?"

He looked away, eyes wandering again for the bartender—who was doing an awfully good job of serving everyone but us.

"Yes," he eventually admitted, gaze bouncing back to mine. His eyelids were heavy, tired. "By association, that unfortunately includes you."

Before I could utter a retort, Cameron slid back into his seat between us. And since I was still hoping to make a good impression on the handsome Mr. Bryant, I swallowed my sass.

"So, Cameron," I started, nervously wiping my sweaty hands on my dress beneath the bar top. "I know you went to law school in Boston with Julian. Where were you before that?"

"New York," Cameron answered with an easy grin. "That's where my mom lives."

"What part? I went to law school in New York City."

Behind Cameron, Julian drew his lips into a firm line before he finally pounced on an approaching bartender for another drink.

"I need another fucking drink," he muttered, interrupting Cameron's answer. "Anyone else?"

"I'd love one," I said, flashing him my brightest smile and hoping it masked my nervous sweat.

To no one's surprise, he did not smile back.

CHAPTER THREE

I CAUGHT A FLASH of pink out of the corner of my eye and spun in my desk chair to see Juniper pause in the doorway to our office. In one hand, she held her phone, staring at it while gripping a bright pink box in the other. I wasn't sure what the hell was so interesting on that phone of hers, but she sure as hell wasn't going to spare me a glance.

That was fine. It was honestly better if we didn't interact because that never seemed to lead to anything good. Never had. Never would.

Tipping my head back, I closed my eyes. I had a fucking headache. Probably from the overpowering cloud of floral perfume that I'd all but lived in since starting at Gardner. It seemed stronger than I remembered from when we were—

Heels clicked across the floor, drawing closer and cutting off my thoughts.

I was about to open my eyes when a weight settled on my lap. Slowly, tentatively.

Distractedly.

"What the *hell*, Daisy?"

I opened my eyes to find them covered by a sheet of brown, sweet-smelling hair. Juniper shrieked, startled as she tried to correct herself before sitting fully on my lap. But it was too late. With her hands full and her balance off-kilter, Juniper's ass landed squarely on my crotch. And hell, that was not what I needed this morning.

"Oh my God, I thought this was—" She broke off, sounding out of breath as she tried to push herself up. But she failed, careening to the side when her ankle wobbled in those goddamn high heels of her. She fell back onto me for a second time, and I had to grab the arms of my chair to keep myself in check.

She seemed like she needed a little nudge. And while I'd love to give it to her, touching Juniper was an awful idea.

"Whatever you thought was wrong," I groaned as she wiggled on top of me.

Goddamnit, I needed her ass to find a new place to sit, and I needed that now. Before things got even worse. For both of us.

I snatched the pink box from her before she dropped it, hoping an extra hand might also help her find her balance.

"I know you want this desk," I said, gritting my teeth in frustration. "But if you're trying to steal it from me, this is not the way to do it."

"I'm not trying to steal your desk," she huffed. Her hand landed on my thigh, the quick touch burning through my pants as she pushed off me. Once she was back on two feet, I breathed a sigh of relief. I saw Juniper do the same, except the burst of oxygen did nothing to tame the blush on her cheeks. "I just—I just wasn't paying attention, Julian."

"Clearly."

I crossed one leg over the other, and Juniper grabbed her box back out of my hands.

"What's that?" I asked.

She flicked the top of the box open and grabbed a plastic plate from her desk. Wordlessly, she began plucking donuts out of the box and arranging them on the platter. I watched her chest rise and fall with quicker-than-normal breaths as she ignored me and fussed with her donuts instead.

"I thought we've been over this, Rosie."

Juniper surveyed her donuts without responding. Satisfied that they hadn't been damaged in the process, her cheeks indented with a tiny smile before she licked some powder off her finger.

She made a little noise of satisfaction, and I shifted in my desk chair.

I cleared my throat. "You can't bribe your coworkers into liking you."

"It's called being nice," Juniper said, words clipped. Her smile faded as it landed on me. "We've already been over that, too."

I suppressed a sigh. God, she was a suck-up. For all her hollering about how she'd gotten here on hard work alone, she sure liked to do a lot of kissing ass and not a whole lot of anything else.

"You were so worried about your *nice* little donuts that you just sat on me, Lily."

"That was an accident," she sniffed, her attention shifting back to the donuts. "Cameron told me that the Happy Hole was his favorite."

"The Happy Hole?" I repeated, disbelieving that any self-respecting establishment would name themselves that.

"They sell *donuts*, Julian."

"I gathered that," I said dryly, glancing at the pile of donuts again.

To my increasing frustration, Juniper had been assigned to the same case Cameron was working on. And now she kept acting like they were friends or whatever.

They were not friends. And they definitely weren't *more* than friends. Cameron just had a sweet tooth.

"You bought two dozen donuts just because Cameron said he liked—" I scrunched my nose in distaste. "The Happy Hole? Don't you think you're coming on a little strong?"

That must have struck a nerve because Juniper made a whole show of ignoring the question. She tucked a wavy piece of hair into the elaborate pearl barrette on the side of her head before smoothing her skirt—black with small, white polka dots. As I watched her, I realized the dots were exactly the size of the pearls she wore as accessories.

Jesus Christ, Juniper.

I had a utilitarian outlook on clothes, which was one reason that I often missed the days of throwing on something comfortable to help my dad in the shop.

"I'm not coming on to him, Julian. Despite your continued belief that I have a one-track mind." She tutted. "I think that says more about you than me."

I pushed the barb aside because *I* wasn't going to be the naive one in this situation.

"Look," Juniper continued, "I know you're upset because they didn't put *you* on Cameron's case."

"I'm not upset," I countered. "We're not kids, Daisy. This isn't some competition."

She raised a brow at me. "Says the man who's calling me by my childhood nicknames."

With a grunt of annoyance, I swiveled back toward my desk. Unable to focus on the case notes I needed to read through, I stared at the cityscape instead. The sun was high; soon, I would be heading out for lunch with one of my visiting college buddies.

"Look, they only picked me because of the experience I have from my internship," Juniper said, her voice softening. Was she *pitying* me? "Cameron doesn't even have much background with the type of case we're working on. But I played a pretty big role in winning a malpractice suit against McKinley Medical," she added, suddenly sounding smug as all hell.

Yeah, never mind. There was no pity there. Not that I wanted it.

I sighed, inwardly realizing that beneath the attitude, she had a point. My internship experience consisted mainly of family law, one of Gardner's other specialty areas.

"Fine." I dragged a hand over my face. "Go deliver your donuts, then, if you feel like it will help win cases."

I didn't bother looking back at her. But I could tell she hadn't moved from her spot beside me. Mostly because her presence was like a weight on my shoulders. But it also had to do with her perfume giving me a headache. Or maybe that was the donuts.

Finally, I felt her shift.

"I was going to offer you one, but I think I've changed my mind," she said before picking up the pastries. Out of the corner of my eye, I saw her fly through the door—as fast as someone holding two dozen donuts could fly through a door, anyway.

Kicking myself beneath my desk, I refocused on my laptop. I had a lot of shit to read before lunch. Better get started.

I almost didn't see my former teammate Grayson when I walked into the Bellflower Bar. He'd camouflaged himself with a ball cap and sunglasses while lounging in a booth at the back. But when he tipped his head to thank the waitress for bringing over his drink—likely nonalcoholic; Grayson never drank when we lived together—I noticed that recognizable sharp jaw and five-o'clock shadow.

Sometimes I forgot he was fucking famous now.

While it'd been fun over the last six or so years to watch many of my college teammates go pro and start successful careers, it also stung. It was a bittersweet reminder of what I'd missed by moving home after graduation.

Grayson rose to his feet when he saw me, pulling off his shades before enveloping me in a gruff hug.

"You can keep the glasses on if you wanna lie low," I said with a crooked smile.

"Nah." He waved the idea away. "People don't usually come

up to me if I'm with someone else. It's when I'm sitting alone that they think it's fair game. Plus, we're in Knights territory now."

"You had that game-winning interception last year when LA matched up with the Knights, remember? Trust me, people know who you are. If anything, you gotta be careful 'round here."

Grayson chuckled, and we both squeezed into the booth. This was one of those places that put more tables on the floor than there was room for.

"No Nessa on this trip?" I asked. "Gabriel?"

"They haven't come to many away games this year," Grayson said, glancing to the side. The way he did it made my stomach sink.

"Why not?"

Last season, Grayson's wife and four-year-old son traveled all over to watch his games. We had a hell of a time at the last one out here; I carried Gabe around on my shoulders and ignored Nessa whenever she glared at me for swearing at the field in front of her son.

The waitress took that inopportune moment to swing by to get my order, and my impatience ticked up while I waited for Gray to reply.

"That's part of what I wanted to talk to you about," he finally said, pinching the bridge of his nose.

"What's going on?"

"They lied, Jules." Only a few times throughout our friendship had I heard Grayson sound so tired. "Or they just plain fucked up."

"Who?"

There was a brief pause while Grayson gathered his thoughts. When he began talking, it was with slow, measured words. To most people, he'd likely sound collected. But he was barely holding his shit together—I could tell.

"I transferred Gabriel to the clinic in Modesto because I wanted him to be seen by the team of doctors who treated me growing up. I requested imaging. Just to check, now that he's older. And it's showing that his heart—"

Grayson broke off, dropping his head into his hands. He didn't have to say more for me to understand, though.

My fingers curled into fists below the table as I realized. *Shit.*

Grayson grew up with a congenital heart defect—some funny word that had to do with his aorta being too small. I didn't know the details; all I knew was that it wasn't good. Freshman year of college, he suffered a stroke, significant enough that he sat out sophomore season, which was also our last chance to play together.

When his son was born a few years later, doctors said his heart was healthy. My friend had been elated that Gabriel wouldn't have to go through what he did. And now...

"Oh, hell. I'm sorry, man."

Grayson lifted his head, shaking it. "I made his previous team pull up his old images from when he was born and—"

He clenched his teeth together, and I figured out the rest.

"And it showed the same?"

He nodded, drawing a deep breath before taking a sip of his drink.

"He's had the defect since he was born, Jules. And they didn't catch it. What if something had happened? What if he—" Grayson inhaled slowly, forcing a bit of calm into his voice. "He's already had the surgery to correct it. It went well, and he's recovering back home."

I relaxed slightly, nodding to the waitress as she dropped off a drink for me.

"Well, that's good news, at least."

"Yeah." Grayson didn't seem the least bit settled, and I knew there was more. "But Nessa...*God*."

As soon as his wife's name left his mouth, Grayson whipped off his hat and scrubbed both hands over his face before dragging fingers through his short hair. Then he shoved his cap back on top of his head.

"You're freaking me out, Gray." I gripped my drink tightly. Nessa was the reason I knew Cameron's sister, Collins. They'd lived together in college, and I became friends with both of them when Nessa started dating Grayson. "I don't know what's going on, but this kind of stress can't be good for you and *your* heart."

He chuckled, but it was mostly humorless. "You sound like Nessa."

"Always did like her."

And I needed to know she was okay.

Mentioning Nessa appeared to settle Grayson's nerves. He relaxed back into the booth.

"This just isn't how I wanted to deliver the news." His lips stretched then, pulling into a smile. The first genuine one I'd seen today. "Nessa's pregnant again."

"Oh *hell* yeah." I leaned back in my seat, too, matching his grin. Relief drenched my nervous system. "I'd be calling for shots if you weren't, you know, *you*."

He laughed openly at that, and it was good to see that twinkle in his eyes. "I'm so fucking happy," he said. "You have no idea."

And then everything dimmed.

"But if I'd known..." He pressed his lips together momentarily. "I don't know if I would have chosen this. They told us there was a risk our kids could inherit the defect, but now we know it's so much more than a possibility. And yeah, I want Gabriel to have siblings more than anything. *Anything*, Jules. But not at the risk of their health."

I struggled to find words, but Grayson said them for me, sounding broken.

"I'm pissed, man. We should have known about Gabriel a long time ago. We should have been able to make an informed decision."

My insides clenched. He was more than pissed; the burning in his gaze gave it away. Grayson Everett had always been incredibly even-tempered, and I'd never pegged him as vengeful. But he was a family man, through and through. God save anyone who threatened Nessa or his kids.

So I wasn't surprised when he added, "And I want to take action."

"Legal action?"

He nodded. "Shit, I know it's a lot to ask, but..."

"I'll do whatever I can to help."

The relief on Grayson's face was palpable. "I don't even know where to start."

"I'll start," I said firmly. "You just worry about kicking ass at the game tomorrow. And for the love of God, promise me you'll get some rest, 'kay? Or I'll have to swing by your hotel tonight and tuck you in myself."

Grayson's lips curled in that rueful but amused way of his.

We'd been friends for years, but our beginnings had never really left. I might just be an associate attorney these days, and he might be the one starring in the NFL, but I'd always feel like his team captain.

"I promise," he said.

My footsteps dragged on my way back to the office. I'd overshot my lunch hour by twenty minutes, too swept up in my conversation with Grayson to realize the time.

I didn't want to admit it at lunch, but with the information Gray told me, I wasn't confident we'd have a case. And I hated the feeling sinking deep in my gut. I was a provider. Being the one people turned to for help? I reveled in that role. I liked doling out realistic, no-nonsense advice to those willing or looking to receive it.

But any advice I could offer Grayson right now was lacking. Medical malpractice suits were determined based on the harm that was caused by negligence, and it would be hard to prove that in his situation. Gabriel was recovering fine from his surgery; he hadn't suffered life-threatening effects from the heart defect before they were able to treat it. And while I more than understood Grayson's concern for their next kid, I wasn't hopeful that *what-if* would be enough.

That didn't mean I wouldn't look into it for him, though. I'd do anything I could. Even if it—*shit.*

Even if it meant enlisting help from Juniper St. James.

I slouched against the doorway to our office, feeling unnecessarily worn out from the trek back. Juniper had her back to me as she rapidly worked through a spreadsheet projected onto her desktop. Apparently, the only times she buckled down were when I wasn't around.

Maybe I should sift my way through research before doing this—before asking her. But surely that would be a waste of time, especially since a quick internet check on my way back confirmed what Juniper said earlier. That McKinley Medical case had a lot of similarities to Grayson's, and she'd been on that team.

"Daisy."

She didn't turn around. Or stop. Just kept click-click-clicking. What was she *doing*?

When she lifted her hand off the mouse, I thought for sure she would turn around. She was probably doing that thing where she paused dramatically before answering me to make it *seem* like she could care less about our conversations. Juniper picked up her polka-dotted tumbler and took a drink. Then she went back to work.

Goddamnit.

"*Juniper.*"

I walked into the office, emphasizing her name. Her real name. She ignored me. Did she realize that she was only reinforcing the idea that I should, in fact, continue to call her any other name besides her real one?

With a step to the side, I hoped I might appear in her peripheral vision. But that was when I realized she was wearing earbuds.

No fucking wonder.

I waved a hand in front of her face, and she jumped. The glare that swung to meet me probably wasn't a good sign, considering I wanted a favor.

God, I couldn't believe I was about to ask for a favor.

"What's got you so plugged in, huh?" I asked as she whipped her earbuds out.

To my surprise, a bit of blush rose onto Juniper's cheeks as she rushed to press Pause on her phone and flip it over.

"Nothing."

She spun her chair to face me, and we were suddenly pressed so close together that I had to take a step back. And sit. Standing above her had delivered an angle confusingly filled with cleavage, and now my subconscious was forcing me to glance out the window. My brain seemed to think the skyline could be a visual palate cleanser and slow my oddly rapid pulse.

"What do you want?" she urged, and the tap of her finger brought my attention back to reality.

"Can I, uh, have a donut?"

Suspicion danced over her face, but she nudged the platter of donuts toward me. "Here."

I picked one up, plopping the sugary, powdery fried dough into my mouth. Juniper's lips twitched as she watched me, making me feel like a goddamn zoo animal with how carefully she studied my approach to eating her donut. But so be it.

"You're getting powdered sugar everywhere," she said. There was a bit of humor in her voice.

"Maybe next time you bring treats, you should pick ones that aren't so fucking messy."

I licked my lips, and Juniper's eyes flicked down to my mouth momentarily.

Heat wrapped around me.

This was annoyingly embarrassing. But somehow, I knew eating one of her precious donuts would soften her up a touch.

"The messier, the better," she said primly. As if messy and Juniper St. James *ever* went together in the same sentence.

After finally swallowing the mouthful of fried dough, I cut to the chase.

"I need your help."

eleven years ago

"What are you doing here?"

Julian stood at the other side of the room, seemingly frozen by my appearance at his kitchen table on Valentine's Day.

"I'm waiting for Gemma to get done with skating practice."

"Where's your date?" he asked.

"I'm sitting at your kitchen table, Julian. Figure it out."

"Sounds like you're here to ask me out, then, huh? Bold move, Rosie, just showing up in a man's kitchen on Valentine's Day."

I rolled my eyes. "In your dreams."

"Trust me," he muttered. "Any dreams I have of you will not take place in my kitchen."

"Let me guess," I said, my top lip curling up in a bit of a sneer. "They'd take place in your car, and you'd be driving me out of town and leaving me on the edge of it. Am I right?"

"It would certainly make my life easier," he said dryly.

"You don't always have to be an ass, Julian," I shot back, leaning forward across the table and meeting his gaze beat for beat.

He mimicked me, leaning my elbows on the table and lowering his voice as he stared back.

"And you don't always have to show up in my fucking house unannounced. What if I was walking around naked?"

I felt my cheeks flushed. "Why the hell would you do that?"

He shrugged. "Because no one was home. A guy with five sisters doesn't get freedom like that very often."

I leaned back again. "Well, don't let me keep you from experiencing your freedom."

His lips twisted. "You always do, Lily. I don't exactly expect it to change much now."

CHAPTER FOUR

SOMETHING WAS NOT RIGHT.

I stared at Julian, repeating his words in my head.

I need your help.

He licked his lips again, trying to catch all the residual powdered sugar from the donut, and I cocked my head to the side. Behind him, the clock on the wall read nearly two o'clock. Had he been gone that long for lunch? I must have gotten carried away listening to my new audiobook. Rebecca Elez was my favorite narrator, and she'd sucked me right into my latest guilty pleasure—a spicy Cinderella retelling. I'd been so engrossed that Julian scared the crap out of me when he came in.

And now he was staring back at me with a strange expression. The crease between his eyes was particularly prominent. And he'd eaten one of my donuts. *Odd.*

"Are you okay?"

"Well, I did just ask for your help," he said wryly, "so I think you can figure it out from there."

He was wrong about that. Because even though I was trying very hard to figure it out, it still didn't make sense.

"No, I mean, like...are you sick?"

Julian sighed heavily and ran a hand through that reddish hair of his. "I'm going to be if you keep this up."

"Fine." Although I was still worried that Julian was either messing with me or terminally ill, I slouched forward in my seat, resting my elbows on my knees to give my very best impression of concern and undivided attention. "What can I help you with?"

Julian stiffened as his eyes flicked over me, leaving me confused. Did he want my help or not?

He looked at the ceiling for a long moment, and I tapped my foot with impatience.

"I need you to fill me in on the details of how your team won the McKinley case," he said with a regretful sigh.

I drew back, leaning into my chair again. Julian relaxed in his, getting comfortable. He seemed to think this would be a long conversation, but he couldn't be more wrong.

"I'm not going to help you take my spot on the case I'm working with Cameron."

"I'm not—" He broke off abruptly with a growl of annoyance. His hands clapped down on his knees, squeezing. "I'm not trying to take your spot on the case."

Based on his reaction, I was almost inclined to believe him. But it would be foolish not to ask more questions. "Why do you want to know, then?"

"It's for a separate case I'm consulting on," he admitted after a brief pause.

"I thought you were assisting Daphne with research for her case."

"I am."

The brevity of his response told me he wanted to leave it there. But I couldn't care less what he wanted.

"But I thought that case was a child custody case."

Although Gardner Law was on the smaller side, it had enough breadth that it was able to provide specialized consultation in more than one area of law. It was one of the reasons why I wanted to work here. My experience with medical malpractice had been what got me through the doors, but the option to branch into family law, specifically adoption law, was what made me want to stay.

"It is."

I wondered if Julian realized that for every short answer he gave me, I'd come back with a follow-up question. On principle, I had to.

"But you're consulting on another case, too?"

He nodded, folding his arms over his chest, which only served to draw my attention to how his suit stretched over his muscled arms. Considering how long it had been since Julian played football, he still maintained himself well. Working in his dad's shop likely helped.

I forced my gaze up to his face. "Why are you consulting on it if you don't have the required experience?"

"Juniper. *Please*." My name came through clenched teeth, shocking me at how desperate he sounded. His eyes didn't shift with mischief, and his dry drawl was absent from his words. This wasn't Julian Briggs, my best friend's brother who always gave me a hard time in everything I did in life. This was Julian Briggs, my colleague...who apparently needed help. Genuinely.

So I gave in. He did say please, after all. And that was an awfully large leap of progress for him. "Sure, I'll help you."

He breathed a sigh of relief before realizing that I wasn't finished.

"But it'll cost."

Julian studied me warily, and I couldn't blame him. I didn't particularly relish the idea of asking him for help. And in this area of my life, especially.

But after doing a mental audit of all my wedding date options after Sofia had messaged me this morning to make sure I'd received her invitation, I'd come up a little short. Okay, really short. I hated to admit it, but between my short-lived undergrad fling and my law school dry spell, I was floating adrift when it came to dating.

Cameron would have been a perfect option—if my professional ethics had not intervened. As soon as I was assigned to work with him on the Waverly case, I knew I had to figure out something else for the wedding. Or rather, someone else. I couldn't mar our professional and personal relationship so quickly.

I wanted a date, yes. And I very much wanted to make an impression on my birth family. But more than that, I was determined to prove to Gardner Law that they'd made the right choice by hiring me.

"You have a lot of...impressive friends," I started.

Both of Julian's brows skyrocketed. "Excuse me?"

"Your friends," I repeated. "I was hoping you could—"

"Most of my friends are married," he deadpanned before I could even finish.

"I just need a date for a wedding," I admitted. "It honestly doesn't matter if they're in love with someone else."

The words tumbled out of my mouth before I really considered them, and now that I had, yep, they sounded bad.

"Um, *I* care," Julian intoned.

"I just meant that it would be *fake*," I quickly amended. "As in, not real. As in, just pretend."

"Juniper..." he started, and I prepared myself for the lecture that was clearly on the tip of his tongue. Ah, just like old times. Reminiscing never felt so annoying.

"Come on, Julian," I said before he could really rev his engines up. "I know you must have at least one friend whose number you could hand over in return for my *superior* expertise on medical malpractice."

To my dismay, Julian looked horrified.

"Forget about it." He threw his hands up in the air, shaking his head. "This was a bad idea."

But now that the opportunity had presented itself, I was starting to think it was a truly wonderful idea. A little trade-off—what could go wrong?

My brain raced down memory lane, looking for potential. It foraged through the hazy, hidden recollections of that night Gemma and I had visited Julian at college in California. One face in particular swam to the forefront, clearer than all the rest.

"What about that one roommate you had?" I asked. "Neil? Nick?"

"Noah?" he choked out.

"Yes!" I crossed my arms over my chest, proud of myself. Maybe a little smug. "That's the one."

If I remembered correctly, Noah was ridiculously attractive, flirtatious, and friendly. Someone who would definitely be comfortable acting as a plus one.

Julian's eyes shot to the ceiling. Exasperation riddled his expression.

"To my knowledge..." he began slowly, gaze dropping one inch with every word. "Noah is single. He's not really the type to ever *not* be single."

He said the last part pointedly, but I didn't care. I wasn't looking to get involved with someone right now, either. Would it hurt if I hit it off with my date and we went on to live happily ever after in our own spicy fairy-tale retelling? Of course not. But it wasn't a requirement.

"Yeah, on second thought...no," Julian said, suddenly standing. But with one glance down at me, he sat again, a look of consternation on his face.

"No?"

"I'm not setting you up with Noah."

"You remember the part when I said it wasn't real, right?"

"I remember," Julian said gruffly.

"I don't care that he doesn't want commitment," I clarified, so maybe he could get it through his thick skull. "So, what does Noah *do* these days? Where does he live?"

I hadn't heard his name come up in conversation at the bar with Cameron, and that meant it was possible Noah was a washed-out, big-leagues reject by now. That wouldn't really bode well for my plan, so it was best to check.

"You don't know?" Julian asked, raising his brows.

I shook my head, and if Julian possessed a larger capacity for positive emotions, I would have said that amused him. His lips twisted as he studied my face.

"I assumed that's why you mentioned him," he said. "Noah London plays for the Knights. He lives here. In Boston."

I immediately straightened with interest. His name did ring a bell. "Your roommate was Noah *London*? The quarterback?"

My standards for dating were not usually so high or so vain. In fact, considering my dating life had been all but nonexistent, my standards were incredibly low. But this was different. This was Sofia's wedding.

"No," Julian repeated, shooting down my hopes. "I mean, yes, he plays professionally as a quarterback. He was my back-up when I played in college and then went on to take my place before going pro. But no—we're not going there. I'm not setting you up with Noah."

"All I'm looking for is his number and maybe a few words of encouragement whispered in his ear," I pleaded, hating how quickly this had changed from him begging me to me begging him. But it was one hell of an opportunity, and it would be wasteful to pass it up. "For how much time I'll be putting in to help with your consultation, that's more than a fair deal."

Julian was quiet for a long moment. He worked his jaw over, rubbing it repeatedly. The air in the office stilled slightly, and with all my nervous energy, I had to keep myself from tapping my finger on my desk while I waited.

"He might say no," he finally pointed out.

I shrugged. "Then he says no."

With a grumble beneath his breath, Julian turned toward his desk again. He started shuffling papers with far too much force, and I had to clear my throat to get his suddenly chaotic attention back.

"So it's a deal?"

Even though Julian loved to call me dramatic, my antics didn't have anything on the sigh he released as he looked gloomily over his shoulder.

"It's a deal."

"What are you doing here?" Gemma Briggs dropped next to me, her ice skates clanging against the cold metal bench as she set them down. Her ice-blue eyes flicked over me in assessment while she pursed her lips. "You're oddly ill-equipped to be at the rink."

"I came right from work." I drew my cardigan around me as though it actually afforded me any warmth.

"But...why?"

"Because it's *cold* here."

A raised brow met my statement.

"And I needed to cool down after making a deal with the devil," I admitted.

"The devil, huh?" Gemma rolled her eyes, her wry expression pulling taut in a way that had to be hereditary or genetic or something because I knew someone else who made that same exact face at least five times today.

"Plus, I knew you'd be here," I added, hoping to sugar her up. "And I need to talk to you."

Gemma had never been one for small talk, unnecessary niceties, or anything that didn't cut right to the chase. So she said, "I don't think I can listen to another rant about my brother, Junes."

Damn.

Gemma took stock of my expression. "He was the devil in the equation, wasn't he?"

She looked a bit disappointed, and I supposed I could understand that. Out of all of her siblings, Gemma was closest to Julian.

In fact, the only thing that wasn't perfect about their relationship was...me.

"Of course not." I flashed a sickly sweet smile. "Julian is an *angel*."

Gemma blinked at me twice.

Okay, maybe I laid it on a little too thick.

"Go ahead, then." She threw her hands up. "Tell me what's going on."

"Do you want to get out of here first?"

Gemma coached the figure skating team at St. Maverick's, one of the many prestigious colleges in Boston. Since I made a habit of coming to the rink when I wanted to pretend it was winter, I usually dressed intentionally. Watching skating practices was the perfect excuse to don my favorite peacoat in early fall.

But today, I hadn't planned to come, and my cardigan wasn't cutting it. Even if I did want to cool off a bit.

After flashing me an *I told you so* smirk while again giving my outfit—my ill-equipped one—a once-over, Gemma stood. "Come on. Let's pick up some food and head back to my place."

"Excellent."

Gemma lived on the outskirts of Boston. She'd moved here about a year ago after landing her job at St. Maverick's. Unlike me, she missed the small-town life and sought as much of it as possible while still working in the city. Usually, I wouldn't drive out to her place on a weeknight, but desperate times called for desperate, suburban measures.

"So tell me about this deal you made with my brother," she said once we'd gotten our hands on a bottle of wine and takeout from the little Italian place near her apartment. It was a mistake to sink so deep into her couch with a bowl of pasta balancing on my stomach; I doubted I'd be able to fight my way out of this comfort trap after a glass of wine and a pound of carbs.

"Actually, it was me who proposed it," I admitted through a mouthful of five-cheese delicacy.

Gemma nearly choked on a sun-dried tomato. "What

happened to keeping your head down and ignoring him?" she sputtered. "That's what I told you to do, remember?"

I filled my mouth with another bite of pasta, afraid to tell her I hadn't been particularly good at sticking to that tidbit of advice. But was that really my fault when Julian was the one who interjected himself into *everything*?

"He asked for help with a case, so I asked for something in return," I explained. "Simple."

"Julian asked for help?" Gemma snorted. "Fat chance that happened."

"He did," I insisted, even though I understood why she doubted it. I'd doubted it, too.

"Julian does not ask for help. He doles out unsolicited advice whenever he gets the chance. But ask for it?" She shook her head, waving her fork around as she chewed a mouthful.

"Believe me, I was just as surprised as you." I shrugged. "But I got him to give me Noah London's number in return, so..."

Gemma stopped chewing. Her eyes grew wide, and—oh my God, was she *choking*? Shit, I was *not* confident enough in my first aid skills for this.

To my immense relief, Gemma swallowed a second later and licked her lips clean. "For the wedding?"

We'd always ridden the same brain wavelength—ever since fighting over the same seat in the cafeteria on the first day of middle school.

I nodded. "If I have to make an appearance at Sofia's wedding, I'm going to do it the right way."

"As a liar?"

I flicked Gemma on the leg, and she laughed.

"I'm here for this. Really, I am, Junes. But isn't London a bit of a player?"

"That's what Julian was concerned about, too."

"Yeah?" She twirled her fork in her pasta, considering my words.

"Yeah, but I'm not looking for a relationship. If he's a one-night sort of guy, then that's perfect for this."

Gemma made a slight humming noise in her throat that sounded a lot like the words *I'm not so sure about that, Juni.* But when she spoke again, she asked, "Did you tell Julian why you wanted Noah's phone number? Does he know about the wedding and Sofia?"

"He knows it's for a wedding date, but I didn't mention Sofia."

I'd only made the connection with Sofia over the last couple years, so unless Gemma had told Julian about her, he probably didn't know I even had a sister.

"I wasn't sure how much you wanted the others to know about your birth family, so I never said anything to him," Gemma said, answering my thoughts for me.

"That's probably for the best."

Julian didn't need to know the details. He'd somehow find a way to use them against me.

"Have you texted Noah yet?" Gemma asked.

"No," I groaned. "I don't know what to say."

After abandoning her pasta bowl, Gemma clapped her hands together. "We need more wine for this."

So more wine we got. But nearly a whole hour and an entire bottle later, we still hadn't figured out how to successfully slide into Noah London's inbox.

"He plays here, doesn't he?" Gemma asked. Her head was in her hands, and she looked stumped.

I affirmed her question with a nod, and her lips stretched into one of *those* smiles. A skinny-dipping on Lock Island past curfew kind of smile. Or a steal your dad's convertible for a midnight drive kind of smile.

But those things hadn't ended well, and I was a bit past my rebellious stage—seven or eight years past it. So I was pleasantly surprised when Gemma's suggestion had me matching her grin.

"You know," she said, "I think they have a home game tomorrow."

I liked the path she was going down, but I had already spotted a few very critical roadblocks.

"There's no way I'd be able to talk to him there, though."

"Maybe." Gemma swirled her wine in her glass, giving me a meaningful glance. "But I think I know someone who could."

"You?" I asked hopefully, ignoring the obvious, gut-curling answer.

She shook her head. "A different Briggs."

Damn.

"And I bet he would just *love* to take you to meet his friend," she added with a wink.

I groaned.

He would definitely *not* love it.

But God help me, I was going to ask him anyway.

CHAPTER FIVE

I WAS REASONABLY CONFIDENT that Juniper had been staring at me for the past ten minutes.

Alright...maybe it had been more like thirty seconds, but it felt like a hell of a lot longer. The heat of her gaze on the back of my neck made it incredibly hard to focus on the files Daphne wanted me to review.

When I couldn't take it any longer, I spun in my chair. And sure enough—there she was. Caught in the act. Staring at me. She jumped as though she actually thought she'd been inconspicuous.

I stared back at her. "Yes?"

Juniper dramatically put a hand to her chest. A finger played with the frilly neckline of her blouse, which today was a peachy color that offset her chesnut hair. At least there weren't any more polka dots.

"How do you do that?"

She said it like an accusation.

"I can feel those lasers you call eyes on the back of my neck." I rubbed below my hairline for extra effect. "You wouldn't believe how difficult it is to get literally anything done."

Juniper dropped her hand with a sigh of exasperation. "Why haven't you just requested a different office already?"

"Are you kidding me?" I swiveled around to point to the cityscape outside the window in front of my desk. "And give up this incredible view? Nah."

"I bet all the offices on this side of the floor have that view, Julian."

I shrugged and began shuffling papers. If she wanted to avoid telling me why she was staring, then so be it. But I had shit to get done.

"So...I can't decide what to text Noah."

There it was.

I slowly turned to face her again. With her hands folded perfectly in her lap, Juniper watched me with an expectant look in her eyes.

"I'm not going to come up with ideas so you can flirt with my friend," I said flatly.

"Oh, I already have an idea."

"Excellent." I clapped my hands on my knees. "Now that's figured out, I can go back to—"

"But I need your help with it."

I squeezed my knees in irritation. "No."

I'd helped my friends with their dating problems before, but this was different. Firstly, Juniper was *not* my friend. Secondly, she didn't even want to date Noah. Hell, she didn't even know him.

"Just listen," Juniper said, jumping to her feet and leaning against my desk, making it impossible for me to turn my chair back around. A wave of her sweet-smelling perfume washed over me, clogging my senses. "It's a win-win situation. You'll love it."

I sighed. "I highly doubt that, Violet."

Did she not realize I hated this entire mess? I hated that I needed her help with Grayson's case. I hated that I'd given her Noah's number. And I was definitely going to hate whatever she was about to suggest.

"You love football, don't you?" She cocked a brow, daring me to deny it as she inched closer.

"Yes," I said slowly, afraid of what I was agreeing to. There was no point lying, though. We both knew that for a large portion of my life, football was what I woke up every day to do.

And now? Now I was sitting in this cubicle-like office with the one woman who had been annoying me since I hit puberty.

Juniper crossed her arms over her chest, which I realized was directly in my line of vision. She was standing so fucking close that I had to recline in my desk chair to see her face and the mischief brewing there.

"Then I can't imagine it would be that much of a hassle for you to go with me to the game tonight." Her bright smile faded by one degree of a sparkle as she added, "And introduce me to your college roommate afterward."

I immediately started shaking my head. The last thing I needed was to spend *more* time with Juniper St. James. And yeah, I might love an excuse to go to a game, but I could only imagine the horror that would be Juniper at a sporting event.

"Look," I said, hoping to level with her because I saw that gleam in her eye that I recognized all too well from high school. It never ended well for me. "Noah is a straightforward dude. You're overthinking this. Just shoot him a text and tell him exactly what you want."

"You have zero tact, Julian." Juniper began tapping her foot on the floor, grating my nerves.

"I have plenty of tact. But I also have a solid understanding of my friends."

"I'll buy the tickets," Juniper offered. Her foot sped up its tapping. "You just have to show up."

I planted my heel and pivoted to place my toes over hers, locking them down. "No."

Her lips grew taut, and I knew she was about to buckle down on her tactics because that was what Juniper did when she didn't get her way.

"I know it's really hard for you to even consider doing something nice—"

"Don't come at me with that shit," I interrupted, feeling heat rise to the forefront. "Stop pretending that I'm an asshole just because I don't want to go to a last-minute football game with you."

Juniper pursed her lips. "I wasn't going to say you're an asshole."

I rolled my eyes. "Oh, just that I never do anything nice, then?"

"For *me*," she emphasized, speaking through gritted teeth now, the anger evident in her bright irises. "You didn't let me finish. Believe me, I know you have the capacity to be nice to other people." Something as outrageous as hurt briefly shone in her eyes. But then it vanished, her face becoming a tight mask again as she continued. "So I was going to ask why you wouldn't want to support your friends."

Her flash of anger momentarily stunned me, and it took me a second to respond. "Friends?"

"Gemma said you have a friend who is a wide receiver for LA. That's who the Knights are playing, isn't it?"

Shit, she was right. I forgot Grayson would be taking the field tonight. I could see Noah play pretty much whenever I wanted, but Gray...

After what a shitty mood he was in yesterday, it would be nice to be there for him tonight. And watching two of my old teammates and roommates face off could make for a hell of a good time.

So to my complete and utter dislike, I gave Juniper what she wanted.

"Okay." I lifted my foot off hers. "But I'm driving, and you're not paying for me."

Juniper shrugged, her satisfaction barely contained. "Fine by me."

Ever since the first day of work, I'd been trying to get back on Tyler's good side. Well, not even his good side, because I wasn't sure I had *ever* been there, so at least his neutral side. But the receptionist couldn't want less to do with me after our first awkward encounter. Not that I really blamed him.

"Any plans tonight?" I asked, leaning on the heightened part of his desk designed for visitor sign-in logs and one too many candy bowls.

He shook his head, leaving it at that.

This was going great.

I blamed this on Juni. If she just hadn't been in my goddamn office...

"You?" Tyler reluctantly asked the return question with all the enthusiasm of someone being asked to work overtime on a holiday weekend.

"Thursday night football," I said. "Just waiting for some—ah, there she is."

Juniper burst through the double doors coming from the office, and Tyler lowered his voice.

"I thought you guys didn't get along," he muttered.

It crossed my mind to lie to him, wash the whole thing over like a bad joke. But I didn't really do schmoozing, and I didn't do lying.

So instead, I tossed him a smile and chuckled. "We don't."

Leaving a baffled Tyler behind, I fell in stride with Juniper as she marched to the elevator.

"I need to stop at home to change. I assume you have other clothes?" I looked her up and down. "Since you planned this and all."

She barely spared me a glance while punching the down button. "No?"

I caught her by the arm. "You look like a walking Kate Spade billboard ad, Lily. Not like you're going to a football stadium."

Juniper smirked as the elevator doors opened, and we both stepped inside. The air stilled as the doors slid shut again.

"I'm not even going to make fun of you for knowing what that is because that might be the best compliment you've ever given me."

"The point just flew over your head," I groaned, releasing her. "You're wearing five-inch heels. You're going to roll an ankle on all the damn stairs."

She straightened. "There are a lot of things that I can do in heels, Julian. You'd be surprised."

I really wished she hadn't said that. Now my brain was taking detours I didn't even know existed as it searched for something else to say.

"We can get you something to wear at my place."

There. That was normal.

"I'm not going to wear your clothes." Juniper's face pinched, disgusted by the thought.

"Not even if it's Noah's jersey?"

The elevator dinged, and the doors slowly rolled open as Juniper considered. Her heels tapped against the lobby floor as she stepped out, and I followed her. When we reached the front door, she muttered beneath her breath. "Fine, I'll wear the jersey."

Feeling a bit satisfied, I grinned.

Fifteen minutes later, we were standing in the entryway to my apartment, and I was really wishing I'd known this was where the night would take us. Because I could practically see the judgment in Juniper's eyes as she scanned my bare apartment.

"How long have you lived here?"

"A few months. Moved in after the end of law school when I decided I'd stay in Boston."

"Does your building have a rule about not decorating?"

"I'm going to get you clothes," I grumbled, pushing past her and down the hallway that led to my room. We didn't have time for lectures on home decor.

Juniper hollered protests at me down the hall, but I ignored her. If she wanted to wear her princess outfit to the stadium, that was fine, but the shoes had to go. For safety reasons.

When I returned, Juniper was leaning against my kitchen counter, inspecting it like she was afraid it carried a disease on the surface.

"Here." I threw the clothes onto the counter, and Juniper jumped back. "Shoes, leggings, and a jersey."

She poked at the leggings. "I'm not going to wear some girl's clothes you hooked—"

"They're Gemma's," I said, exasperated. "Her rink is around the corner, so she stays here sometimes."

That surprised Juni. I could see the little tick of annoyance making her eyebrow twitch. She didn't like that there was something she didn't know about her best friend.

"I knew the rink was around the corner. But...how often does she stay here?"

I shrugged. "Depends. Sometimes she practices late, and I don't like her driving home when she's tired and it's dark."

Something softened slightly in Juniper's expression. If there was one thing we could agree on, it was that Gemma Briggs was important to us. But Juniper's moment of neutrality didn't last long. Her eyes rolled up as she snatched the leggings off the counter.

"You're so overprotective. You know your sister is a competent woman, right? You can't make her—"

"I don't make her do anything. I offer her the option, and she sometimes decides to take me up on it." I threw off my suit jacket, and Juniper's eyes widened in horror like she thought I was about to get naked in front of her. "Now, can you please change? The traffic is going to be awful."

"Fine, but I don't know if these will fit." She gave the leggings a skeptical glance. "Gemma is at least two sizes smaller than me."

"Just try them," I said, giving her a little push toward the bathroom. Leggings stretched, didn't they? Weren't they like one-size-fits-all or something? Besides, Juniper was exaggerating their differences. Sure, Gemma had a more slender frame while Juniper had curves I tried not to think about, but they used to always share clothes growing up.

When I heard Juniper mumble something beneath her breath, I added, "You're being awfully obstinate, considering I'm doing you a favor."

Juniper's expression shuttered at that, and she closed herself in the bathroom for an ungodly amount of time. But it allowed me to change, too. I threw on a different jersey—Grayson's, since Juniper had my Knights one—and slid into a more comfortable pair of shoes because I wasn't a fucking hypocrite.

Just as I began searching which route we wanted to take to the stadium, Juniper finally emerged from the bathroom. "Okay, I'm ready."

I wasn't. I definitely hadn't been ready for the moment when I glanced up from my phone to see Juniper looking like a completely different person, drowning in my jersey. It appeared like she tried to tuck it into the leggings—which fit, by the way—but the jersey was too long and fell around her hips.

She'd tied her hair up in a high ponytail that bounced when she walked toward me.

"That looks..." I cleared my throat. "Uh, good on you."

"Wow, don't sound so convincing," she drawled, but there was a thread of nervousness there. And for some reason, I felt the need to make it disappear. I wasn't used to a nervous Juniper, and I didn't like it. It put me on edge, too.

"Noah will like it," I said briskly while walking to the door. "Now, come on. Let's go."

Juniper nodded as she steeled herself.

"Let's go."

eleven years ago

"Have you ever changed a flat tire?" Gemma hissed.

"Of course not."

"Then do you really think it's a good idea to try to learn in the middle of the night while you're naked at the beach?"

I propped a hand on my hip.

"It's not my fault someone stole our clothes while we were swimming. What do you suggest?"

Gemma looked down, and the slight movement was so guilty that I immediately knew what she was about to say.

I groaned. "No way, Gems. That's an even worse idea."

"I didn't even say anything!" Gemma cried in her defense.

"He'll be pissed, and you know who he'll be pissed at."

"Oh, just ignore him."

She said those words like it was the easiest thing to do.

But it was impossible to ignore Gemma's broody brother. He didn't like me, and if he came to get us right now, it would be another reminder of that.

"We're naked and stranded, Junes," Gemma pleaded.

"No," I insisted. "We're not calling Julian."

We called Julian.

CHAPTER SIX

JULIAN NOT KEEPING HIS hands off me was the last problem I expected to have tonight.

After I felt his fingers grip my hip for the third time, I glared at him over my shoulder.

"What is your *problem*?"

"Would you—" He pushed me to the side. "Would you look where you're fucking going?"

A whoosh of air going by my ear and the cough of a nearby person explained it. I'd been about to run into someone. Again.

"You distracted me with your grabby hands," I accused, swatting him away.

He let go of me but moved closer as we maneuvered through the crowds entering the stadium. When he spoke, his voice was grumbly and gruff. Warm breath brushed the shell of my ear. "I grabbed you because you were walking straight into the oncoming traffic of people. Again."

He was being overdramatic, which wasn't much of a surprise. Did I clip someone's shoulder while crossing the street to the stadium? Maybe. Did they give me the finger while yelling a derogatory word that I refused to repeat in my head? Yes, that might have happened.

But as a small-town girl who'd only left her home zip code for a bank-draining education, I'd never been to a stadium of this magnitude. The size of it distracted me, looming even larger as we approached.

Julian's heavy sigh startled me back into awareness. "Why didn't you tell me that you were such a hazard to take into public?"

"Why didn't you tell me that professional football spectators were such a hazard?" I shot back at him. "I might have bumped into him a little, but that man was—"

"He was an ass," Julian growled in my ear, his fingers squeezing my hip again as he directed me through the stadium traffic.

Finally, something we agreed on.

Julian seemed eager to find our seats, and I noticed the appreciation in his eyes when he realized how good they were. I wasn't sure if these tickets would be worth ruining my monthly budget, but the entire point of coming tonight was to sit close to the players and the field.

"How much do I owe you for the tickets, Rosie?"

I shook my head. "Don't worry about it."

Julian's displeasure with my response was evident. That starry-eyed look he'd showcased a minute ago vanished as he looked down at me. "Part of our deal was that—"

"I don't remember what I paid for them off the top of my head," I said, which was technically the truth. I couldn't remember the exact amount, not down to the very dollar. "But they weren't that expensive. I'll let you know."

"You're lying."

Okay, yeah, the second part was definitely a lie.

I didn't know why I was trying to let Julian off the hook for the tickets. God knows I could use the money, but part of me felt bad for dragging him here last minute when I knew he wasn't precisely a last-minute person. Besides, relying on him to help me talk to Noah made my stomach churn unpleasantly. I shouldn't need his help, but here I was anyway. And refusing his money somehow made me feel better.

"I don't know why you want to pay so badly."

"It's weird having you pay for me to come see my friends play." He wrinkled his nose, eyes moving to scan the field. "And it won't cost money to uphold the other side of our bargain."

That was the thing about Julian. While I'd been pegged for law school because of my sharp tongue and determined spirit, Julian had always held a firm philosophy of fairness. Justice. Not that I didn't believe in those things, too, but sometimes it seemed the people we grew up with thought Julian had gone into law for all the right reasons while I'd pursued it for all the wrong ones.

My passion for my career had nothing to do with my aptitude for arguing. Even if it did give me a little adrenaline rush from time to time.

"Let's just enjoy the game," I encouraged, turning back toward the field.

"Do you think you will?" Apparent curiosity lingered in Julian's voice.

"What?"

"Enjoy the game?"

"Of course I will."

Julian glanced sharply down at me. "What do you mean, *of course*? I've never once seen you interested in football before today."

I crossed my arms over my chest, slight irritation coursing through my veins. "I went to every single one of your games in high school, didn't I?"

His brows furrowed. "You did?"

"You might not remember me, but I was that girl who sat with your family in the crowd and tried to blend in with all the redheads."

"I—" He opened his mouth, shut it again, and frowned. "I knew you came to some of them. But I didn't know you went to *all* of them. Pretty sure you called me an empty-headed jock on at least one occasion. I took that to mean you weren't exactly a fan of the game."

"Oh, I'm not."

Julian rolled his eyes and muttered something that undoubtedly wasn't in my favor beneath his breath.

"I don't like the game itself very much," I explained, "but I do like going to them."

"God, you are so confusing sometimes," he groaned, rubbing his forehead like he was about to get a tension headache.

"I *mean* that I like their energy. The atmosphere is fun. I loved those fall Friday nights at high school games. It's that camaraderie part, ya know?"

Julian dropped his hand, his face clearing a bit. There was a slight pause. "Yeah...I do, actually."

With that second unusual agreement, Julian turned his attention back toward the field, likely looking for Noah. When he spotted him, he nudged me—as if I wasn't already paying attention to exactly what he was doing.

"Right there." He pointed to a lean, golden-brown-haired player wearing a number nine jersey, similar to the one I had on.

I nodded, squinting to make him out as Julian returned to surveying the field like he was a coach taking stock of the situation. He put his hands on his hips, twisting to glance down to the opposite end zone, and I was left looking at his back.

"You're wearing an LA jersey." The gold lettering on his jersey spelled *EVERETT*, and a bell rang in my head. "Is that your other former teammate?"

"Yeah, you just noticed?" He spun back toward me, exasperation painted on his expression. "Keep up, Lily."

I bit down on my tongue to try to keep from snapping back—he'd already called me out for being obstinate once today. "I really try not to look at you as much as possible, Julian."

Guess I didn't bite down on my tongue hard enough. But if we were keeping score, I'd give myself a little point for that one.

"Oh, yeah?"

He said it like it was a challenge.

Luckily, it was an easy one. "Yeah."

"It must be hard if you have to put so much effort into it," he said with a smirk.

My cheeks flamed in response, which was so startling that I eagerly sought an escape.

"You know what? I think I'm going to go get some food."

Julian straightened, his demeanor immediately shifting. "Do you want me to come with you?"

I shot him a glare over my shoulder as I began to retreat back down the row of seats. "That would defeat the purpose of why I'm leaving."

His dramatic sigh cut through the crowd's chatter before he called after me. "Just watch where you're going for once, will ya?"

"Believe it or not, I can survive in public without you," I shot back.

"Fine." I saw him throw his hands up from the corner of my eye. "Prove it."

I did prove it. I got a little turned around on my way back from the concession stand and lost some popcorn while descending the stairs, but I survived.

Julian had his hands on top of his head while intently staring at the field when I reached him, and I saw an odd bit of relief when he glanced over to find me in my seat again. He'd likely been worried he might have to tell Gemma he lost me at the game.

"You're back." His relief morphed into judgment. "All you got was popcorn?"

"For some reason, I just had this *feeling* you would judge my food choices, so I went with popcorn. Absolutely no one can hate on popcorn." I scowled. "Except you, apparently."

"I'm not hating on popcorn, and I don't give a shit about what you eat." He grabbed a few kernels from the top of my tub and tossed them in his mouth. "But unless I missed it, you didn't have lunch today. And I don't want you passing out on me before I can watch Everett score."

That reasoning tracked. "True, I would hate to inconvenience you."

"Since when?" He snorted. "We're here, aren't we?"

"You're enjoying yourself," I pointed out.

Because it was true. He had a brightness in his eyes that reminded me of the energy I used to see when I went to his games in high school. It was like someone had cranked a hidden dial, and now he was in sport mode, his eyes critical as he watched the movements around us. The first quarter began, and our conversation came second to the game. He didn't even bother to refute my point. A youthful smile wormed onto his face instead.

That was fine with me, though. I wanted Julian to have a good time. If he enjoyed himself tonight, there would be less for him to complain about tomorrow.

The minutes ticked by surprisingly fast. Julian's attention stayed glued to the field with the exception of halftime; he used that small window of opportunity to sprint to the bathroom and load up on food, which he insisted on sharing with me. And since it was true that I hadn't carved out a good lunch schedule at work, I stole a few of his french fries during the second half of the game.

"Okay, follow me."

After the final seconds disappeared on the scoreboard, Julian ushered me down the few steps toward the sidelines. We zigzagged around departing fans as we made our way to the corner of the field, spotting where athletes took off for the locker rooms. And then, like a beacon of sweat, muscles, and tight, shiny pants, there he was. Noah London.

I'd definitely kept my eye on him during the game. Even though my football knowledge was limited to high school games and the things my dad shouted at the TV screen, I knew Noah's performance was impressive. And now, seeing him up close was overwhelming.

Suddenly nervous, I took a step in the opposite direction—backward.

What was I thinking? Noah London probably got asked on dates every hour of every day. Why did I think that he would ever go on a date with *me*? Even if it was fake.

Noah was only a few steps away from us when Julian noticed my retreat. His brows furrowed as he jerked his head toward the railing, mouthing for me to get my ass over there.

"This was a bad idea," I hissed beneath my breath.

"Too late." Julian grabbed my hand, pulling me to stand beside him. He locked his arm behind my back, gripping the railing on the opposite side of me. "This is your chance, Daisy. We're not doing this again."

Stuck with no hopes of escaping, I began fidgeting with my hair.

"Juniper."

Julian's sharp voice caught my attention. His eyes were piercingly blue beneath the stadium lights as they roamed my face. We were so close that I could count his strawberry blonde eyelashes if I wanted to. I hoped he couldn't feel my heart pounding. More importantly, I hoped he didn't dare think it was because of him.

"Yeah?" I asked, my breathing shallow.

"Stop acting un-Juni-like," he muttered. "I don't like it."

"Un-Juni-like?"

"Yeah." He looked away. "You know."

I did know. Only Julian didn't realize that this *was* me. This nervous, sweaty-palmed girl was me most days; I just never let him see it. He was used to a different Juni. But he was right about one thing. If I could turn my confidence on at work, I could do it here, too.

Noah waved a security guard away with the assurance that we were welcome and greeted Julian heartily. They shared a slightly awkward handshake, considering our position above him, and I plastered on a smile. But before I could say anything, another ridiculously hot football player jogged over to join us.

"Looking good out there, Gray," Julian called as the brown-haired, sharp-jawed man stopped beside Noah.

He smiled broadly, and when Julian and Noah returned it, I felt sweat tickle my brow. The fall weather had been warm today, but not *this* warm. Not warm enough for me to become this much of a mess.

There were too many handsome guys in too small of a space, and my nerves weren't sure they could handle it. I probably would have snuck away if it weren't for Julian's strong arm behind my back, locking me in at his side.

"Why didn't you mention you were coming yesterday?" Grayson asked, running a hand through his hair.

"Last-minute plans," Julian said. "Juniper and I work together now, and she had an extra ticket."

And then, looking like he was truly pained to do it, Julian opened the conversation up to me.

"Daisy, this is Grayson Everett and Noah London." He pointed out each player as if they didn't have their names embroidered on their jerseys. Or on ours. "They were my teammates and roommates, so you might remember meeting them when you and Gemma visited California."

"The names certainly ring a bell," I said with a smile and a wave over the railing, trying to look more enthused about this awkward meet and greet than I felt.

"Yeah, the looks might not, though," Noah said with a chuckle. "I've definitely put on a few pounds since college."

Making jokes about gaining weight wasn't what I'd expected from a professional athlete, but honestly, it put me a little more at ease. I could relate. Post-college me had a different body shape than college me.

"Same."

Noah waved off my admission and drew back, looking me up and down in an obvious, over-the-top way. "Jersey looks damn good. That yours, Briggs?"

Oh, so he *was* a flirt. And was I misreading the silent communication between the two guys, or was Noah asking if *I* was Julian's?

Because I certainly was not.

"The jersey," Julian said tightly. He shifted on his feet before dropping the arm that had been around me. "The jersey's mine, yeah."

Noah raised a brow, and he grinned cheekily. "Well, it looks better on her than you anyway."

Julian's eyes rolled, but he was back to wearing that silly, goofy grin of his again—the one I couldn't ever really remember seeing. "Nah, I just think I look better in an Everett jersey."

"That's what we like to see," Grayson laughed before clapping Noah on the back and complimenting him on the game—which Noah and his team had won. My heart warmed as I watched the exchange, and I wondered if maybe Cameron had been right when he said his sister had found good people in California.

"How ya feeling, Gray?"

Julian leaned on the railing, pinning his friend with a meaningful look. The tone of the conversation shifted, and I wondered what context I was missing.

"Good." Grayson nodded, putting his helmet beneath his arm with a sigh. "Ready to be back home, though."

"I'm sure Nessa's ready to get you home, too," Noah said, elbowing his friend and opponent.

A heated grin split Grayson's face, and I quickly concluded that Nessa—whoever she was—was a lucky lady.

We parted ways soon after that, which was fine with me. I knew we wouldn't be able to talk to Noah for very long, but I was hoping that even that quick introduction would help me when I mustered the courage to slide into his inbox. Now maybe it wouldn't seem so out of the blue to message him.

Julian was quiet on the ride home, but I didn't have it in me to analyze his silence. I'd prepared myself for a few snarky comments to punctuate our evening, but they never came. Instead, I was left with my thoughts, contemplating exactly what my next move would be where Noah and the wedding were involved.

"What's your address?" he asked when the glowing lights of the city grew closer.

"I'll just walk home from your place," I said with a yawn. "It's not far."

"It's midnight."

"So?"

"So, you're not going to walk home." He readjusted his hand on the steering wheel, gripping it tightly. "Tell me your address, Juni."

"632 Oliver Street," I recited.

But only because he called me Juni, and it wasn't even the first time tonight.

Julian nodded, flicking his blinker on in preparation for the upcoming exit.

A few minutes later, we parked in front of my apartment building. "There she is," I said with a sigh, pointing to the balcony above us on the second floor. "Home sweet home."

Julian ducked his head to look out the passenger window, following my finger toward my dark apartment. When I thanked him for the ride, he turned his attention from the building to me. It was hard to make out his expression in the dark, but mostly he looked...tired. My lips parted as I sat on the verge of saying something more, but he stopped me.

"Good night, Daisy," he muttered.

Sensing he wanted to get home, I quit lingering and jumped from the car. I assumed he'd drive off right away, but he didn't. It wasn't until I made it into my apartment, turned on the light, and walked past the window that I noticed him drive away.

eleven years ago

"Please tell me you're wearing a swimsuit under that towel."

Juniper shook her head slowly.

"No swimsuit, no clothes...so can we please just get—"

I cut her off with an irritated groan, scrubbing a hand over my face. When I dropped it, my eyes flicked over Juniper, unable to resist myself.

"Where the fuck are your clothes?"

"Jace stole them from the beach when we were swimming."

"Fucking asshole," I grunted. "He didn't see you, did he?"

Both my sister and Juniper shook their heads.

But I was still going to kick Jace's ass.

"Can we just go?" Juniper whined with a defiant little stop. "We can fix the car later."

I watched as a little shiver worked through her. Without thinking, I whipped my shirt off, walked it over to her, and stuffed it over her head. She didn't complain as she snuck her arms through the sleeves and wrapped them around her, hugging my shirt to her chest.

I turned around, not liking what the image did to me.

"I'm fixing it now. I'll be quick," I mumbled. "I'm not letting you drench my fucking car in lake water."

"Can I help?" Juniper offered as I crouched in front of her busted

tire. I heard the sound of gravel crunching as she took a step forward, and I gritted my teeth.

"No, just—stay over there," I rasped. "Please."

Juniper's sigh was like a cool breeze on this otherwise hot summer night.

"Fine."

CHAPTER SEVEN

LATE NIGHTS WITH JUNIPER St. James were not a new concept.

From the minute Gemma introduced us, Juniper and I communicated in various forms of insults. I didn't like her always being *there*, squeezing her way into our already overcrowded house. And she didn't like...well, me. I never took the time to figure out why Juniper didn't like me because the feeling was mutual. The *why* didn't matter.

Deeper irritation didn't start until later in high school, though. Mostly because I liked my sleep. And Juniper liked being the reason for me not getting it. She had a bad habit of barging into my room at all hours of the night. Even after years of sleeping over at our house, she never learned how to correctly count the goddamn doors in the hallway. She also had a bad habit of winding up in unbelievable predicaments. Like when she and Gemma wound up stranded and naked on Lock Island.

Christ, that night.

Juniper's flat tire might have been easy to change and relatively easy to patch, but I'd still had to stay up until three in the morning to do it. The last thing I'd needed was for her to have an excuse to still be at my house when I returned from football practice the next morning.

Hell, that was the shittiest practice I ever ran. I was nearly an hour late from being so goddamn exhausted, and it hadn't exactly been a good look, not when there had already been people saying that Greg fucking Kennedy should have been captain over me.

Tonight was just another one of those nights—the ones where Juniper kept me from getting enough sleep. I was in bed by a little past midnight, but annoyingly, I couldn't get comfortable. Noah had already texted me like five times since I made it back to my apartment.

Okay, fine. It was once so far. But the words kept repeating in my head, making it feel like more.

LONDON: Juniper single?

This was why it hadn't been necessary for us to go to the game. Besides almost throat-punching that guy after he said shit to Juniper in the street, I'd had fun. Grayson and Noah both scored, and Juniper was surprisingly nice enough not to interrupt my concentration on the game. But the Noah-Juniper meet and greet didn't need to happen.

Noah was a straight shooter, as evidenced by his text. I was positive he would have just texted her himself...if he had her phone number.

Yeah

LONDON: Number?

Some people have regular jobs they have to get up for in the morning, Noah

LONDON: If you don't want to give it to me, that's fine. I'd also take your sister's.

I didn't have to ask which one. I knew it was Gemma. He'd hinted at it more than once after she visited our senior year in college.

I punched my screen with my fingers as I typed a response, feeling exhausted and irritated.

Fuck off. You might be in the pros, but I can still kick your ass.

This was the exact reason I'd hesitated when it came to setting Noah up with Juniper. He was a good guy with a good heart, but damn if he wasn't still a player. Noah and I lived on different planets. Every time I talked to him, he sounded like he was still in his college party era while I was firmly in my work-eat-sleep-repeat era.

LONDON: You think so, huh?

Yeah

Maybe if I gave him one-word answers, he would get the picture that I was trying to get some rest. I should have known sleeping tonight was a useless effort, considering Juniper was involved.

LONDON: Enough to bet on it?

LONDON: I'll make it easy. All you have to do if I win is hand over the numbers.

No deal, no numbers

LONDON: Maybe I misunderstood at the game, then.

What do you mean?

LONDON: You made it seem like you weren't interested in her.

JULIAN: I'm not.

LONDON: ...

I sighed into my pillow. Truth was, when he'd asked at the game if the jersey was mine and then trailed his gaze over Juniper appreciatively, I'd fought the urge to tighten my hold on her. I didn't like how Noah looked at her. That jersey she wore tonight might have had his name on it, but it was from my closet.

I'm not giving you her number without her permission

Somewhere in the back of my mind, I recognized that Juniper would undoubtedly give permission. After worrying over what to say to him—which was weirdly un-Juni-like—she'd probably love it if he texted her first.

Not to mention, I hadn't precisely asked Noah's permission before handing over *his* number. But this wasn't the first time a girl had asked for Noah's digits. When I was living at home after college, everyone seemed to know—likely from my bigmouthed sisters—that I was friends with Noah London, the newly drafted New England quarterback. I couldn't go out for a goddamn drink without a girl, usually one I went to high school with, approaching me to ask for Noah's number.

When I told him about it once, he flashed a smile.

"Eh, give it to them," he'd said.

LONDON: Oh, why didn't you just say that? That's fine, man.

I'll talk to her. Night, London.

Unfortunately, talking to Juniper was a given these days. More than likely, I would walk into the office tomorrow, and she'd bombard me with talk of Noah. But I'd deal with that tomorrow.

For now...sleep.

JUNIPER WAS ARRANGING A TRAY OF MUFFINS WHEN I WALKED INTO OUR office the following day.

"Let me guess," I grumbled, "Cameron told you that he was a big fan of the Mighty Muffin or something."

"No." Juniper scoffed like it was absolutely ridiculous of me to suggest that. "This is *my* favorite bakery."

"Dirty Desserts?"

"What? No."

"Naughty Kneads?"

"Julian."

"Creative Cream Pies?"

"Oh my God. It's just called Georgia's Bakery," she huffed. "Grow up, Julian."

"You're the one who keeps buying breakfast foods as a way to flirt with someone." I threw my stuff on my chair. "By the way, can you stop flirting with my friends? It's getting annoying."

"Oh!" Juniper jumped a little. "That reminds me. I've been talking to Noah all morning."

A knot formed in my stomach as she grabbed her phone, intent on showing me the evidence. But I couldn't care any fucking less about what she and Noah had been talking about.

"What do you mean *all morning*?" I glanced at my watch. "It's eight o'clock."

I'd been awake for less than an hour.

"Not everyone rolls out of bed at the last minute, Julian."

Sighing, I dropped into my chair and pulled out my laptop. "I don't know why they don't."

"It's called productivity," Juniper chirped, now staring down at her phone as she scrolled through what I assumed were messages with Noah. "Have you heard of it?"

"Have you?" I gave her a pointed look. Which, of course, she didn't see because she wasn't paying me any actual attention. "It's business hours, and you are astonishingly off task."

Juniper's eyes found mine as she swiped a curl out of her face to glare properly. "You just walked in the door, and I've been here for a half hour already. So I don't think you're really one to talk."

She never fucking gave it up, did she? Never had, either.

Shaking my head, I focused on my computer. Maybe I didn't come in early or bring in food and drinks to kiss ass, but when I was at work, I got shit done.

Except it was pretty hard to do that when Juniper's phone went off every three minutes. I considered texting Noah about giving it a goddamn rest, but bugging Juniper was more accessible.

"You're going to have to put that on silent, Daisy."

"I'm telling him I can't talk anymore," she said, not even looking up from her phone. Rude, if you ask me. Her peach nails kept tap-tap-tapping. "I have a lot to get done today."

I watched her text Noah for a second before letting my curiosity get the best of me. "So you actually figured out what to say to him, huh?"

Juniper put her phone on the desk and focused on me. Finally. "Well, it was easy after last night. I just texted him this morning and told him it was nice to meet him and he played a great game."

Yeah, that'd do it. Noah loved any chance to get a fucking compliment. I was sure he was all over that.

I nodded, shoving down the odd itch to ask more. Hopefully, Noah wasn't acting too forward. He tended to do that, and Juniper had said she wanted the date to be *fake*. Considering Noah's interest last night, I hoped she led with that.

Maybe I should check.

"You told him that you want a *fake* date, right?"

She gave me a funny look. "Why?"

Didn't want him to get any ideas, that was all.

"Just making sure everyone is on the same page."

"I'm being very straightforward." Juniper crossed her arms over her chest, clearly affronted. "Don't worry. I can handle it."

"You do remember yesterday, right?"

Her implication that she didn't need my help was awfully annoying, considering how she'd begged for it less than twenty-four hours ago. I was starting to regret the hell out of introducing Juniper and Noah.

With a huff of annoyance that I very much felt, Juniper spun around to face her desk. Luckily, I didn't hear her phone ring for the rest of the morning, and I could get some case notes done before I met with Daphne. When I returned to our office after grabbing lunch with Cameron, I found Juniper in the same place I'd left her.

"So, can we start next week?" I asked, leaning against the doorframe. It felt good to stretch my legs.

Juniper swiveled in her desk chair and blinked at me, her long lashes fanning up and down as her brows drew together. All doe-eyed and confused, I didn't recognize her for a second. There was an innocence there that surprised me. She slowly crossed her legs while thinking, which was a miracle in and of itself, considering how tight that skirt was. Christ, Juniper.

I cleared my throat, urging her to answer.

"Start what?"

"Looking at my case," I said, shoving my hands in my pockets with irritation. Of course she'd forgotten. Now that she had what she wanted from our deal, she probably—

"Oh, of course." Her sharp features returned as she nodded. "Do you want to meet after work? I'm free to stay late on Wednesday. I have plans with Gemma on—"

"Sure."

I just wanted to get this deal over with.

Noah could return to being my friend and only *my* friend, and Grayson could get some case-winning legal advice.

Fingers crossed that we could quickly determine an approach

to his malpractice lawsuit. Working in the same room as Juniper was one thing, but working overtime *and* on the same case as her was another.

Fuck, this had to be a bad idea.

But we were doing it anyway.

CHAPTER EIGHT

juniper

"OH, *HELL* NO."

I stiffened at the sound of Julian's voice behind me. Shit, why was he here already? He was consistently five minutes late for work, but *today* he decided to show up early? Of course he did.

"Take the goddamn plants off my desk, Poppy."

Julian's anger had always been easy to detect by how often he swore. So I probably should have taken the goddamn plants off his desk. But did I?

Nah.

Turning to face my *lovely* colleague, I found him standing there, eyes narrowed on me. His worn messenger bag was slung over one broad shoulder as he overwhelmed the doorway with his frame. If I didn't know any better, I might have been a little intimidated.

But I *did* know better. So I squared my shoulders in preparation for another week where Julian did that thing he always did to make me feel like I was a nuisance who didn't belong. Luckily, I was used to it.

"They need direct sunlight," I said. "And your desk is the one by the window."

Julian pushed a hand through his hair, which was darker, more auburn this morning. Clumped strands fell over his forehead, and I realized they were still damp. Which also explained why our office suddenly smelled like soap. Masculine soap with hints of musk and spice.

"I don't give a shit what they need," Julian grunted. "They can die for all I care."

"I was going to move them back to my desk in a bit," I explained. "After a little sunbath."

Julian grabbed the top of the door frame with one hand before resting his forehead against his bicep in a moment of clear frustration. His words were muffled when he spoke. "Your plants, your desk."

I rolled my eyes at his dramatics. "I thought you liked flowers. You know, considering how often you reference them in conversation."

"That's not even a flower." Julian lifted his head, eyes scrutinizing my plants. "It's just a bunch of leaves."

"It's a moonflower, Julian."

He dropped his arm again. "Why are you saying that like I'm supposed to know what it means?"

"Oh, moonflower isn't on your curated list?"

Julian's lips twitched, pulling into a smirk. "No, but I can add it."

Just once. Just once, I wanted to have a conversation with Julian that didn't backfire on me. I glared at him when I said my next words so he knew I was serious.

"Do not start calling me that."

"I can't make any promises." He shrugged, noncommittal. "Not while that's sitting on my desk."

"Fine."

Picking up one pot and then the other, I moved them back to the corner of my desk that was most likely to get some sunlight. I wasn't counting on it, though. Julian's desk faced the only window in the office, while mine was tucked into the corner with only blank walls to keep me company. Together, they made a squished L-shape. Sometimes it felt more like we worked in a closet than an office.

Julian nodded with approval before he crossed the space and started unpacking his bag. I watched him for a moment, my good mood from earlier slowly transcending into annoyance. This happened most mornings, and it usually only worsened the longer Julian and I had to stay within the same four walls.

"You're doing that staring thing again," Julian said without even bothering to look at me. I was sure he purposefully tried not to on most days.

I crossed my arms over my chest, knowing I wouldn't be able to get back to work until I scratched that combative itch inside me that only Julian seemed to spark. "I was just thinking that an alternative solution would be for us to switch desks."

"Hell no." He shook his head, keeping his eyes on his computer as he opened it. "If you wanted to litter your desk with plants, you shouldn't have brought ones that need full sun. It's called planning ahead. How did you get through law school without critical thinking skills, Daisy?"

I scowled, hating when he made some small thing I did into a bigger, professional slight. Did he forget that *he* had come to *me* for help with a case?

"I'm trying to declutter my apartment," I confessed, ignoring his comment. "I didn't realize you would be so much of a curmudgeon about it. My mistake, honestly. I should have expected you'd be the Ebenezer Scrooge of the office."

Even as I said it, I knew the words weren't entirely true. This behavior of Julian's would never extend to the entire office. Only *our* office.

"The last thing I need is you invading my space with your shit. I had to deal with that for like ten years, and I'm over it." He sighed heavily, hunching over his desk. "Leave your clutter at home, okay?"

Often when we argued, there was a hint of a smirk on Julian's face. A smirk that told me that he enjoyed irritating the hell out of me. But this was not one of those times. I couldn't even see his face, but I knew. The tone of Julian's voice was sharp. Pointed.

I sighed as a familiar, embarrassing sense of rejection swirled in my gut. I shoved it down, refusing to let Julian bother me.

"Right now, my apartment looks like I'm unhealthily obsessed with plants, books, and clothes and have no friends," I said, doing whatever I could to *not* get sucked into the past. "I don't want Noah to see all that."

Although, it was an accurate description. My life was a collection of outlet malls, romance novels, enough plants to have my own greenhouse, and Gemma. Because I did have *one* friend. In Boston, anyway. The few friends I'd made in college were now scattered throughout the country, and it was scary how quickly we'd drifted apart.

Julian turned abruptly in his chair to stare at me. His face had twisted even more than I imagined. Eyebrows pulled together, mouth flattened in a rigid line, the tone of his voice still sharp.

"What is that supposed to mean?"

I frowned, not sure what had been unclear. "It means I invited Noah over and—"

Julian's entire body seemed to tense, though I didn't understand the reason behind it. "Why did you do that?"

"Because," I began slowly. Maybe if I enunciated it more, he'd understand me for once. "If Noah and I are going to act like we're in a relationship at my sister's wedding, we need to get to know each other first."

From my very first text, Noah had been super friendly. All my nervousness about talking to him vanished as soon as he started texting back, asking me questions about working with Julian and moving to Boston, making it seem like he was genuinely interested to know more about me. There was an ease to talking to him that I enjoyed. Sometimes I couldn't tell if he was being flirtatious or if he just had a natural bit of charm to him, but I liked it. We could definitely survive one night together.

"Hold on. Hold on." Julian lifted a hand while raking the other one through his damp strands. "Hold on, Rosie."

He paused, and it felt theatric, as usual. I tapped my foot, impatient.

"Holding on," I said dryly. "And waiting for the point."

"Sister?" His confusion verged on something...more. Something I couldn't put my finger on. "You don't have a sister."

"Sofia," I said, swallowing the sudden lump in my throat. I hadn't meant to let that slip to him, but it was the least of my concerns at the moment. The wedding was only a month away, and just thinking about it made my palms sweat. "My biological sister."

I watched as the neurons fired in Julian's brain. He relaxed, softening, looking like he wanted to ask more. But then the gears in his head turned faster, and we skipped right past the questions to something else. A dark mask of irritation replaced his momentary understanding.

"And you want Noah to pretend to be your *boyfriend*?" His lip curled on the last word like he couldn't imagine anyone wanting to date me. "That's not what you told me."

"I told you I needed a fake date."

"A fake date is different from a fake boyfriend, Juni."

His incredulity was somewhat satisfying today, considering Noah had already agreed to my plan without seeming bothered by it. Our conversation from Friday had extended into the weekend, and while I was a little overwhelmed by how flirty and forward he was, Julian had warned me that he was a bit of a player, so I wasn't too surprised or bothered.

"It's just for one night." Why did he care so much? "It'll be fine."

"Why?"

"What do you mean *why*?"

The exasperation on Julian's face told me he thought the question should be obvious.

"Why does he need to pretend to be your boyfriend?"

I stiffened, having no desire to explain that particular *why* to the man in front of me.

"*Because*, Julian."

That was all I had in me today.

Julian opened his mouth to undoubtedly call out my nonanswer when a friendly face popped into the door of our office. One that was more than welcome at the moment.

"How do either of you get anything done when you spend half your time at work arguing?"

Cameron gave a megawatt smile, clearly teasing.

Julian, on the other hand, did not seem amused.

"Wanna grab some coffee quick?" he asked, sending Cameron a look that pleaded for a reason to get out of this office.

I was positive that Cameron's reply would only piss Julian off more, and I grimaced in preparation. Sure enough, Cameron lifted his coffee cup from Georgia's—the one I got him earlier this morning—and gave a regretful response.

"Juniper already brought me some." An awkward silence filled the room for only a second before Cameron rushed to add, "But I'll go with you, man. Just gotta be back to meet with our team by nine."

He glanced at me—because I was on said team—before checking Julian's reaction. Which was to wave it off and turn back toward his desk.

"No worries," Julian said. "Maybe another time."

Cameron winced, and I hated the guilt that washed over his expression. How I helped put it there.

Poor Cameron was a people pleaser. Well, to an extent. In meetings, he was assertive and confident with the perspective he brought to the table, even if it differed from others. But as soon as we'd revert to small talk, he softened into a different version of himself. It was easy to see how his family background might have influenced him into that—an actress for a mom and an artist for a sister while his late father was in the military.

Cameron sighed, lingering in the doorway, and I gave him a

wave to let him know I'd see him at our meeting. Once he left, I got to work, ignoring Julian while he ignored me.

At one point, that might have been easy, but today, something wasn't sitting right. I felt oddly *bad*. Our deal was hanging over my head, too. We'd made plans to stay late tonight to look at Julian's case, and now I was dreading it.

I shook my head and put my earbuds in, needing to think about anything or anyone but Julian Briggs. At least until I had to.

I could do that...right?

I SAW THE PIZZA BOX WAITING FOR ME ON TYLER'S DESK AS SOON AS I walked into the reception lobby. When I grabbed it, Tyler paused what he was doing to glance my way, curiosity woven into his expression.

"Working late tonight," I said simply and turned around before he could ask any questions that I couldn't—or didn't want to—answer.

Julian didn't move a muscle when I slid through our office door. Unsurprisingly, my presence meant nothing to him. I put the pizza on his desk, followed by paper plates and napkins I'd grabbed from the commons area.

"I ordered pizza."

It was an obvious statement, but it was the first thing I'd dared to say to Julian since we bickered this morning. He didn't like that I got things for Cameron—that much was obvious. Was it because I never got anything for him? I doubted that was the case, but something still churned in my gut, similar to the guilt that flashed across Cameron's face earlier.

Not knowing how else to fix it, I bought pizza. For Julian.

When he didn't respond, I nudged the box closer to him. "It's pepperoni and pineapple. You still like that, right?"

That captured his attention. He turned his head slowly and

examined the pizza box, probably wondering if I'd poisoned the damn thing.

I cleared my throat. "I assumed you still wanted to stay and look at that case tonight."

After drawing out the moment in his own personal brand of dramatics, he spoke.

"You remember what kind of pizza I like?"

"Saturday pizza nights at your house were a staple of my childhood, Julian." Was it surprising that he forgot I was there for those? Not even a little bit. "How could I forget the way you domineered the weekly ordering process?"

Julian hesitantly opened the box, frowning.

"You didn't have to buy dinner," he muttered, ignoring my critical comment. Typical. "How much was it?"

"Don't worry about it."

Julian shot me a glare while snapping his computer shut. I was sure it had to do with the sudden unbalance of what he perceived was *fair* in our deal, but he took a slice of pizza anyway.

"Are you going to eat, too?" he asked after swallowing the first bite and licking his lips. "You always get food and drinks for other people but never yourself."

It took me a minute to find any words. Considering how much time Julian spent actively ignoring me, his words struck me as surprising. No, more than that. Shocking.

"I'll eat."

I didn't want to argue about it, nor did I want Julian to go down a sudden rabbit hole that involved dissecting my relationship with food. So to prove it to him, I grabbed a slice of pizza and dropped into my desk chair. I kicked my feet up in a hopefully casual attempt to brush past his comment, and Julian's gaze flicked over to me before immediately training on the ceiling instead.

"What?" I asked, ragged exasperation filling the word. What the hell was his problem *now*?

Julian coughed, managed to swallow a bit of pizza, and then cleared his throat. All without looking at me.

Drama king.

"Your dress," he admitted hoarsely.

Huh? My polka-dotted wrap dress was one of my favorites. Flimsy and comfortable, it covered my thighs entirely, even as I sat back in my chair. But as I smoothed the hem and followed it around to the back, I realized that with my legs propped up, the underside of my legs—and maybe even a bit of my ass—were exposed. Unlike the skirt I had on yesterday, this dress didn't stick to me like a second skin.

I hastily flattened my feet back on the ground. "That better?"

Julian lowered his gaze, assessing me in a way that warmed my cheeks. Not warm from embarrassment or warm from the hot pizza in my hands. It was warm in a way that tripped a confusion wire in my brain and caused goose bumps on my arm. My palms grew sweaty. I hated being sweaty, but this? I didn't know how to feel about this.

Finally, Julian responded by making a noncommittal noise in the back of his throat, and I snapped out of it.

"Didn't realize you were afraid of a little bare skin," I said, hoping that the heat inside me might fade to embers if we reverted back to our status quo.

My hopes lasted all of two seconds.

"Afraid?" Julian chuckled, but it was deep, and there wasn't much humor there. His voice tickled the already raised hairs on my arm. "Daisy, no."

Breathing was suddenly something I had to concentrate very hard on.

"So tell me about this case," I said, hurrying to find a topic of conversation that wouldn't make my palms sweat even more.

Julian nodded, clearly relieved that I'd brought it up. He launched into a description of the case, which focused on an undetected heart defect—coarctation of the aorta, to be precise. His eyes lit up as he spoke, his passion more than apparent. It wasn't something I'd seen in Julian, not in a long time. Except for maybe at the football game last week.

"There's something you're not telling me," I said when he finished, though I couldn't articulate precisely what it was. "Why haven't I heard anything about this? I was just talking with Daphne about—"

"It's being kept on the down low."

"Why?"

"The client is..." Julian bit his lip, looking like he didn't want to finish that sentence.

"Famous?" I offered. "A celebrity? Politician?"

He shrugged. "You could say he's well-known, yes."

Sensing that Julian wouldn't drop his insistence on being tight-lipped, I let it go.

"Okay." I rubbed my hands together, eager to get started. It was these moments that I lived for, the reminder within me that knowledge *was* power. And I had it. "This is what I know."

We walked through my experience with a similar case until the sky was inky outside the window. It was strangely nice. Even though I'd been working in this office with Julian for weeks now, tonight was the first time we shared a professional, working conversation.

"We can look at it more tomorrow if you want," I offered once I realized the time. The pizza was cold, the office was dark, and I had just yawned three times in a row.

"That'd be great. Thanks, Juni." Julian nodded absently, still shuffling through medical reports that his client had sent him while I stilled, shocked at how he'd *thanked* me. "I'm taking Friday off to help Mom prepare for the party," he added.

The Briggs Family Annual Halloween Party—I'd almost forgotten.

Julian glanced up, cocking a brow. "I assume you'll be crashing."

My stomach soured, feeling the progress we'd made over the past few hours going down the drain.

"It isn't crashing if you're invited, Julian." I sniffed, turning my attention to organizing my desk. "Your mom sent me a text as a reminder last week."

"Of course you're texting my mom," he mumbled beneath his breath.

"Your mom loves me."

He sighed. "I know."

"Gemma has practice Friday evening, so we're driving to Whitebridge after she gets done."

He shot me a look, his eyes narrowing and jaw twitching, and I immediately regretted opening my mouth. I knew what he was about to say, and I would do anything to escape the upcoming conversation.

"Which one of you is driving?"

Yep, there it was.

From the beginning, Julian thought I was some sort of imposter into their family—like he couldn't fathom having yet *another* girl in the house. While the rest of the Briggs family treated me like I was the sixth sister, Julian had always rejected that idea. Instead, he liked to pretend I didn't exist.

But then there were times that he was forced to acknowledge me, never for good reasons. And the car accident Gemma and I were in on a snowy night in high school was the worst one. He still blamed me for that, for what happened. He went from thinking I was annoying to hating me because of it, but not more than I hated myself.

"Gemma is driving," I said icily, knowing it would be what he wanted to hear. "Something is wrong with my car's brakes right now, so I'm riding with her."

His previous concerned expression twisted visibly.

"Why didn't you tell me?"

"Why didn't I tell you what?"

"That your brakes aren't working."

"Why would I tell you?" He acted like we had the kind of relationship where we shared personal life details even though we usually just tried to get through the workday without biting each other's heads off. "It's not *that* bad. Just whenever I drive, they—"

"Jesus Christ, Juniper," he cut me off, and I jumped from how sharply he said my name. My real name. "You're still driving with bad brakes?"

"Why do you care?" I shot back, instantly defensive as I careened into memories of that night in high school and all the other nights, too. Anxious energy filled my words. "As long as I'm not driving Gemma around, it's not like it'll matter to you if I end up in a ditch with a broken neck."

Julian flinched at my harsh words, his eyes darkening as they swept over me. When he spoke, his voice was eerily low. Unsteady. "Don't ever say something like that again."

I looked away, unable to handle the intensity of Julian's stare or how it made me feel. My heart was already in my throat from thinking about the accident, and now—

"Did you drive to work?" he asked, the sharpness returning to his tone.

I shook my head, peeking over to find him looking more relaxed. Relieved.

"Your car's at your apartment?" he clarified.

Still not trusting myself to speak, I nodded. And with that response, Julian quickly packed his belongings and made for the door without even glancing at me. I breathed a sigh of relief that the conversation was over until Julian checked back over his shoulder.

"Coming?"

I frowned. "You don't need to wait for me."

"Yes, I do." He momentarily pinched the bridge of his nose. "I need you to show me where your car is so I can look at it."

He wasn't serious, was he?

"I have an appointment with a mechanic next week."

"I'm a mechanic."

"You're an attorney, not a mechanic."

This man really liked to act like he was all-powerful sometimes, and it drove me up the wall.

"I'm as good as one after how many years I worked in my dad's shop, and you know it." The longer Julian lingered in the doorway, the redder his face seemed to grow. Maybe it would match his hair soon. "How are you planning to get to your appointment if your brakes don't work?"

I shrugged. "Well, it's not far, and my brakes should work enough to get me there—"

Julian interrupted me with a grunt. "Let's go."

When I hesitated, debating if I should dig my heels into the ground even more, Julian insisted.

"Now."

"It's late." I emphasized that with a yawn.

His lips curved. "Our specialty, right?"

"Fine," I huffed.

As much as I hated once again relying on Julian to help me with something, I found it hard to argue with him when it meant I might save money on repairs. Every once in a while, I was practical.

But also, I was tired. My combative itch had been scratched for the day, and my desire to argue disappeared from all the barbs that had stuck and hurt.

Sometimes it wasn't worth it. And this was one of those times.

So for the second time in a week, I followed Julian out into the night and let him take me home.

CHAPTER NINE

KEEPING UP WITH JULIAN as he took long strides across my parking garage was nearly impossible. The still air made breathing difficult, and sweat began gathering in all its typical spots while I tried not to fall too far behind. My bed and my to-be-read pile of books were calling to me from a few floors above, but Julian was insistent. Arguing with him further would only involve a risk I wasn't willing to take. If I opened my mouth now, he'd likely hear how wildly out of breath I was, and I didn't need to give him another reason to make fun of me.

"It's the white one, right?" he asked over his shoulder.

Luckily, I was able to answer with a nod.

Julian marched the rest of the way to my car without saying a word. My apartment complex allotted me the parking space in the furthest corner, which I didn't mind unless I had groceries to haul in. Or unless I'd been wearing the same pair of heels for nearly twelve hours. Like right now.

"You should request a better spot so you're not walking across this entire garage by yourself at night," Julian said, assessing the situation with his hands on his hips.

I wiped my sweaty palms on my dress as I came to stand beside him, hating how sticky I felt. Usually the dankness of the garage felt cool on my skin, but the humidity stuck to me tonight.

"Why do you assume that I'm alone?"

I raised a brow at Julian and hoped I didn't sound like I was still trying to catch my breath from keeping his ridiculous pace.

Julian's gaze cut to me, sharp in its perusal. He pressed his lips together, his jaw clenching before he switched his attention to my car again.

"Maybe because you needed my help finding a date?" he muttered, chuckling beneath his breath as he held out a hand. "Give me your keys so I can back it up."

Goddamn him. A flush rose from my neck to my cheeks, and I straightened in defiance.

"I can back it out myself," I snapped, getting in my car before Julian could be more of a demanding ass. After reversing enough for him to have plenty of working space, I rolled to a stop and winced at the horrible squealing noise that happened whenever I so much as touched my brakes.

Julian had his arms crossed with his brows furrowed when I got out of the car.

"That's the concern, I take it?" He glared at my front wheels and then my back ones as though he had the power to fix the brakes with laser vision. "Anything else you've noticed besides the squeaking?"

I shook my head.

"I tried to tell you it wasn't an emergency," I said, sensing he was about to say something to belittle the problem or indicate I was wasting his time—even though this was his goddamn idea.

But as I leaned against my car, Julian remained quiet. I could see the gears in his head turning, winding up. I waited, trying to be patient. But patience had never really been my forte, and when at least a minute had gone by without Julian saying a word, I dropped my keys on top of my car, hoping the loud clanking would get his attention. When it didn't, I sighed.

"Just forget about it."

"I'm not going to forget about it." He jerked out of his trance and tipped his head toward my trunk. "I assume there's a jack in here?"

I looked pointedly at his attire, sweeping my gaze up and down. "You're really going to jack up my car and look at my brakes in your little attorney getup?"

Julian replied by stepping forward while shrugging off his suit jacket, dropping it to the garage floor. I frowned while staring at it, unable to think of anything but how dirty it would get, and when I looked up again, Julian was even closer. His eyes bored straight into mine while he hooked a finger in his tie, working it down until it was loose enough to yank one end out of the knot. His tie joined his jacket on the ground before Julian undid the top buttons of his white dress shirt.

If I thought I was sweating before, it was nothing to the stickiness on my palms once Julian began intently rolling his sleeves without breaking eye contact.

To my shame, I looked away first—just for a second—to watch his fingers capably fold fabric over veiny forearms. *Shit.* I knew he was trying to make a point, but I hated how effectively he was doing it.

"Didn't realize you were afraid of a little bare skin, Rosie," he said, repeating my words from earlier in a low-toned challenge.

Accepting Julian's dare, I flicked my eyes over him and all his exposed skin, which rippled over an annoying amount of muscles. "I'm not, Julian."

"Okay." He cocked a brow, gesturing to his refreshed attire. "Is this better, then?"

The shrug I gave him was a definite attempt to act like I wasn't bothered by his unbuttoned shirt, rolled-up sleeves, and annoying smirk.

"I mean..." I cleared my throat. "If you manage not to get that white shirt dirty, I'll be impressed."

The corner of his mouth kicked up even further, and to my horror, he damn near closed the distance between us, causing me to stumble back into the side of my car. Julian's sharp eyes danced with amusement as he placed a hand on the car roof behind me, leaning in. His lips found my ear, his breath fanning across my skin.

"I'm not afraid of getting dirty, Lily," he murmured before snatching my keys from the top of my car and stalking off to pop the trunk.

I swallowed past the sudden dryness in my throat. "Then have at it."

Julian glanced up, smiling at me above the popped trunk. "I will."

Leaving it at that, he began pulling equipment from the spare tire compartment, and I was abundantly relieved that there was some space between us again. Not nearly enough, but it would do for now. My attention switched to my feet, aching in my favorite pair of pumps. They were perfectly comfortable for a typical day in the office, but today was anything but typical.

Unable to bear it any longer, I kicked them off. Julian glanced quizzically at my feet as he walked by with his arms full, and I shrugged. "If you're going to get comfortable, so am I."

Even though dirt undoubtedly covered the ground, the cool concrete felt good on the bottoms of my feet. I'd just have to take a long, hot—well, maybe cold—shower tonight.

"Feet hurt?"

I nodded. "They're killing me."

"Maybe if you didn't wear torture devices for shoes." He scowled at my heels as if they'd personally offended him.

I decided not to dignify that with a response. Julian had made it clear on more than one occasion that he didn't understand fashion in the slightest. Instead, I watched as he began jacking up the car to remove the front driver-side tire.

"How do you know it's that one?" I asked.

"Heard it when you braked earlier," he grunted, the muscles in his now-bared forearms flexing while he tried to loosen the lug nut. He gripped the breaker bar with both hands, throwing his whole body into it while he pulled his lower lip between his teeth in concentration. I watched with far too much fascination until Julian finally got the bar to twist with one final heave.

"Front driver side was the loudest one," he continued as though he hadn't just acted like a total muscleman show-off. "Although they all squealed. Hold this, will ya?"

I held my hand out without thinking, and Julian dropped the lug nut into it. Then I bit down on my tongue as I stood there for the others, hating that I was letting Julian—of all people—tell me what to do. It would benefit me in the long run, though.

"Have you had someone else look at this recently?" he asked, twisting back to look up at me after he'd removed the tire and some other car parts I couldn't name. His auburn waves fell back from his face as blue eyes scrutinized me.

"I had my brake pads replaced—"

"They used cheap ones," Julian cut in before I could even finish. "They're not ceramic, and they should be."

And with that, Julian began putting the wheel back together again.

"So I should go back and request ceramic brake pads?" I asked, wanting to make sure I understood my next steps.

"Don't bother." Julian stood, wiping grease-covered fingers on his black slacks, making me cringe. Before I could ask for clarification on what he meant by that, he jumped in the driver's seat to pull the car back into its parking spot. When he slid back out, he added, "I'll take care of it so it's done right. I can pick up the supplies from my dad's shop when we're home this weekend and fix it next week."

"You don't have to—"

"I'll do it Monday," Julian insisted, swiping his jacket and tie off the ground. "Now, come on. It's getting late."

Couldn't argue on the late part. I grabbed my heels without hesitating, eager to put an end to this night. But when I tried to straighten, shoes in hand, my entire world momentarily tipped. *Careened.* My scream bounced off the walls of the parking garage as a strong arm looped beneath my back and my knees, and I realized—with a fair bit of horror—that Julian was *carrying* me.

"What the hell are you *doing*?"

When he spoke, his words brushed across my hair. I felt them —like a breeze. "Seems a bit obvious, doesn't it?"

"Maybe not as obvious as you'd think," I hissed before trying to shift, wondering if I could roll out of his arms and back into a more composed position. But Julian's grip tightened. His fingers pressed securely into my sides, just like they had at the football game last week.

"Julian, put me down," I demanded when I realized I couldn't escape on my own.

"No."

"*Julian*."

"I saw at least two broken bottles earlier," he said plainly. "And I don't know about you, but I'd like to get home. Which means I really need you not to slice your feet open."

"If you had just *told* me that, I could have put my shoes back on."

"You mean the torture devices?" he corrected. From the corner of my eyes, I saw the wry twist of his lips.

"You're going to get my dress dirty." I flicked his fingers, hoping he'd let go. He didn't.

"No, I'm not. My hands are clean enough." His voice dropped. "I'd never dare otherwise with you."

"Sometimes you are absolutely infuriating," I grumbled, hating how his body heat seemed to be pressing in from all sides. God, I hoped he couldn't feel how sticky I was. A shower. I just needed a shower. And I needed Julian to stop getting so goddamn *close*.

The rumble of Julian's soft laughter vibrated in his chest. I felt it—like an earthquake, shaking my world. I leaned into the comfort of it without thinking. What was wrong with me?

"Sometimes?" he questioned.

When he didn't put me down even when we got to the elevator, I amended, "All the time."

The doors slid open, and Julian stepped us beneath the fluorescent bulbs of my building's outdated elevator. He tipped me back toward the ground slowly, and I had to fumble with my dress to keep it from riding up again as I slid down his front.

Infuriating. Absolutely infuriating.

He stepped back as soon as he could, undoubtedly scrambling to get away from me, and when I'd composed myself, I glanced around the elevator to find Julian on the opposite side of it. His eyes were trained on the ground, but they lifted when I faced him.

Julian and I were like magnets—always had been. We were two same-sided magnets, and the repulsion force was overwhelming. Undeniable. There were times, though, that one of us... flipped. And suddenly, there'd be a *pull.*

"All the time?" he repeated, eyes bright.

Caught in a magnetic force I was trying to fight, I found it hard to respond.

Julian's expression tightened. He looked like how I felt inside. "Feeling's mutual, Daisy."

CHAPTER TEN

BY TWO O'CLOCK THE next day, I started looking forward to the evening. Or, more accurately, when the office would be empty besides Juniper and me.

It had nothing to do with the high-heeled princess I shared my office with and everything to do with, well, everyone else. I hadn't been able to go more than five minutes without an interruption today, and all I needed was some fucking peace and quiet.

Peace, quiet, and Juniper St. James were not a usual combination, but working together on the case last night had been an odd relief of sorts. We got along better when speaking a common language, and law was it.

As the bustle of the office slowed, I shifted my focus from the new case I was working on with Daphne to Grayson's lawsuit. I didn't like deceiving Juniper about the full story surrounding our work, but it was better this way. Grayson had asked me to keep it under wraps until we had a better idea if there was even enough potential for taking action. He had enough spotlights on him already during the middle of the football season, and I understood that.

Not wanting Juniper to beat me to the punch this time, I ordered dinner from an Italian restaurant around the corner. I overheard her raving about the restaurant's gnocchi to Cameron earlier today—one of my many interruptions. But at least it gave me an idea for dinner; the last thing I needed was for her to spend even more money on me during a deal that was supposed to be an even trade.

First, the football game, and then dinner. It was one reason I felt justified in fixing her brakes: it would cancel out the cost of the tickets from last week. And tonight's dinner would make up for last night's.

"Oh, I love this place!" A smile stretched onto Juniper's face as she looked inside the paper bag I set on her desk, and I quickly pushed down the satisfaction that rose inside me at seeing it. "Thank you for this. They have the best—"

"Gnocchi," I finished for her. "I know."

"You've had it?" She looked up at me with surprise and hope in her eyes. Like I might suddenly become bearable if I also understood the wonders of Victoria's Eatery. Was I invisible? Did she forget that I could hear everything she said all day, every day, in this goddamn office?

"No." I rolled my eyes before looking away. "You told Cameron that earlier."

"Oh." Her voice deflated. "I didn't think you were listening."

"Kinda hard to focus on work when you're rambling about pasta."

"Cameron asked me for a restaurant recommendation because his mom's in town," Juniper said defensively. "Also, gnocchi is not pasta, Julian."

"Are you sure about that?" I muttered. "It definitely looks like pasta."

Juniper pursed her lips together. "It's a debatable topic that, in my opinion, is hardly debatable at all."

I bit down on my tongue to keep my reply in check. I didn't give a damn what it was actually called, and frankly, I shouldn't be annoyed at all. It wasn't like Cameron could have asked *me* for recommendations. We both knew I wasn't the person to go to for that sort of thing. My palate was less than refined, and Cameron knew it. We'd survived on whatever cheap food we could find in law school.

"Let's just get to work," I said, pulling out the reports I'd reviewed last night.

Out of the corner of my eye, I saw Juniper nod. And then, just like that, the mood shifted. She asked me about Gabriel's initial scans when he was an infant, scribbling notes between quick bites of pasta. Sorry, *not* pasta. And then we moved on to looking at Gabriel's most recent scans, and before I knew it, the sky was a hue of navy. The lights in the hallway outside the office were off. I'd learned they were motion sensor activated, which told me no one else was here but us.

When I glanced back at Juniper, she was in the middle of a massive yawn.

"Time to call it a night, I think," I said, even though I had an urge to keep working. We'd made progress, but if Grayson called me tomorrow, I still wouldn't have good news to tell him. And that bothered me.

Juniper soundlessly began to pack her things. I waited until she'd slipped on her light pink blazer, the one that distinctly reminded me of when my sisters forced me to watch *Legally Blonde*, before I spoke again.

"Come on," I said, "I'll drive you home."

I expected an argument, but all she did was blink twice at me before nodding. An unbidden chuckle slipped from my lips.

"Tired, Daisy?"

She nodded again, and her lack of energy, the way the corners of her lips tipped down, made me fight the urge to scoop her back up into my arms like last night. I wanted a reaction; I wanted her alive again.

But I didn't do anything more than jerk my head toward the door. She followed me silently to the car, saying very little on the drive to her apartment, too. Only once she stepped out onto the sidewalk did she glance back at me and cock her head to the side. "You're taking tomorrow off, right? For the party?"

I nodded slowly, feeling a surprising amount of unease settle in my gut.

"See you on Saturday, then," she said.

And then she was gone. Before I could even thank her for the extra work she put in tonight. The long hours deserved gratitude, at the very least.

Our deal wasn't fair, and it irked me. Even with the dinner, even with fixing her brakes. Her exhaustion tonight made that more than clear—it wasn't fair. And I'd have to find a way to change that.

With a sigh, I waited until I saw her light flick on in her apartment before heading home. Once again, I couldn't sleep after crawling into bed, and this time, it had nothing to do with texts from Noah. It *did* have to do with Juniper, though. Juniper and Gemma. Driving home together. At night. Tomorrow.

I pulled out my phone, checking the weather.

It was going to rain. It wasn't snow, but it wasn't nothing, either.

I squeezed my eyes shut, willing my brain not to think about Juni's tears or the beeping of hospital machines. It was years ago now, but the memories had never faded. Not even a little, and tonight was no different. My brain wasn't listening to my request to forget; it never did when it came to anything involving Juniper.

That accident changed everything. Juniper thought it was because I blamed her for it, and that was honestly for the best. Better than her knowing the wake-up call it gave me, the realization it caused me as a teenager of why she got so under my skin, of why her determination to sneak into my family bothered me so much when I—

It didn't matter anymore. The confusion. The anger. It launched a resolution in me, and I hadn't been able to escape it since.

Fuck.

With the flick of my thumb, I switched to my messages app and sent a text to my mom. There was a change of plans for tomorrow.

THE SHOCK ON JUNIPER'S FACE WHEN I WALKED INTO THE OFFICE THE following day was enjoyable. Her expression was back to being animated and scrutinizing. Irritation and confusion swept over her features, and I sat back, watching her try to piece the puzzle together. She wanted to know why I was in the office when I said I'd be gone, but she was visibly trying not to care. Not to ask.

It was all very Juni-like.

So was her reaction when she walked into Gemma's apartment later that night to find me sitting on my sister's couch. Her jaw came unhinged as she gaped at me before pulling herself together and facing Gemma with a look of disgust.

"Do you realize you have an interloper on your couch?"

Gemma winced apologetically. "Julian asked if he could get a ride at the last minute, too."

Juniper's sharp gaze jerked back to me. I smiled, twirling Gemma's car keys around my finger. "I think something might be wrong with my brakes, too."

A lie, and she knew it.

"And you couldn't fix them?" she challenged. "Imagine that."

"I'll be in the car," I said, getting to my feet and striding toward the door. When I brushed past little Miss Elle Woods, I choked a bit on the sudden cloud of floral perfume. God, that was going to fuck with my concentration while driving, wasn't it?

As soon as the apartment door shut behind me, I heard Juniper groan to Gemma.

She could be mad. I'd let her rant to Gemma all she liked about me; that was fine. I didn't care if she was angry. I cared that we didn't relive the Halloween weekend from nearly a decade ago, when thick snow had blanketed the ground and the two of them hadn't made it to the party.

Unsurprisingly, the car ride was quiet. But not in the way that it was yesterday. Tension simmered beneath the silence tonight. Anger and anxiety—a mix of it. Rain pelted against the windows, reaffirming my decision to drive Juniper and Gemma home. As proud as Gemma was, I knew driving in bad weather made her nervous. Actually, I suspected any kind of travel made her nervous. And Juniper was so eager to prove herself all the damn time that it led to disastrous decision-making.

Gemma made Juniper sit in the front, trying to be nice. Or something. But it made the entire ride awkward and unpleasant. All I could smell was *her*. All I could feel was her irritation, her presence. But after two hours of breathing in bouquets of roses, we finally made it to Whitebridge.

Juniper huffed exaggeratedly as she got out of the car in front of her parents' house—an idyllic two-story in the center of our small town. She promised Gemma she would see her tomorrow at the party before giving me a quick glance filled with bitterness.

Feeling's mutual, Lily.

I pulled back into the road, and it took Gemma approximately half a second before she jumped on me.

"I thought maybe since you were working together, the two of you might have...fixed things."

"Fixed?"

Gemma was delusional if she thought that Juniper and I could be fixed. That would imply that we were broken, which couldn't be further from the truth. This was just the way we were. This was the way we always would be, too.

"You know." Gemma sighed. "Figure things out."

"What's to figure out?"

I saw Gemma throw her hands up in the rearview mirror. "Why you hate each other."

"I know why I hate her."

"And why's that?"

Gemma's tone turned slightly hostile, which always happened when we broached this subject. It was the only reason I ever felt bad about my less-than-ideal relationship with Juniper —because it bothered Gemma to no end that we didn't get along.

"Because no matter where I go, I can't fucking *escape* her."

There was a slight pause. A silence that had a pulse in the car.

"That's why you went to California for college, isn't it?"

I scoffed, ignoring how my stomach flipped. "Yeah, I moved across the country to get away from Juniper. It definitely had nothing to do with the D1 football scholarship."

Gemma hummed, raising her brows. She tapped her fingers on the car door armrest like she was contemplating my answer. Wasn't sure what there was to contemplate, though.

"How was the football game last week?" she asked, abruptly changing the subject.

"Good." I turned the last corner of our trip, driving down our childhood street until I saw the old Victorian we called home looming before me. Leaves swirled to the wet ground, painting autumn on the pavement. "Knights won."

Gemma's eyes connected with mine in the rearview mirror. Blue met blue.

"And I hear that Juni is hitting it off with Noah."

I looked away, focusing on parking in our driveway beside the other cars of our siblings and parents. "I don't know about *hitting it off.*"

A scoff sounded from the back seat. "You haven't seen their texts."

I put the car in park with more force than I probably needed to before turning to narrow my eyes at my sister. "What's that supposed to mean?"

My sisters rarely pissed me off. A little annoyed or irritated, sure. But that skin-crawling vexation was reserved for other people in my life. Right now, though, as Gemma shrugged and jumped out of the car without answering me...I found my fingers wrapping tightly around the gear stick. Hard.

"Gemma!" I called after her, but the door slammed anyway.

I watched her skip through the light rain and the fall gloom, disappearing into the shelter of the open garage.

Fuck, I needed a drink. But I knew I probably wouldn't get one, not until our house was party-ready. God, I hoped everything went off without a hitch this weekend.

Many years, it didn't. Nine years ago, it was the accident. Four years ago, it was Johnny Lewis climbing on top of the kitchen table to belt out *Thriller* before falling and earning a trip to the hospital. And last year, we almost had to cancel the party because my parents struggled to afford it.

All we needed this year was no snow, no tabletop belters, and no last-minute cancellations. Luckily, I had enough in my bank account to help fund the annual get-together this year, so I wasn't concerned about the last one.

But the other thing I needed to happen? Juniper. I needed Juniper at the party, even though I hated admitting that. If she was at my house, in my kitchen, downing the apple pie shots my mom always recruited me to make, she wouldn't be spending time weaseling her way further into my friends' lives. Into *my* life.

Halloween had already been established as something I had to share with her.

My friends, though? That was new. And I didn't like it. Actually, I hated it.

I hated it a fucking lot.

THE BRIGGS FAMILY HALLOWEEN PARTY WAS A WHITEBRIDGE STAPLE.

My parents invited nearly the entire town...which had its pros and its cons. Pro: I got all my catching up done in one night; no need to make multiple arrangements to see high school classmates or family friends. Con: There were people in town I had absolutely no interest in catching up with.

For one, I hoped Kelly didn't show tonight. We dated for about nine months during our senior year of high school before going through what I *thought* was a mutual breakup. She'd planned to attend a university in New York, and with me going to California, we hadn't wanted to attempt a long-distance relationship. But for the last ten-some years, she'd acted like I was a cold-hearted asshole who dumped her out of the blue.

I was standing in the kitchen with my dad when the first guests arrived—who luckily were *not* Kelly. With a peek down the hall, I was unsurprised when Juniper strolled through the front door with her parents a little past eight o'clock.

I also shouldn't have been surprised to see her wearing that familiar short and pleated skirt, but *hell*, I still did a double take.

Gemma and Juniper had been dressing as Girl Scouts for Halloween for *years*—ever since they were kicked out of their fourth-grade troop for shady under-the-lunch-table Girl Scout cookie dealings during the infamous Whitebridge scandal of 2005.

Okay, maybe not that infamous.

I wasn't sure if they started the Halloween costume tradition as an act of rebellion or as some sort of consolation—since they had been allowed to keep their green sashes and berets. But now, it was undoubtedly an act of irony. One I could usually appreciate.

Juniper ran into Josie and Genevieve first—my two youngest sisters—giving them both hugs before making her way into our living room. Tall, black candelabras and glowing jack-o'-lanterns lit the space, giving it a spooky glow. My mom was next in the line of greetings, giving Juniper a big hug before accepting a platter of cupcakes from her.

Juniper hadn't been lying the other day; my mom loved her. Jenny Briggs had never been a very strict parent. She maintained firm boundaries, but her concern was first and foremost for her children's happiness. And whenever Gemma was with Juniper, she was happy. Which was all fine and whatever...until Gemma ended up in a hospital bed with a bad concussion and a collection of broken bones. And Juniper...well, there wasn't anything happy about that night.

"You haven't told us much about the new job."

At my dad's gruff voice, I turned to face him. He was busy filling a barrel with an assortment of beer that likely cost more than a day's work in his shop.

"I share an office with Juniper," I said, thinking that should sum it up.

Dad gave a hearty chuckle. "Small world, isn't it?"

"Too small," I grunted.

"You could always come back home," he offered. "I miss having you around at work."

"I miss being around the shop," I said honestly. "But..."

But Gardner Law was a good place for me. Even with Juniper there. They cared about their clients, and I felt like I was doing something with truly meaningful impact. I didn't know how to say that to my dad, though. I didn't want to diminish what he did or his service to this community. He was here for people when they needed him, and that was important, too. Working with him *had* been meaningful to me, just in a different way.

"But you have big fish to fry," he finished for me. An inkling of a smile appeared on my dad's face, the most I ever really saw from him. Not because he wasn't happy but because he showed it in his eyes. They swept over me with a look of pride that affected me more than I dared to admit. "I know you do, Julian, and I'm excited for you."

"Thanks, Dad," I said, feeling my throat tighten with emotion I wasn't expecting. He nodded, clapping me on the shoulder before bringing the beer into the living room for people to grab.

More and more guests flooded into the house, and I refilled the punch pitchers while sipping on a beer. I used to treat myself to an entire row of apple pie shots, but my party days ended the moment I left my undergrad days behind. Those four years had been my escape, my break from being the third parent in the house. Ending up as captain had been like transitioning to a different type of big brother, but it still wasn't the same. It wasn't picking Josie up from play practice before getting Gianna from soccer and bringing them home to make dinner while my mom graded papers and my dad finished changing someone's oil in the garage.

I sometimes wondered if I had taken a chance on the pros, would I be where Noah was? Still living in a party? Sometimes I regretted not finding out. Sometimes I was happy that I didn't. I probably could have been on that field with Grayson and Noah. I didn't admit to being damn good at much, but I was one hell of a quarterback.

Football was a gamble for so many reasons, though. There wasn't always control over where you played nor where you traveled. The income was great, but it wasn't reliable. What would happen if I got injured in my first season? My career could end in the blink of an eye, all while I had people counting on me.

I needed something where I could be here consistently for my family. I needed something I could be passionate about for the rest of my life, not just through my prime years.

"You're quiet tonight," my mom commented. I hadn't even noticed her enter the kitchen, but she stood next to me, watching the house fill up. I knew this was the one pause she'd allow herself before going off to mingle and greet guests.

"Busy mind," I said with a shrug.

"Anything you want to get off of it?"

I shook my head. It wasn't the time, and it wasn't anything I'd dare tell my mom. I never wanted her to think I wasn't happy where I was or with the choices I made. Because I was.

"Are you—"

Interrupting my mom, I swore beneath my breath as a short guy with dark hair slipped in the front door. He wore our hometown football jersey and jeans, which had to be the most unoriginal Halloween costume I'd ever seen. Even more unoriginal than wearing the same thing for the last seventeen years.

But that wasn't what bothered me.

"What the hell is he doing here?"

My mom made that familiar judgmental noise in her throat. "You need to learn to let go of grudges, honey. You hold on to them way too long."

I scowled, gritting my teeth as Greg fucking Kennedy sidled up to Juni, doing that thing where he put a hand on the wall behind her and leaned in, being a blatant flirt.

"He's an ass."

I ignored how my mom tsked in response. Not because of my swearing. She couldn't care less about that. But she did have a very no-nonsense policy on name-calling.

"Who is?" Gemma popped up next to me. I didn't look away from Greg and Juni, but I'd know her curious voice anywhere. I didn't need to answer for her to figure it out, though. After a few beats of silence, she sighed exaggeratedly. "Oh, I should have known."

"Do they still talk?" I asked while studying how Juniper tucked a strand of hair behind her ear and flashed a smile that couldn't be genuine. Could it?

When Gemma withheld an answer, I turned to see her grin.

"Why are you looking at me like that?"

"Why do you care?"

I glanced back at Juniper; she seemed to be shrinking into the horrendous floral wallpaper that had been there since the '90s. "I *don't* care how you look at me," I said to Gemma. "I just—"

"No, why do you care about Juni and Greg?"

I immediately busied myself with restacking the pumpkin-printed napkins. "I don't care about that either. I'm just curious. As her best friend, I'd think you'd be discouraging this. She doesn't exactly look enthused." I waved a hand in Juniper and Greg's direction. "Plus, he cheated on her at least once in high school."

"Is Jules ranting about Juniper again?"

Josie popped up beside Gemma, her short auburn curls

bouncing beneath her wizard hat. Big *Lord of the Rings* fan, that one.

Gemma nodded, almost proudly, as she stuck her chin in the air. "Yep. I'm about to rescue her from Greg Kennedy, but honestly, I think Julian should do it. You know, since he feels so strongly about the two of them."

"He sure gives her a lot of attention," Josie said, tapping her finger on her chin. Drama was Josie's thing, and she sure was leaning into it tonight.

"He really does." Janie joined us in the kitchen, leaning on the countertop with that goddamn mischievous expression I adored and hated all at once.

Mostly hated, at the moment.

Janie was the second oldest after Gemma and the sister I affectionately referred to as my mini-me. Bound for law school while currently playing D1 soccer, Janie had followed closely in my footsteps.

I stopped listening to all my sisters as Greg stalked away from Juniper, bursting through the door leading to our garage. I liked that he'd disappeared, but what the hell was he planning to do out there?

Leaving Josie, Janie, and Gemma behind, I followed Greg into the garage, and the minute he turned around to reveal that face I'd grown up despising, I started saying shit I probably shouldn't.

"What are you doing, Kennedy?"

His lips curled as soon as he saw me, but he nodded at the cigarette in his hand. "Smoke break."

The garage door was open. My parents had decorated the space as an area for the party to spill out into, but the rain of the last few days left a severe chill in the air, and I doubted anyone would leave the warm house. Meaning it was just me, Greg Kennedy, and a few bedsheet ghosts out here.

"Don't you think it's a little embarrassing how you throw yourself at Juniper every time she comes home?" I asked, shoving my hands into my pockets.

"Fuck off, Briggs," Kennedy snarled, flicking his cigarette ash to the ground.

"Did you forget this is my house?"

His eyes rolled up, and I immediately had to resist the urge to punch him. "It's none of your business."

I begged to differ. "Shit that happens at my house is, actually, my business."

"Fine," Kennedy conceded, "but nothing else involving Juniper is."

"False."

As much as I hated it, for the past two decades, *everything* involving Juniper involved me. We all but grew up in the same house, graduated from the same high school, pursued the same careers, and now started at the same job. The *exact* same job.

"False?" Greg puffed his chest out, clearly feeling challenged. I reveled the hell out of that because there was nothing I loved more than watching guys who were full of shit attempt to flash nonexistent peacock feathers. "Is that so?"

God, I wanted to deflate this son of a bitch so bad. He was always on my ass in high school, a sore goddamn loser about not being team captain our senior year. It irked me to no end because I tried so damn hard to make our team into a family, and he always wanted to ruin it.

"Yeah." My heart raced at the prospect of bringing him down a peg or two. "You don't even deserve to look at her, Kennedy. Leave her the fuck alone."

Greg shoulder-checked me as he stepped into my space. "Since when did you start admitting that you give a shit about Juniper?"

Words danced on the tip of my tongue, and I knew I shouldn't say them. They'd come back to haunt me.

But it *was* Halloween. Let the haunting begin.

Besides, seeing the hopeful light drain from Greg's eyes would be so sweet and so worth it. What kind of guy thought he could waltz back up to a girl after cheating on her ten years ago? Juniper had talent and success—especially compared to this waste of space. She was all pretty and perfect and *Juni*. Of course *now* Greg wanted her.

Of course Noah wanted her.

Of course—*shit*.

My lips curved upward as I stared down my high school football teammate. If he thought he would go back in there and breathe down Juni's neck again, he was dead wrong.

"See, you don't care about her," Greg scoffed when I didn't say anything.

I squared my shoulders. "Wrong."

"Since when?" he repeated, taking the bait exactly how I wanted him to.

Because I never, ever passed up the opportunity to make Greg Kennedy regret cheating on Juniper.

"Since I started fucking her."

ten years ago

Julian's various sports trophies glinted at me from their place on his shelves, alerting me that I was in the wrong place. But before I could close the door, Julian came into view. He peeled his shirt over his head before swiveling in my direction.

"It's called knocking, Lily," he said dryly.

He threw his shirt onto the ground, resulting in a half-naked Julian.

Oh, God. Heat worked through my veins, my palms immediately growing clammy.

"You think I was trying to come talk to you?" I scoffed. "Wrong room, sorry."

"Again?" Julian rolled his eyes. "Learn to count one of these days, will you?"

"Doesn't matter. You won't have to worry about it much longer, will you?"

Wanting to end the conversation there, I went to close the door again.

"Rosie, wait."

I should ignore him. I should shut the door in his annoying face and sprint back to Gemma's room, but my curiosity outweighed all the other warning bells in my head. So I opened the door wider and stepped inside Julian's room.

CHAPTER ELEVEN

I BREATHED A SIGH of relief as Greg walked away from me.

If he'd approached me anywhere else, I would have told him to fuck off. But causing a scene at the Briggs' Halloween party was the last thing I wanted to do. I knew how much tonight meant to their family, and I'd already been the one to ruin it once. I didn't need to ruin it again.

"Was that Greg Kennedy?"

My mom took Greg's place beside me, and I had a feeling she wouldn't let him steal it back.

Katherine St. James had always been overprotective like that, a bit of a helicopter parent. Gemma and I were both raised with educators for moms, but Gemma's was the free-spirited English teacher while I'd been gifted the middle school principal who loved control. I'd often wished for a sibling when I was younger—just so I had someone to share her attention with. Just so I could breathe a little. But I knew everything my mom did came from a loving place.

I loved my parents. I loved our home and even this town on most days. I would forever be grateful for the spin of fate that allowed my parents to find me.

Chance played a part in everyone's lives, but it felt different for me. So many decisions and doors needed to open just to match me with my own parents, my own house, my hometown.

But being adopted sort of worked like that.

I nodded, taking a long sip of Julian's famous "apple pie"—longer than was smart, considering how the sweetness of the drink likely masked an ungodly amount of vodka.

My mom made a noise of disgust in response to my affirmation that Greg Kennedy was lurking around the party. She flicked a single blonde curl over her shoulder as my dad joined us, an easy smile on his face that I knew was somewhat fake. Parties weren't his thing, but he knew how to make people believe they were.

"I heard Kennedy was engaged to that Kelly girl who was a year ahead of you in school," he said, always the casual gossiper. It would probably surprise people that my dad, the hardworking businessman, had a propensity to run the rumor mill. But that was Brooks St. James.

"Huh," I said, simultaneously intrigued with Greg's engagement to Julian's ex and, well, that Greg was engaged at all. Maybe I'd misread his intentions when he approached me.

"Think you'll be invited to the wedding?" Dad teased, a sliver of a smirk appearing just before he tipped his beer back to hide it. He knew I had no interest in attending Greg Kennedy's wedding, nor did I want to talk to him. I suspected that was why he'd joined my mom over here—to stand guard in case Greg returned.

"Definitely not."

Out of the corner of my eye, I noticed the door to the garage swing open, and I prepared myself for Greg's return. But a flash of auburn hair told me no one was coming back into the house. No, Julian was leaving. Following Greg? Unlikely, considering how much he'd always disliked him.

Putting both irritating men out of my mind, I faced my parents. And took a deep breath.

"Speaking of weddings," I began, "I was invited to Sofia's."

"Oh?"

My mom's eyebrows rose. Meanwhile, my dad took another slow drink of his beer, his poker face holding its place.

"Are you going?" he asked.

"Yeah, I want to." I tapped my fingers on the glass in my hands nervously. "I hope that's okay."

"Of course it's okay, Juniper."

My mom's response was swift, but I caught the tension in her stance. On the other hand, my dad leaned against the wall, a picture of neutrality.

I'd never met my half sister, but since my adoption was open, my parents had told me everything they legally could regarding my birth family. I imagined a part of them had always been waiting for this day to come.

Receiving Sofia's invitation shocked me. It probably wasn't how I would have gone about our introduction, but I saw it as an opportunity, an open door to have something I'd always wanted: a sister.

Gemma had always been *like* my sister, but I was painfully aware that she *wasn't* my sister. My hair wasn't red; my eyes weren't blue.

"Whatever you want, Juniper," my dad said earnestly, almost like he could sense my hesitation on their behalf. I met his green eyes and saw that he meant it. Of course he meant it. He had a lot of chances to hide my birth family from me, but he never did.

A loud clattering from the garage interrupted our moment at the same time Julian's mom hollered across the room at my parents. Something about the desserts they brought. I stopped listening, staring at the garage instead. My curiosity led my feet toward the sound, leaving the party behind and my parents to talk with their friends.

The cool air caused goose bumps to erupt on my skin as I stepped into the garage. Julian stood a few feet away, a look of smug satisfaction on his face as he watched Greg walk down the driveway to his car.

A slight drizzle interrupted the silence, pattering softly

against the pavement until Greg drove off, and the wheels of his car squealed through the night air. The street was lit by dim streetlamps. One flickered. Just like orange string lights flickered in the garage, making it glow.

I turned to Julian, and his expression fell upon seeing me.

Typical.

"I heard something." I surveyed my surroundings, wondering what it might have been. "I thought I'd come out to the two of you fighting."

Julian scoffed. "You think I'd waste my time fighting Kennedy?"

"Then what happened?" My curiosity rose. It thrummed in my veins, powered by alcohol. "He told me he would be back."

His brows shot up. "Did you want him to come back?"

"Of course not." The attack in his tone brought out my defensive side.

"Good," he mumbled before staring back at the street with a stormy expression fitting for Halloween.

"So, what happened?" I pressed.

"He kicked that chair." Julian pointed at a folding chair, his lips twitching with amusement. "Then he took off to buy more cigarettes or something."

"He kicked the chair? Why?"

Julian winced. How odd.

"I might have said something," he admitted. He took his hands out of his jeans pockets before crossing bulging arms over his jean shirt. It made his red puffer vest puff up even more, momentarily derailing my curiosity.

"What's happening with your outfit?" I wagged a finger up and down. "That is far too much denim to wear at once."

"I'm obviously Marty McFly." His look was accusatory when he trailed his eyes over me. "But you can't really judge, Ms. Same-Costume-Every-Year."

I wrinkled my nose at him, adjusting my beret, even though I had perfectly placed and pinned it earlier.

"What did you say to Greg?" I asked, reverting the conversation again.

Julian released a stream of air between his teeth. A near whistle. "It was about us."

"Us?"

"You and me."

"You and me?"

"Yeah." Julian met my gaze before calmly answering. "I told him we were fucking."

He said it so naturally that it took a few seconds to register, maybe even more. The words swam in my head, bouncing off the walls of my brain. That we were *what*?

I stared at him, unblinking. Julian ran a hand nonchalantly through his hair, clearly not caring about my internal meltdown as I processed what he admitted. He waved a hand in front of my face, looking for a reaction I didn't have.

"Daisy?"

My mouth tried to make words, sounds, anything, but the apple pie had caught my tongue, that god-awful sneaky drink.

Julian took a step toward me, brows furrowing. "At least give me a sign that you're breathing, 'kay?"

Nope, couldn't do that. This was an impossible-to-breathe moment.

Julian lifted a hand when I didn't reply, pressing his fingers along my neck. His touch, gentle but firm, jolted me into awareness.

"Strong pulse, at least," he murmured. Did his eyes get bluer somehow? Bigger? Why was he looking at me like that? "Kinda quick, actually."

Finally, my words sputtered out. "You told Greg Kennedy that we were *sleeping together*?"

Julian dropped his hand, but his fingers slid the length of my throat before disappearing from my skin. Yeah, my pulse was definitely quick. More than quick. Racing.

"No."

Oh, thank God.

"I told him we were fucking."

Jesus Christ. He needed to stop saying it like that. It was not helping anything.

"Why the *hell* would you do that?"

The words had no problem tumbling out of my mouth now. They were loud and clear. Very loud and clear. Probably too loud and clear.

"Look," Julian said, inching forward in a deliberately soft voice that was obviously meant to remind me to keep my voice down. "I—"

"*Why*, Julian?"

This entire scenario didn't compute in the slightest. Julian hated me. Why he would want anyone to think we were associated even more than we already were was beyond me.

"Because I wanted to piss him off," Julian hissed, throwing his hands up. "Because it's Greg fucking Kenn—"

I stabbed my finger into his overly puffy vest. "You wanted to piss him off, or you wanted to piss *me* off?"

More likely, it was a two-in-one deal for him.

"Him," Julian said firmly. "And don't pretend like you didn't want to do the same. I saw your face when he was talking to you. I saw how you felt."

"You don't need to do that overprotective thing with me, Julian." I stabbed him even harder with my finger. That would surely show him. Right? "You have five sisters you can do that for, but I'm not one of them."

"Trust me." He tossed his head back with a laugh that stung because of its implication. Then he looked down at me, lowering his voice. "I'm well aware you're not my sister."

I spun on my heel, walking toward the edge of the garage. God, *why* did he have the ability to make me feel this way?

The rain broke the tension, coming down harder against the pavement.

"I'm sorry, Juni." Julian's sigh was ragged, echoing in the empty space. "I know you're mad."

"I'm..." My sigh matched his as I came down from my initial shock, feeling deflated. "Not," I finished, surprising even myself. I was confused, yes. Pissed at the things he'd said, yes. But I wasn't really *mad*.

See, there was an irony here that I appreciated. Greg had a multitude of excuses for cheating on me in high school, but there was one that hurt more than others: I wouldn't put out. Sex hadn't been on the table. I wasn't ready for it. Not with him. So, of course, he had to get it elsewhere.

If allegedly sleeping with Julian was what got Greg Kennedy to finally leave me alone, well, that was rather poetic, wasn't it?

He didn't need to know it wasn't true. He didn't need to know I still hadn't put out for anyone. Ever.

"You're...not." Julian said the words with slow disbelief.

I shook my head. "If it keeps Greg Kennedy as far away as possible, it's hard to be mad."

He had been sliding into my DMs and lurking around my house whenever I was in town for far too long.

"I'll drink to that," Julian grunted, lifting his beer to clink it against my plastic cup.

I rolled my eyes. Did he think he was off the hook? Because I was still working very hard to resist punching him square in the nose.

"If Greg starts running his mouth about us, I will personally end you, Julian Briggs."

The town was small, and word of mouth spread fast.

"I'd like to see that." His lips curved up. "But he won't," he added, seeming pretty sure of himself. But of course he had to be sure; he wouldn't want more people to think he actually *liked* me.

Before I could reply, Greg's squealing car tires returned. Oh, shit. I'd hoped he was gone for good. But he just kept coming back —like a goddamn boomerang. I tipped my cup back, trying to drown myself in sickly sweet alcohol.

"Easy there, Lily." Julian's voice was husky and incredibly close—the only reason I didn't jump when I lowered my drink to see him directly before me, only inches away. "Stuff's strong. I would know. I made it."

I licked my lips before frowning. "Maybe you should lighten up on the vodka next time."

"Stop making that face," he muttered. A light chuckle filled the space between us. "If you want Kennedy to fuck off, you'll need to do a better job than that."

"A better job?"

"A better job pretending you like me."

"Oh my God," I groaned as a car door slammed behind me. "Do I have to?"

Julian chuckled again, appearing to find this far more amusing than I did. I couldn't be sure, though, because I refused to look at his face. Not when we were so close like this. But then he slid an arm behind my back, yanking me closer, and murmured, "Come on, Rosie."

Begrudgingly, I raised my gaze to meet his. Those bright blue eyes were already trained steadily on me.

"This is ridiculous," I hissed, unnerved by his direct attention. "Why did Greg even come back?"

"I think he was here with his parents. He probably returned for them."

"Did you know he's engaged to Kelly Mcvarish?" I asked, remembering the conversation with my parents earlier. I was curious how Julian would react, considering how much he hated Greg and how he'd dated Kelly.

Julian's brows rose. "Really?"

I shrugged. "According to my dad."

"Your dad would know," he said with yet another chuckle, surprising me. That was three times now. A noise resembling laughter had come out of Julian's mouth three times while talking to me. Could *he* be drunk? That would likely explain everything.

Especially how his thumb was rubbing my side slowly, his touch burning through my thin shirt.

"Yeah."

Yeah. All I could think to say was *yeah.*

A knowing smile lit up Julian's face, but it quickly dimmed. His eyes darted over my shoulder as footsteps splashed through the pools of rainwater. "That makes me hate him even more if he's engaged and still pulling this shit," he breathed, shocking me yet again. He didn't seem to care that Greg was marrying his ex, but he did care that...what? That Greg had talked to me?

We were so close that I felt Julian's words against my hair, similar to the night he carried me through the parking garage.

I still couldn't believe he'd carried me through the parking garage.

"Me too," I agreed, and before any other words could be ripped from my throat, Julian tugged me into his side instead so we were both facing Greg as he trudged back through the garage. A breeze blew in with him, and I shivered. Julian's grip tightened. The alcohol turned my limbs to jelly, and I melted against him.

"Back so soon?" Julian asked, a clear challenge in his voice. I would know. I was used to hearing that challenge.

Greg's eyes narrowed as they shifted from Julian to me, tucked beneath Julian's arm. I could tell he hadn't believed it until this moment—that I would ever get into bed with Julian. Or, more likely, that Julian would get into bed with me. His lips flattened as he visibly bit down on a response.

But his self-restraint only lasted a moment.

"You never could shut up about him when we were dating," he said to me, bringing heat back to my skin.

And then he walked away, returning to the party before I could tell him to fuck off. Goddamn Greg Kennedy and his massively annoying mouth.

Julian only waited a second before he turned to me, dropping his chin with a smirk. "Aw, you talked about me?"

I pushed Julian away with a hard shove, scowling as a flush

worked further up my neck and into my cheeks. "Believe me, it was nothing good."

"Of course not."

It was hard to tell if he meant that. If he did, in fact, believe me. Considering his slight grin, I doubted it.

After a glare over my shoulder, I put as much distance between Julian and me as possible without walking into the cold autumn rain. "Right now would be a good moment to hop into your DeLorean and find a time warp to get stuck in, McFly."

Julian leaned against the side of the garage, shoving his hands in his pockets. "Oh, yeah?"

"Absolutely."

"Sorry." A bit of wistfulness snuck into the word like he really did wish he could jump into a car and disappear from this garage. "My DeLorean's in the shop at the moment."

"Guess you'll have to make do with something else." I glanced around the space, looking for other escape options.

Julian nodded toward the motorcycle leaning against the back of the garage—the only choice around. "I doubt Noah will like it if I take his bike to a different decade."

He walked over to it, running a finger over the handlebars and then the shiny leather. I sipped from my cup, watching him closely as he appreciated the motorcycle.

"It's Noah's?"

A nod. "He bought it at some auction, but it needed a ton of work. So it's been a project of mine for a while."

"Are you finished with it?"

"Yeah." Julian's eyes swept over the motorcycle, apparent pride in them. He looked like he wanted to hop on it and ride, escape. So I gave him the option to. The buzzing in my veins told me it would be a good idea. I sidled up to the bike, putting one palm flat on the seat and leaning on it.

"We should probably test it out, huh?"

There was a spark in Julian's eyes as he digested my comment, and something odd, something akin to hope, spread in my chest.

But it vanished when he began shaking his head, rejecting the idea. Rejecting me.

"No, we shouldn't."

His demeanor shifted while he took a familiar stance in front of the bike. Of course he would protect his special project from me. I'd find a way to fuck it up, wouldn't I? I'd find a way to ruin something else for him.

"You would drive," I said. I assumed that'd be obvious, but maybe Julian thought *I* wanted to test it out, and that was his problem.

"Obviously, I would drive."

Goddamn him.

Julian's expression was stern, final. And it brought back my irritation from yesterday when he wouldn't even let me and Gemma drive home from Boston without him. After all this time, I couldn't believe he was *still* like this.

I shrugged, trying to let it go. "When are you giving it back to Noah? I'll ask him to take me for a ride, then."

Julian stiffened. More than I thought was possible. But there he was, in all his six-foot-three glory, standing rigidly in front of me, his jaw ticking with evident frustration.

Usually, I did a better job at controlling myself, at keeping my mask firmly in its place on my face, especially when Julian was involved. But my tongue felt a little loose, my fingers a little tingly. And my lips started to curve with a ghost of a sly smile.

"I'll text him right now," I added before remembering I didn't even have my phone on me. Apparently, Girl Scouts didn't believe in pockets.

Julian took a quick step toward me, seeming ready to intervene. But when I didn't take out my phone, he sighed.

"We can take it for a spin when you're sober," he said while slowly assessing me. And at that very inopportune moment, the world swayed around me. Or maybe *I* was swaying. Because Julian's hand shot out, settling firmly on my waist to steady me. "I don't trust that you can hang on to me while on a moving vehicle right now. That's all."

I automatically opened my mouth to argue before the image of what he'd said started to conjure in my brain. Me, behind Julian. My arms, around his waist. Us, sitting on the same seat. Close. Too close. The thrum of the motorcycle engine. The thrum of—

He was right. It wasn't a good idea. None of this was a good idea. Not how he was touching me, not how I was proposing ideas for us to touch *more*.

"Okay," I whispered, refusing to meet his probing gaze. Instead, I darted away, back into the safety of the Briggs' house.

The crowd, the music, the sprinkling of redheads amongst guests—I could hide here. This was familiar and safe. The garage was officially off-limits, and the person inside it had always been off-limits. But it was good to remind my tipsy self of that.

I didn't see Julian for the rest of the party. I saw every single Briggs except for him. And that was okay. I was fine with that. I was *relieved* by that. I didn't see Greg, either. Another reason to be relieved.

Yet unease spread like a web within me, catching all my worries and holding them there. I couldn't even put a finger on what they were, just that they were *there.*

Not even alcohol seemed to release them. But I kept trying.

I tried until everything was fuzzy, spinning, warm. A bed—I needed a bed. To lie down. I told my parents earlier that I would be staying with Gemma, but all the doors in the hallway were closed when I made it to the second floor. God, this hallway. It felt like home. It smelled like sleepovers in high school and mischief and the vanilla bean candles Jenny Briggs always lit.

I counted the doors as I walked down them. Gemma's was the third on the left, and I sighed with relief as I found it, ready to sink into her mattress.

I didn't bother turning on the lights. I wanted it dark, like a mask. I wanted to escape in it.

A body turned on the other side of the bed when I slid beneath the covers, and I frowned, wondering when Gemma had gone to bed and why she hadn't told me. But asking her didn't seem worth waking her up. And it definitely didn't seem worth delaying my sleep or the release of my worries. Not tonight when they crawled over me, getting stuck in that web.

We'd talk in the morning. For now, I pressed closer to the familiar warmth in the bed, to the feeling of home.

And let myself fall.

CHAPTER TWELVE

THERE WAS SOMEONE IN my bed.

Fuck, had we slept together? Under my parents' fucking roof?

I might have been going through the longest dry spell in the history of dry spells after that fling I'd had in law school, but had I really stooped this low? Was I this desperate for a hookup that I slept with a Whitebridge local, someone I risked seeing every time I returned to town?

The apple pie was too strong. Next year, I needed to tone it down a little bit. I drank more last night than I had in a long time. Janie found me in the garage, and I'd let her talk me into refill after refill while I listened to her college roommate drama. I'd needed a distraction, and it had worked.

But how I ended up with a girl in my bed was beyond me. I didn't remember talking to very many people last night. My family.

Kennedy.

Juniper.

Shit, I was afraid to open my eyes and see who it was. She was soft, though—whoever she was. One leg draped over my hip, and hot breath warmed my skin as it hit a sensitive spot right below my ear. I nearly moaned from the feeling, wanting more than that tease.

Goddamn. If we'd fucked, how was I still this ready to go?

She just felt so good. Her weight was delicious, the perfect blanket for a chilly morning, and I tucked my head deeper into the crook of her neck. If I'd tasted her last night, then it wasn't enough. Because hunger unraveled deep in my gut, a want I wasn't prepared for. I let my lips brush soft skin as I nuzzled deeper into hair that smelled like—

My eyes flew open.

Roses. Her hair smelled like fucking roses, and it was the same smell that invaded my office every Monday through Friday.

Juniper was in my bed.

Juniper was in my bed, and I was *tangled* in her.

Juniper was in my bed, and she'd just gasped delightfully at the hint of a kiss—a kiss, for fuck's sake—that I brushed along the curve of her neck.

"What the *hell* are you doing here?"

Her head jerked upward at the sound of my voice, wavy dark hair flying everywhere. It was on my pillow. It was on me. Juniper squinted sleepily, and I ignored the pang of softness in my chest.

No, no, no.

"Julian?"

Saying my name aloud seemed to do the trick, to make the realization sink in, and then the air rang with her ear-splitting squeal.

I clapped a hand over that mouth of hers, but noises still flooded out, so I rolled us over, pinning Juniper down on the bed and giving her a glare. A glare that said *shut the hell up.*

"Greg Kennedy isn't the only one who's going to think we're fucking if you don't quiet the fuck down," I hissed. "Do you want my entire family to burst in here?"

A gasp and then silence. Those brown eyes grew wide as Juniper shook her head aggressively. It caused her body to wiggle a little beneath me, a reminder that *my* body did not need.

I didn't think Juniper's eyes could grow even rounder, but they did a moment later, and I knew she felt my erection. Pressing right into her soft stomach.

Fucking hell.

That was not an erection meant for her. It was an erection meant for the mysterious woman draped over me, whose breath had grazed my skin as I woke up, thinking we'd fucked.

Now that my brain was clearer, I knew there'd been no fucking.

I'd remember sex with Juniper St. James.

Frankly, I was afraid to move. Any tiny movement would make my situation worse. Even though this erection hadn't started as something meant for Juniper, it sure was appreciating the fuck out of her now.

I lowered my hand slowly. At the very least, it would help if her full goddamn lips weren't pressed into my palm. But that had been wishful thinking; now, those lips were parted in some kind of wondrous expression, and my cock pulsed with the need to see if I could get her to open them more. To see her breath hitch, her jaw drop.

But I restrained myself. I didn't move.

Juniper did, though. She scooted up in the bed beneath me. Which was all fine and whatever, except she still wore her Halloween costume, and her shirt was bunched beneath my bare chest. And then my skin brushed her skin. Heat on heat. But it wasn't nearly as mind-boggling as when my erection fell between her legs as she settled in her new position.

She gasped.

And there it was—that expression my cock had wanted to see.

Juniper wiggled again, but I grabbed her hip with one hand.

"Stop," I rasped. "You can't—just stop."

She did. She froze, all except her eyes. They darted around my face. That gaze was hot as it traced the outline of my mouth and then up my nose to my eyes. Oh, *hell*, Juni.

I'd promised myself that just because I told Kennedy I was

fucking Juniper didn't mean I got to *think* about fucking Juniper. I'd spent many, many years distinctly *not* thinking about fucking Juniper. And that wasn't going to change.

At least, I hadn't been planning for it to change.

But I also hadn't been planning on waking up to find her on top of me. I hadn't planned to pin her to my bed. I hadn't planned on her moving beneath me until she had my cock positioned *just* right. It was almost like she wanted it there.

And the way she was looking at me—God, the way she was looking at me made it really hard to keep my shit together. Juniper St. James wasn't supposed to look at me like that.

"Julian," she whimpered.

That got through to my brain. That little plea—or whatever it was. In a single swift movement, I flung myself off her, sprawling on my back instead. Only once I regained control of my breathing did I turn onto my side to face her, feeling angry and wildly aroused.

"*How?*"

Bewilderment passed over her face. "How?"

"How did you pass the Massachusetts Bar when you can't even count the doors in this goddamn hall?"

Because I knew that was precisely what had happened.

"It's your fault," she groaned, rolling over to leave me staring at her backside.

Very unhelpful.

"My fault?"

"You made the apple pie, didn't you?" Her voice was muffled against my pillow.

I couldn't help but notice she hadn't jumped out of my bed yet. She hadn't scrambled away and out of the room. But I shoved that thought down. Deep, deep down.

"I told you to take it easy with that stuff."

"Well, I didn't," she snapped, abruptly pushing away from me. Ahh, there she was. There was that escape I'd been expecting.

It couldn't happen, though. Before she could get very far, I circled her waist and pulled her down again. Her back collided with my chest. "Where do you think you're going, Daisy?"

"Home." The word squeaked out of her.

"How are you getting there?"

"I'll go wake Gemma." She squirmed, but my grip was firm. For her own good. "Or someone else."

"Gemma probably thinks you went home last night," I pointed out. "What's your plan when she asks why you're still here? Where you slept?"

Juniper relaxed with a heavy sigh, convincing me to let go. Put a little space between us. Some much-needed space.

"You're right," she said.

I perked up. "What was that?"

I could *feel* her scowl, and my lips twitched.

"*You* can give me a ride home, then." She glanced back at me, and a teasing smile lit her face, illuminated further by the soft glow of dawn. "It seems to be one of your favorite things, after all."

"I don't know about *that*," I grumbled before rolling out of bed anyway. I'd take her home; God knows I couldn't keep having this conversation while lying in bed with her.

"We can take Noah's motorcycle," she said, and hell, was that hopefulness in her eyes? I didn't understand it. Didn't know why the hell she thought that was a good idea after what had just happened. The idea of Juniper wrapping her arms around me from behind while we huddled together on Noah's bike was a torturous one. And it wouldn't be happening.

I shook my head. "No."

"Why not?"

"Because that sounds loud, cold, and uncomfortable. I'm hungover and need at least two more hours of sleep. The last thing I want to do is get on that bike."

It wasn't a lie. But it wasn't precisely the truth, either. Parts of my body were aching, but I wasn't convinced it was from alcohol.

Trying to ignore the urge to check Juniper's reaction, I

turned and focused on finding a shirt. Spotting an old football tee on the top shelf of my closet, I threw it on before facing Juni.

She was still awfully close. None of the rooms in this house were very big, and because I got my own room—not all of my sisters did—I also had the smallest room. Fair was fair, and I had no complaints. Except now.

Because even though I stood on the opposite side of the room from my bed, I was still within a few feet of Juniper St. James while she curled deeper into my bed, wearing nothing but her Halloween costume.

At least she'd pulled up the blanket now—the plaid comforter my mom bought for me in high school wrapped around Juni's shoulders. But Christ, I needed to get her out of here. She didn't belong here between my football trophies and the college textbooks I didn't know what to do with. I'd spent a lot of energy over the years making sure she didn't come anywhere close to where she was right this very second.

Never again. I would never make apple pie ever again. I'd find a new festive drink for next year's party.

"Come on," I said. "I'll drive you home. In a car."

She raised a brow. "You don't think anyone will see?"

"Usually, I wake up to my mom grinding coffee. That hasn't happened yet, so I bet she's still asleep. And if Mom's asleep, everyone's asleep."

"Hmm." She made a purring noise in the back of her throat. "Sounds like you've done this before. I'm not the first girl you've snuck out in the morning, huh?"

Not the first, but it definitely wasn't a common occurrence. I tried to keep girls very far away from this house, and for good reason; my family could be overbearing, and the walls were guaranteed to be thin—a problem when the women I brought home weren't quiet.

"Juniper," I growled, not wanting to have this conversation with her. "Let's go."

Whether it was the use of her full name or the tone of my voice, I couldn't be sure, but she sprang right out of bed.

As suspected, the house remained quiet as we tiptoed through it. Which made sense, considering I checked my phone to find it was six o'clock in the morning. Six o'clock in the morning. On a Sunday. Why had I thought I would get any sleep this weekend? I should have known it'd be a lost cause as soon as a certain brunette with brown eyes and a forest-green beret appeared in my living room.

I sighed as Juniper slipped into the front seat of the car.

No rest. Not ever.

TWELVE HOURS LATER, I WAS BACK IN A CAR WITH JUNIPER. AND GEMMA.

Thank God Gemma was here, too.

Very little happened between Whitebridge and Boston, and I had no complaints about that. An uneventful evening was the best I could wish for at this point. Gemma had an early morning skating practice tomorrow, so she planned to stay at my place tonight, saving us a stop in the suburbs. We pulled up to Juni's apartment building a little after 8:00 p.m., and I swiveled in my seat to look back at her.

"What day do you want to stay late to work on the case this week?"

While I'd made some exceptions this month, I didn't typically like making plans last minute. I liked figuring shit out ahead of time so I could puzzle together all the other parts of my life—running errands, hitting the gym, socializing. Spur-of-the-moment plans always put me off-kilter. Probably explained a lot of how I'd been feeling lately.

Juniper thought about it for a moment. "Noah's coming over Wednesday, so maybe Monday or Tuesday?"

Noah. My expression quickly dipped into a scowl. Because

Noah. Or, more specifically, Noah going over to Juni's place. Juniper talking about Noah. Noah and Juniper.

But there was no time to get stuck on that at the moment.

"I'm working on your brakes tomorrow," I reminded her.

"Right." Juniper glanced out the window before concluding, "Tuesday, then."

"Tuesday," I agreed, and she climbed out of the car, seeming more than eager to escape.

She'd been subdued the entire ride back. Not Juni-like. And while it had led to an uneventful trip that I shouldn't bother second-guessing or caring about, I wondered why exactly that was. She might have been hungover and tired—like me. But...

I shook my head. It was nothing. Nothing but a 6:00 a.m. wake-up call and a bad apple pie hangover.

When we pulled away from Juniper's apartment building, Gemma cleared her throat. "You're working on Juni's brakes?"

A nod. "Yeah, someone put shitty pads on them the last time she took it into the shop."

"I see."

That note in Gemma's voice, I didn't like it. Especially when she continued. And brought up Noah.

"And I take it you're pissed that she's hanging out with Noah?"

I bit the inside of my cheek to keep myself from replying too quickly. "Who said I was pissed?"

Gemma snorted. "Your face."

"I'm gonna make you walk home," I threatened, feeling the urge to pull over and kick my sister to the curb.

"You won't," Gemma said proudly.

She was right.

I wouldn't.

CHAPTER THIRTEEN

julian

APPROXIMATELY EVERY SEVENTEEN MINUTES, I opened a blank email and stared at it for at least thirty seconds while considering requesting a new office.

About every hour, I contemplated pulling up Indeed to search for associate attorney job openings in Boston. Or, you know what, maybe it wasn't too late to get my shot in the NFL after all. It was unlikely, but the risk might be worth it. Especially when the alternative was continuing to work with Juniper.

To be clear, *working* with Juniper was never the problem. On more than one occasion, she proved to be a valuable asset to our team.

No, the problem was *being around* Juniper. Specifically, sitting two feet away from her for the entirety of every single workday. For the love of God, breathing wasn't even an option, not without being suffocated by the smell of flowers, both from the plants she continued to pile on her desk and from that goddamn perfume that seemed to follow me home.

I didn't know how to look at her without remembering Sunday morning. The arousal in her eyes. The way her lips parted eagerly. Her skin. Her soft fucking skin when I kissed her neck. *Shit*, these were not things I was supposed to be thinking about.

But she was *right here*. Right next to me. How was I not supposed to think about it?

It had been so much easier in college, when she was on the opposite side of the country and I could forget her.

Spending even more time with Juniper was the last thing I'd wanted to do Monday night, but fixing her brakes was nonnegotiable in my book. I refused to let her talk me out of doing it. Or let me talk myself out of doing it. Whoever replaced her brake pads when she took it into the shop clearly didn't know what they were doing, and while they really should fix the brakes for free, I didn't trust them to do it right.

Much to my relief, Juniper didn't wait around in the garage while I worked on her car like last time. However, she did bring me a sandwich and a beer around six o'clock before marching back to the elevator.

Dinner Tuesday night was on me. At precisely seven o'clock, I put a container of sushi in front of her while she looked through a pile of Gabriel's medical documentation.

When I'd first handed over the documents, I worried Juniper would put two and two together regarding our client's identity. But then again, it didn't list Grayson's name. And *Elez-Everett* barely made an appearance in a sea of *patient this* and *patient that*. In a way, it dehumanized the little boy with big, hazel eyes I'd come to love.

Gabriel Elez-Everett was going to be one talented little fucker. He already was, from what I'd heard about him. The musical talent, the athleticism, and the good nature in his genes were one hell of a combination.

"Eat, Violet," I reminded Juni when she still hadn't looked up from the notes.

Her nose wrinkled, but she didn't say anything.

She'd been uncharacteristically quiet the last day or two, and I couldn't help but wonder if it had anything to do with that...thing I wasn't going to think about.

"You don't like sushi?" I asked, thinking I should have

checked with her before ordering from the restaurant across the street. But if I'd asked her, she would have argued about who was buying dinner. Just like she didn't ask if I wanted my sandwich last night because she knew I'd have told her not to bother.

"No, that's not it." She sighed, putting down the paperwork. "I love sushi. Thank you."

I raised a brow.

Juniper noticed. Sighed again. Wrinkled her nose a second time. "It's just..." she started. "Violet? Really?"

I chuckled, relieved dinner wasn't the problem. "Oh, you don't like that one?"

"I don't like *any* of them."

A forbidden smile wormed its way onto my face from her declaration, one I didn't believe.

"Okay, Daisy."

Juniper glanced at her sushi while biting down on her own smile.

"Did you find anything?" I asked, ignoring an odd invasive warmth.

She shook her head. "No, but I'm not giving up. We need to request more of the patient's records between birth and the date of their proper diagnosis. While all of the records surrounding the corrective surgery indicate there will be no lasting harm to the patient, perhaps we can prove that the delayed diagnosis still caused worsening symptoms or other such damages during the years prior."

I nodded, having thought the same thing earlier. To my knowledge, Gabriel had been presenting as a healthy child until they'd learned the truth, but maybe there was something Grayson hadn't bothered to tell me.

"I'll work on that."

Satisfied with my answer, Juniper returned to scouring papers while quietly eating.

But selfishly, I wanted to keep her talking. Because, well, I wasn't sure why. A quiet Juniper was a cause for concern, I supposed.

"Do you think the lack of proper diagnosis and its implication for their new baby, given they now have confirmation of genetic predisposition for a heart defect, could support the case?"

Juniper's head lifted abruptly. "Their baby?"

"They learned Nes—the mom was pregnant with their second child after receiving the correct diagnosis."

If Juniper caught my slipup, she didn't react to it. She was too busy glaring at me for another reason. "You didn't tell me that."

"Yes, I did."

"No, you—" Breaking off, Juniper shook her head while rubbing her temples. "You know what, never mind. I should probably get going anyway. I have to tidy up a little bit before I have company tomorrow."

My mood immediately soured. I hadn't forgotten who her *company* was.

Even though Juniper claimed she needed to leave, she sat there for at least another minute, staring out the window. A frown seemed stuck on her face. She twisted a ring on her finger. Round and round.

"You're doing it again," I said finally.

"What?"

"Acting weird."

Her lips curved. Slightly. "You mean un-Juni-like?"

"Yeah." The word was dry. I needed a drink. "That."

A frown swallowed her whole again, and I tried not to let my mind get ahead of myself as I wondered what prompted it. Instead, I took a stab in the dark.

"Cameron and I are planning to grab a drink after work tomorrow." I cleared my throat, still wishing I had something to lubricate it. "Maybe just invite Noah to join us."

I studied Juniper's reaction, thinking I saw a hint of relief there.

"I don't know if that would work."

It was my turn to frown. "Why not?"

"That would mean I would *also* have to be invited," she said, a bit of challenge entering her tone. There she was. That was Juni-like.

"No, you don't." I grinned. "You invite yourself to places all the time."

"Cameron invited me last time," she countered. And while she rolled her eyes, she also fought a smile. "I didn't invite myself."

"Whatever, Rosie." I stood, feeling better now that the status quo had been restored. "The Bellflower Bar. Tomorrow. Five o'clock. Invite London, or I can."

Wariness lingered in Juniper's gaze, but she nodded. "I'll think about it."

My brain didn't like imagining Noah and Juniper together. It made my gut roil in weird ways I didn't totally understand. All I understood was the irritation bubbling inside me, caused by Juniper's continuation of stealing away the people in my life. But I wasn't sure if this was any better. This, right here in the bar, had to be worse. At least my imagination had left room for doubt, for the chance that maybe the sight of them together wasn't completely sickening.

In reality, there was no room for doubt.

They were completely sickening.

Juni's laugh was over-the-top as she tossed her head back at everything Noah said. And *Jesus Christ,* had she undone a few buttons on her blouse? No, that wasn't it. Upon closer inspection, there were no buttons at all. It was the bow. Earlier at work, she had one of her ridiculous bows tied at her neckline, and only an oval-shaped glimpse of skin was exposed on her chest. Now, the ribbonlike strings on her shirt lay untied, the fabric gaping.

I didn't like it.

It wasn't a Juni-look. It was all...wrong.

I couldn't even hear what they were saying. The four of us sat at the bar, Juniper on the far end and me on the other. And this was the first time in a very long time—possibly ever—that I wished the distance between us could lessen. But only so I could hear what she was saying and know for certain I had the right to be annoyed by it.

Cameron sat next to me, with Noah on the other side of him, and even he kept getting drawn into their conversation, which appeared increasingly animated and featured a lively, transformed Juni. Nothing like last night's version of Juniper St. James.

I tossed back my beer, a light lager with not nearly enough alcohol to numb the feeling in my chest. Why the hell had I suggested this or thought it was a good idea?

"Don't worry." Cameron nudged me just as I was about to order another drink. "They're not talking about you."

"I'm not worried."

"...besides Julian being a killjoy."

Juniper's voice suddenly carried across the bar, loud enough for me to make out the words.

It was almost as though she wanted me to hear her.

Cameron winced. "Okay, I take that back."

Despite knowing better than to take Juniper's bait, I leaned forward over the weathered, wooden bar top to glare down at her. "Excuse me?"

She smiled, but it was wicked. An invitation to spar. "I was telling Noah about the party this past weekend."

A quick glance at Noah told me my friend was having difficulty holding his tongue.

Just like Grayson had when he met us at the Bellflower, Noah wore a hoodie and a ball cap pulled low over his face. While he hadn't escaped notice, the attention wasn't overwhelming, either. Not yet, anyway.

"*I* was the killjoy?" I glared down the bar at Juni, wondering how she figured that when she was the one who fell asleep in my goddamn bed. She'd certainly killed the joy of sleeping. And not for the first time. And not for the last, considering how little I'd slept this entire week.

"Gotta admit," Noah cut in. "It's hard to imagine that, knowing Jules."

Juniper kissed her teeth. "There was a perfectly good motorcycle in the garage, and he wouldn't even take me on a ride."

Noah laughed heartily, cutting me a look. "My motorcycle?"

I nodded. "We were drinking. Didn't think you'd appreciate me taking it out like that, considering all the work I put in on it."

"You'd be right." Noah looked back to Juniper. "Safety first, sweetheart."

Biting my tongue, I sat back in my seat. But not before I grabbed Cameron's drink and finished the rest of it off. This was his fault. He'd interrupted me before I could order another one and then jinxed this entire conversation.

With the alcohol drained and my self-restraint hanging on by a thread, I pushed back from the bar. Fuck this.

The pulse of the bar thumped around me as I dodged around the other patrons of the Bellflower, needing to get away. Needing to be alone. But only a few seconds after stepping into the alleyway and soaking in the crisp evening air, Cameron joined me. I walked away from him, though, not really wanting to hear anything he had to say.

He let me, staying by the door. A silent watchdog. At least until he couldn't keep it in any longer.

"Julian..." His sigh echoed between the rising brick walls. "Come on, man."

"It was stuffy in there," I said, my hackles rising in automatic defense.

"I don't get you," Cameron said, ignoring me. "If it bothers you so much, why'd you set them up?"

"It doesn't bother me," I grunted, knowing Cameron would see right through that lie.

"I've never known you to be a bullshitter, Briggs."

Yep, that reply checked out.

When I started to shake my head—despite knowing he was right—Cameron continued.

"No, I'm serious. It's what I've always liked about you. You were a genuine straight shooter in a sea of law school brats. But this?" He walked toward me slowly, giving me a once-over. "This is a lie. One that you're selling me. And Juniper. And Noah. And most importantly, yourself."

Shit, I forgot how intense Cameron could sometimes be. I forgot how much he'd whipped my ass into shape when I needed it in law school, and he certainly wasn't holding back now.

"I set them up because Juniper asked me to," I managed to say. Sticking to the facts seemed like a safe bet. "In exchange, she's helping me with a case."

For reasons I couldn't fully explain, I hadn't confessed this to Cameron yet. It was partly because I didn't want to hurt his feelings about going to Juniper for help on the case instead of him, but I knew it was more than just that.

I didn't want to have to explain...everything.

"Juniper needed a date for her sister's wedding," I added, "so I found her a date."

Cameron stared at me for a long moment before a laugh exploded out of him. A rueful laugh. One that lacked genuine humor, perfectly fitting for this shittastic moment. "Your chance was staring you straight in the eye, and you really went and fucked it up, didn't you?"

I swallowed, hating how he'd arranged those words and what they'd implied. "I didn't fuck up anything besides inviting Juni even further into my life by setting her up with my goddamn friend."

"Okay." Cameron nodded, but the twist of his lips told me he didn't buy a single word I'd said. "I'll let you believe that for now." He leaned in closer, clapping a hand on my shoulder. "But that denial will keep biting you in the ass if you don't do something about it."

He made it sound easy. Like the fight within me was something that could be easily tossed aside. But he didn't know the half of it. He didn't understand the number of years she'd made me suffer.

"It's not too late," he added beneath his breath, seeming to sense the battle going on in my head.

It's not too late.

I wasn't sure I believed that.

I wasn't sure I even wanted to believe it.

In the end, it didn't matter. Not in the way Cameron meant it.

The only thing that mattered was making sure I never had to hear Noah call Juniper *sweetheart* ever again.

ten years ago

"What?" I sighed.

Julian crossed his arms over his bare chest, his mouth opening and closing with words that wouldn't come out. Hating how my eyes kept wanting to drift lower, I looked away from him.

Eventually, Julian cleared his throat. "Kelly and I broke up."

My eyes shot over to his face, noting the drained expression and tight, clenched jaw. Even more than usual. He took a step closer to me, and without even consciously realizing it, I took a step closer to him.

Weighty silence fell over the room. The house was quiet, except for the slight creak of the floorboards as I shifted my weight from one foot to the other. The moonlight flooded through Julian's open window, that soft summer breeze making the curtains dance around the frame. And the oddest sensation settled in my chest.

"You and Kelly broke up?" I prompted, feeling like walking out on him now would be rude.

He nodded. "I thought..." He rubbed his jaw in thought for a moment. "I thought we were on the same page. About not wanting to do long distance. She...didn't feel the same."

I stared at him, unsure if I was comprehending correctly. "So you broke up with her? I thought you really liked her."

Me? I wasn't a big fan of Kelly Mcvarish, but I didn't have a good reason. She was fine. But there was just something about her that grated on my nerves whenever I saw her. Over the last few months, sometimes I would show up at the Briggs house and collide with a smiley blonde. And I always had to pretend to be happy to see her.

Julian shook his head, his eyes avoiding mine. "I liked her, but..."

He never did finish his sentence.

CHAPTER FOURTEEN

THERE WAS THIS SOCIETAL misconception that people were either created as early morning risers or late-night owls. That if they went to bed late, they hated waking up early. That if they woke up early, they never slept in. That their night-time preferences had everything to do with sleeping and nothing to do with living.

I stayed up late because nights were when freedom existed.

And I was always so reluctant to give it up. To resign myself to the morning when the sun tended to bring an immediate agenda —one I had never known how to *not* stick to like glue.

I liked having my to-do lists, but sometimes I didn't know how to live until everything was checked off.

Tonight was one of those nights, the ones I was reluctant to end.

Saying good night to Noah meant saying good morning to Julian tomorrow, and I wasn't sure I was ready for that after how he acted tonight.

Well, even if it weren't for tonight, I wasn't sure I wanted to go into the office tomorrow. Being around Julian the last few days had been *exhausting*. I didn't know how else to explain it because I didn't know where to place the feelings I'd experienced Saturday night. Or worse, Sunday morning.

Sunday morning.

I was between ninety and one hundred percent certain that Julian had kissed me. His lips on my skin, making me gasp. He'd found that spot, the one that caused all-over shivers and an unraveling in my gut.

Based on his reaction a second later—his accusations and unbridled irritation—he hadn't realized *who* he'd been kissing. But that didn't matter. The moment happened, and the memory clung to me. A constant reminder that Julian wasn't that annoying boy from my childhood anymore.

He was a man, a full-grown man who was mind-numbingly attractive when shirtless and sleepy-eyed. The rumpled hair and the rippling muscles pinning me to the bed had only added to it. And just when I thought I might have been dreaming, his hips had shifted and—

Man. A man.

And on that Sunday morning in Julian Briggs' bed, I was a woman who wanted him.

When he'd abruptly pulled away, I'd hated myself for feeling that way, but it was too late. And now it kept haunting me, worse than any Halloween horrors.

I'd learned the best way to hide from the dark was to bask in the light, and that was exactly what I was doing. Tonight, I'd clung to every little compliment Noah had tossed my way, every smile. Because I knew exactly where we stood and what our status quo was. And while Noah was still every bit a stranger, that was so much more comfortable than exploring something new that hid in the old.

Noah held open the door as we left the Bellflower, letting me walk into the night first before skirting around to bump me away from the curb and take his place beside me.

Poor guy had wanted to wait for Julian to come back, and I didn't have the heart to tell him that his friend probably wouldn't return. Plus that it was my fault. Only after Noah checked his phone to find confirmation that Julian had left did he give up, pay for our drinks, and insist on walking me home.

Sensing Noah's confusion, I sighed. And admitted the truth.

"You know, he's just mad at me about...this."

I wiggled a finger back and forth between us, hoping he'd get the hint.

But Noah only frowned. "You think he's mad at *you*?"

"He's always mad at me."

With a slow nod, Noah shoved his hands into his pockets. The bar had grown stuffy and warm, and Noah's sleeves were now pushed up, highlighting the tattoos covering his forearms.

"Okay," he said, drawing out the word, "but why do you think he's mad at you *this* time?"

Wasn't it obvious? "He thinks I'm stealing his friends. Just like I stole his sisters."

"You think—" Noah cut off with a laugh. "I don't know about that, Juniper."

"Trust me," I insisted. "He'll definitely make some comment about it tomorrow in the office."

Noah smiled. *Genuinely* smiled, and it confused me. "Kind of a twist of fate that you two ended up working together, huh?"

I wasn't sure why everyone found this particular fact amusing when it was, in fact, incredibly irritating.

"We don't just work together," I corrected. "We share an office."

Noah's lips curved even further, his grin a reminder of how handsome he was—in and out of his jersey. "Like I said...fate."

"Do you mean karma?" I asked, raising a brow. "Because I did have a rebellious streak when I was younger, so maybe this is retribution for my wrongdoings."

Noah laughed, eyes twinkling as he looked over at me, but he didn't seem entirely convinced. Luckily, he kept from arguing the point further, and we fell into a companionable silence while strolling through Boston.

Things with Noah were easy. We didn't have much in common, but he still had that charm I remembered from college that translated into relaxed conversations and a sense of ease. It gave me hope for the wedding, which was close enough now that the ball of anxiety grew in my stomach every time I thought about it.

When he stopped in front of my apartment, Noah turned to face me. His eyes flicked over my face, and I grew warm, even considering the brisk fall air. Noah studied me closely, an obvious assessment that made me wonder what he was thinking. I probably wasn't half as pretty as the girls he usually took out for drinks, but he was far too nice to ever let me realize that.

I opened my mouth to excuse myself, not wanting him to think I expected anything more than a whispered good night, when he cut me off.

"For the record, Juniper." His voice was soft. "I would kiss you if I knew it wouldn't cause problems with your coworker."

"Oh, I—"

He put a finger to my lips. "Trust me on this one. Okay?"

All I could really do was whisper in reply.

"Okay."

I WAS RIGHT.

I should have done more to keep last night from ending.

My morning so far had been unforgiving. So much so that I was tempted to call in sick. Or ask if I could work from home.

But I didn't do either of those things. Giving up wasn't on the to-do list for today. Instead, I picked up coffee for a handful of my colleagues—Julian included with his dreadful plain order—along with a menagerie of pastries before heading into the office. And after I'd delivered my morning treats to those who were already there—Julian was not, of course—I returned to my car. Two of my favorite houseplants, a peace lily and a pothos, sat in my trunk.

Julian would be annoyed. And that was fine. Perfect, actually. He could spend the morning pestering me about my plants invading our office, the donut powder coating our keyboards, and how I bought Cameron coffee again. He could scowl and call me all those flower nicknames he loved so much and forget about last night. He could forget about the weekend.

And we would forget everything.

Everything except what we already knew.

I'd still help him with the case if he needed it, but I enjoyed that kind of work, so it wasn't a big deal.

"How was the rest of your date with Noah?"

Goddamnit. It had been hours now, and Julian hadn't said a word about my plants. He hadn't said anything about the coffee and donuts except *thank you*, and he hadn't called me Daisy once. Not once.

Of course when he finally decided to open that annoying mouth of his, it was to ask that. He'd tossed the question into the office without even looking away from his computer. I barely heard it over my audiobook, though I had the volume low while I picked at my lunch.

The last thing I needed was for Julian to overhear and add my books to his list of things he pestered me about.

I pressed Pause and cleared my throat. "It wasn't a date."

Julian swiveled in his desk chair, seeming taken aback by my sharp tone.

"Okay..." He grappled with finding words for a moment. "Then, how was the rest of your *night* with Noah?"

I busied myself with watering the moonflower, using a desk-sized watering can I'd found at the farmer's market last year. "I don't want to talk about Noah."

The rustle of movement behind me should have been my clue, but I still jumped when I turned to find Julian standing a breath away.

"Did he do something?"

A strange fire danced in his eyes. A tick jumped in his jaw. Anger flashed across his face. Anger at...Noah?

"He didn't do anything," I assured. "Not last night."

Frowning, Julian took another step closer. I really wished he wouldn't do that. Being so close to Julian made it hard to focus on...anything. Thinking. Talking. And frankly, I was afraid of liking it.

"What's that supposed to mean?" he pressed.

All of this—it had been what I was trying to avoid. But clearly, it was unavoidable.

"It means he texted me this morning to let me know he can't go with me to Sofia's wedding anymore."

My words lingered between us, hanging there. Julian sucked in a breath, almost like he needed to absorb what I'd said to make it true. Then his mouth opened and closed at least twice before he could say anything.

He was reacting better than Gemma had, although that was to be expected. Gemma had cursed Noah out in a string of text messages. But Julian was surprisingly calm.

"Why not?"

I shook my head. "Something to do with his football schedule."

Julian's frown deepened. "When's the wedding again?"

"Not this weekend but the next."

He nodded. And then kept nodding. Until finally, he cleared his voice. And for some reason, I realized he was about to say something that would mess with everything. It would make it harder to ignore the new mixing with the old.

"I'll take you."

Silence followed, broken only by my heart, which felt like it was hammering loud enough for the entire office building to hear.

No.

He couldn't have said that. Julian volunteering to spend time with me? No.

"What?"

"Look, I know I'm not an NFL quarterback or anything, but..." He sighed, throwing his hands casually into his pants pockets and rocking back on his heels. And then an unexpected little smirk broke onto his lips. "But I clean up pretty well in a suit. And I owe you a date."

Of course. It was his damn sense of fairness. His pride. The *deal.* But it wasn't really fair. He likely didn't realize exactly what he was offering.

"You'll...go with me to New York for the weekend?" I clarified.

His restrained, nonchalant demeanor immediately shifted like I'd known it would. "It's in New York?"

"It's in New York," I repeated, an odd mix of relief and regret filling me as soon as I said it.

He wouldn't come with me to New York. There was no way.

"Noah was going to go with you to fucking New York? For the whole weekend?" He ran a hand through his hair, shaking his head. "Goddamn, Daisy."

The first nickname of the day, and I didn't even understand what it meant.

"It's really okay, Julian," I said, trying to slide away from him, scooting along the edge of my desk. It would be easier to have this conversation if I couldn't see how blue his eyes were. "You don't have to come with me. I don't even think I'm going to go anymore, so—"

"If you want to go, you're going." He said it stubbornly, a finality in the words as he crossed his arms over his chest. "And I'll go with you. If I'd known I was setting you up to spend an entire weekend away with a guy who you've just met, I wouldn't have done it."

"Oh, I—" My throat momentarily closed as I took in his insistence, his commanding presence that I usually found over-the-top and unnecessary, irritatingly so. But now...I didn't know what to think. "And you'll pretend to be my boyfriend?"

Skepticism laced the question. I wasn't ready to accept this. A few hours ago, I convinced myself that I wouldn't even be attending the wedding. In a moment of overwhelming rejection, I swore off taking risks—risks like fake dates and meeting new siblings.

But Julian shrugged, unfazed. "We've already had some practice pretending. What's a little more?"

A lot more. Did he not realize that it was going to be *a lot* more?

My skin began to heat up when Julian crowded me against my desk, and I tried really hard not to think about those moments in his garage. In his bed. What it felt like when his—

"I know you, Juni," he said, knocking over my defenses with the sheer tenderness in the sentence. It caressed my skin like his lips had that morning. I froze as he swiped a piece of hair out of my face. "If you think anyone could fake being your boyfriend better than me, you're dead wrong. Name one guy who's known you as long as I have. Who knows you as well as I do."

I blinked. There wasn't anyone. But that wasn't my concern.

"Yeah, but you have to be *nice* to me."

Julian smiled, and goddamn, it seemed genuine. "I can do that."

"No, I mean the whole time, Julian." Anxiety threatened to storm on me, waltzing straight over my already lowered defenses. "Not just in front of other people. I'm already nervous enough about this wedding without—"

"I'll be nice." There he went with that soft voice again, confusing all my senses. "I promise. But you have to do a better job pretending that you like me than you did in front of Greg Kennedy."

I gulped, lifting my gaze only to get assaulted by the brightness in Julian's. I fought the urge to look away, to shield myself. But his apparent sincerity washed away my last bits of doubt.

"I can do that," I whispered.

The expression that blossomed on Julian's face at my answer shouldn't be allowed. Not in this office, not near me. It told me, in very explicit terms, that this was a terrible idea. And his next words only confirmed that.

"Should we practice?"

"Oh, I don't think we have to practice."

I needed him to drop this idea right now. It was a terrible one. Julian had to realize that, right? He'd been there, in that bed. He should understand why we didn't need any more blurring of whatever lines existed between us.

Although maybe he hadn't felt what I had this weekend. Maybe the large-and-in-charge thing that had landed between my legs was nothing more than a sign that Julian had a healthy, functioning nervous system and superior blood flow. You know, normal manly morning things. Or maybe he'd been thinking about the woman he seemed to think was in his bed—whoever was on his mind when he kissed me.

That might explain why Julian smiled at me and said, "I'd disagree."

"Why?"

"Well," he drawled, sliding in closer with his hands in his pockets. "For starters, you need to work on loosening up a little bit when I touch you."

"I'm loose," I said defensively, resisting the urge to smack the cockiness off his face. He was making it sound like *I* was the only one here who needed practice. "I'm relaxed."

"Really?" His smirk didn't let up.

"Yes," I insisted, trying to prove it to him by perching on the edge of my desk nonchalantly.

My attempt to look at ease failed when I didn't know what to do with my hands, though. Finally, I settled with folding them awkwardly in my lap, placing them tactically over the tummy roll that appeared whenever I so much as slouched.

Okay, so maybe I wasn't loose. And goddamnit, he wasn't even touching me yet.

Julian looked like he was trying really hard to hold in his laughter. And while I appreciated the attempt not to laugh straight in my face, it would have been better if it weren't so obvious.

"You look ready to spring off that desk, Lily," he said once he finally managed to swallow his amusement.

"Well, it isn't exactly a comfortable position," I snapped.

"Then stop shrinking away from me and come over here." He raised a brow. "I won't bite."

He might not bite, but that didn't mean getting closer to him was a good idea. We already had enough confusing moments dancing around in my head. We didn't need to purposefully add more.

So I wrinkled my nose and snarked at him—my go-to first defense. "You don't bite, but you do smell."

Julian's lips twitched. "Am I the only one who's required to be nice in this fake relationship?"

"Yep, pretty much," I said, giving him a satisfied nod.

"I think I'll still survive."

At least that made one of us.

When I didn't reply, Julian held out his arms like he expected me to dive into them, and I stilled.

Okay, *fine.* Maybe I did need some practice with this. *This* being voluntary movement toward Julian Briggs. Presently, my body seemed to require a little coaxing. Or maybe that was my brain.

After sliding off my desk, I warily closed the distance between Julian and me, trying to ignore the odd, encouraging smile he flashed me. And once my face was in the perfect position to stare straight at Julian's neck and his bobbing Adam's apple, Julian closed his arms around me. A hand settled on the base of my spine. The feeling of it burned through my dress, but pleasantly so. I could do this. I could handle this.

But then Julian began trailing his fingers up the length of my spine like he was tickling keys on a piano, and I immediately changed my mind.

"Relax, Daisy."

Easier said than done, but I took a deep breath and let myself lean into him.

"See?" Julian breathed. "That's not so bad."

When I didn't reply, he added, "I bet I don't even smell bad, do I?"

I shook my head, breathing in the masculine musk of his cologne. And then my eyes fluttered shut as Julian's caressing hand put some sort of drowsing spell over me. It must be the lingering Halloween spirit from the weekend. It had to be.

"How late were you out last night?" he asked, voice soft, humor apparent in it.

"Not that late."

There was a beat of silence.

"Did Noah walk you home?"

"Yes," I whispered.

"When?"

"Not long after you left."

"But then you stayed up. Didn't you?"

I nodded against his chest, hoping I didn't get my makeup on his crisp, white shirt. If I did, he might revoke his kindness rule, and I was a little bit banking on that at the moment.

His chest rose and fell beneath my head in a steady wave. Hard and soft at the same time.

This wasn't supposed to feel this good.

Shit, bad idea. Such a bad idea.

"When we go to New York, I'm going to make sure you get plenty of sleep." His voice was husky. It had a soothing quality I didn't ever imagine possible.

That woke me right up. Because I hadn't thought that far ahead to realize that if Julian was my date to Sofia's wedding, then we would be staying together. Sleeping together. Well, not *sleeping* sleeping together, but sleeping in the same room. And we'd already done that once, and to put it mildly, it would be dangerous to repeat.

"I don't need you to tuck me into bed, Julian."

"Someone clearly does."

"Should I have asked Noah to do it last night?"

"Absolutely fucking not," Julian snapped, his tone low—so low that something burned inside me.

"Noted."

"You're tense again," Julian muttered, which I thought was hypocritical considering how rigid he suddenly felt against me. His breath brushed the top of my head as his touch grew firmer—like he was trying harder to comfort me when, in reality, it made my head spin. "Does the thought of a good night's sleep freak you out that much?"

"Of course not."

It had nothing to do with sleep.

Julian released me, but he did it slowly. First, his hand dropped from my back. Then his arm released its hold around me. And finally, he stepped away.

I'd hoped that the step away would help me breathe better, but here I was, still thinking about sharing a hotel room with Julian.

Indecision reared its ugly head as my brain analyzed my options in a rapid-fire fashion. It quickly came down to only three: share a room with Julian for a weekend, go to the wedding alone without knowing anyone else there, or don't go to the wedding at all.

I sighed.

Sharing a room with Julian, it was.

"Gracias por su tiempo. ¡Qué tenga un buen día! ¡Hasta pronto!"

I ended the call with my client, feeling eyes on the back of my neck as I put the phone down. Sure enough, I found Julian watching me when I spun in my chair. He leaned against the door frame, arms folded over his chest. Before I could call him out for being creepy, he tilted his head and smiled.

He'd smiled a lot in the last week and a half. I half wondered if I needed to let him know that he didn't need to start being nice to me until the weekend, but at the same time, I didn't want to jinx anything. Or give up the smiles.

"I didn't know you spoke Spanish."

"Really?" I matched him, cocking my head to the same side. "And here I thought you claimed to know me better than anyone."

"I didn't say better than *anyone*," he corrected. "I said better than any other *man*."

I hated that that was true. It was an indicator of all my failed relationships. The guy who knew me better than anyone shouldn't be my best friend's brother.

Leaning back in my chair, I crossed my arms over my chest and gave Julian a pointed look. "Well, my last boyfriend knew I spoke Spanish, so..."

His eyes flitted over me quickly before meeting my gaze. "Evan?"

I raised a brow, surprised he knew his name. I nodded.

"So he knows more than me, huh?" Julian clarified.

"Yep."

I said it definitively.

And like a challenge.

Julian, of course, accepted.

"Guess we'll have to change that." He grabbed his chair, pulled it toward my desk, and then sat. We were close enough that our knees nearly touched, and Julian folded his hands in his lap like he planned to interview me. "So, when did you learn Spanish?"

I should have known that interviewing me was *precisely* what he planned to do.

I cleared my throat. "In high school."

His brows furrowed momentarily. "I remember you taking French in high school."

He was right. I did. But what an odd thing to remember.

"My parents and I learned together at home. And then I continued in college. Did you know there are over half a million Spanish speakers in the Boston area?"

"I knew there were a lot, but I guess I didn't know it was *that* many. You learned in undergrad?" he asked.

I nodded.

"Did you take courses?"

"No, I did it on my own time."

That seemed to stump him. "Would have made sense to get credit for that on your transcripts."

"Not all of us had a full ride in undergrad, Julian," I scoffed. "Those extra credits would have cost a pretty penny."

"Good point," he said.

"Good point?"

Had he just agreed with me?

"Yes, Rosie. Good point. I might not have had to pay for my own tuition, but I know how much college costs. I'm paying for Gianna's degree."

"I—you're what?"

"We're getting off topic." He waved my confusion and disbelief away. "So why did you choose to learn Spanish in your free time?"

"My birth dad was Mexican American. I thought maybe I'd feel...closer to that part of myself if I learned the language and more about my heritage."

Julian's slow nod was an understanding one that put me a little bit at ease. His voice shifted slightly when he asked his next question.

"Have you met him?"

I shook my head. "He died while my birth mom was pregnant with me. They were newlyweds, and my mom..."

I struggled to finish the sentence because I didn't really know what went at the end of it. I didn't know what exactly happened, and while it was hard, I tried not to let myself think too much about it. Because I likely wouldn't ever know, and the speculation helped no one. Besides, I had landed exactly where I was meant to be—with my parents in Whitebridge.

"Juni..." Julian's expression shuttered. He leaned forward. One finger brushed over the top of my knee. "Have you met her? Your birth mom?"

"No." I sighed. "I wonder...well, I don't know."

Julian waited patiently, clearly hoping I'd continue. So I did.

"It was an open adoption, but there hasn't been much contact. All I really know is that Isabella has minimal health history concerns, and she's a white woman with Western European ancestry—German, I think, a lot like my parents. They were the ones who wanted me to know about my background while still respecting Isabella's privacy since she rarely reached out."

Julian's single finger made another soothing pass over my knee, and I had to steel myself beneath the intensity of his gaze.

"I know more about Sofia because we follow each other on social media," I added because talking was easier than thinking about Julian. "She's a couple years younger than me, born once Isabella remarried. I'm not sure what she does for a living, but considering how her wedding is at a five-star hotel in Manhattan, I'd say someone in that family is making good money."

Julian didn't ask about the wedding. I thought he might. I thought it might get us off this track of my family history. But instead, he asked, "And you haven't met Sofia either?"

A phone rang in the office next to ours, the only interruption to the silence that lingered between Julian and me while I thought about how to best answer that question. I bit down on my lip, chewing on it. Julian's attention dipped to my mouth before flicking back to my eyes.

"No," I whispered finally. "I connected with her when I was living in New York for law school, thinking maybe I'd get the guts to ask if she wanted to meet. But I never did. And I know it's probably ridiculous that I'm going to her wedding even though we've never met and that I'm trying to make such a good impression, but—"

"It's not ridiculous. I wish I'd known all of this. I wouldn't—" He stopped, rubbing a hand over his face.

"That's what happens when you let my college boyfriend know more about me than you," I teased, trying to lighten the dark look on Julian's face, the one that frankly shocked me after his hand dropped. "Guess it's a reminder to work harder on it from here on out."

"Guess it is." Julian's face was set, eyes blazing. It felt like he'd taken my teasing joke and turned it into a promise. One that wasn't a joke at all. "Are you packed for the weekend?"

I nodded.

"You still want to leave right after work tomorrow?"

"If that works for you." I tried to roll my chair back—put some space between the two of us—but I quickly hit the desk behind me. "Although I know that means we won't get into Manhattan until well after dark, and we might hit rush hour."

"That's fine." Julian shrugged, and to my immense relief, he wheeled himself and his chair back to his desk. "More time for me to increase my bank of knowledge on Juniper St. James. Since it's apparently lacking."

"You know I was just kidding about—"

"I take getting to know my fake girlfriend incredibly seriously." Julian tossed me a smirk over his shoulder. "Don't ruin my fun."

"Oh, now it's fun spending time with me?"

This was a new development that I didn't know how to handle. Although, I also didn't think it was true.

"That depends. Are you going to get donut powder all over my car?"

"No, donuts are a morning thing, Julian." I rolled my eyes. "We're going in the evening."

He chuckled while packing his messenger bag, clearly

intending to head out after he was done irritating me. "Are you going to bring another one of those damned plants?" he asked.

"No, you know very well that's an illogical question. Why would I bring plants—"

"Are you going to make me listen to your audiobooks for over three hours?"

I gasped. "How do you know about my audiobooks?"

Julian stood, throwing the strap of his bag onto his shoulder and crossing the office to leave. But before he did, he swiveled and grabbed the top of the doorframe, leaning in as though whatever he was about to say was a secret he'd been holding on to for a long time.

"You need better headphones, Daisy."

And then he smiled knowingly and walked out the door.

CHAPTER FIFTEEN

I DIDN'T KNOW HOW to stop what was happening.

Part of me wondered if I should reach out to Noah, get to the bottom of why he'd ditched Juniper. Because I highly doubted it had anything to do with football. But the last thing I wanted was to give him a hard time only for him to change his mind.

Like hell did I want him taking Juniper to this wedding.

Which left me as her only option.

This was a bad idea. For fuck's sake, I'd spent years keeping Juni at arm's length, and now I was pretending to be her boyfriend for a weekend?

Bright fucking idea.

But Halloween had fucked me over, and now escorting Juniper to the wedding was exactly the excuse my brain needed to justify being close to her. I couldn't shake the itch to touch her. I couldn't stop thinking of how it had felt to have her beneath the sheets. Christ, I thought about her more than any man should think about a woman who was his coworker and sister's best friend. And it was damn annoying, honestly.

There were so many reasons why this was a terrible idea. And incidentally, one of those reasons was blowing up my phone.

GEMS: You better be nice to her this weekend.

GEMS: She's really nervous about meeting Sofia.

GEMS: She doesn't need your ass to be moody on top of it.

GEMS: Maybe, you know, be encouraging for once. Give her a smile. Or a hug. You might actually enjoy it.

I did fucking enjoy it. That was the problem. I hated how much I enjoyed it.

Not that Gemma needed to know that.

I'll be nice, Gems. I'm not an asshole. I know this is important to her. Otherwise, I wouldn't be doing it.

GEMS: I know you're not an asshole. But sometimes you act like one when Juni's around.

GEMS: Thank you for taking her.

I owed her.

GEMS: For what?

She's helping me with something for work.

GEMS: I still can't get over that you guys work together.

"Ready?"

I pocketed my phone at the sound of Juni's voice, ignoring Gemma's last text. Everyone seemed to think Juni and I working together was amusing as all hell without realizing just how much of my sanity it cost me.

And now I was about to lose more of it.

Juniper, looking almost unrecognizable in jeans and a sweatshirt, rolled her bags toward where I waited outside her apartment. I took her suitcase, sliding it into the trunk of my SUV before opening the front passenger door for her to get in.

She rolled her eyes. "I feel like you're taking this whole nice thing too far."

"Oh, so now I'm *too* nice?"

She looked from me to the open car door pointedly, chewing on her lip in a way that made it nearly impossible not to stare at her mouth and those soft lips. *Shit.*

"Get in the fucking car, Juniper," I growled.

Her eyes, wide and wondrous, flew to mine. Pink lips parted in surprise. She hesitated only a moment before settling in the passenger seat, but that single moment made my pulse tick up.

After putting on her seat belt, Juniper looked at me from beneath her lashes. "That better?"

"Much."

She held my gaze for one more beat before glancing down and clearing her throat. When she spoke, her words were crisp and diplomatic. That single moment from before had vanished, and God, I was thankful for it.

"You know, I think you could work on finding a middle ground, Julian. Between nice and...whatever that was." Her manicured hand waved in my direction, a finger flicking up and down.

"Noted."

Ten minutes later, we were on I-90W, undoubtedly headed toward a catastrophe. Juniper connected her phone to my car's Bluetooth and had her head down, searching for a playlist. Meanwhile, I could barely think because of all the fucking flowers dancing around my head.

"What's it called?"

"What's what called?"

"Your perfume."

"Bloom. Why?"

"I'm going to buy out their entire stock so you can't torture me with it anymore."

"I regret saying that you were being too nice." She sniffed, pursing her lips. "Why did you even volunteer to be my date?"

"Because I didn't want anyone else to."

The words were out before I could stop them, but I wasn't sure how much I cared.

Noah taking her to this wedding was a ridiculous idea, and I didn't know why we had ever run with it. He barely knew Juniper, had probably only wanted to see if he could sleep with her, and likely wouldn't have stuck around afterward. It had been a shit idea. And setting her up with anyone else would have been a shit idea, too.

While *this* idea was still absolutely a bad one, it was better than all the others that didn't involve, well, me.

"Anyone else?" Juni questioned. "You mean any of your other friends, right?" When I failed to answer that question, she added, "I think you're just afraid they're going to get to know me and realize they like me better than you."

"No, Rosie," I grunted. "That's not it."

"No? Then maybe I should have asked Cameron." She paused. "Although the professional boundaries would have been a definite concern."

My grip on the wheel tightened at the mention of Cameron. "Professional boundaries? *We* share an office. And here I am."

But she hit the nail on the head on the second reason I shouldn't be doing this. Whatever happened this weekend, I still had to share an office with Juni for the foreseeable future. And I liked working at Gardner Law. Despite how often I perused job ads these days, I didn't really want to get a new one.

"Our boundaries aren't the same, and you know it."

I did know. I fucking knew it all too well, and I doubted it was a good thing.

"Why is it important that you bring a date anyway?" I asked, changing the subject. "I obviously understand not wanting to go alone, but why do you want Sofia to think you're in a relationship?"

Juniper snuggled lower into her seat, crossing one leg over the other. "Different question, please," she said.

After quick consideration, I didn't ask a different question. I really wanted to know the answer to this one. So I waited, tapping my finger on the steering wheel and keeping my eyes on the road.

Eventually, Juniper sighed. "Look, I'm well aware that there is absolutely nothing wrong with being a single woman. There are many, many impressive single people in this world."

"Yes." I side-eyed her purposefully. "Yes, there are."

"But..."

Juni hesitated. Meanwhile, I trained my eyes back on the road, hoping it would make it easier for her to find words. But then a booming male voice broke through the silence in the car, cutting off whatever Juni might have said. And shocking the hell out of me.

"Georgia leaned back on the bed, spreading her legs wide. I sat back on my knees, taking in her glistening pussy, wet and waiting for me. Fuck, she was gorgeous. And she looked at me with those eyes—"

"Shit, shit, shit," Juni muttered as she fumbled with her phone. "That was not what I—"

"By all means," I half yelled, half laughed over the man telling me exactly how he planned to fuck some lady named Georgia, "don't turn it off on my account."

"I'm *trying*—ah, there."

The car abruptly fell quiet again—quiet enough that I could hear the tires spinning on the highway beneath us. Out of the corner of my eye, I saw Juniper glance sheepishly toward me.

"That was, uh, supposed to be a diversion," she admitted before that familiar twinkle brightened in her eye. "Plus, I know how much you were looking forward to listening to my audiobooks."

The ridiculousness of it all made me laugh again, harder this time. I'd known she spent her lunch hours listening to audiobooks; the cadence of the narration was just loud enough to make out. And while her reaction yesterday made me wonder exactly what she thought I overheard, I hadn't imagined it would be *that.*

"Well planned," I said. Except it wasn't, of course. Juni looked slightly mortified that the book had picked up in that spot, and meanwhile, it diverted me to my next line of wondering, one I knew she wouldn't like anymore. "I think you should let the scene finish. Ya know, to give me a better idea."

"A better idea?"

"Of what my fake girlfriend likes."

"Oh." Juni shifted in her seat. "Well, as you can tell, I mostly read romance books. I'm not sure we need to listen to the rest of the scene to explain that."

Luckily, my many years of knowing Juni had given me the practice I needed to keep my expression motionless, even though my lips itched to curve in a knowing smile.

"I wasn't talking about books, Lily."

It took exactly five seconds before I heard the quick intake of breath and felt a simultaneous slap on my arm. "*Julian*!"

"This is your mistake, honestly. You blasted an explicit sex scene in my car," I pointed out, giving in to the smirk that wouldn't stay off my face. "We could go back to the conversation about impressing your family if you want."

"We are *not* talking about my sex life."

"Are you sure?" I shrugged, ignoring my internal irritation at the thought of Juniper sleeping with other guys—most of whom I bet didn't deserve even a hug from her. Case in point, Greg Kennedy. "Seems like something that two people who are fake fucking and fake dating should talk about."

"No, it does *not.*" She crossed her arms over her chest, pouting in her seat. "Remember those professional boundaries we were talking about earlier? This is very much crossing them."

"You said our boundaries aren't the same," I reminded her. "And even if they were, *this* is where we draw the line? It wasn't when you crawled into my bed on Halloween?"

"I thought we agreed not to talk about that," she hissed, glaring at me. The heat of her look singed my skin.

"We never agreed on anything." I raised my brows. "We've never talked about it at all."

"Exactly!" Juni threw her hands up. "We never talked about it. Ergo, we never were going to. It was an unspoken agreement, Julian."

I chuckled, hoping that maybe she wouldn't see how much it affected me to even think about Halloween weekend. She didn't need to know that I'd reimagined her beneath me far too many times by now. "I don't think that's how it works."

Juniper huffed in a very Juniper way. "If you're so eager to have this discussion, why don't you share first, huh?"

I glanced over at her. Despite her sulky appearance as she slouched in my car, her eyes shone. And if I wasn't mistaken, curiosity simmered there.

There she was—the girl from my bed that morning. I'd been scared to confirm it, but she was there. And I wasn't sure exactly what, but she wanted *something*.

"What do you want to know?" I asked.

Considering how my pulse couldn't seem to find any consistency during this car ride and how my palms were starting to sweat on the steering wheel, I probably shouldn't encourage this conversation. But she'd presented this rabbit hole, and I'd dragged us down it. So here we were.

Juni thought for a moment, tapping her nose adorably. Her cheeks had grown pink, matching her lips, and I wished I wasn't driving so I could keep watching her.

It was precisely that fact—that I had to look back at the road—that made me miss the change in her expression. My only warning of her next words was the low tone of her voice when she started speaking.

"As your girlfriend, how satisfied would you say I am?" she questioned, stirring up heat within me. "I need to know how to act."

I adjusted my grip on the steering wheel, wishing I could do something else with my hands. "You're more than fucking satisfied."

I could feel Juni watching me, but I didn't dare turn to look at her. I had a feeling it would ruin everything. So I bit my tongue, keeping myself from saying anything I'd regret.

"Well." Her voice was forcefully light. "That's an awfully bold statement without any pro—"

"Don't ask for proof unless you're ready to get it, Juniper."

Fuck. Speaking of words I'd regret, there they were. She'd been right. We shouldn't be having this conversation. Because while I still refused to look at her, I heard Juni suck in a breath, and suddenly, the car was stiflingly hot.

"You could have proven it to me on Halloween," she said quietly, a low murmur beneath her breath. But I heard it loud and clear. "There was a moment when I wondered if you were going to."

Oh, God. Hearing Juniper talk like that made all my nerve endings feel like they were about to explode.

"I thought you didn't want to talk about Halloween," I said, matching her tone.

Juni twisted to look out the window, avoiding my attempts to capture her gaze. "You're right."

This weekend would absolutely destroy me.

I softened my voice. "If you change your mind, let me know."

As much as I wanted—and had been trying—to ignore whatever this was between us, it was really fucking hard. And the fact of the matter was that we were two adults who had to work and exist around each other. Eventually, we might have to talk about it. Ignoring Juni might not be an option for much longer, even though I hated to admit it.

Juni nodded without taking her eyes off the passing landscape, and I took that to mean that the conversation was over and closed. For now.

"We should stop for something to eat," I said, changing the

subject. "You skipped lunch again today."

"I was too anxious to eat."

"About the weekend?"

She nodded, and I noticed how her shoulders were slumped. Guilt instantly sank into my gut, heavy as a rock. I was being an asshole, doing exactly what Gemma had told me not to do. Juniper was undoubtedly worried about meeting her sister, and here I was, probing her with uncomfortable topics.

I watched as Juni fiddled with her phone, popping the case on and off in the corner. I reached out and grabbed that fidgeting hand, forcing it to still. Her fingers slowly relaxed, letting mine thread between hers. I squeezed, ignoring the heat of her skin. And how soft it was. She stared down at our hands for a moment.

"You can turn your book back on if you want," I said.

"Oh, no." A nervous giggle cut through the tension in the car. "No, that's okay."

"I was only teasing you yesterday," I said, holding her hand even tighter, not wanting her to slip away. "I don't really mind if you want to listen to it."

"I don't want you to ruin all the best moments."

"Me?" I pretended to be affronted. "I would never."

Juni flashed me a look that told how much she believed me: not one bit.

I couldn't help but laugh. She was right; I probably would end up ruining something.

"Tell me about it, then," I insisted. "Are you enjoying it?"

"I am," she said, and I watched as a light switched on in her eyes. In her whole face, actually. "It's the third book in a series, and I think this one might be my favorite. But I'll probably say that about the next one, too."

"How many books are there in the series?"

"I think there's going to be five, but only four books have been released."

"What's this one about?" I nodded toward her phone.

Juni smiled brightly.

And then she told me all about it.

IT WAS LATE WHEN WE FINALLY MADE IT TO MANHATTAN.

Our hotel was a stunning high-rise with room rates that were likely more than Juniper could reasonably afford. And even though it would cause an argument, I made a mental note to pay her back for our stay later.

After Juni checked us in, I followed her to the elevator, where we shared a quiet ride up to the sixteenth floor. She was more than tired; I could tell from how she dragged her feet as she pushed open the door to our room. A full day of work and hours of stop-and-go traffic had made my eyelids droop, too. We'd been forced to take at least four detours due to construction.

Sometimes detours were nice. A surprise diversion. New sights that you wouldn't have noticed otherwise. Old sights but in a new light.

These weren't those kinds of detours.

Juniper's obvious fatigue made me frown with worry when she stopped short just after entering the room. Her purse dropped to the floor with a loud thunk.

"Juni?"

I stepped beside her, looking over her shoulder to catch a glimpse of her face. She stared blankly ahead, causing my frown to deepen.

That is, until I followed her gaze.

The room was nothing short of elegant. The finishes screamed luxury and unheard-of expenses. But most importantly, in the middle of the room sat a large bed with fluffy white linens and a sleek, black headboard.

One large bed. One set of fluffy white linens. One sleek, black headboard.

One.

CHAPTER SIXTEEN

THERE WAS ONLY ONE bed in our hotel room.

It had been enough of a disaster when I thought I would have to share a room with Julian. Now I had to share a *bed* with Julian? After that car ride, when we'd skated around the topic of the last time we'd shared a bed? When Julian said that thing about *proving* he could leave me more than satisfied?

Oh, hell no.

Julian pushed past me, dropping one of our bags—because he'd insisted on carrying both—onto the armchair in the corner. He set the other on the ground.

"I'm sorry that you're not going to be able to sleep with my friend like you'd clearly been planning on."

His words were sharp, and his features pulled taut as he unzipped his jacket and wrestled out of it in an overly aggressive manner.

I barely managed to find my voice. "It wasn't like that. I made these reservations before asking Noah to go with me. I don't remember booking one bed, but then again, I didn't expect to need two."

Julian exhaled heavily. Dramatically. He was always so dramatic.

"At least the bed is big," I added.

Julian's gaze met mine, and I immediately knew that it didn't matter how big the bed was. A forbidden heat lingered between us, and it would only fester beneath the sheets.

When Julian finally looked away, it was to search the room. His eyes landed on the nightstand, and he strode toward it to pick up a leather-bound booklet.

"I'm ordering room service because you need to eat something." His movements were brisk as he began flipping through the pages. "So either tell me what you want, or I'll pick for you."

"You can pick."

I hadn't been hungry when Julian pulled into a rest area with a few different food options earlier. It was hard to focus on food when I was too busy reliving The Car Incident™. God, I was so tempted to delete all my audiobooks off my phone to make sure there was no way that could ever happen again. But I was too afraid to even open the app.

Meanwhile, Julian had glared at me when I told him I still wasn't hungry. But eventually, he let it go.

He wouldn't let it go this time; I knew that. He got overly stubborn with things like this, and I didn't have any more fight left in me tonight.

Julian nodded absentmindedly while he perused the menu and then, before I knew it, had ordered more food than his entire eight-person family could eat.

I stared at him as he hung up the phone.

"Who's going to eat all that?"

"You," he replied flatly. "And me."

"Jul—"

"If anything, I came this weekend to make sure you eat and sleep. So pick which side of the bed you want, and relax until the food comes."

So that was that, huh? We were actually going to do this. *This* being sleeping in the same bed. Although, there weren't very many other options unless the velvet armchair in the corner counted. Or the floor.

I dropped onto the side of the bed closest to me. "You're bossy when you're hungry."

"Sure am." Julian crossed his arms over his chest as he looked me over, seeming satisfied now that I'd designated which side of the bed was mine. "You should remember that for the future, Daisy."

I rolled my eyes, ignoring how my stomach flipped when he kept staring at me with such a ridiculous amount of intensity.

"I think I'm going to take a shower," I muttered before diving into the bathroom.

An intermission was a necessity at this point. I needed a break from Julian and how he made my blood pressure rise, my hands ball into fists, and my skin tingle. It was confusing and infuriating.

But even more infuriating was the realization halfway through my shower that I'd forgotten to bring a change of clothes into the bathroom.

Goddamnit.

Although maybe this was presenting an opportune solution: I'd just sleep in the bathroom. That way, I wouldn't have to walk into the room in just my towel, I wouldn't have to sleep in the same bed as Julian, and I could prolong my intermission. It was—

"Juni?" A single knock on the bathroom door. "You good in there?"

Hurrying from the shower, I wrapped myself in a towel. Judging by the amount of moisture on the mirror and steam in the air, I'd extended my intermission longer than I realized.

"I'm good," I called. "Can you like...close your eyes, though? I'm coming out."

There was a slight pause followed by a choked voice.

"Are you naked?"

"No!" Great, now the thought of accidentally dropping my towel in front of Julian Briggs was firmly in my brain, and it was even more mortifying than The Car Incident™. "I'm wearing a towel. Just—just close your eyes, Julian!"

"Fine." Was that a sigh I heard *through* the door? It was hard to tell, but I definitely made out footsteps leading away from the bathroom and dared to open the door.

Julian was on the bed, propped against the pillows, with a hand covering his eyes when I came out. "You *do* know I've seen you in a towel before, right?" he muttered as I made a beeline for my suitcase.

"What? No, you haven't."

Pretty sure I would remember something like that happening.

"Yes, I have." Julian cleared his throat. "When you and Gemma got stranded on Lock Island."

I couldn't help but laugh as I dug through my luggage, searching for clothes. "Which time?"

Even though I couldn't see Julian's eyes, I could feel him rolling them. "The skinny-dipping time," he said tersely.

Oh, that. Yep, I was definitely naked except for a towel that time.

"This towel barely covers my ass, though."

Julian remained quiet for a moment, and I hurried back toward the bathroom with my clothes, standing around the corner from the bed so he wouldn't be able to catch glimpses of me while I dressed. Although, I doubted he'd try to look.

"Your skirt barely covered your ass on Halloween," Julian grunted after a pause, sounding...irritated by that memory.

I peeked around the corner, clutching my towel tighter. "I thought we were trying *not* to recreate Halloween."

Julian didn't respond. He made a slight humming noise in the back of his throat like he had something to say but knew he shouldn't say it.

When I finished changing, I hung my towel on the shower door before reemerging into the bedroom.

"You can look now."

Julian lowered his hand, and with my attention entirely on

him for the first time since leaving the bathroom, I suddenly realized that all his muscles were on display, along with his golden, slightly freckled skin.

"You're not wearing a shirt."

Julian had been in the middle of appraising my pajamas—a cute, striped set of pants and a short-sleeved top—when his gaze flicked up to mine. "I never wear a shirt to bed."

"But we're...eating." I gestured to the pile of trays on the bed that must have arrived while I was in the shower. And now that I could smell it, *fuck*, I was hungry.

"And then going to bed." He raised a brow. "Didn't realize you were afraid of a little bare skin, Rosie."

Damn him for using words from that night in the garage. Bristling, I walked around to my side of the bed and sat on the edge of it. "I'm not."

"Then why are you perched on the bed like you were the other day on your desk?" I could hear the slight humor in his voice. "I don't bite, remember?"

Wordlessly, I scooted closer to Julian so my whole body was on the bed. But there was still a good distance between us as I crossed my legs and tucked my feet under my body.

"Feeling better after your shower?" Julian asked as though he wasn't the exact reason why I'd disappeared into the bathroom, why I'd stayed there so long, and why I already wanted to go back. He busied himself with uncovering each plate of food while he waited for my response.

"Yeah, I am."

Or at least I had felt better until I realized Julian was half-naked.

He put my dinner in front of me—a pasta dish with grilled chicken that made my mouth water. "You sure were in there a long time," he said.

I shrugged. "Well, I had to ensure I washed all my perfume off so it doesn't suffocate you tonight."

He laughed, but it was humorless. "Your perfume is the least of my worries at the moment."

"What are you worried about?"

"That you eat." He shoved a fork into my hand. "Eat, Daisy."

I ate.

But only because my hunger was finally showing.

Not because of Bossy Julian.

He turned on the TV while we ate, but we weren't really paying attention to the sitcom reruns that cycled through. It was just background noise filling the silence that hung between us. Julian must have been trying his best to ignore me because when he finally glanced my way and said something, he sounded surprised. "You ate your whole plate."

I nodded, suddenly a little embarrassed that I'd wolfed my food down.

Julian's lips pressed into a small smile as he reached to clear my empty plate for me. "Good girl."

Something warm unfurled inside me as I slipped under the covers. This was ridiculous. I shouldn't need encouragement and praise just to eat a goddamn meal. I shouldn't have needed anyone to come with me this weekend at all.

But I was relieved not to be alone. And as bummed as I was when Noah had texted me that he couldn't make it, I was shockingly glad Julian was here with me instead. Even though he did it in a bossy and overbearing way, he was good at ensuring people were taken care of. He'd been doing it his whole life—as a brother, son, captain.

Julian cleared the rest of the plates before disappearing into the bathroom. When he returned, he got beneath the covers—the same covers I was beneath—and turned off the lights.

My heartbeat immediately tripled. The darkness of the room closed in around me, pulsing. I could *feel* Julian's heat radiating toward me beneath the sheets and comforter.

The likelihood that I'd sleep tonight was slim to none. The memories of waking up in Julian's arms a few weeks ago, combined with our current scenario, paralyzed me with emotions I didn't dare unpack.

I didn't know how many minutes—or even hours—had gone by while I lay awake before Julian exhaled loudly. The covers rustled as he readjusted himself.

"Come here, Juniper."

I winced, wondering if my tossing and turning had been louder than I realized. "I'm sorry if I'm keeping you up, but—"

"Come here," he repeated. "Put your head on my chest."

"On your chest?"

Did he think that would help me sleep? I had very little confidence that would be the case.

"Yes." Exasperation touched his voice. "Like you did when we were in the office and you practically fell asleep standing up."

"You had a shirt on then."

That felt very necessary to point out.

Julian chuckled. It was hard to see his face in the cloaked, dark room, but I could just make out the trace of a smile on his lips.

"You're very stuck on this no-shirt thing," he said, his voice low. "I can put one back on if you need me to."

Need, not want.

It was like he knew that I very much *wanted* to see him without a shirt, but I very much *needed* him to be wearing clothes so I could function normally.

But I didn't need to confirm that thinking for him. So I shook my head.

"No, it's fine."

"Then what are you waiting for?"

I paused, holding my breath because I refused to let him hear it. I knew that sounded ridiculous, but if he heard my breath and how it kept coming quicker, he'd hear other parts of me, too. Parts I didn't want him to know about.

I had to remind myself that this was the caretaking version of Julian. This was Julian being *nice*, playing his part. This was Julian doing what I'd asked him to do and nothing more.

As soon as I started to scoot closer to him, Julian lifted his arm, beckoning me to curl up beneath it. Cuddling. We were cuddling. His skin was warm to the touch as I rested my head on his chest and placed my hand awkwardly beside it, trying not to consciously notice how hard of a pillow he was.

Like so many of our other ideas in the past weeks, this was a bad one. I doubted I'd ever be able to fall asleep in this position, not while I couldn't help but count every single one of Julian's breaths as his chest rose and fell beneath me. As I settled into him, wiggling until I found a comfortable spot on my side, they seemed quick, shallow. Then they slowed.

My breathing did the opposite. Because the arm I'd snuck beneath curled around me, caging me in before Julian's fingers started stroking my hair. First lightly. Then more confidently, threading through my damp strands like a massage. It was more soothing than I wanted to admit, and my heavy eyelids drifted shut.

"You smell different," he muttered. "Like mint."

It took me a moment to find my voice. "I used the hotel's shampoo and conditioner and didn't reapply my perfume. You're welcome."

Julian didn't say anything, continuing to play with my hair. I felt myself melting into him, that slow awareness that sleep had a partial grip on you. Reality and dreams mixed. I couldn't be sure if it was real or in my head, but I thought I felt something press against the top of my head.

And I thought I heard words that didn't make sense.

"You know, I think I like the flowers better."

ten years ago

"You're going to stay out of trouble when I leave for college, right?"

Julian's eyes burned into mine.

"Wouldn't want anything to happen to my girls when I'm not around," he added.

"Nothing is going to happen to your sisters," I said dryly, crossing my arms over my chest.

Julian looked at me oddly, his suddenly dark gaze wandering over my face.

And for some reason, I held my breath, waiting to see what he was thinking.

Waiting to see why he was looking at me like that.

Waiting for...something.

But that was all he said.

CHAPTER SEVENTEEN

juniper

I WOKE WITH A very stiff neck, courtesy of Julian's hard body.

And I was sweaty. God, I hated being sweaty. Honestly, it was challenging to tell if the sweat was coming from me or if it was coming from Julian, but it was there. Oh, it was there, causing my cheek to stick to his chest. My palms, too, were damp as they dragged down his stomach over slick abs.

To clarify, *I* hated feeling sweaty. But experiencing Julian as a sweaty mess? That maybe wasn't so bad.

In peeling open my eyes, I found minimal sun filtering through the hotel room curtains, which meant the heat in the room was caused by...something else. It wasn't exactly a mystery. Last night, the way Julian's body had pressed next to mine was soothing. This morning, it was sending my hormones into overdrive. He was very much everywhere right now. I could feel him *everywhere.*

Suddenly, the massive body that was both beneath and beside me shifted, and his grip wrapped around my wrist.

That was the moment I realized my fingers had been absent-mindedly tracing muscles that were awfully close to the waistband of Julian's pajama bottoms. It was also the moment I realized that his hand, the one that had been in my hair when I fell asleep, was tightly gripping my hip.

"Careful with that hand there, Lily."

His voice was raspy and guttural, only making this entire situation worse.

Why did he have to be so...so hot? Literally, of course. It was roasting beneath these sheets.

"I wasn't trying...I'm sorry."

I couldn't come up with a good explanation for what I'd been doing.

Julian's low chuckle rumbled beneath me, an earthquake to all my senses. He still held my wrist, plucked between his fingers, and used his hold to carefully return my hand to his chest. His skin felt feverishly hot, and I tried to pull my touch away and sit up. But Julian's grip was unrelenting, and I ended up smashed against his chest again.

"Go back to sleep," he grunted.

"I'm hot, Julian."

"I know you are." He cleared his throat. "Peel back the top layer, then. We still have two hours until our reservation."

"Our reservation?" I tried sitting up again, and this time, Julian let me, heaving a big, resigned sigh. It was the sigh of a man who knew he wasn't getting back to sleep.

He rubbed a hand over his face before answering. "Yes, I made a reservation for brunch."

"When?"

"It's for eleven o'clock."

I squeezed my eyes shut for a second, hoping if I just couldn't *see* Julian and how he was stretching his arms behind his head leisurely while lying half-naked in bed next to me, I could think clearly.

It was a lot to ask.

"No, when did you make a reservation?" I clarified, opening my eyes again.

"Oh." Julian's head tilted thoughtfully. "On Wednesday, I

think. It was after you gave me the itinerary for the weekend, and I noticed there was nothing scheduled this morning until the ceremony."

"Yeah, that was purposeful." This morning had been set aside for mental preparation. And physical, of course. But mostly mental. "I need to get ready."

"I'm not letting you obsess and worry about this wedding for eight hours. You don't need that long to get ready, Daisy. But you do need to eat."

"You're really taking this whole eating thing seriously, huh?"

He nodded. "You'll feel even more miserable going into this with an empty stomach. Especially if you plan on drinking tonight."

I supposed he had a point; I needed at least one stiff drink to get me through this night, and I didn't want it going straight to my head. Besides, I needed Julian to put on clothes. Like, immediately. Leaving would help with that.

"The fresh air will be good for you," he added.

"We're in New York City," I said, even though he'd already convinced me. "I'm not sure *fresh* is the best way to describe the air."

"At least it won't be as hot as it is in here, *Jesus*," Julian muttered, kicking the sheets the rest of the way off.

Nope, having Julian further exposed while lying in bed did *not* help the heat situation. I hadn't noticed last night, but dear Lord, his pajama pants were gray—of all colors, they were gray—and they were also way too thin for this situation. The morning after the Halloween party, I'd felt more than my fair share of Julian Briggs, but seeing all that outlined was—

Julian cleared his throat, interrupting the free show I was enjoying. Fuck, and he knew it. When he spoke, it was with a gruffness that tickled my nerve endings. "Save those looks for tonight when you're trying to fool everyone into believing we're dating."

I opened my mouth to say a downright lie. "I wasn't looking—"

"It's okay, Juni." He pushed off the bed without looking at me. "I was, too."

THE BRUNCH SPOT WHERE JULIAN MADE RESERVATIONS SAT AROUND THE corner from the hotel, so we walked. The November air bit through my coat as we strolled the Manhattan streets, and when I shivered, Julian put an arm around my shoulders, pulling me into his body heat. Practice for later, right?

I asked Julian to order for me again, despite realizing it was an uncharacteristic move. Asking a man—a man who was Julian Briggs, of all people—to make my decisions? I didn't know what was happening to me, but letting him pick my food meant one less thing I had to worry about today.

Julian happily ordered me a massive stack of spiced apple pancakes with a side of bacon and scrambled eggs. When I glared at him on account of the sheer amount of food in front of me, he merely shrugged and told me we could take the leftovers back to the hotel.

I hated to admit it, but the pancakes were quite possibly the best thing I'd ever tasted, and Julian's lips twitched noticeably when I moaned after taking a bite. But instead of gloating—which I'd assumed he would—he asked me more about Sofia and what I knew of the wedding. And since Sofia had been so active with sharing details of her life and upcoming nuptials on her social media, I had a surprising amount to report. She'd been putting out teasers about the ceremony's live music for a while now. Supposedly, the artist was a big up-and-coming name, and Julian and I spent a few minutes trying to guess who it could be.

After that, I informed him he was getting a steak entree because that was what I'd RSVP'ed, and he made a joke about how the tables had turned. And lastly, I told him that—based on the venue and the seeming cost—I expected to see at least one or two high-status guests. Julian, of course, put his money on some football player I'd never heard of, while I thought a famous influencer or two was more Sofia's style.

I was halfway through a review of the timeline for the afternoon when a wash of anxiety surrounded me. But before I could spiral too much, Julian abruptly asked about the plot of the first book in the series I'd been reading, and I forgot all about the weekend. Fiction was always more fun to talk about than real life anyway.

Unfortunately, though, at a certain point, fiction faded.

My heart pounded as we strode back into the lobby of the hotel. Julian had been right—ugh, another thing I couldn't believe I was allowing—that a trip out into the city had been a good distraction and a much-needed break from the stuffy air inside our room. Now that we'd returned, though, I knew it was only a matter of time before my nerves returned.

Sofia likely wouldn't even have more than seconds to spare to meet me, so I didn't know why I was so anxious about it. It was her *wedding*. Our interaction wouldn't last more than a quick congratulations, but even knowing that, I still couldn't escape the feeling that tonight was a big deal for me, for us, for the possible beginning of something more.

Giving myself three hours to get ready for an event that was only an elevator ride away seemed like it should be plenty of time. But, no surprise, it wasn't. We had to be out the door in the next fifteen minutes, and I was stuck staring at myself in the mirror. Full face of makeup. Hair still in curlers.

Using curlers equaled rookie mistake number one. I never should have tried something new right before an important event. But my little black dress, the one I still had to stuff myself into, inspired me to go for a classic glam look. I wanted big, swooping waves, and my curling iron had never been able to achieve that. I was almost too afraid to take out the curlers now.

What if it looked horrendous? There wasn't enough time to start over.

"Do you need help?"

Julian's voice made me jump. He stood in the doorway, leaning against the frame while wearing a spotless, crisp tuxedo. It fit him perfectly. I saw him in suits all the time, but this was different. The midnight-colored jacket contrasted with the brilliance of his auburn hair, emphasizing the hue. He pushed a hand through it, letting it fall back over his forehead in a perfect, styled wave.

I was going to look ridiculous standing next to him.

His eyes drifted visibly up to my crown of curlers.

"Don't make fun of the curlers," I warned.

I really needed Nice Julian right now. Not any other versions.

"I wasn't going to," he said earnestly. "I wanted to know if you need help. You look beautiful, but I'm guessing this isn't the final look."

I ignored my stomach flipping and kept strictly to the topic. "Do you know how to take out curlers? You have to sort of twist them when you unroll them, so the curl falls the right—"

"Do you know how many sisters I have, Rosie?"

Without hesitation, Julian stepped behind me and started plucking the pins from my curlers, dropping them on the countertop in the bathroom.

"I don't usually do my hair like this," I admitted.

"I know."

"How do you know?"

"Because this isn't what your hair usually looks like." He nodded to the curls he had already taken out, acting like it was obvious when it had taken all my ex-boyfriends *weeks* to notice every time I got a haircut.

When I tried to help Julian with the curlers, he swatted my hand away and told me to take a few deep breaths. So I stood there, watching in the mirror as Julian's brows furrowed in concentration. Barely a minute later, I was left staring at the finished product. Except something still wasn't right. Sure, the curls looked good. Really good, actually. But, it also seemed plain.

"It isn't right," I said.

Julian raked his eyes over me in the mirror, assessing the result, and I suppressed a shiver at how focused his attention was on me.

"It isn't you," he muttered before lifting a single finger. "Hold on."

After darting out of the bathroom and then darting back in, Julian held up one of my bows. My favorite bow. I loved it because it wasn't so floppy that it just looked like shapeless ribbons, and it wasn't too stiff that it looked like it should be on top of a present. But how and why did he have it?

"Did you go through my suitcase?"

"Yes," Julian said without any further explanation.

We didn't have time to argue about that now. "I don't know if that will go with my dress."

"I saw your dress in the closet. It's black. This is black. Ergo, it goes."

"Julian—"

"Trust me."

Oddly enough, I did. I supposed it had something to do with confidence, and Julian had too much of it. Yes, he did have a plethora of sisters, but that didn't mean that he was a hairstylist. He really shouldn't be trusted.

Still, I let him start pulling and twisting my hair until it was pinned with my bow in a loose, low pony. A few curls draped my face, styled but not *too* styled. They bounced a little as I shook my head, testing if everything was adequately secured. It was. And I was in *awe.*

When Julian finished, he stepped back, appraised his work, and then muttered three words beneath his breath that momentarily halted mine.

"There she is."

My mouth opened and closed once before any words could come out. "How did you do that?"

My hair was classic and glamorous, but it also had a touch of *me*. Incredible.

He spoke quietly, eyes on me in the mirror. "Remember when Josie was cast as Glinda in the school's production of *Wicked*?"

I nodded mutely, and he lifted one shoulder casually.

"She'd get so nervous before the shows, and I'd help with her hair so she could focus more on reviewing her lines." He backed out of the bathroom, and I was still so shocked that I didn't move until he returned a few seconds later, holding my dress out for me. "Let's finish off the look, huh?"

Speechless, I took the hanger from Julian and closed the door to change. After shimmying into the dress, I quickly came to the conclusion that I wouldn't be able to zip it on my own. Of course not—that would be too easy. Resigning myself to my fate, I walked backward into the bedroom, hoping that Julian would get the picture so I wouldn't be forced to ask for more of his help.

He did. I didn't even need to say a word. I felt his stilted breath on my neck and the slight tug on my dress as he worked the zipper up. His fingers brushed against my skin, and I assumed he was slipping the eye hook into place.

"All done," he muttered. "Ready?"

The words lingered on my skin, and I closed my eyes.

He was close—too close. And this was...this was all going to go terribly, wasn't it?

Julian breathed my name.

"Juni."

A slight pause, and my heart skipped a beat.

"Juni, turn around for me."

I did. Slowly, one step at a time.

As soon as my eyes met Julian's, he noticeably sucked in, taking all the air in the room with him.

"*Fuck*, Juniper."

"What?" My hands flew to my dress, smoothing it over my body self-consciously. "Is something wrong?"

Julian shook his head, his shoulders shaking as he pinched the bridge of his nose. Was he laughing right now? Honestly, at a time like this?

"*God*, yes—"

"Yes?" I repeated in horror.

"I mean *no*." He reached out, grabbing my hands to steady them because they started smoothing even harder. Such an oxymoron and so useless. "No," Julian intoned. "Nothing's wrong. You just shocked me."

Shocking wasn't really what I was going for tonight, and I stared at Julian, looking for more. Shocking *how*?

"In a good way or a bad way?"

Julian smiled as he stepped closer. Goddamn, this man. Was my panic that amusing to him? His eyes shone as he brought one of my hands to rest on his arm like he planned to escort me from the hotel room. Like we were a couple. Well, that was exactly what we were, I supposed. At least for the rest of the night.

His lips brushed against my ear as he leaned in to whisper his response like it was a secret no one else could know.

"A good way, Daisy."

CHAPTER EIGHTEEN

I WAS SO FUCKED.

Juniper wore dresses all the time to work. But there were dresses, and then there were *dresses.* And the one Juni had on looked so unbelievable that I couldn't look at her for more than five seconds without imagining things I shouldn't be imagining.

Namely, taking it off.

Fuck.

Was she trying to torture the hell out of me with that thing? It was silky and tight and highlighted all those curves pressed against me this morning.

We absolutely could not sleep as closely tonight. Not after feeling her fingers trail lower and lower earlier. Not after seeing her in this dress. And that was honestly a damn shame. I fucking hated to admit it, but it was a bit nice holding her all through the night—even though my arm fell asleep more than once, and I woke up aroused as all hell.

There was no mystery woman to blame it on this time. Only Juniper. Juniper St. James and her striped, button-up pajamas.

What was happening to me?

Juniper's movements were stiff as we stepped into the elevator, and I squeezed her hand, the one still resting on my arm.

"I've got you, okay?" I reassured her softly. "It's going to be a good night."

She nodded while staring blankly ahead. I wondered if she was too deep into her own head to hear me, but then she relaxed.

I couldn't imagine being in her shoes. Meeting new people was hard. Meeting new people closely related to you for the first time on one of the most important days of their life...well, her anxiety was warranted.

This wedding business showed me a side of Juniper that I didn't fully realize existed. I grew up with a Juniper St. James who was brash, confident, and sharp-tongued. She was a pain in my ass. She *knew* she was a pain in my ass but never seemed to care.

This Juniper St. James was still bold and beautiful, still witty and sharp. But she was also vulnerable. And she did care. She cared that her tossing and turning had kept me up last night. She kept apologizing for things she didn't need to apologize for.

After making it to the lobby, we followed the signs for Sofia and Marc's wedding until we found ourselves standing in a glass-covered atrium in the middle of the hotel. Pastel-colored flowers burst from every corner, piling fragrance into the air until it was nearly hard to breathe.

Luckily, I was used to being suffocated by beautiful things.

Hundreds of other guests flooded into the atrium, and I felt Juniper relax further. I understood; it was easier to blend in when there was a crowd. But it still didn't stop her leg from bouncing after we found our seats, and I placed a hand on her knee to soothe her. Bare knee, bare skin, bad idea. But Juniper stilled and shifted in her seat. My touch dipped, my thumb rubbing the inside of her thigh while my fingers curved beneath her knee. I squeezed, meaning for it to be reassuring. But Juni's breath hitched, and *goddamn*.

She was so responsive. She reacted, lit up, to every tiny touch. Was she that unused to having a man's hands on her? Or was it just me?

Honestly, I was fine with either option.

"Is that...?" Her murmuring broke through my thoughts. "No, that—that wouldn't make sense."

"What?"

Tearing my attention away from how perfectly my palm fit her inner thigh, I followed her gaze to the front of the ceremony space. There were so many people milling around that it was hard to determine exactly who she was looking at.

"The piano player," Juni said. "It's just he looks a bit like your other old roommate. I know how ridiculous it sounds, but for a moment, I thought it was him."

My face split into a wide grin. "Actually, it's not ridiculous at all."

"It's not?"

I shook my head, unable to contain my grin from spreading further as Nessa walked to a microphone in front of the piano, adjusting it before returning to a hidden spot off to the side. Meanwhile, Grayson continued to play a familiar soft melody as guests streamed into the atrium, finding their seats with the help of the ushers.

It was hard to believe, and yet—

"You know that up-and-coming artist you were talking about?" I glanced over at Juniper, who was still looking thoughtfully at the stage.

"Yeah?"

"It's Nessa."

"Nessa?"

When she still looked confused, I realized my mistake.

"Sorry, you probably know her as Wednesday Elevett."

Juniper's big, beautiful eyes grew even bigger. And, unfortunately for my sanity, even more beautiful.

"When you and Cameron were talking about your friend in the music industry, it was *Wednesday Elevett*?"

"Yep," I said, resisting the urge to wave Nessa down, even though she was very clearly busy. "She's married to Grayson. Elevett is a combination of her last names, Elez and Everett."

"The wide receiver for LA?"

"Correct." I nodded toward Grayson on the stage. It was fucking good to see him in his element again. I watched him playing football all the time—whether in person or on TV. But this was rarer. This was the lesser-known side of Grayson Everett. "And the roommate. Who is, in fact, playing the piano."

"He's playing the piano," she repeated breathlessly. "Why is a football star playing the piano at my sister's wedding?"

"Grayson was a music education major in college," I said, trying not to laugh at Juniper's expression. Her eyes flicked between the dynamic duo on stage and me, and I relented, giving her a better explanation. "If Sofia's goal was a trendy wedding, Nessa *is* the trend. Even I'm with it enough to know that. And Grayson just sort of comes as a package deal. Nessa really got her footing performing at events like this in the LA area, and Grayson would always tag along to accompany her. So while I'm surprised to see them, I'm also not. Especially with how big this wedding is."

Juniper nodded absently for a few seconds. When her brows were still scrunched, I gave her a little nudge, curious what was going on in that head of hers. She turned slowly to look at me.

"Did you say...Elez?"

"Yeah. Why?"

With a quick clear of her throat, Juni looked away. "Nothing."

It was absolutely not *nothing*, but I decided I'd bug her about that later.

Within ten minutes, the atrium had filled to the brim. Nessa was the one who kicked off the ceremony, confidently singing her heart out as the first family members started walking down the aisle. And while the entire crowd watched Nessa or the procession, I watched Juniper.

Her eyes shifted between her hands and her surroundings as the bride and groom's parents started walking down the aisle. Indecision danced in them, but Juniper's gaze finally locked on the middle-aged woman with golden-brown hair, brown eyes, and a nose the same shape as Juniper's.

I rubbed my thumb soothingly over her knee while she stared, fixated. It wasn't until Sofia emerged to walk down the aisle and the guests around us stood that Juniper switched her focus.

The ceremony itself wasn't long. Vows were exchanged, and Nessa performed another number, one of her rising hits. Before I knew it, the newly married couple made their grand exit.

"Let's get you a drink," I said to Juni as soon as the guests started to exit the aisle.

When she nodded enthusiastically, I put my hand on the small of her back and led her toward the bar. Two drinks later, we were safely tucked to the side of the pandemonium, sipping our cocktails.

"*Lavender* vodka lemonade," I muttered, glaring at the purple drink in Juni's hand. "Do you have to be so goddamn predictable?"

"It was the bride's specialty drink," she shot back, although I didn't miss the twist of her lips that hinted at amusement. "Probably because lavender is one of their wedding colors. Have you ever been to a wedding before, Mr. Briggs?"

I grimaced. "Don't call me that. It's weird."

"Oh, so you can call me whatever nickname you like, but I can't call you by your last name?"

Rocking back on my heels, I nodded. "That would be correct, Lavender."

Juni looked ready to unleash another comeback when we were bombarded by a mountain of white lace and squeals.

"Oh my *God*! Juniper!"

When I say that the bride of this ridiculously extravagant wedding jumped on my fake girlfriend, I mean *jumped*. Sofia's arms looped around Juniper's neck, leaning into her with so much force that I had to apply some extra pressure on Juni's back to keep her upright.

While she was crushed against Sofia, Juniper's expression

flitted between shock, relief, and worry as she flashed a wobbly smile. I could tell she hadn't been prepared for this. Not yet, anyway. Not before she'd finished her first drink. But Sofia wore such a bright enthusiasm that I doubted she noticed her half sister's reaction. And the tighter Sofia hugged, the wider Juniper's smile seemed to grow.

"It is so amazing to finally meet you!" Sofia squealed, finally pulling back. "I am absolutely delighted that you were able to make it."

"Thank you for the invitation," Juniper replied, her smile still growing with each passing second. "It meant a lot."

"Of *course*. After months of stalking you on social media, it's so exciting to actually see you. I've always hoped we could meet up, but..." Sofia drifted off, checking over her shoulder. Her smile faded slightly, and in turn, so did Juniper's. "Mom's just not quite ready, and I wanted to respect what she needed." She brightened again. "But today's my wedding, and I wanted my only sister here."

"I'm thrilled to be here," Juniper said earnestly, a bit of shininess in her eyes.

I hoped it was happiness. I hoped it was because her sister seemed genuinely ecstatic to meet her. I hoped that was it and nothing else.

In case it wasn't, I grabbed her hand.

Unsurprisingly, Sofia took note of the movement and turned her attention toward me.

"This must be your man," she said slyly to Juniper while beaming at me.

I knew. I knew I was coming here to pretend to be Juniper's boyfriend, but being referred to as *her man* hit me harder than any tackle I'd endured during my college football career. I hadn't been prepared for that. Not a single bit.

Juniper cleared her throat, and her voice sounded slightly strained when she spoke. "This is my boyfriend, Julian. Julian Briggs."

"It's a pleasure to meet you and be here," I said, extending my hand. "Congratulations to you and Marc."

"That's so sweet. Thank you." Sofia shook my hand, even though it looked like she was considering pulling me into a hug like she had with Juniper. "I would introduce you to Marc, but he's off with the photographer for a few pictures with the groomsmen."

"Completely understandable. We wouldn't want to monopolize his time, anyway." I wrapped my arm around Juni's waist and pulled her right into my side. "Or yours, of course."

"Oh, nonsense." Sofia waved that thought away. She was a tiny thing, and her whole body seemed to move with every word. But while she was smaller and a bit more animated than Juniper, they had the same brown eyes and hair. "I do hope you enjoy the rest of the evening, though! I made sure to seat you next to Grayson for a little college reunion."

Sofia winked, and a laugh of disbelief slipped out of Juniper. "How did you know about that?"

"Oh, girl." Mischief oozed from Sofia's grin. "It would be embarrassing to admit the amount of research I did for tonight's seating chart. It's all I've done this week. I never should have waited until the last minute to sort through the RSVPs. Although I wish I'd known you had an in with Wednesday Elevett all this time! It's impressive, I gotta say."

"I—"

Juniper didn't appear to know what to say to that, so I brushed a hair out of her face before muttering my own response.

"Juni has a way of surprising everyone."

But it had nothing to do with *knowing* impressive people.

And everything to do with being one.

"Julian—"

Knowing she was about to protest, I cut her off. And just to make her a little extra speechless so she couldn't argue, I dropped a kiss on her head.

"It's true, baby," I said.

"Oh, he's *dreamy*." Sofia laughed before leaning in to give Juni one more hug. Her next words were said below her breath, but since I'd refused to let go of Juni completely, we were close, and I still heard it. "Hang on to that one."

"I plan on it," Juniper replied breathlessly.

Sofia beamed, pulling back. "See you on the dance floor later?"

Juni nodded wordlessly before Sofia vanished into the crowd. I studied my date, wondering how she was recovering from that whirlwind. When she didn't say anything, I gave her a prompt.

"So...she seems nice."

Nervous laughter flitted around us. "You're just saying that because she called you dreamy."

"Hey, don't fault her for that. I *am* dreamy."

Juniper took a long, overt drink of her lavender lemonade instead of replying. When she was done, she pursed her lips before opening her mouth and—

"Jules?"

I turned to find Grayson standing a few feet away with a drink.

A drink?

"You don't have to drink it," Nessa was muttering as she rummaged around in a small purse, clearly having missed what her husband had just said. "People just keep *handing* them to me for some reason—"

Grayson glanced away from me momentarily to side-eye his wife. "It's because you're famous, darling."

"—and I can't drink it, but we haven't announced our *you-know-what*."

A smirk lit up Grayson's face as he stepped closer to Nessa, smoothing his hand over her stomach. "I do know what."

On any other day, I would have rolled my eyes. But I was too busy being happy just seeing them. Meanwhile, Nessa huffed before turning toward me for the first time and—

"*Julian?*"

"You two were looking good up there earlier," I said, closing the distance to pull Nessa and Gray in for a hug before returning to Juniper's side. My hand found its place on the small of her back again.

"What are you doing here?"

Nessa sounded like she'd had the wind knocked out of her.

"Sofia is Juniper's sister."

"Half sister," Juniper corrected.

"Wow, really?" Grayson's brows lifted, his eyes moving slyly from me to my arm around Juniper. "It seems Julian and I have some catching up to do."

"Oh, I think it's pretty obvious without any catching up, Gray," Nessa said with a laugh before I could correct Grayson's assumptions. "It's been obvious since that party our sophomore year. When she came to visit. I mean, come on."

Goddamnit, I should have cut Nessa off. Obvious? What the hell did she mean by that? I remember being pissed beyond reason that Juniper crashed one of my last college parties.

Nessa turned to Juni, whose eyes were wide. "I'm sure you don't remember meeting me," she said, "but I'm—"

"Nessa," Juniper finished, looking a little awestruck. Which I found adorable and funny all at once. "It's so lovely seeing you again. Your performance during the ceremony was amazing."

Nessa's cheeks grew rosy. "Thank you. That's so sweet of you."

Juni's whole face was glowing. She was downright radiant now that her nerves seemed to have slid away. I squeezed her side, and she tipped her head back to meet my gaze. Those sparkling eyes nearly took me out. Dusk had settled outside, meaning that the natural lighting in the atrium was dimming, and ropes of string lights lit up the ceiling instead.

I raised a brow. *See, Daisy? This wasn't so bad.*

She shrugged before breaking our eye contact to take a sip of her drink.

"The four of us should go on a double date sometime," Nessa added cheerily, and I knew I needed to set the record straight before Nessa got too carried away.

"We should." Grayson nodded as he put one arm around Nessa's shoulders while the other went to protectively palm her stomach. She was showing, although barely. "I owe you dinner, Jules. It's the least I can do after everything you've done to help me with Gabe's legal case."

Juni tensed in my arms, and I could tell it wasn't a good tense.

It was the kind of tense that told me I had some fucking explaining to do.

Shit.

CHAPTER NINETEEN

THIS WEDDING WAS A roller coaster. It kept hitting me with twist after twist that I didn't expect, and for some reason, it still felt like we were gearing up for a big drop.

The clients of Julian's case were his *friends*?

Julian continued chatting with Grayson about Gabriel, the little boy I had read so much about through his endless medical reports. And the more they talked, the more my perspective began to morph.

From the outside looking in, Nessa and Grayson were a powerhouse celebrity couple. But at their core, they were concerned, loving parents who had clearly been through a lot. It didn't escape me that Gabriel being Grayson's son meant the star football player had also suffered a congenital heart defect his entire life. And what an impressive story that was, considering where he was now.

"Where's the little man tonight?" Julian asked Grayson, his thumb still moving in circles on my lower back. If he seemed bothered that his friends thought we were dating, he clearly didn't show it. He hadn't made any attempts to let the truth be known.

"He's with Uncle Beau," Grayson said with a little roll of his eyes. "Getting spoiled for the weekend."

Julian chuckled. "At least Collins can be the voice of reason, right?"

"True," Grayson agreed without hesitation, making me think Cameron's sister, Collins, was a lot like him. He was always our voice of reason at work, too.

We parted ways with Nessa and Grayson so they could grab drinks—nonalcoholic, it would seem—and walked to our assigned seats before I finally broke my silence.

"Why the hell didn't you *tell* me?"

Julian didn't reply, guiding me by the hand toward our table in the ballroom attached to the atrium. I wondered if I should tell him that he could probably cool it a bit with the dating act, but at the same time, I didn't *hate* it. His touch was...distractingly nice.

"*Julian*," I persisted.

He heard me. And he couldn't pretend like he didn't know what I was talking about.

Once we were both seated, he exhaled dramatically. "I was respecting Grayson's privacy. He asked me to keep it under wraps since they haven't announced Nessa's pregnancy."

I brushed that excuse aside. "He just brought it up in front of me. Clearly, he isn't all that concerned."

"He also thinks we're dating," Julian pointed out. "So now you're part of the inner circle. If you're important to me, you're important to him. It's how it works with us."

"I noticed you didn't correct him, though."

Julian cleared his throat and sipped his drink before responding. "The conversation got away from me."

There was a lull while people milled around us. The wedding tables were decorated extravagantly with piles of lavender and baby's breath and perfectly matching linens. Across the ballroom, Nessa and Grayson were stopped by fawning fans. Not for the first time tonight, Grayson slid his hand protectively over his wife's stomach. Watching it made something in me swell and then sink.

"If I'd known..." I began before cutting off and shaking my head, turning back to Julian. "If I'd known that this case was about your friend's son, I would have helped you—"

"Gabriel's actually my godson."

I had to look away again because something was very wrong with that annoying thing inside my chest. It was aching. Hurting. And my eyes, something was wrong with them, too. They were leaking.

"Juniper."

Julian's voice was soft. He grabbed my chin, forcing me to meet his gaze again. Goddamnit. Maybe if Nice Julian disappeared, I'd be able to get a hold of myself. But this was almost too much.

"Why?" His brows furrowed as he flicked a tiny tear off my cheek. "I don't understand why you're so upset."

"Because I feel like such a bitch," I admitted, trying to blink the tears away. "I made you take me to that game, made you set me up with Noah, made you drive all the way to New York, and you were just trying to support your best friend. He's probably not even an official client, is he?"

"No, he's not. But Jun—"

"*God.*" I dropped my head into my hands.

Julian leaned in. I could feel it from how his breath grazed my cheek.

"You didn't make me do anything, Daisy. You didn't ask me to drive all the way to New York. I offered, didn't I?"

"Because you felt obligated," I muttered, refusing to look at him.

"Because I knew it meant a lot to you," he said like it was a correction. Like it was the truth.

But I knew better than that.

"You can drop the nice act, Julian."

I appreciated that he was trying. The effort he'd put into respecting my requests for the weekend was more than appreciated. But I needed the real Julian to help set the record straight because I didn't know what was up or down, what was real or pretend.

He wasn't here for me. That couldn't be the truth.

"Stop hiding for a second, Rosie."

The tenderness in Julian's voice convinced me to drop my hands and lift my head. I hated that I fell for something so obviously not real, but I couldn't help but listen to him when he talked to me like that.

"I'm not acting," he said when our eyes met.

And then he didn't look away. It must have been an illusion caused by the lighting, but his eyes were an unusual deep shade of blue, midnight sparkling in them. They warmed as he held my gaze.

I warmed.

I wanted to ask him more about what that meant. Exactly *which* part of this weekend hadn't he been acting for? But then the DJ announced for everyone to take their seats, and we were interrupted by Grayson and Nessa scooting in beside us. Grayson said something to Julian about football, and their conversation quickly directed into something I easily tuned out.

Dinner was a plated affair. Decadent and delicious, but I was finding it difficult to stomach anything at the moment. I spent more time pushing it around my plate than eating it. Julian noticed; he kept shooting looks my way. Thankfully, he kept his mouth shut, though.

Once the plates were cleared and the speeches finished, I excused myself to go to the bathroom for a few moments alone and away from Julian's scrutinizing gaze. But I didn't make it more than thirty seconds before I heard my name being called.

Even while standing under unfavorable bathroom lighting, Nessa Elez-Everett was an extraordinarily stunning woman. It was downright intimidating.

Except her expression was...not. It was warm and full of concern.

"Hey, is everything okay?"

"Oh, I—" Biting my tongue, I questioned how to answer that. Was everything okay? "I'm just a little overwhelmed. I apologize if my silence during dinner was rude."

"It wasn't." She looked appalled that I would even think that. "Julian was worried about you."

Worried? That was a stretch. Although, Julian undoubtedly thought of me as his responsibility this weekend, and he did get a little strung up over his responsibilities.

"Look, about Julian..." I sighed. "He's not... we're not dating. I don't want to give you the wrong impression."

She blinked twice. "I don't think I have the wrong impression."

"Noah was going to be my date this weekend," I said, hoping to explain that, yes, she did have the wrong impression.

Nessa tucked her brown, shoulder-length hair behind her ear, cocking her head to the side in apparent confusion. "Noah London?"

I nodded. "Something came up at the last minute, though. Julian offered to take me so I wouldn't have to come alone."

I decided to leave it at that, not wanting to go into how I asked him to pretend that we were in a relationship, how everything she thought she saw was a huge misrepresentation. It was fake, all of it. Telling her that would have helped her understand the truth, but this was embarrassing enough as it was.

Nessa walked toward the sink, pulling lipstick out of her bag. Then she leaned against the countertop while looking at me sideways in the mirror, seeming unconvinced. "Well, he's worried."

"He's overprotective sometimes," I reasoned. "He's like that about everyone."

Nessa considered that. She knew I was right; I could see it in her expression. Julian *was* like that with everyone.

"I had to stop him from coming into the bathroom after you," Nessa said, shocking me.

"What?"

After reapplying her dark red lip color, Nessa grinned into the mirror before turning to face me again. She rubbed her slight baby bump, smoothing a hand over her short dress, which she'd paired with black, shimmery tights.

"He's waiting on the other side of the door," she said.

She appeared delighted by this fact, even though I thought it was a little mortifying. Her smile grew, and there was a touch of something in that smile I didn't understand. Without another word, Nessa walked back out of the bathroom.

It took me another minute to follow her, needing to prepare myself for whatever was on the other side of that door.

Julian—I needed to prepare myself for Julian.

But all the preparation in the world couldn't have readied me to see his expression as soon as I stepped back into the wedding reception.

Relief. He was relieved to see me. Possibly because he was tired of waiting, of lurking by the restroom, but possibly not. I didn't detect any of his usual irritation as he leaned against the wall, hands in his pockets.

He pushed forward, looking me up and down as he closed the distance between us. "The DJ is calling all couples onto the dance floor."

"We're not a couple, Julian."

Suddenly, I wasn't as eager to pretend. We'd put on enough of a show in front of Sofia earlier that I was sure it didn't matter anymore.

"You told Sofia that you'd see her on the dance floor later," he pointed out.

"I'm sure she's forgotten all about it."

Did I want to spend more time getting to know my sister? Of course I did. But Julian had already done enough for me, and all of it had been unnecessary. I never should have let him come with me this weekend. It wasn't fair to make him do anything more. I was sure the last thing he wanted to do was dance with me.

Julian stared at me, searching my face for...well, I wasn't sure what.

"It drives me nuts that I can't read your mind sometimes," he eventually muttered.

"It's not that interesting," I promised.

"I doubt that, Lily." His low chuckle was dry and raspy. "Come on."

He grabbed my hand, charging back through the ballroom to the atrium doors where the chairs had been cleared, and a dance floor took up most of the moonlit space.

"*Julian*," I hissed. "What the hell are you—"

With one final tug, he launched me into his arms. They circled my waist, holding me close as we found a spot between dancing couples.

"I'm dancing with my girlfriend," he muttered. His fingers ran down my spine, similar to how they did in our office that day. "Now, loosen up, will you? This is why we practiced."

Julian didn't get it, did he? It didn't matter the amount of practice we had. When he touched me, the world spun faster on its axis. And I didn't know how to slow it down.

Julian's determined expression told me that all I could do was hope to get through this night without letting him see how much he could affect me.

But a second later, Julian squeezed my hip, and I heard the sharp gasp that flew out of my mouth. In response, Julian made a noise that sounded like a cross between a grunt and a groan. He murmured my name with a tone I didn't fully understand.

The world spun faster.

Yeah, I definitely wasn't going to make it through tonight.

ten years ago

Her lips parted in surprise when she saw me, which was ridiculous considering she knew I lived in this house, and she knew my bedroom was right next to Gemma's.

And then, right on cue, her pretty features immediately transformed into a scowl.

She wiped at her tears, clearly not wanting me to see them.

I didn't want to see them, either. I hated seeing them.

"Julian," she said, the word clipped as it came from her lips.

"Daisy," I murmured back.

Her mouth flattened into a straight line at her nickname.

I didn't know what to say to her. I wanted to ask if she was okay.

I wanted to ask about Kennedy's cheating ass and if I could kick it.

I wanted to say a whole lot of things, but Juniper was scowling at me like all she wanted was for me to disappear.

But while my usual snide comments were sitting on the tip of my tongue, I couldn't deploy them. Not while the streaks from her tears were still visible on her face.

I didn't know how to talk to Juniper in situations like this. Our relationship wasn't built for these moments.

"I'm sorry Kennedy's such an asshole," I finally settled on.

Juniper just rolled her eyes, which pissed me the fuck off. Because

Kennedy had just cheated on her. How could she honestly deny the truth now?

"Yeah, you've told me about how he's an asshole...many times," Juni drawled.

"Well, now maybe you'll believe me."

"Yeah." Juni was nodding now, blinking rapidly in a way that told me she was holding back fresh tears. Her eyes shone, but not in that happy way they did sometimes. Fuck. God fucking damnit. "Congratulations on being right, Julian," she whispered.

CHAPTER TWENTY

I JUST WANTED TO get inside her.

As in, her brain.

What the hell was going on in there? Why the hell was she hiding in the bathroom?

Not to mention, I needed to get rid of all the other thoughts in *my* brain that kept circling around how good she felt and that goddamn noise she'd just made when I pulled her closer.

"If it makes you uncomfortable, I can stop," I muttered.

Juniper frowned. Only inches separated us as we swayed slowly on the dance floor. "Uncomfortable?"

"When I touch you," I clarified, keeping my voice low. "You freak out a little bit every time we get too close."

I strongly suspected she was just like me; she was bothered because she liked it, not because she didn't. But since I couldn't figure out what she was thinking, I had to check. I needed to know.

"I don't *freak out*."

I should have guessed that the way I said it would make her get defensive. Sighing, I backpedaled.

"Juniper, I'm trying to make sure you feel safe with me," I said, and she stilled in my arms, halting our dance.

"Safe with you?"

"Yeah, well...You didn't want to dance. You were quiet at dinner. You ran away into the bathroom."

"Julian..." Her mouth opened and closed while she tried to find words. "That's not it at all. You've always kept me safe, and tonight isn't any different."

My relief, the blossoming in my chest, was short-lived because it *was* different. Tonight was unlike any other night. We both knew that.

Luckily, she kept talking, and I didn't have to find a reply. Juniper stepped into me, circling her arms around my neck and continuing our gentle sway. She tipped her head back as she gazed up at me. The twinkling lights above us reflected across her face.

"I'm feeling guilty and overwhelmed," she confessed.

I understood overwhelmed, but... "Guilty?"

"That you're here."

"That I'm—*Juni.*" I exhaled, tightening my hold on her. "I told you already. I'm happy to be here."

It was fucking terrifying how true that was.

"I know what you said. But I don't know how to just turn off my feelings." She sniffed and looked away. "I told Nessa that we weren't really dating. It was embarrassing."

"I'm sure Nessa thought nothing of it."

A single nod. "Yeah."

That was the most unconvincing *yeah* I'd ever heard.

"You know..." I started. "You never told me why it was so important to you. To pretend to have this relationship."

I was venturing into murky territory, especially considering what this same line of questioning had instigated in the car on the way to New York. But I had a strong feeling that if I got her to explain this to me, then I wouldn't need her to explain anything else.

Juni laughed harshly. "Didn't you see it?"

"See what?"

Her face screwed up, twisting with some emotion I didn't understand. "Sofia's reaction to you, to how you knew Grayson, to my false connections."

"I saw it," I admitted. "But I think she would have been just as excited to meet you without it."

"You don't get it," she muttered.

"No, I don't. Explain."

For years, I thought I had Juniper all figured out. I put her in a box, slapped a label on it, and then put it out of reach. Easy. Simple.

Juniper was anything but *simple*. This weekend had been a slow unwrapping of her many layers, and now that I'd started, I couldn't figure out how to stop. Goddamn, did I even want to?

"I've always wished I had a sister, Julian," she whispered. "Or any sibling."

I nodded encouragingly, wanting her to continue. Thankfully, she did.

"And I know it sounds silly, but if Sofia believes someone like you thinks I'm good enough to keep around, to date, to...to love, then maybe she will too. Maybe she'll keep me around. Maybe I can convince her I'm worth that."

Christ, hearing those words was one hell of a blow. My chest ached as I searched Juni's face, urging her to look back at me. When her eyes finally lifted to meet mine, there was a yearning there that killed me to see. These thoughts were the ones she'd been hiding from me, huh?

"Juniper..." I breathed, knowing I needed to respond, even if I didn't know what to say. "Of course you're worth that."

"Since when?" She cleared her throat. "You've never wanted me around."

Shit. She hadn't been hiding these thoughts from me at all. I just never saw them for what they were.

"Not to mention..." Her eyes darted away, searching for something. Someone. "*She's* in this room, Julian. She's in this room, and she doesn't want to meet me."

Goddamn. My grip on her tightened, hoping it might communicate that people did want her. People, as in...*fuck.*

"I'm okay with that, though," she rushed to say. "Really, I am. I love my parents endlessly. I have the best mom. It's a sister I don't have. That's why I wanted to meet Sofia."

The song that had been playing began to fade, and another took its place, also slow, also perfect for holding your girlfriend—or fake girlfriend—close. And I thanked God for that. Letting go of Juniper now would crumble the last remaining unbroken piece of my heart.

"You can let go if you want," she whispered. "We can sit down."

"I don't want to let go."

She blinked up at me. Once. Twice. I saw stars in her eyes.

"Okay."

We danced through the next song without talking. I pulled Juniper in close enough that eventually she rested her head against my chest, similar to last night. I tried really hard to think of something to say that would fix those thoughts in her brain, but I realized my words didn't matter.

It was my actions.

They'd caused it—or had a hand in causing how she was feeling.

So they were going to fix it.

"So Nessa said you are not, in fact, dating Juniper."

Grayson dropped those words into my lap as soon as I returned to my seat. Juniper had gone off with Nessa, sidling up to the bar to get another one of those purple concoctions.

I shook my head. "It's complicated."

"Didn't look that complicated just now," he said, leaning back in his chair. "Or when you stormed over to the bathroom earlier."

"Gray..."

I couldn't do this right now. Everything was a mess, and I couldn't wrap my head around any of it.

He made a show of settling further into his chair. "Tell me how it's complicated, Jules."

We were really going to do this, huh?

I glanced over toward Juniper. She was smiling now, pulled into a conversation with Nessa as they stood near the bar with their drinks. Sure enough, one of those lavender lemonades was in her hand. She turned as she talked, leaving me with a view of her backside and a reminder of how fucking tight that dress was.

I couldn't do this anymore.

"I've spent years fighting my attraction to this woman," I admitted.

Grayson didn't react except for a tiny twitch of his upper lip. "I know."

Fuck him.

"I've watched you fight it on more than one occasion," he added.

I sighed. "I thought I was *supposed* to fight it, to give her the cold shoulder. It became ingrained in me, even though she made it impossible at every turn. When we were young, I resented that she acted like she was a part of our family because I never saw her as a sibling like my sisters did. I saw her as—*fuck*. But now..."

"But now...?" Grayson prompted when I couldn't finish the sentence.

That was the whole problem, wasn't it? I had no clue how to finish that sentence.

"And now, nothing," I sighed. "She still knows exactly how to drive me up a wall—"

"Maybe you should drive *her* up a wall," Gray muttered.

"And she's still Gemma's best friend," I continued, ignoring him. Mostly because I couldn't allow my brain to linger on his words. "Actually, she's friends with *all* my sisters. My parents think of her as their sixth daughter, for fuck's sake."

My asshole best friend seemed to think that was funny. "Maybe because they knew one day she would be," he said with a smile.

"Shut up, man." I glared at him. "Our history is complicated, and our present is even more intertwined. We're colleagues, and I've put so much into getting this job. You don't get it."

"You're right." He shrugged. "I don't. Because to me, it seems like you're currently taking the advice you gave me a long time ago."

"What's that?"

Grayson's devilish grin widened. "You're running laps on a practice field to prove you're worth something so she'll give you playing time in the game."

"I was drunk when I said that," I pointed out flatly.

"Still the best damn advice I've ever gotten."

Grayson was a confident fuck in college. Not cocky, but definitely confident. His natural talent and good looks afforded him every opportunity. Scholarships and women all but fell in his lap. For the most part—besides the whole heart defect thing—he got exactly what he wanted.

Except Nessa.

Nessa made him work for it. She made him prove himself on the practice field before giving him playing time. But this was far from the same situation.

"I'm not trying to get playing time," I said.

"You're not?"

"I can't."

That had never been an option.

Wholly unconvinced, Grayson folded his arms over his chest. "Well, I hope Juniper knows that. She seems nice, and Nessa is already attached, so don't hurt her."

"Stop." Grayson warning *me* about not hurting Juniper made my hands ball into fists. "I'm not going to hurt her. She knows it isn't like that. She wanted to be here with Noah, not me."

"Yeah, Nessa told me that." He crossed his legs, shifting in his seat. "It made me curious, so I texted him."

"Who, London?"

Grayson nodded.

And then he fucking smirked.

"What?"

"We got shots!" Nessa's voice interrupted whatever Grayson was about to spill. The arrival of a handful of small glasses followed her announcement. She placed them on the table between Grayson and me.

"You can't drink, my little whiskey girl," Grayson said dryly. His expression appeared split between amusement and concern as he pulled Nessa onto his lap.

"Okay, we got *you* shots."

"I don't drink," Grayson pointed out, smile inching upward.

Nessa glared back at Grayson. "Would you just—"

"I don't think shots are a good idea," I cut in, turning to talk to Juniper specifically. But it was too late. She was already tossing one shot after another down her throat.

When she went to grab a third, I snatched it from her hand.

"Hey now," she chastised, eyes glittering. "Nessa tells me you were the life of the party in college, and suddenly you think shots are a bad idea?"

I slowly lifted the shot glass to my lips while keeping my eyes on her over the rim. Tipping it back, I let the burn of alcohol slide down my throat. Juniper watched. Her gaze on me added to the burn.

"They are when you barely eat dinner," I muttered after slamming the empty glass back on the table.

Juniper rolled her eyes, and it sparked something inside me. I was surprisingly grateful for that attitude. She was coming back into the version of herself I recognized, and I liked to believe it was because of more than the alcohol. Maybe getting things off her chest earlier had helped. Maybe I'd convinced her that we were meant to be here, both of us.

"I'll be fine, Julian."

She sounded like she was trying to reassure me about more than just the drinks, and goddamnit, she shouldn't be reassuring me. It should be the other way around.

"No more," I warned.

She lifted a brow. "Or what?"

I narrowed my eyes at her, and she grinned.

I could really get used to seeing Juniper St. James smile at me.

It was a radiant fucking smile.

Mimicking Grayson, I looped an arm around her waist and pulled her down to sit on my lap. Juni released a small shriek, and I ignored the looks on both Nessa's and Grayson's faces as I welcomed a new form of hell: Juni trying to find a comfortable way to sit on top of me.

This was ten times worse than when she'd accidentally sat on my lap in the office. Because now I wasn't too afraid to admit how much I liked the feel of her. And I wasn't as good at keeping thoughts I shouldn't be thinking out of my head.

When she shifted into a position that put my slightly stiff cock in direct contact with her ass, I stifled a groan. Juni still heard. Or at least, I assumed she did, considering how she tried to scramble off my lap.

When I didn't let her, she glanced back over her shoulder. "I'm squishing you—"

"You're not. Don't insult me."

"I would never dream of insulting you."

"Well, *that's* a lie."

"Juniper!"

Juniper's whole body jerked toward the sound of her name, causing me to suck in sharply at the jolt. Juni didn't seem to notice this time, though. She was too busy smiling back at Sofia, who was trying to coax her onto the dance floor again.

"Go," I said, tapping her on the hip. "Go celebrate with your sister."

She hesitated, which would have surprised me about the old

Juniper. The one I thought I knew. But I understood things differently now.

"Do you want me to come with you?" I asked.

I wasn't much of a dancer outside of the easy sway we had done earlier, but I would become one if Juni asked it of me.

"No, you can stay," she said.

"Are you sure?"

She nodded, more confident now. "Yeah, I'm sure."

And then, because I knew Sofia was watching, I kissed her on the cheek. "I'll be here," I breathed in her ear.

Juniper shot off my lap so fast that my body, once again, nearly went into shock. But I used another one of Nessa's shots to help myself recover.

For the next fifteen minutes or so, I chatted with Grayson and Nessa while keeping track of Juni in my peripheral vision, dancing with Sofia and the other wedding guests. But apparently, I wasn't watching closely enough.

"Jules," Grayson said, interrupting Nessa's explanation of her new tour schedule. His tone of voice—and how he'd cut his wife off—immediately had me leaning forward, tense.

Without saying another word, Gray pointed to the dance floor. One look and I saw it. No explanation necessary.

A guy with slicked-back hair and an ill-fitting suit was way too fucking close to Juniper. Close enough that he could reach out and—

"Oh, *hell* no."

My vision went hazy, and I was on my feet and across the room.

CHAPTER TWENTY-ONE

SOMEONE JUST TOUCHED MY ass. And based on how Julian was now storming toward me, he *saw* someone touch my ass.

His eyes pinned on something—more likely, someone—behind me, and I spun, looking for the culprit. I didn't spy them until Julian had pushed his way onto the dance floor and grabbed the shirt collar of a guy to my right.

"Give me one good reason I shouldn't break all your fucking fingers."

Julian's low snarl made goose bumps rise on my skin and my jaw drop.

Did I—did I hear that correctly?

"I'm waiting," Julian growled, reaffirming that, yes, I did hear it correctly. He gave the man a shake while keeping a white-knuckle grip on his shirt. When the man stammered something about it being an accident, Julian scoffed and released him with an eye roll that made it clear he didn't believe that excuse for a second.

"Stay away from my girlfriend if you don't want to go to physical therapy. Got it?"

The man—who looked to be a little older than me but with considerably less fashion taste—nodded. Once he split, Julian slid in casually behind me, circling his arms around my waist as though he hadn't just threatened someone for getting too close to me.

"Are you okay?"

I nodded, even though a slight tremor coursed through my bones. Honestly, it had a lot less to do with the guy who'd invaded my space and more with how Julian handled it. It wasn't a surprise in the sense that Julian Briggs had always had an over-protective streak. But not with *me*. And not while calling me his girlfriend in the same breath.

Although that was probably why he did it. Just another part of the show, huh? That made sense, even if knowing the truth of it did nothing to stop my heart from hammering.

"How long have you two been together?" Sofia's voice brought me back to reality. If she saw Julian threaten one of her guests, she didn't seem annoyed by it. In fact, she appeared utterly unfazed as she twirled the straw in her glass, her body twisting slightly to the beat of the music. "I was surprised when you said you were bringing your boyfriend because I've never seen you post any pictures together."

I stiffened, realizing she was right. Maybe she knew—she'd already figured it—

"Not long," Julian replied easily, his lips brushing my ear. "But we've known each other forever."

"We grew up together," I added, relaxing into the truth. "Julian's sister is my best friend."

"That explains why you seem to know each other so well, even though your relationship is new," Sofia said with an easy smile. Her gaze flicked over my shoulder to Julian. "What does your sister think about it?"

God, that was a good question. How would Gemma feel if she could see us right now? How would she feel if she knew the way

Julian had held me last night? How would she react if she heard some of the things he said? Some of the things *I* said?

For the first time in a while, Julian seemed speechless until he cleared his throat.

"She's getting used to it," he replied, making Sofia laugh before someone cut in and stole the bride away from us.

The funny tone of Julian's voice sparked curiosity. I spun in his arms, wanting to see his expression, but it caused me to momentarily lose my balance. Julian's hold on me closed in, keeping me steady. Once the world straightened again, I tipped my head back, looking up his six-foot-plus frame to find him staring back at me, face wiped blank.

"Did Gemma say anything to you about this weekend?" I wondered.

"Just told me to behave."

"Behave?"

Why was I suddenly curious to see what Julian acted like when he *didn't* behave? Surely, Gemma didn't think he'd misbehave in *that* way. Right?

Julian cleared his throat. "Be nice to you."

Of course. Well, that certainly made so much more sense. My brain was running wild tonight with far too many assumptions.

"I told her I already promised you I would be," he added.

No wonder he was being especially nice. Not only had I asked him, but he knew I'd report back to Gemma if he was an ass. I supposed I had her to thank for the sweet, protective version of Julian that was my date tonight.

I'd miss him.

We were dancing very noncommittally. It was one of those awkward songs that lacked a good beat to dance to. Not fast, not slow. Julian and I shuffled from side to side. He likely wished he could be back chatting with Grayson and Nessa, but he didn't say anything.

"Have you ever actually broken someone's fingers?" I cocked

my head to the side, asking the first question that popped into my head. It was swimming a little bit, my head. Those shots were finally doing something.

Julian looked away, biting down on his lower lip like he had a confession he didn't know if he should share.

I sucked in with surprise. "You *have*, haven't you?"

He shrugged. "He deserved it."

"Who was it?"

I was suddenly absolutely sure that I'd never wanted to know anything more than this information about Julian Briggs.

Julian's gaze swooped down to mine, intense. "Greg Kennedy. Luckily, we were at football practice in high school, so it was easy to pass it off as an accident."

"What?" I gasped. "But...*why*?"

Julian's feelings about Greg Kennedy were far from a secret, but *breaking bones*?

Another shrug. "Don't like the guy."

"Not liking someone isn't a good enough reason to break their fingers, Julian." A questionable statement at times, but usually, it held true. "I mean, you don't like *me*, but—"

"He cheated on you."

I stopped moving, my hands falling to my sides as I stared blankly at Julian. His jaw ticked, irritation threading through his tense features. He plucked my arms back up and threw them one after another around his neck again. Then he grabbed my hips, tugging them tighter to his.

"And I do like you, Daisy," he breathed, dipping his head to press it against mine. "Stop telling me how I feel."

It took everything in me not to ask him more.

But all my thoughts and wonderings flew out the window when the song changed. With a racing beat that matched my pulse, it was the type of song meant for dancing. Julian's hips picked up on the switch in tempo, and suddenly, they were grinding against mine.

The feeling of his body made it hard to think, much less talk. We danced wordlessly. Julian's fingers dug into my hips, urging them to move with his. Heat seeped through my dress, warming my skin. Warming *all* of me. Julian's hot, short breaths hit the side of my neck, urging on the flames licking my insides.

His last words rang in my head. *I do like you, Daisy.*

They repeatedly rang until I knew I needed to do something about them. I pushed myself up the front of Julian's body, my lips finding his ear.

"I can't believe I'm saying this," I breathed. "But I like you, too."

Julian made a noise in the back of his throat, and I felt it everywhere. It reverberated into my body, making my skin tingle. I could become addicted to that sound, to that feeling. I slid back down until my feet were flat again, and Julian crushed us closer together. He extinguished the space between us in such a desperate, raw way that my breath vanished, and I suffocated on my sudden need for him.

Our bodies rocked, Julian's hands started to roam, and the ache—

"We should take a break," Julian gasped, taking an abrupt step back.

"I don't want to."

I should be ashamed of how quickly those words flew from my lips, but this dance was intoxicating, and I wasn't done getting drunk. I wanted to stay right here in this bubble, with Julian's hands all over me, forever. I wanted my breaths to keep matching his. I wanted to feel his pulse against my temple, racing beneath his skin. I wanted this—this right here.

"Juniper, you need water," Julian said, more demanding this time. He let go of me, and I relented as he started pulling me off the dance floor. I followed behind him, admiring how sweat had gathered at the base of his neck, causing that auburn hair to curl. I wanted to wrap it around my fingers.

"Wait here," he said, sticking me in a seat next to Grayson before stalking off.

I slunk back in my chair before spotting the remaining shots that Nessa had grabbed earlier. The alcohol had nothing to do with my high right now, but it certainly hadn't hurt. And, hating to see them go to waste, I tipped one back.

My face immediately contorted at the rush of alcohol.

"Did you just—" Julian's familiar voice lapsed into a growl as he pushed the remaining shot glass out of my reach and pushed an overflowing cup of water into my hand instead. "Drink, Juniper."

"I *was* drinking," I mumbled before gulping greedily. Admittedly, the water tasted a whole lot better than the whiskey had.

"Water," he clarified. "You've had more than enough alcohol."

Julian punctuated his statement by glaring at Grayson, who threw his hands up in defense.

"She was too quick about it," he said, looking apologetic.

I lifted a brow, staring at the fuzzy NFL player sitting next to me. "Aren't you supposed to have good reflexes or something?"

Nessa howled with laughter, which made me smile.

I liked her.

Julian shook his head, his lips curving up as he leaned down next to Grayson, pulling him into a hushed conversation I couldn't make out. A few seconds later, he sat in the available seat beside me, scooting close so he could speak in hushed tones.

"If you would feel more comfortable, you could stay with Nessa tonight," he said. "Their room is just down the hall from ours. Grayson and I could share."

I frowned. "Are you trying to get rid of me, Julian Briggs? Tired of having me around?"

Honestly, I was surprised it took this long. But now I wondered if I should have grabbed that last shot just so I could dull the pain.

His eyes widened with alarm, more than I would have expected. "Juni, no. It's just—" He sighed raggedly, looking away while running a hand through his hair. "I just wanted you to have the option."

"Why?"

He lowered his gaze, peering at me beneath feathery lashes before saying my name. Just my name.

"Juniper..."

The unspoken words that should have followed told me all I needed to know. He thought that whatever had just happened on the dance floor was dangerous. But I'd already told him; he always kept me safe. Tonight would be no different.

"I want to stay with you," I whispered, "if you're not sick of me."

His eyes fluttered shut momentarily as though my words had tortured him. When he looked at me again, his gaze was bright.

"I'm not," he said firmly.

I wasn't sure if I believed him, but I wasn't sure how much I cared. He was too hard to figure out tonight. And I was still too focused on his eyes. How were they so blue even when the lighting was so low?

"Juni," he prompted when I continued to stare silently at him.

"You have pretty eyes," I said beneath my breath—like it was a secret.

It sort of was.

"Jesus Christ," Julian cursed as I swayed a little in my chair, trying to put my drained cup on the table. He put a hand out to steady me.

"Come on," he muttered. "You, bed. Now."

I suppressed a grin, thinking I didn't hate hearing those words come out of Julian's mouth.

God, what was *wrong* with me?

This entire situation should be mortifying. It *was* mortifying last night. Well, in the beginning, maybe. Then, it was nice. It had been nice like Julian had been nice, and now I was having a hard time trying to be upset that there was only one bed in a hotel room that I needed to share with Julian Briggs. In fact, my body ached pleasantly at the thought of it.

After saying quick goodbyes to Grayson and Nessa, Julian led me by the hand out to the hotel lobby and up to our floor. When he pushed open the door to our room, I shivered. There was a draft.

Or something.

"Sit," Julian commanded, pointing to the bed.

I sat.

And then I watched as Julian shrugged off his tux jacket and tossed it on top of the dresser. Without it, his muscles tensed through his white dress shirt as he knelt before me.

I held my breath, not releasing it until Julian picked up my foot. His fingertips brushed lightly over my bare ankle as he unbuckled my heel and slipped it off. When he moved to take off the other shoe, I snuck my phone out and took a picture.

"What are you doing?" Julian muttered without taking his attention away from my foot. His fingers seemed to move higher this time, up the back of my calf and down again.

"Photographic evidence," I said, trying not to focus too much on how heat consumed me with each of Julian's touches.

"Photographic evidence?" he repeated.

"For Gemma when she asks if you were nice to me this weekend."

Julian sighed as he stood and pulled me up with him. "Don't take a picture of the next part, Daisy."

Something about how he said it, about how his voice washed over me, made my breath hitch.

"Why not?"

"Because my sister doesn't need to see a picture of me taking your clothes off," he grunted.

My heart leaped into my throat, my mouth running dry. But it only lasted a second before Julian added, "Now, turn around so I can unzip that dress and get you into those ridiculous matching striped pajamas of yours."

"My pajamas are adorable, thank you very much," I said breathily, twisting so Julian could unzip me. I felt his fingers fumble a little with the eye hook at the top of my dress before the fabric around my bodice started to give way, loosening.

"You're right," Julian said, voice husky.

I held on to the front of my dress to keep it from falling while carefully spinning to face him again. Julian's taut expression took me in slowly before he took one step back and then another, his back hitting the wall with a thump. He rolled up his shirtsleeves, eyes surveying me from top to bottom while he did.

It hit me that this was probably the last time I would experience Julian looking at me like that. Taking off my shoes and unzipping my dress would be his last little acts of kindness before returning to the real world where we didn't exist like this.

"I'm not ready."

It took me a second to realize I had said it aloud.

Julian's brows furrowed.

"Ready?"

I tried to take a step forward, but I stumbled over my feet, and Julian caught me in his arms. God, why did it have to be so nice being in these arms? Why couldn't it have been unbearable so I wouldn't have to miss it? It would be easier if I could continue to hate him in peace, wouldn't it?

Blinking up at Julian, I gave my truest confession. "I'm not ready for it to be over."

He swallowed, his throat working as his eyes danced all over my face. But he didn't speak.

"Can we stay like this until morning?" I whispered, my tongue too loose to hold it in. I didn't want the bubble to pop yet. I liked it too much. All the little fake moments were so much better than the real ones.

Julian tucked a strand of my hair behind my ear and then trailed his finger beneath my chin, tipping it up.

"Sure, baby," he rasped. His gaze dropped to my mouth and

then back to my eyes, burning me up inside. "We can stay like this as long as you want. Whatever you want."

Thank God.

I pushed myself onto my tiptoes and did what I'd wanted to do all night, every time he looked at me like he was looking at me now. I did the thing that people who were dating did. And even if it was fake, even if it was our last minutes of pretending, I wanted to spend them feeling something.

I wanted to spend them kissing Julian Briggs.

ten years ago

Today, I walked into practice pissed at Kennedy for yet another reason. I stewed about him and Juniper all last night. I kept replaying the conversation I'd had with her, over and over again, until I was damn near ready to drive over to Kennedy's house at midnight.

Fuck him for creating another reason for Juniper to hate me, and fuck him for hurting her.

I brushed by the asshole himself while leaving the locker room, making sure to shoulder-check him the way he always did to me.

"What's your problem?" he grunted at my back as I kept walking away from him.

"You're my problem," I muttered, but I knew he wouldn't hear it.

Apparently, though, Kennedy really wanted to hear what I had to say about him, jogging after me until we were making our way across the field, and he was nipping at my heels.

"Not gonna turn around and fucking face me?" he called at my back.

I was the baby? When he'd been pissing and moaning all season long?

When he spoke again, he'd dropped his voice. "It's about Juniper, isn't it?"

I stopped in my tracks and slowly turned to face him. A few drops of rain splattered to the ground between us, and I hoped the skies opened up so I could watch Kennedy act like a baby about that, too.

"I'm not talking to you about her," I said, trying to keep my voice steady.

Kennedy's expression reeked of exasperation. "She came crying to you, huh? Careful, Briggs. Your jealousy is showing. Your sister might not realize how badly you want my girlfriend, but I sure do."

Losing it a little, I took an intimidating step closer to Kennedy, satisfied when he quickly took a step back.

"She's not your fucking girlfriend," I reminded him. "Not anymore."

That was the one good thing to come from him being a cheating asshole.

CHAPTER TWENTY-TWO

IT ONLY TOOK ONE brush of Juniper's lips against mine to know that this kiss would haunt me forever.

Considering how close I'd been to kissing her on the dance floor, I should have predicted this. I *had* predicted it in a way. It was why I'd asked Grayson if Juniper could stay with Nessa; my self-restraint was so fucking weak that I barely trusted myself around her.

But what I *hadn't* predicted?

Juniper saying all the things she'd just said. Juniper kissing me like this.

Fuck, her lips were heavenly. They swept over mine once, twice, waiting for my reaction. Waiting to see if I would push her away.

As if I could ever.

If she was going to offer up her mouth for me, I was going to fucking take it.

I gripped her chin between my fingers, holding her there to ensure I could kiss her back and kiss her good. Juniper's breath hitched when my mouth moved over hers. I traced the seam of her lips with the tip of my tongue, back and forth, until she opened for me. And when she did, that was all it took for me to lose it.

With a moan, I crushed my lips to hers, needing to kiss her deeply and soundly. She deserved a kiss like that. She deserved all the kisses, but this was the only one I could give, so I was going to do it well.

Juni kissed me back just as aggressively, throwing one arm around my neck while the other stayed tucked between us to hold up her dress. She tangled her fingers in my hair while her tongue played with mine, flicking into my mouth and driving me wild.

Of all the times I'd imagined what it would be like to kiss Juniper St. James, I never conjured up *this.*

"*God,* Juni," I groaned before diving back in.

This wasn't just a kiss; it was Juniper consuming every inch of me. My skin *burned.* My body *ached.* My hands *moved,* finding curves I'd been dying to touch all night. She felt criminally good. My lips had a mind of their own, trailing from Juni's mouth and kissing her jaw, neck, collarbone. She arched for me, gasping when I found a particularly sensitive spot. She tugged harder on my hair like she wanted more.

I wanted more. I wanted *her.* I wanted to taste every inch of this woman.

The need, the want, the desire that I had pushed away and denied for so long—this kiss was unleashing it.

Holy shit, I wanted her. So. Goddamn. Much.

I pressed my lips in a line ascending her neck before catching her lips with mine again. Fuck, I could feel her smile in the way that she kissed. *Of course* she smiled when she kissed. How very Juni-like of her.

"I need you to take kissing me as seriously as I take kissing you," I mumbled, my lips curving up to mimic hers.

"I do," she gasped. "It's just that you're good at this."

Heated, foolish pride burned in my chest. "I'm good at a lot of things, Rosie."

She laughed, lightly and beautifully, and then I stole that

laugh with my mouth, not releasing it again until we were both breathless.

"Julian," she whimpered between barely parted lips. "Show me. Show me what you're good at."

Fuck.

Her voice slipped and slurred, and hearing her say my name like that brought me to my senses. I wrenched my lips off hers.

"Juni, you're drunk," I gasped, pushing the words out of my mouth as a reminder to myself. "You're drunk, Juni."

She stumbled back a step, and I took that opportunity to put a bit of space between us even though it felt like it would be the goddamn end of me.

"I'm fine, Julian," she said through heavy breaths, still clutching her dress to her chest.

I couldn't help but notice she didn't try to tell me she *wasn't* drunk.

"You're drunk, Juniper."

"You already said that."

"It warranted being repeated."

And I'd keep repeating it to myself if I had to.

Juniper plopped back onto the bed. Both dress straps were falling off her shoulders, and God help me, I wanted to strip her of that black, silky thing.

Temptation. Hell, the *temptation*. If Juni hadn't made it abundantly clear that it would hurt her feelings, I would be hightailing it to a different room to stay for the night.

Juniper's pouty, kissable lips were an utter distraction, so I forced myself to turn around and search for her pajamas instead. Thankfully, they weren't hard to find, tossed on top of her suitcase.

"Arms up," I muttered, bringing her pajama shirt over to her with shaky hands. There was too much adrenaline coursing through me.

Her brows furrowed. "You're going to kiss me like that and then put my clothes *on*?"

Although I was equally frustrated, I didn't say anything. Something told me that if I gave Juniper an inch of how I was feeling, she'd run a mile and ruin me forever.

"You kissed me, if you recall."

Juni rolled her eyes. The shots of booze had made all of her movements seem increasingly dramatic—more than normal. Regardless, she lifted both of her arms above her head, and by some miracle, I slipped her shirt over her head before that dress fell completely. It bunched beneath her pajama top.

"Are you wearing a bra?" I asked, wanting to make her as comfortable as possible. I couldn't do anything about the raging headache she'd likely wake up with, but I could do something about this. "Did you want to wear one to bed?"

"I'm not wearing one." Her eyes swam drunkenly as she looked up at me. "But do your hands count? Because I wouldn't mind wearing *them* to bed."

This was a torture unlike any fucking other.

"My hands do not count," I said woodenly. "I'm putting you to bed, Juni."

Juniper smiled, and all I could think of was how that smile had felt pressed against mine. "I think you said that sentence incorrectly," she said.

"Oh?"

"I think you meant to say... I'm *taking* you to bed, Juni." She cocked her head to the side. "Is it too late to ask for that proof? Because I think I'm ready for it."

I hung my head for a second while collecting myself, my hands balling around her pajama pants in frustration. She wanted to joke about me taking her to bed, huh? She wanted proof that I'd leave her satisfied as all hell? God, she had no idea the things I would do to her in this bed if I could. She wouldn't be smirking at me like that when she couldn't walk after getting what she asked for.

"Here." Taking a deep breath, I lifted my head and threw her pants at her. "Put these on."

"I'd rather not." She threw them back at me, hitting me square in the face. "It was roasting in here last night. I'll just wear my shirt. It's long."

It was *not* long. Juni stood, wiggling her hips to shimmy out of her dress, and I suppressed a groan. Her shirt barely covered her ass. One little bend and I'd be able to see everything.

"You have to wear the pants, Juniper," I said, desperate now. I needed every bit of barrier between her and me. Because that kiss...*shit*. If her mouth tasted that good, I couldn't even begin to imagine how good her pussy tasted. And the longer she stood there without pants on, the harder it was not to find out for sure.

I couldn't, though. I knew I couldn't, and I wouldn't. I could go to bed tonight dreaming about going down on her, but I couldn't touch her. I couldn't taste her.

"Fine," Juni huffed, ripping her pajamas back out of my hands. "I'll wear the pants and take off my shirt instead."

She had to be fucking kidding me.

"You can't sleep without a goddamn shirt on, Juniper."

I would lose my mind and never get it back.

"Why not?" She arched her brow. "You didn't wear a shirt last night."

"Is that what this is about?" I threw my hands up in frustration. "You're still mad about that?"

"I was never *mad* about it," she clarified, making a face like that was a ridiculous assumption even though she'd brought it up at least three times last night. Although, if she wanted to admit she'd been worked up about it for another reason, that was fine by me.

I smirked. "Not mad, huh?"

She gave me the sheepish version of my expression. Coy and timid all in one. "Not mad."

"So you're saying you liked it."

I wanted to make her say it.

Juniper's eyes narrowed before she plopped back onto the bed, nearly missing the end of it when she did. Christ, she wouldn't be able to walk tomorrow regardless of what we did—or didn't do—in bed.

"That is *not* what I'm saying," she argued. "I'm saying that if you can sleep half-naked, I should also be allowed the same courtesy."

Technically, she had a point. Even if it was one that I hated.

"Fine." I shook my head in defeat but started to unbutton my shirt in the same movement. Juni's mouth snapped shut as she suddenly gave me her full attention, studying my hands. The heat in her gaze nearly made them fumble.

"You don't have to wear the pants, but will you at least wear this instead?" I asked, shrugging off my button-up and thrusting it into her lap.

She picked it up thoughtfully. "Instead of my shirt? Why?"

"It'll cover more of you," I muttered before striding to the bathroom and shutting myself inside it, needing a goddamn minute to cool down.

I splashed water over my face before doing it again more aggressively; the first time hadn't been enough of a shock. Water sloshed over my neck and shoulders before dribbling down my chest.

It didn't do anything, though. I could take a freezing cold shower and still be running hot for Juniper St. James.

Steeling myself, I walked back into the bedroom.

I should have steeled myself harder.

"Fuck."

"What?" Juniper did a little spin for me, pirouetting sloppily. She nearly tipped over completely before catching herself with a laugh. "Don't you like it?"

I fucking loved it; that was the problem. Seeing her in my shirt sparked possession in me even fiercer than on the dance floor earlier. She should get rid of those striped pajamas and wear this every night. Even if I never get to see it again, at least I could imagine it.

"What's that?" she asked when I couldn't find an appropriate reply. She pointed at my hand.

"Oh." I cleared my throat. "This is a washcloth."

"A washcloth?"

"If you want to take your makeup off." I held it out for her to take. "I know that's like...important or whatever."

She walked toward me slowly, waiting to grab the washcloth until she was close enough that I could see her pupils dilate.

"That was very...nice of you. Or whatever."

I didn't know what she was doing, but I couldn't handle the wash of emotion that accompanied her thick voice. I turned around, grabbed my own pajamas, and ducked back into the bathroom to finish getting ready for bed. When I returned, Juniper stood before the mirror, her shiny and renewed face full of concentration while she tried to pull the bow out of her hair.

"Here," I said softly, helping her untangle it.

Juni's eyes followed my every movement in the mirror, and it took everything in me not to look back at her.

Once the bow had been removed, Juniper spun slowly to face me again. It reminded me of what she'd done not thirty minutes earlier. And although it pained me to interrupt the cycle, I couldn't relive the torture, even though some of it had been bliss.

"Bed," I said with a grunt before scooping Juniper into my arms and carting her off to the mattress. I dropped her onto it, and she squealed as the mountain of blankets and pillows consumed her. With a huff, she covered herself before peeking out above the comforter with eyes that told me everything.

"I promised I would put you to bed and make sure you got lots of sleep this weekend," I whispered, a reminder to both of us.

She nodded and opened up the covers, welcoming me to get in. "Get lots of sleep with me?"

I inhaled slowly, unsure I was ready for what this night would bring. But when I turned off the lights and dipped beneath the covers, the comfort of being near her warmed me in an entirely different way. So annoyingly familiar and sweet and perfect.

Once I snuggled in toward her—close enough to feel her but not close enough to touch her—I heard Juniper sigh. It was a contented sigh.

"Your shirt smells good," she breathed.

I snorted into my pillow. "You told me I smell. Remember?"

"That was a lie."

I figured it had been. But still, it made me wonder...

"How often do you lie, Juniper?"

A quiet moment passed.

"With you or in general?"

"With me."

"All the time."

She didn't hesitate to answer that question.

"Did you lie to me tonight?" I asked before holding my breath and waiting for a reply.

I didn't have to wait long.

"Not at all."

Daring to get closer to her beneath the covers, I curled an arm around her waist. She settled right into me.

Yeah, I was going to miss this.

I transferred my head from my pillow to hers to whisper in her ear. "Ironic, isn't it?"

"Yeah." She didn't turn around, but I could tell she wanted to. I wondered if she could tell what I wanted, too.

"Yeah?"

"Yeah." Her voice started to disappear into the night. "It's ironic, Julian."

CHAPTER TWENTY-THREE

I NEEDED JUNIPER'S ASS to be further away from my crotch.

This was the first time that being someone's big spoon had caused me physical anguish. Juni kept readjusting herself like she couldn't get comfortable even while sleeping, and it was even more distracting than yesterday morning when I caught her tracing my abs with her fingers.

When I couldn't take any more torture, I slid out of bed and padded toward the bathroom.

I needed to take a long, cold shower.

Unfortunately, it didn't end up giving me very much relief, and I left the bathroom feeling equally as...tense.

Not to mention, when I made the decision to only wear a towel riding low on my hips, I assumed Juni would still be passed out. But now I stood at the foot of the bed, about to break out in a sweat. God, it made me want to dive back under the cold shower spray when she looked at me like that.

"You're awake."

Juniper blinked at me, and I ran a hand through my hair nervously, slicking back my wet locks. Water trickled from the ends of my strands down my back and shoulders. Juniper's eyes widened as she watched, similar to when I was stripping my shirt off last night.

Jesus Christ.

"Juni, do you..." I cleared my throat. "Do you remember last night?"

Her eyes darted to my face and lingered for a moment before she answered. "Yeah," she whispered and then straightened herself in a hurry. She flung the covers off and scrambled out of bed, mumbling something about how she was going to take a shower. Her eyes stayed downcast, watching her feet as she tiptoed around the bed.

When she went to dart past me, I hooked an arm around her waist to stop her without even thinking twice about it. I should have, though. She looked at me with pretty but alarmed eyes, her hair hanging limply around her face.

"All of it?" I asked, needing to know. "Or just some of it?"

I couldn't help it; my gaze fell to her mouth, my own memories nearly doing me in.

"All of it," Juniper said, a hushed confession.

I dropped my arm like her words burned me, and Juniper ran off to the bathroom. I didn't move from my spot until I heard the shower turn on, and then all I could do was quickly dress and pack my suitcase.

The thought of Juniper stripping down on the other side of that bathroom door was enough to drive me to my breaking point. I scribbled her a note that I would be waiting for her in the lobby and then left to get some fresh air.

JUNIPER AND I LISTENED TO ONE OF HER AUDIOBOOKS ON THE WAY BACK to Boston. She picked a new story so we could start from the beginning and promised it was advertised as a slow burn. In other words, the explicit sex scenes would be minimal, if not nonexistent.

I'd never admit it aloud, but the story did a damn good job of sucking me in by the time we arrived in front of Juni's apartment. I parked the car, feeling a bit reluctant to turn the book off. To say goodbye, if only for a night.

A frown settled on my face when Juniper waived my offer to help bring her bags upstairs, and I didn't bother insisting. It couldn't be more clear how eager she was to escape my presence.

I supposed now I knew how she felt last night when I suggested she stay with Nessa.

I didn't like it.

Admittedly, though, I let out a sigh of relief as soon as she was out of my sight. Maybe I'd be able to fucking breathe now. Maybe I could go more than thirty seconds without thinking about that kiss. Maybe I'd be able to forget about how this weekend made me feel.

Or maybe not.

I tossed and turned all night, and then, before I knew it, I was walking into the office on Monday morning. Early. I hadn't been able to sleep anyway, so I figured I might as well get some stuff done before Juniper arrived and consumed all my goddamn brainpower.

This was precisely why I'd always kept her at arm's length. Otherwise, it was a slippery slope, and now I was falling down it.

The sun shone brightly this morning, and without any clouds to trap the heat, it was a cold one outside. Luckily, warm air blew in full force through the vents in our office, and that, combined with the sun beating through the window, caused sweat to trickle down my back.

It had absolutely nothing to do with the fact that I was preparing to sit next to Juniper for an entire eight hours and pretend everything was normal after she moaned into my mouth this weekend. Nothing to do with that.

Shit.

It was odd being at work before her. I glanced over at her empty desk, noting the line of polka-dotted coffee mugs and her arrangement of plants. Half of them seemed to be wilting. With a sigh, I moved the plants to my desk, situating them in the sun, hoping the light might resurrect them.

A minute later, Juniper strode through the door.

"Oh!" She jumped back with such surprise that the cup of coffee in her hands sloshed in her cup, nearly spilling all over her frilly, white blouse. "What are you doing here?" she gasped.

"I...work here?"

Did she think I'd resign over one little kiss?

Fuck, who was I kidding? I'd definitely considered it.

Juniper rolled her eyes as she shuffled into the office and kicked the door shut behind her. It was impressive, considering how much she was carrying, the height of her heels, and the length of her skirt. "I mean, what are you doing here before me? You're never here before me."

"Oh." I shrugged. "I don't know. Just got up earlier today, I guess."

More like never slept at all.

After cocking her head to the side and examining me for a moment, Juniper crossed our small office and placed the coffee cup on my desk.

"I got this for you at the place across from—" Her words vanished as she caught sight of her plants lining my desk. "I swear I didn't put those there," she rushed to say. "I'm sorry. I'll move them back."

The worried look on her face stomped all over my heart.

"I know you didn't put them there. I did." I shifted in my seat, swinging my attention back to my laptop so I wouldn't have to keep watching Juniper's expression. "They looked like they needed some sun. Although I don't think that one's going to bloom no matter how much sun or water it gets," I added, pointing to the one in the middle.

Juniper was silent, and I risked a glance over my shoulder at her. "It's a moonflower," she said. Round and filmy eyes stared absently at the plants while that voice of hers sparked in exasperation.

"You keep saying that like I'm supposed to know what it means," I muttered before picking up the cup. "Thank you for the coffee, Daisy."

She blinked twice before looking away from the plants. "You're welcome. It's plain and boring. Like you."

I smirked but hid it by lifting my coffee cup to my lips slowly. "You don't think I'm boring, Juniper."

She flushed, and it was beautiful. It brought heat to my skin, too. Heat that had nothing to do with the warm air coming from the vents or the sun streaming through the window.

Juni didn't reply. She turned promptly on her heel, hurried to her desk, and unloaded her bag. Her reaction immediately made me regret my comment. Because while I did love watching Juniper blush, I hated when she shut down. When that Juni-like wonder faded. And that was exactly what happened.

Juni was silent for most of the day after that. When she did talk to me, it was strictly professional, strictly work-related. Reestablishing those boundaries was likely good for us, but still. It bothered me. I wished it was as easy for me to stay focused on work as it apparently was for her.

Around five thirty, she turned to me with a pleasant smile, and I thought that maybe I was going to get something else out of her besides a clipped comment or question, but once again, I was disappointed.

"Do you want to stay late tonight to work on Grayson's case?" she asked. "Or maybe tomorrow?"

Surprised, it took me a second to reply. "Let's do it tomorrow. I'm pretty tired from the weekend. I'm sure you are, too."

Although she'd probably slept a hell of a lot better than I did last night.

"I am," she admitted, "but I want to ensure that we give the case enough attention. Gabriel deserves that."

"Okay." My throat tightened with emotion. Gabriel *did* deserve that. "Tomorrow it is."

Juni nodded but continued watching me curiously as I started packing my things. It was nearly dark outside; the clocks rolled back a few weeks ago, and now the nights were long and came early. At this hour, the rest of the office was quiet. A few people had left for client dinners tonight, and most everyone else had called it quits for the day or brought their work home.

I was about to call it quits. It had been a long day with a busy mind. But Juniper's voice stopped me in my tracks before I could reach the door.

"Julian, wait."

I turned slowly. Something about how she said my name made all the hairs on my arm stand on end.

Juniper stood, aggressively smoothing down her black, silky skirt, and I just knew right then and there—

"Can we talk before you go?"

Yep. There it was.

"Talk about what, Juni?"

I fucking knew what.

Juni sucked in a breath and then swallowed.

"The kiss."

CHAPTER TWENTY-FOUR

juniper

"I SHOULDN'T HAVE KISSED you, and I'm sorry."

Despite my words, Julian's face remained a blank slate as he stared at me from his position halfway out the door. His lack of reaction made me wary. I should be apologizing for a lot more than the kiss, but I couldn't get myself to bring up any of the other embarrassing things. I shouldn't have kissed him. I shouldn't have asked to wear his *hands* as a *bra*. I shouldn't have goaded him to touch me while asking for proof.

To say I'd been dying of mortification for the last thirty-six hours was an understatement.

Yes, he kissed me back. Thoroughly, too. But then he pushed me away. And I wasn't *that* drunk. I wasn't too drunk to *kiss*. All I wanted was a few more moments with his lips on mine.

Okay, *fine*. That was a lie. But still, Julian had been steadfast in his refusal to kiss me, to touch me, to even look at me. My memories might have been fuzzy, but I would never forget how stiff he'd grown when I tried to sleep half-naked—another thing I shouldn't have done.

Once upon a time, he told me he wasn't afraid of a little bare skin, but he proved that statement dead wrong over the weekend. Afraid, repulsed...who knew exactly how Julian felt about me sleeping without a shirt, but he sure as hell didn't want it to happen.

Always good enough to kiss, never good enough to wait around for anything else—that was my story.

I cleared my throat. "I think I just got carried away with all the fake..." I trailed off when a muscle in Julian's jaw clenched and tried again to explain what I meant.

"I know all those moments on Saturday night were just for show. I know that, Julian. I just forgot for a split second, got swept away in them, and I'm sorry. You don't need to worry that—"

"Juni."

"—that I'm going to act differently around you," I continued, ignoring Julian's low voice. He took a slow step toward me, and I dodged him, inching sideways until we were stuck in a moving circle while I rambled. He tried to get closer with every step, crowding me. "You don't need to worry at all. I'm certainly not delusional in thinking that you—"

"Juniper."

"—want me like that. Trust me, I am more than aware that you don't have any *real* interest in me. Not like that. I mean—"

Julian stole the rest of my words with his lips, kissing me and knocking me back into his desk in a single swift movement that left me reeling.

His talented lips broke from mine for one split second to grunt, "Shut up," before he dove in again, capturing my mouth with his for a second time. I kissed him back recklessly, momentarily losing myself in how our tongues tangled and lips clashed. *Why?* Why did he have to be so good at this?

I slipped away with a gasp as reason returned to me. "Jul—"

"God, you drive me up the wall." Julian grabbed me by the throat and wrenched us back together. "I said *shut up.*"

I shut up.

Our lips fused back together.

Although, I was torn. Because even though *I* loved the feeling of his lips on mine, I didn't want him to think that he had to do this. He didn't have to kiss me. He didn't have to do anything. That was the whole point of this conver—

"Now, stop thinking," Julian grumbled against my lips, giving my neck another frustrated squeeze before running his hands reverently down my body. "I want you. I desperately want you like this. You have no idea, Juni baby."

Chills ran across my skin. Maybe I was easily convinced, but those words combined with his mouth, his hands, his hard body —it wiped all my other doubts away.

I desperately want you.

I couldn't comprehend it, but I didn't care. Not right now. I stopped thinking and threw my hands around Julian's neck.

Julian made a gruff noise of approval in the back of his throat. Continuing to kiss me, he slid both hands beneath my ass to hoist me up before kicking the door shut and pressing me up against it. His hips anchored us there, rocking against me while his lips trailed down my neck. I wrapped my legs around his waist and held on tight.

"It wasn't fake," he breathed, his lips fanning my skin. "The kiss, the things you said in the hotel room... Tell me it wasn't fake. Tell me it was more than getting swept up in the moment."

"I thought you wanted me to shut up," I retorted while fighting to catch my breath.

He moaned in frustration, fingers curling into my hair and tugging, forcing my head back to expose more of my neck. His voice dropped to a tone I didn't dare disobey. "Well, now I want to hear your pretty little mouth tell me it wasn't fake."

"It wasn't fake."

None of it was fake, not a single moment.

"I know," Julian groaned into my neck, and my stomach flipped. He peppered kisses on my hot skin, his lips never leaving for long, making me feel *wanted.* Like he had on Saturday night. Until he pushed me away.

"Don't stop," I whispered. "Don't stop tonight."

Julian did the exact opposite of what I wanted him to do. He stopped. He'd always been infuriating like that. He'd always done exactly what he wanted to without a care—

"You know I didn't want to stop, right?"

Julian's piercing blue eyes were only inches from mine as he stared at me. His breaths were deep, chest heaving beneath his white button-down, his hands shaking as they left my hair to travel over my skin.

But his eyes were steady.

"Pushing you away this weekend was the hardest fucking thing." His husky voice made my insides swirl and my head spin. It felt like a dream, like something I'd imagined. "The things I would have done to you if you hadn't been drunk, Juni...*God.*"

My mouth ran dry, and I could barely get my words to leave my throat. "That wasn't how you were acting."

Those blue eyes darkened, turning hazy with lust. "It was all I could do to keep my fucking shit together with how you were teasing the hell out of me." His voice lowered. "You're gonna pay for that, by the way."

I dropped my voice so it matched his. "I already told you not to stop, Julian."

He smirked before kissing me again, and the perfect way his lips moved across mine proved this was some version of heaven. Every inch of my body screamed at me. My hands needed to move, needed to feel more of Julian. My muscles tensed, doing everything to hold on to him and never let go. The pulse between my legs ached.

God, it *ached*, and it was hard to comprehend that it was all for Julian. *Julian*. But now that I wasn't drunk, I felt it with such clarity, such intensity. It would destroy me if I wasn't careful.

What happened when magnets resisted their pull? It couldn't be good.

"Fuck, this wasn't supposed to happen," Julian cursed harshly, suddenly mad. Not at me, though. At himself. But it didn't keep him from kissing me. It didn't stop his hand from running up my leg, from inching beneath my skirt. "But I just want to feel you, Juni. Just once," he rasped. "Please."

At this point, nodding between kisses was the only thing I could do. Yes, I wanted to feel him. Feel *all* of him. A hardness pressed between my legs, but I wanted to feel more. It wasn't enough to soothe the ache, the pulse.

"Please," I repeated, the only word in my brain at the moment.

I felt Julian smirk beneath my mouth again. God, I absolutely hated how much I loved his mouth. How much I loved kissing him. His hand rode higher beneath my skirt while letting me slowly slide back to the ground. But even once my feet landed on the floor, it still felt like I was floating. Our kisses grew lighter, less frenzied. Instead, we exchanged rough gasps and continual brushes of lips against lips like we wouldn't survive if we separated completely.

"Juniper." He spoke my name between us, sounding gravelly, desperate. "I'm going to touch you. I need to touch you."

I tugged on his hair in response, a signal to hurry the fuck up.

Julian's light chuckle grazed my lips while his fingers inched upward. They traced the top of my underwear slowly, and I wanted to know what the hell he was waiting for.

"Payback, remember?" he breathed.

"Touch me," I pleaded, and my request had Julian folding in an instant.

"Christ," he groaned, slipping his hand beneath the fabric of my underwear. "Open up for me, Juni."

Knowing what he wanted, I widened my stance, thinking about nothing except how badly I hungered for what he was about to give me.

"Good girl," he murmured appreciatively before sliding his fingers between my legs and swearing under his breath. The rest of Julian's reaction was lost on me, though. I was too distracted by the brush of his fingertips over my clit and his breath over my skin.

I whimpered his name and felt his lips twitch in response.

"So wet," he whispered, sounding awed. "You're so wet. Was it like this before?"

"Before?" I repeated breathlessly while he stroked deeper and deeper before coming back to play with my clit more.

"At the hotel. Did you drench your underwear for me then, too?"

"Yes," I admitted, tired of taming the truth or reworking it in my head. "Why do you think I said all those things to try to get you into bed?"

"I thought maybe you were trying to kill me. You always are." He cupped my cheek with his free hand, angling my head to the side so he could swoop in for another soul-satisfying kiss while continuing the magic he was doing between my legs. My knees nearly buckled, and I groaned into his mouth.

"I'm sorry, baby," he said tenderly after pulling back again. "I'm sorry I didn't give you what you needed this weekend, but I'll do it now."

I didn't get a chance to respond before Julian curled his fingers inside me. A wordless cry flew from my lips as bliss fired through every inch of me.

"Oh, Fuck. *Juni*."

I couldn't agree more with Julian's rough curse. *Fuck*. Fucking hell. But unlike him, I couldn't talk. Julian's voice growled in my ear as he pumped his fingers faster, making me see stars.

"Your sweet pussy is gripping my fingers so fucking good. I can only imagine...shit."

"Julian," I gasped as I comprehended his words. "You should know that I'm—oh my *God*."

My words descended into a moan as he hit a spot inside me that had to be forbidden with how good it felt. My eyes rolled back, my legs weakened, my fingers grabbed onto his shirtsleeves with desperation, nails digging into his muscular upper arms. And then his thumb grazed over my clit, and my body tightened in response.

Somewhere in my consciousness, I realized Julian was

pressing little kisses all along my jawline until he made it back to my ear, nipping my earlobe as he murmured bits of sweet, dirty encouragement while finger-fucking me against our office door.

"That's it," he muttered gruffly. "Come on, love."

"I—oh—*Julian*." My attempts at words were reduced to pants. I squirmed against his hand, against his entire body. So close, I was so close to finding—

"Come for me," he commanded, voice filling with an authority that made my pussy weep even more than it already was. "Stop being so goddamn stubborn, and come all over my fucking fingers, Juniper."

I wanted to. I wanted to more than anything I'd ever wanted. It felt like I was running along a cliff's edge, and I needed freedom. I needed to fall, and I needed to fall into him.

Julian covered my mouth with his again. This kiss was drenched in need and hunger, incomprehensible and wild. But when his tongue flicked against mine at the same moment he pinched my clit, I screamed into his mouth, pouring cries down his throat.

My world exploded with rapid bursts of hot pleasure that only Julian could cool. His kisses grew tender and soft as he slowly brought me back to reality, soothing the intensity into something more bearable but equally exquisite.

Julian drew his fingers out of me gradually, like he was savoring the last tremors of my body. Wet arousal coated my inner thighs, and my face flushed as I realized exactly what had just happened. But while slight embarrassment trickled up my spine, Julian had a satisfied smirk plastered on his face. He kept one hand on my hip to steady me while bringing his other hand to his lips, slipping his fingers into his mouth to taste me. He sucked on one finger after another, groaning before swearing abruptly under his breath.

With an eagerness that took my breath away, he grabbed me by the waist and spun us around, pressing me against his desk again. And then I was on top of it with my skirt bunched up around my hips.

"It's not enough," Julian gasped, his wild eyes trailing over me. "That taste, that amazing fucking taste—it's not enough."

He pushed his desk chair out of the way, and it rocketed across the small office on its wheels.

Then Julian dropped to his knees.

All I could do was watch his head with all its tousled auburn hair dip between my legs. He kissed the inside of my knee before looking up at me.

"I couldn't sleep last night," he said, his breaths coming in short spurts. "Ask me why."

"Why?"

Another kiss was pressed against my skin. His eyes flicked up to mine, piercing me. "I couldn't stop imagining going down on you."

All of the satisfaction, all the melting perfection of the last few minutes, vanished. And the hunger returned. His words bounced inside my brain, fueling it.

"Let me," Julian groaned, his tongue swirling up my inner thighs like he wanted to give me a preview of what it would feel like. "Let me taste more of you."

I was torn. I wanted that. *Really*, I did. But I also wanted to have my turn.

"Me first," I gasped, trying to ignore how goddamn good it felt to have his lips and tongue on my skin.

When Julian didn't listen, continuing his ascent, I kicked my foot out, placing it on his chest to stop him.

That worked. He paused, glancing at my high heel keeping him in place. Then he sat back on his knees with a burning look that made me question my decision to stop him. I ran my gaze over him, appreciating every little bit of Julian Briggs in a way I usually didn't get to. I watched as he ran his hand through his hair and licked his lips. I watched as anticipation shone in his eyes. And then my eyes lowered further, and I took in his impressive erection. *Shit.*

"Me first," I repeated, slower this time, so he couldn't miss it.

I wanted to taste him, too.

But to my dismay, Julian shook his head.

"You can't touch me." His words were whispered and tortured.

"Why not?"

That hardly seemed fair.

"If you touch me...I won't survive, Juni." He swallowed before slowly standing. "I'll never get over it."

"Why do you have to?"

Julian's expression morphed at my question, and a heavy dose of reality washed over me. The magic vanished, and something cruel and heart-wrenching took its place.

"Juniper..."

God, I usually loved when he said my full name, but I hated this.

Julian took three steps backward, leaning against the office door. He stared at the ceiling for a few moments, catching his breath. Eventually, he lowered his gaze.

"We can't."

He said it so quietly that I almost didn't hear it.

"We can't *what*?"

I knew the answer, but I wanted him to say it, to spell it out.

"Do this." He waved a finger back and forth. "Let it happen again. You're Gemma's best friend. We share an office, for fuck's sake. We're... It's not a good idea."

"So...why—why did you kiss me?" I asked, my voice sounding hollow. I pressed my fingers to my lips, feeling the ghost of his.

"It was the way you were talking about yourself," he replied in a low voice. "As if it was out of the realm of possibility for me to want you, when in reality..."

He didn't finish his sentence, and it tore me up inside. If the reality was that he wanted me, why was he pushing me away?

"But we're just not a good idea, Juni," he finished weakly.

He was right about that. None of this had been a good idea. But it seemed a little too late, didn't it?

"Maybe taking me to Sofia's wedding wasn't a good idea, either," I said testily, awkwardly yanking my skirt down, fully covering my legs again. "While I appreciated it, maybe you shouldn't have bothered."

"I didn't want anyone else taking you," he said evenly. "I told you." When I glared at him with barely concealed irritation, he added, "If it hadn't been for Gemma and work, I probably would have told Noah to fuck off myself."

His admission made me suck in with surprise. He—*what?*

Julian's heated look remained steady. It was something close to a dare—daring me to deny the truth of his words. I didn't want to, though. I desperately wanted them to be real.

"I don't know how to go back," I said, admitting the very thing I'd been trying to figure out since yesterday when he dropped me off at my apartment. It was the reason I'd prepared my little speech, which he'd naturally interrupted. Julian liked to ruin things for me in the best and worst ways. I didn't know how to go back, but I'd been ready to try.

But now? We couldn't go back now.

"We can't go back," I said more forcefully.

"We have to," Julian insisted, and I scowled. He noted my expression and grew exasperated. "Yes, we kissed, but—"

"Twice," I interjected.

Not to mention everything else he'd just done to me.

My cheeks flamed, and I hoped to hell Julian didn't notice.

"Twice," he acknowledged. "We kissed twice. Impulsively. Unplanned. And now we can *plan* to not do it again."

"That's what you want?" I probed, trying to ignore how much it hurt to hear those words.

Julian just stared at me, jaw clenching.

"There's a difference between impulsivity and living in the moment, Julian."

He exhaled loudly, but his eyes didn't move from mine. "Explain it to me."

I slid off the desk and back to my feet, even though my legs felt like jelly. I wanted to be on the same ground as Julian. "Sometimes it feels good to prolong moments where you can really live before being crashed back into a reality where you just exist."

Julian held my gaze for the longest time. It was the worst sort of anticipation, nothing like this weekend when I knew we were moments from kissing.

Now I knew we were moments from breaking.

"It wasn't impulsive," I added in a breathy whisper.

"What?"

"When I kissed you at the wedding? That wasn't impulsive. It's not like I never thought about you...like that before," I confessed, opening myself up to even more pain and embarrassment. "But I guess it wasn't the same for you."

Julian shook his head sadly, and I didn't know how to interpret it. "Kissing you feels like living, Juniper."

I nodded, hating how I'd felt so high and now I felt so low. "But tomorrow, we're just going to exist, aren't we?"

He paused, and a wave of nausea hit me at his silence.

"Tomorrow, we're just going to exist," he said.

To his credit, the words were pained and sharp. Which explained why they cut so deep.

Unable to handle it any longer, I looked away. Silence filled the office, replacing the gasps and groans from minutes earlier. When Julian spoke again, his voice scraped against my heart.

"The flower," he said throatily. When I glanced at him, he pointed over my shoulder. I followed his finger to my row of plants on his desk. "It finally bloomed."

I closed my eyes momentarily, feeling like we were on a Ferris wheel that was slowly losing control.

"It's a moonflower, Julian," I said, repeating the same thing I'd said numerous times before.

He took a step closer, his body cradling mine. His words whispered across my hair. "Tell me what that means, Daisy."

Tipping my head back, I traced his face with my eyes, loving and hating every inch of it. Julian's attention dropped to my mouth, but he didn't move. He waited for my answer, which came in the form of a confession.

"It only comes alive at night."

ten years ago

"I'll bring you to your sister," the nurse said, the words swimming around my head.

"She's okay," she continued, looking over her shoulder. "But she has a pretty nasty concussion and a broken collarbone. I believe she'll be returning from X-Ray soon."

Relief, pure sweeping relief, made it easier to breathe. And yet...it still felt like something was stuck in my throat. In my chest.

"She'll recover?" I asked, thinking that maybe I just needed to hear it a second time.

The nurse nodded reassuringly. She stopped by the door to a room, giving me a kind, sympathetic look. "You can wait in her room for her if you want," she said, gesturing to the doorway before walking away.

My feet wouldn't move. She didn't say anything about Juniper. Juniper must be in the room, then, right? She was fine; she was waiting for Gemma. I'd see her in just a few seconds when I finally got my feet to move.

My heart strained against the wall of my chest, pounding so hard that it felt like I was about to have the medical emergency. For every rapid thump, her name repeated in my brain.

Juni, Juni, Juni, Juni.

My feet broke free, rushing toward the hospital room the nurse gestured to. It was empty, and something inside me cracked open. I spun around, desperately searching for a flash of brown hair, but nothing...there was nothing. Chaos surrounded me as I pushed my feet forward, following in the direction the nurse went. The flash of her blue scrubs rounded the corner, and I picked up my pace, shouting after her.

"Where is she?"

The nurse paused and then backpedaled. Her brows furrowed. "Your sister will be back from X-Ray soon."

I shook my head, wringing my hands together as I tried not to scream. "Not Gemma. Where's her friend...the one who was in the car with her when they crashed."

The nurse's confusion doubled down, and I threaded my fingers through my still-damp hair, pulling at the ends in frustration.

"Juniper," I clarified, feeling like my knees were about to give out. "Juniper St. James. Brown hair, brown eyes, so fucking pretty. Please tell me someone knows where the hell she is."

CHAPTER TWENTY-FIVE

julian

THE PAST WEEK HAD been torture, and frankly, I deserved it.

Being in the office with Juniper was more impossible than usual. In a way, it proved my point. If we continued whatever the fuck we'd started at the wedding, and then again the other night, there was no way in hell I'd be able to concentrate on work. Existing around her was distracting enough, and at the moment, our interactions were only clipped greetings and necessary case updates.

I hated it.

So, as it turned out, Juniper was also right.

We couldn't go back.

We rarely got along to begin with, but now we existed in an entirely new dimension. This wasn't anything like it was before. It wasn't mild irritation or playful teasing. This was painful. It felt like every breath I took was only enough air to get by until the next inhale, and I'd never get back to fully living unless I had her.

But I had some faith that our relationship would come back around if I waited long enough.

At least until Thanksgiving. Then, that faith quickly vanished.

Thanksgiving was one of those yearly constants. My whole

family would spend the morning in the kitchen, we'd eat dinner together midafternoon, and then the St. James family would come over at night to kick off the Christmas season by watching a movie picked by one of our moms. Sometimes we'd even start pulling out decorations, and Juniper and Gemma would run around our old house with strings of lights.

I watched Katherine and Brooks St. James walk in the front door, eagerly waiting to see Juni follow them inside. I'd seen Juniper for the last ten days straight, and after one whole day without her, I was fucking miserable.

But she wasn't there. My heart sank.

And then a hand slapped my chest.

"What did you do?"

"Jesus, Gemma." I rubbed the spot she slapped and crossed my legs while sinking deeper into the couch. "I didn't—"

I couldn't even finish the sentence because it was such a fucking lie.

I did do something. I did a lot of somethings, including pinning Juniper to our office door and thrusting my fingers inside her until she cried into my mouth while coming.

And then I told her it could never happen again.

I shouldn't have done it, shouldn't have done any of it. But at least now I could live and die knowing what Juniper felt like, what her little gasps of desire sounded like. Fucking exquisite, all of it. Her *taste*. Christ, her taste.

"You're such an ass."

True, very true. After all, I was sitting next to my sister, thinking dirty things about her best friend. Reliving them, actually.

I felt Gemma's eyes bore into the side of my head while I stared longingly at the door, hoping Juni would still walk through it.

"Oh, where's Juniper?" I heard my mom ask Katherine in the background, followed by a quick explanation of how Juni hadn't been feeling good.

"Ate too much turkey?" my dad joked, and light chuckles followed.

That wasn't it. I knew Juni.

"What did you do?" Gemma hissed, repeating herself. "Did something happen at the wedding that Juni didn't tell me?"

Everything happened at the wedding.

But I was curious...

"You talked to Juni about the wedding?"

"Of course I talked to Juni about the wedding."

"And did she...what did she say?"

Gemma's eyes narrowed. "Julian John Briggs, what did you *do*?"

I cleared my throat and looked back at my eldest sister, noticing how all my other sisters seemed to be leaning toward us with interest, too.

"I had a great time at the wedding," I said, the biggest oversimplification and understatement all in one sentence. "And I think Juni enjoyed herself, too."

It wasn't a lie. Technically.

"There's something you're not telling me," Gemma grunted, folding her arms across her chest.

"There might have been some problems at work this week," I allowed.

Also not a lie. Not technically.

Gemma scowled. "I knew you did something. You're always so hard on her for no reason. But she's never not shown up before, so whatever you did this time..."

Her voice trailed off in an attempt for me to fill in the blank. But that wasn't going to happen. I couldn't tell Gemma what happened when I still hadn't fully wrapped my head around it.

Gemma's lips pressed together firmly when I remained quiet. Her eyes pleaded a bit, but all I could do was shake my head apologetically, and she flicked her gaze down to her lap, giving up.

Fuck.

Gemma had been critiquing my relationship with Juni for years, but something about this time hit differently. Maybe because I realized how right she was. Maybe because the thought of anyone being hard on Juni, myself included, made my hands ball into fists. Juni didn't deserve that. She deserved the world.

I wanted to give her the world. I wanted to give her the world so fucking bad, but I didn't know how to juggle that and work and my relationship with Gems.

Although, right now, I was dropping every single ball anyway.

I stood, pulling out my phone. "I'll text her."

"You better," Josie piped in this time. She was twirling one of her short curls around her finger while shooting me an icy look.

"Yeah, I was excited to see her," Genevieve added, her small voice nearly cracking my heart.

"Fix it. She better be here at Christmas, Julian," Gemma warned, pulling my attention back toward her again. "Or else."

Disappointing my sisters was the *last* thing I wanted out of this mess, so I heaved a sigh and walked off toward the garage, finding solace in the cool air and the quiet. I stared at my phone, unsure where to even start.

After a few minutes, I decided to text what felt most natural. What felt most true.

We miss you.

DAISY: We?

My sisters. But mostly me.

DAISY: You saw me yesterday.

It isn't the same.

DAISY: I thought you'd be happy. You finally get a holiday without having me around to annoy you.

Reading those words made me feel like punching something. My fingers shook as I texted her back.

I'm not happy, Juniper.

I could have said so much more. I owed her apologies on top of apologies, but that wasn't a conversation to have over text. So I pivoted to the more important thing for tonight.

You should be here.

DAISY: I needed a little space.

Okay. I'm going to be in the garage for the next couple of hours, tweaking a few things on Noah's bike. There's a spot for you on the couch next to Gemma if you start feeling better.

I had a hunch that it wasn't space from Gems that she needed.

Juniper belonged here, and I realized I had to overcome years of telling her she didn't.

If I needed to leave to make her feel comfortable, then I would leave.

I'd do anything.

JUNIPER WAS TRYING TO KILL ME.

Since destroying little bits of my heart wasn't good enough, she was now attacking my dick. No surprise there. As if the first day back at work after a long weekend hadn't been brutal enough on its own, Juni left about five minutes ago after finishing her last meeting of the day and came back wearing a short and flirty dress designed to tease the hell out of me.

I unashamedly stared at her.

To be honest, I'd been doing it all day. Although my sisters told me Juni had made an eventual appearance on Thanksgiving, I stuck to my word and stayed in the garage. Meaning I hadn't seen her since last week, and now I was soaking up every little glimpse of her.

But this...this was too much. She seemed to have come back from our weekend in Whitebridge on a mission.

"What are you wearing?"

She didn't give me her eyes when she replied. "What I'm wearing doesn't concern you, Julian."

"Maybe it doesn't concern me, but that doesn't mean I can't be concerned," I grunted, wondering where the hell she planned to go in that.

"You wanted to just *exist*, Julian." She slammed her laptop shut before looking up at me beneath her lashes. "Let me exist."

I closed my eyes momentarily to get my shit together. This existing thing? I hated it. Didn't she realize I hated it?

"Juni—"

"It's a dress," she cut me off before bending down to grab her purse from beneath her desk.

My cock stiffened to an unbearably painful degree.

Standing again, Juniper swiveled back around to flash a smirk in my direction. She knew exactly what she just fucking did to me. "Do you have a problem with it?"

"Not a problem, no," I said, trying to keep my voice steady. "But there isn't much of it."

That was the mildest way I could think of reminding her that it would only take half a second for me to get beneath any fabric she put on her body.

She raised a brow. It was done mockingly, and somehow, that made it even hotter. "I thought you weren't afraid of a little bare skin, Julian."

"I'm not." I stood, slamming the door to our office shut as I stepped toward her. If she noticed my obvious arousal, it didn't register on her face, which was likely for the best. "Your skin, your lips, any little bit of you, I'm not afraid of any of it."

Juniper leaned back against her desk slowly. Her back arched seductively as she drew her bottom lip between her teeth.

I closed the distance between us, not wanting this conversation to be overheard. "I fucking crave it," I said in a low voice. "But I'm afraid of what it'll do to me if I let it. What it will do to you. What it will do to the people around us."

"Julian..."

She said my name like a warning, and I understood. My blood was running hot, and I needed to find a way to cool it. But Juni's stare was equally bold and audacious. She was flashing warning signals while simultaneously daring me to continue.

"It's not about me, Juniper," I pleaded. "It's not about what I want. You have to understand."

"Oh, I understand. I know you, Julian." She shrugged, pulling her hand away to create a void where her touch vanished. I watched as her shoulders deflated. "You've been pushing me away for years. It's not like I'm not used to it."

"Juniper, I—" My words cut off at her stony glare, and I knew anything I had to say would fall flat.

"You haven't changed," she muttered with a sigh. Disappointment was written all over her face.

"Yeah...I'm still the worst." I stared back at her, sinking into that deep look in her eyes.

"Look who's being self-deprecating now," she breathed, but her lips twitched slightly in amusement.

"Well, it's true."

My mood dropped as I reminded myself that this was our reality. While I'd lusted after Juniper for years, she'd been thinking of me as *the worst* for many more. Why would she even think it would be a good idea to continue what we started the other night? Juni had made no indication that she wanted me in the way I wanted her. She seemed eager to start something physical, sure, but I doubted that would be enough for me. Once we started, I wasn't sure I'd be able to stop.

"You've never liked me, Juni," I reminded her softly, trying not to sound so goddamn sad about it but likely failing. "Remember? What happens when you realize that you still don't?"

I'd avoided letting myself get close to her for all these years for a reason.

Those brilliant brown eyes blinked at me, almost like she was *trying* to remember. Then she abruptly sucked in as if it all came flooding back.

"I told you, Julian. I told you at Sofia's wedding that I liked you. And then, if I remember correctly, you made me admit that nothing about that night was fake. So it wasn't a lie. But you know what...it doesn't even matter." She looked down, pushing me away with her words, and I supposed I deserved that, even if it fucking hurt. "Not anymore."

"It doesn't?"

"No, I have a date I need to get to."

I took a step back, feeling sucker punched with that information. "You have a date you need to get to," I repeated.

Juniper looked down at herself thoughtfully. "You didn't think I put this dress on for you, did you?"

I honestly hoped she had.

"Who did you put the dress on for, Juni?" I asked through gritted teeth, falling back into my desk chair like she'd pushed me. I spun around to face my computer. How could I keep staring at her when she was looking so perfect for someone else? But I waited, bated breath, for her to answer.

"Noah," she said, her voice sweet. "He asked me to dinner tonight."

Oh, *fuck* no.

I turned back around with such force that I had to plant my feet on the ground to stop the momentum of my chair.

"Excuse me...*what*?"

CHAPTER TWENTY-SIX

I DEFINITELY SHOULD NOT be enjoying the anger on Julian's face this much.

But I had an inkling that it didn't stem from irritation like I used to believe. This wasn't him trying to gatekeep his friends. This was something far more than that, and in my personal opinion, something Julian deserved to experience at the moment.

Jealousy looked good on Julian Briggs.

It really took this moment and the way he was looking at me to fully realize the extent of it. Or that it existed at all. Jealous. He was actually, legitimately jealous.

Had I taken advantage of this well-timed opportunity? Played it up a bit? Of course I had. And I refused to feel guilty after everything that had happened in the last couple of weeks. I'd gone to the wedding thinking that meeting Sofia would help fill a hole of loneliness in me. I thought that meeting someone who was blood-related to me would give me a sense of belonging in this world. And for a few hours, it did.

But then Julian happened.

Now I was back in Boston. And Sofia wasn't here, Julian was pushing me away, and I had no one to talk to about any of it. Gemma had tried to get more out of me at Thanksgiving, but I stuck to the story I'd told my parents—that I didn't feel well. As much as I would have loved to vent to my best friend about her brother, I couldn't. No matter how mad I was, the last thing I wanted to do was damage his relationship with his sisters. I couldn't do that to him.

But I could do *this* to him.

"I'm going to dinner with Noah," I repeated for him, even though I was positive he'd heard me correctly the first time.

"Noah London," he clarified through clenched teeth.

"Noah London," I confirmed. "You know...tattoos, professional football player, lived with you in—"

"I know, Juniper." The growl of his voice sent a thrill through me that I chose to ignore. "What I don't know is why the hell you're going to dinner with him."

I arched a brow. "Is that so unbelievable of an idea?"

"Of course not, but—"

"He felt bad that he couldn't take me to Sofia's wedding and asked to make it up to me."

"And you said yes?"

"Clearly." I motioned to my outfit, which I'd picked out specifically for this occasion. "It's not like anyone else is asking me on a date tonight."

Julian's lips clamped shut at that, and to his credit, pain bled into his eyes, mixing with apparent fury. It was hard to look at, so I grabbed my coat, spun on my heel, and exited the office before I changed my mind.

Those eyes of his had been begging me not to go, but he'd have to say the words to get me to stay. He'd have to say a lot of words to get me to stay, and since his mouth wasn't moving...

"Juniper!"

Oh, goddamnit.

My feet faltered, but when Julian didn't say anything more, I continued forward.

Dinner with Noah would be good for me. I wasn't naive in thinking it was an actual date. Just dinner with a man who wasn't confusing, utterly infuriating, and made my entire body react uncontrollably when we were in the same room.

My hormones had *not* gotten the memo that I was upset with Julian this past week. All they wanted to do was relive the moments when I was pressed against him, crying his name. It really put a damper on my efforts to freeze him out when I got all hot and bothered every time he even glanced at me. My knees shook when he so much as slipped out of his coat in the morning.

Jesus Christ, I was a mess.

But it was time to put thoughts of Julian out of my mind.

A short walk through light snow later, I stepped into a trendy restaurant and pretended to be far more confident than I was while walking across the dimly lit dining space. Noah immediately caught my eye from a table in the corner, slightly sheltered from the rest of the restaurant. Celebrity status was good for some things, I supposed.

"Juniper, you look great," he greeted me as soon as I approached him. His enthusiasm didn't seem fake, nor did his movements when he brought me in for a brief but firm hug. After pulling back, he offered to take my coat, hanging it on the rack behind him.

"Thank you," I said, flashing him a smile. "You know, you didn't have to do this."

Might as well get it out in the open right away that I knew what this was and what it wasn't.

"Do what?" He frowned, settling into his seat across from me. "Have dinner?"

"Yeah, I hope you don't think that just because you weren't able to make it to the wedding, you owe—"

"Of course I don't think that," he said, waving away my concern. "But I still wanted to make it up to you. After all, I heard you had to go with Briggs." He winked at me over his menu. "Must have been a rough weekend."

The twinkle in his eye told me he didn't mean a word of what he'd said, but I still had the oddest urge to defend Julian.

"The weekend was actually...a lot of fun."

"Was it now?" Noah had a prying look worse than Gemma's. "I heard you saw Gray and Nes."

I leaned in conspiratorially. "Who I learned was actually Wednesday Elevett."

Noah leaned back and laughed. "Did Jules tell you how much she hated being called Wednesday in college?"

I shook my head. "Why did she pick it as a stage name, then?"

"Grayson made her love it. Took a while, though."

"That's sweet," I said with a smile before looking down at my menu. Noah also fell quiet across the table, taking a minute to peruse the options. The only thing that interrupted our momentary silence was the continual buzz of his phone. I was sure it always did that, rang off the hook.

With a sigh, Noah put his menu down and glanced at his phone. Not wanting to stare while he responded to girls or fans or whoever was hounding him, I buried myself in the menu again. But my stomach turned, and I wished we had agreed to get drinks, not fine dining for two.

A waitress swung by, grabbing our drink orders. Hard to say if she caught mine, though. Noah had most of her attention.

"God, I'm starving," Noah commented, leaning back in his chair. His phone had disappeared, and I didn't hear it anymore, so I wondered if he had silenced it. "I seriously want to order everything. But don't worry, it's all on me tonight."

"Oh, you don't—"

"Juniper, I asked you to dinner. Now, let me *take you out* to dinner, okay?" He put a hand up to stop my protest. "What looks good to you?"

"I'm not sure," I said truthfully. "I ate a big lunch, so I'm really not that hungry."

Noah fixed me with a stare before opening his mouth and saying something I honestly didn't believe at first.

"Julian says you *barely* ate lunch, and I have to make sure you have something for dinner." He glanced back down at his menu. "He says you like gnocchi. Or pasta. But I shouldn't imply they are the same because, according to you, they are not."

"It's a debatable topic," I mumbled, trying not to let my lips curve up. "When did he say that?"

"Just now. He's been blowing up my phone nonstop for a half hour now." Noah cocked his head before stabbing a finger at the menu. "They have a creamy penne alla vodka. How does that sound?"

"I—good." Food was the last thing on my mind, now more than ever. But it seemed that Noah was taking his task of making sure I ate seriously. Just like someone else I knew. "That sounds great, actually."

"Excellent." Noah put the menu down again, fixing me with a look. His eyes had a smokey quality to them. That, combined with his crooked smile and sleeves of tattoos, made him seem more mysterious than he really was. And attractive, of course.

But knowing someone was attractive was far different than having an attraction to them, and I realized Noah was firmly in the former category for me.

Shit. That look he was giving me was a dare, and I folded far too quickly. I took a sip of my water to buy myself time to change my mind, but my words came out the same regardless.

"What else did Julian say?"

Noah's lips slowly formed into a shit-eating grin. "He's threatening what he'll do if I touch you. And the longer I go without answering his threats, the more creative they seem to be getting."

"Oh my God," I groaned. "I'm so sorry. He's so incredibly infuriating."

Of course Julian would try to domineer situations just the way he wanted them. But Noah appeared far from bothered that his friend was threatening him, which I struggled to comprehend. He grinned the entire time we paused our conversation to let the waitress place glasses of wine in front of us.

As soon as she left, he leaned forward onto the table. "Let me explain Julian for you."

"Oh, I understand Julian." I took an overly large gulp of my Chardonnay. "I've known him for over a decade, and most of it has not been pleasant."

"I'm not saying he doesn't have his faults, but you gotta realize he's a good guy. *More* than a good guy."

Wow, not only was Noah not bothered by Julian's incessant threats, but he was also going to *bat* for him?

When I quietly took another sip of my wine, Noah insisted.

"He is, Juniper."

"He's threatening you," I pointed out, in case he'd forgotten.

"Because he knows *my* faults and wants to protect you."

Protect me. How funny it was that Julian always tried to protect me from everything and everyone...except himself.

"You would touch me if I didn't want you to?" I asked, not believing that I needed protection from the man across the table, who was far more kind-spirited than I'd initially given him credit for. He'd seemed so genuinely apologetic when he canceled on me for Sofia's wedding that I wasn't even surprised to get his text the other day about tonight.

"Of course not." Noah looked affronted. "But I am aware I have a reputation."

"Then he has nothing to protect me from." I glanced away. It was hard admitting truths when looking people in the eye. "I don't know why he thinks he gets to want nothing to do with me and also tell other guys that they should want nothing to do with me."

When I looked back at Noah, he was sitting back in his chair, crossing his arms over his chest. It emphasized his biceps, which were trying to bulge their way out of his white dress shirt. "These are not the texts of a man who wants nothing to do with you, Juniper."

"He doesn't think we're a good *idea*," I admitted.

This was such an inappropriate conversation to have with a

guy who'd asked me out for dinner, but again, we both knew what this was: not a date. And it felt good to say those words aloud after repeating them in my head for the last week.

"Of course he doesn't," Noah said softly, taking me aback.

"Of course?"

"Because it's *Julian*." His sigh made me feel like I was supposed to understand what that meant, but I didn't. Which forced me to the realization that maybe, just maybe, there were parts of Julian that I didn't fully comprehend. "Julian's life revolves around his family," Noah added.

Okay, yes, *that* I did know.

"And you are in the unfortunate situation of being very close to that family."

"I love the Briggs family," I defended because he made it sound like something was wrong with them.

"Exactly." Noah tapped his finger on the table pointedly. "His entire life, he's made decisions based on what he thinks is best for the people he loves. He could have easily made a career in the NFL, but he didn't think it was the responsible choice. He could have easily gone into law school immediately after undergrad, but his dad needed his help back home. He could have asked you out eons ago, but he didn't want to get between your relationship with his family, the one you love so very much."

"Eons ago?" I repeated, getting stuck on that little part. "Julian never made any indication that he liked me growing up."

An understatement.

"Oh, sweetheart." Noah picked up his wine, peering at me over the rim of his glass. "You're wrong. That's why I was so surprised when he introduced us, but he insisted it was fine. Until it so clearly wasn't."

"I—I don't know about that, Noah. Really, I—"

"And now you both work together," Noah continued. "And Julian's goal his whole life has been to secure a long-term, well-paying career that can support his family. He has that job now, the one that will help make sure Genevieve or Josie or whichever one it is goes to college. The job that is sustainable enough to take care of his parents when they get older and his dad can't crouch under cars anymore for a living. That job is really fucking important to him. It doesn't mean *you* aren't."

"Doesn't it?" I cringed as soon as the thought came out of my mouth. "Sorry, that sounded really self-centered."

"No, it didn't," Noah reassured me. "Look, I'm not going to sit here and say he isn't making some big mistakes, but that's just how I see it."

I took a deep breath, absorbing everything he'd said. I understood that Julian was self-sacrificing, but I'd never *dream* of doing anything to put his job at risk. Nor would I ever think to get between him and his sisters. Gemma hated when Julian and I argued. And here I was, for some incomprehensible reason, trying to end that era of us.

"You sound like you've talked to him about this," I hedged.

If he did, I'd be a little upset. I wished Julian would talk to *me*. And not just cryptically or condescendingly. But honestly.

Noah shook his head, though. "No, I didn't talk to him." He gave me a sympathetic little smile that was sweet but painful. "I just know him."

His answer made me wonder...did I know Julian? I thought I did.

But I also thought he hated me, and the last few weeks certainly didn't feel like hate. I thought he was cold, but recently, I'd never felt so warm. When it came to me, I thought he only knew how to be hard and unfeeling, but then there were those moments when he was oh, so soft.

God, just thinking about those moments made my heart beat faster.

Before it fell into my stomach because I remembered the rejection that followed.

If I was honest with myself, it was a gut-wrenching realization. Wanting him like this was gut-wrenching. The want kept growing and growing the more I thought about it. But it wasn't anything more than a whole new way for him to hurt me.

"How about that pasta?" Noah jerked his head to the side, capturing my attention again. "Should we flag down the waitress and order?"

I took a deep breath. "Yeah, let's do that."

But before we got the chance, Noah's phone buzzed again. He sighed, glancing down at it. His lips pressed together in a repressed smile.

"What?"

I couldn't help it; I needed to know.

Noah read from his phone without looking up. "He's reminding me that he's broken bones for you before, and he can do it again."

"He's so dramatic," I scoffed, despite my stomach flipping.

Noah chuckled before giving me a curious look. "Do you want me to cave and tell him where we are?"

I thought about it for a second before shaking my head. "He can have tonight to figure out what he wants. And then, just maybe, I'll give him a chance if he realizes it's me."

Noah tucked his phone away with a soft smile. "He knows it's you, Juniper."

He sounded so sure of himself.

I wished I could be that sure, too.

CHAPTER TWENTY-SEVEN

A FEW MINUTES AFTER Noah dropped me off at my apartment, there was a knock on my door. I frowned, wondering if he'd come back for some reason. Although it was odd that he wouldn't have just sent a text or—

"Oh, thank fuck."

I opened my door to find Julian leaning against the frame. His chest heaved while snow melted into his gingery locks. And he was peering up at me with such angry relief. I didn't know how else to describe it. Tension rolled off his shoulder in waves, his movements stiff as he straightened. And then, without another word, he grabbed my hips and walked me back into my apartment again.

"What are you doing here?"

My words were breathless as a snow-covered Julian guided me through the entryway and into the kitchen. Once he had me pressed against the counter with a thrilling sort of roughness, his attention turned to the rest of the apartment, scoping it out.

"He's not here," I said dryly.

Julian ran a hand through his hair, pulling a bit on the ends before he looked down at me again. His hair was wet now, hanging over his forehead.

"He better not fucking be here," he said, eyes wild as he slid so close to me that his damp clothes—the same suit he wore earlier at work—brushed over my bare skin. I repressed a shiver.

Instead of entertaining that comment, I repeated my earlier question. "What are you doing here, Julian? It's late."

"Noah wouldn't tell me what restaurant you went to for dinner." His hand returned to my side, gripping it between his fingers as though to check if I was actually there. "In fact, that ass barely responded to me at all."

"Because we were *eating dinner*," I emphasized before holding my breath as Julian put his hands on the kitchen countertop and slid them forward. Meaning that all those little brushes of his body against mine were obliterated. He was firm and hard, and his hips held mine captive.

"What did you have?" he whispered, his tone growing soft.

"For dinner?" I whispered back. "Pasta."

"And did you eat all of it?" His eyes wandered my face, ready to detect any signs of a lie.

"Most of it."

Julian's lips curved slightly. "That's my girl."

My girl.

I wanted it. I wanted to be someone's girl, but mostly, I wanted to be Julian's girl. I wanted this fierceness of his and the tender way he held me when we shared a bed. I wanted to talk to him about my books and tell him what I had eaten for dinner. I wanted him to fix my hair when it wasn't right and dance with me when I felt lonely.

But he thought all of those things were a *bad idea.*

And yet, here we were.

"Julian, what's happening?" It was a good thing he was so close because I could only seem to make my words so loud. "What is this?"

I worried his answer would break me, but I also worried that not asking would break me more.

"It's nothing new," he confessed, his jaw continuing to clench angrily even though his eyes were soft and imploring. "Not for me. I spent so many years pushing you away because of it, and I'm sorry. I'm so sorry, Juni." His apology was marred by a curse beneath his breath. "But you have to understand what it was like."

"What *what* was like?"

"You were everywhere, Juniper." His voice scraped my soul. "Every time I turned the corner, you were *there.* Your stacks of books, that perfume, clothes—all over my house. Everywhere, all the time. Such a goddamn tease. Because even though you were there, you hated me. And even if you didn't, I couldn't have you."

My head swam with his words. Unbelievable, world-altering words. But somehow, I managed a reply.

"I only hated you because of how you made me feel. You were the only one who never accepted me, who didn't consider me welcome. All I wanted was more family to call my own."

I loved my parents to no end, but being an only child grew lonely sometimes. The chaos, the connectivity of the Briggs family...it drew me in and held me tight.

"I know." His face screwed up. "And I didn't know how to give you what you wanted, Juniper. Because it didn't feel like we could be...that. Not with how I wanted you." He sighed. "Do you remember the car accident you and Gemma were in?"

"Of course I do." How could I forget when he brought it up so frequently? When he'd never let me forget the moment that seemed like the breaking point between us. "You were so mad at me. Because of what happened to Gemma—"

He shook his head before piercing me with a look so intense that my breath vanished. "No. I was so mad because of *you.*"

"Me?"

"My sister was lying in the hospital bed, and I couldn't stop obsessing over *you.* Over what could have happened to *you.* I love Gemma to no end, but you—*you*, Juni..." He grasped my face between both of his hands. "I felt so guilty. About all of it. Those feelings didn't feel fair to Gemma. They didn't feel fair to you because I knew what you wanted, and it wasn't *that*. I was mad; you're right. I was mad at all of it, and after that, I pushed you so far away until I couldn't feel *you* anymore, and instead, all I felt was *anger*. That was what I held on to in the end."

I was wrong. In his own twisted way, Julian did protect me from himself. He just didn't realize it wasn't necessary. And it was futile.

Because here we were.

"Being around you these last few months, Juniper..." He closed his eyes momentarily, seeming nearly remorseful. His hands fell back to his sides. "It's like little pieces of you are coming back to me. And it's not that I'm realizing how much I want you. I'm *remembering* it. Bit by bit, I'm remembering it. Even though I tried really fucking hard to hold on to the anger, I just couldn't."

"Why, Julian?" I shook my head, practically speechless. "I don't want you to feel that way anymore. I don't want that for us."

"Because I thought it was better for you, Juni. And for my family."

"It isn't," I insisted. "It isn't what's better."

I was so sure of that. I was so sure that we could live in a world where Julian and I didn't hate each other, and I was so sure we could do it in a way that didn't disrupt any relationships, not with work, not with Gemma or any of his other sisters. If things didn't work between us, the worst-case scenario was reverting back to what it was before: arguments, hurt hearts, and irritation. And we would survive. We would exist.

I had a feeling we could live, though.

"I know that now," Julian admitted, leaving me speechless. "It's not better. It's awful, Juni. It's awful because I want you so badly. I want you more than I know how to explain. And I can't... anymore. I can't."

His words made me feel like I was soaring, but then his

expression pulled inward again, and I immediately knew my high wouldn't last.

"But you went on a date with fucking Noah, and now I—" Julian cut short, like he couldn't even stand to finish the sentence. All of his fire dredged back up again, simmering in every movement. "What happened after dinner?"

At his accusatory tone, my own anger flared. I was still reeling from his words, but in a way, they made everything worse. He had all that bottled up inside him, and he *still* pushed me away last week?

It made it seem that much more hopeless.

And I refused to exist hopelessly.

"He drove me home."

"He better not have fucking touched you," Julian growled, raking his gaze over my body as though he'd be able to *see* if Noah's hands had touched my skin.

I shivered. And then something unexplainable possessed me to reply, "Unfortunately, he didn't."

"Unfortunately?" Julian forced the word out in a deadly whisper.

"Well, no one else is touching me," I said, rephrasing my words from earlier about the date. He had to understand that if he was going to stick to his convictions about how we couldn't be, I'd need to move on. I was tired of feeling unwanted. "And I'd rather not remain a virgin forever."

Julian's eyes snapped to my face. "What did you just say?"

His voice was eerily soft.

Mine was even softer.

"You heard me."

He stared, unmoving. His breathing grew shallow, and I wished I knew what he was thinking. I wished I could gauge his reaction, but his expression remained stoic and stunned. When he spoke, his voice was taut.

"You're a virgin?"

"It's not a big deal." I swallowed, suddenly regretting my impulsive confession. "Virginity is just a social construct, Julian."

"You brought it up, not me." He leaned closer, a new kind of heat burning in his eyes. "And now I need you to answer the question."

"You know the answer," I replied breathlessly.

Despite the cold, snowy night, sweat began to gather on the small of my back beneath my dress. Usually, I hated the sensation. But tonight, I welcomed the warmth that brought it.

"Fuck, Juni."

Julian abruptly dropped his head. Almost like it had been too heavy to hold up any longer. I felt the absence of his gaze so acutely, my blood instantly cooling. He swore again under his breath as I remained caged between his arms against the countertop. I wasn't sure what was about to happen, but something was. Something that would either hurt or heal me.

"Juniper," Julian murmured, raising his head slowly.

"Julian," I whispered, trying not to look away. I likely should, though. His look was so hazy with lust, and the last thing I wanted was to make the same mistake I'd made before when he looked at me like that.

He brushed a hair out of my face. The tenderness of it completely contrasted his body's hard angles and delicious weight as it crowded me against the countertop. I barely dared to breathe while waiting for him to say something more, and when he did, his husky voice kissed my skin.

"From now on, if you want someone to take you on a date, it's going to be me," he muttered, his fingers dragging along my jawline to my chin, holding on to it so I wouldn't look away. "And if you want someone to fuck you, that'll be me, too." He rocked his hips against mine, letting me feel how ready he was for it. "Not anyone else. Me, Juni. Understood?"

All my nerve endings lit up, blazing, and I had to swallow a groan before speaking. "What happened to just existing?"

"At this point, I don't even know how to do that without you," he grunted, dropping his forehead against mine. "I've never not wanted you, Juni. I've tried for years not to want you, but I can't do it anymore. I want to be around you *constantly*."

"Constantly?"

Despite the desperation in his voice, I found that hard to believe.

"Constantly, Daisy." The confession brushed against my lips. "I think about you constantly. I want you constantly."

My eyes fluttered shut as I felt Julian's lips press against the corner of my mouth. And then my jaw. And then I tipped my head back slightly to allow him to trail his open mouth down my neck. He tugged the ends of my long hair to keep me exposed for him before groaning my name into that spot where my pulse thumped faster and faster. My breathing came in short spurts as his free hand slid up my back and fisted my dress like it was all he could do to hold on to his restraint.

I didn't want him to restrain himself, but I knew he was waiting for me to say something. And while I longed to demand that he put that talented mouth to work, I'd learned my lesson.

"That's an awfully bold statement without any proof," I said breathlessly.

I needed proof. More of it. Or a different kind of it, at the very least.

I felt Julian's dark chuckle against my skin as he released my hair. His face emerged from the crook of my neck again, gaze meeting mine. It was bright. He smirked. "Don't ask for proof unless you're ready to get it, Juniper."

"I'm ready." I licked my lips, trying not to pay too close attention to how Julian's eyes dropped to my mouth.

"Tell me more," he encouraged.

"What do you want to know?"

"I couldn't give you what you wanted when we were younger. What do you want now?" His eyes glittered, hopeful. "Is it something I can give you? I need to know what you're ready for. I need to know what proof you want."

Years. I'd wanted this version of Julian for years—the one who looked me in the eyes and told me I belonged in his life, in any capacity. But now I didn't want to just exist in his life. I wanted to live it *with* him, which was a terrifying realization.

Although it made my answer easy.

"I want you, Julian," I admitted. My voice sounded raw to my ears, but it also sounded real. "I've *been* wanting you. So now I want you to prove that you want me, too. Completely and constantly, like you claim. Not just in these moments."

Julian's lips split into a satisfied grin, reminding me how ridiculously handsome he was. "Not just in these moments?"

I'd thought that maybe he'd feel rejected by those words—that this, right now, wasn't enough for me to move forward. But he seemed giddy about it.

"It's hard to trust that things that happen at night will still feel real in the morning," I explained.

Julian nodded, taking a step back, and my body ached with the separation. He'd come back, right? He had to.

"Don't be a moonflower, Julian," I whispered.

But his grin only grew. "I won't be. I'm going to give you proof morning, noon, and night, Juni. Trust me. This is the easiest thing you've ever asked of me."

I didn't know what to say to that. I'd never witnessed Julian with this sort of elated expression on his face before, and it was leaving me speechless. He didn't seem bothered by my silence, though. Leaning forward, he gave me the briefest kiss on the forehead before striding off toward the door again.

When he reached it, he glanced back. His lips curled as he trailed his gaze over me, making me regret not kissing him when I had the chance.

"See you in the morning, Juni baby," he murmured.

And then he was gone, leaving me excited to fall asleep for the first time in a decade.

ten years ago

"Julian?"

That voice. God, I knew that voice. It washed over me, a sweet relief.

And then, there she was. Standing on two feet at the other end of the hall, though she seemed unsteady. Her eyes were wide and red and pretty. Tear tracks stained her cheeks, mixing with streaks of mascara. Her face was as messy as her hair, but fuck, I couldn't stop looking at her.

I stared, unable to even get her name out, my mouth opening and closing in shock.

What the hell was happening to me?

"Gemma's in here," she said quietly, jerking her thumb toward the hospital room.

I nodded absently, striding toward her before I could second-guess what I was doing. And then my hands were on her face, my fingers in her hair, my breath skimming the top of her head. I felt her stiffen and gasp and then momentarily melt beneath my hands.

I tipped her head back so she was looking up at me, my eyes and fingers focusing on the stitches sticking out from beneath a bandage along her hairline.

"You're hurt."

She swallowed, her throat working slowly in a way that I understood all too well. "I'm fine," she whispered. "Gemma—"

"Did you hit your head? You should sit down."

"The seat belt." She gasped as I brushed my thumb beneath her eyes, wiping the streaks of mascara away. "The seat belt cut into my forehead when the car flipped. I didn't hit my head, Julian."

Her words bounced around in my brain.

When the car flipped.

An image of it flashed before my eyes, and I didn't even realize I was gripping Juni's face too tightly until she squirmed in my grasp. I dropped my hands, balling them into my pockets instead. "What the fuck happened?"

She flinched, and I immediately regretted my tone. But I didn't know how to control the emotions tangling inside me. I didn't understand them, but I had to try.

"I hit a patch of ice when I was merging onto the highway, and it sent us flying toward the median—"

"You have to slow the fuck down, Juni," I cut in, wringing my hands anxiously in my pockets. "You have to slow down when the weather gets like this. What were the two of you even doing out?"

"I know that," she snapped, taking a step back as she glared at me. "I was taking it slow."

"Clearly, you weren't taking it slow enough," I pushed back. "Jesus Christ, look at what happened to Gemma. And you, you could have—"

I bit down on my tongue, hard enough that the taste of metallic spread through my mouth. But Juni didn't need to know how badly I'd been falling apart seconds before she called my name. She didn't need to know that I was halfway down a spiral right now. She didn't need to know anything.

I just needed her to never do that to me again.

CHAPTER TWENTY-EIGHT

I WOKE UP TO a text from Julian, and I smiled into my pillow —two events I never thought would happen.

JULIAN: Can you meet me at Georgia's before work?

Georgia's? Why?

JULIAN: I need help with something. And you said it's your favorite.

I'd told him that Georgia's was my favorite bakery once. *Once.* And he had been making fun of me during the entire conversation. How did he possibly remember that?

What time?

One glance at the clock told me that I'd already slept longer than usual, and if I planned on making a stop before work, I should leave soon.

JULIAN: I can be ready whenever.

Since when did you become an early riser?

JULIAN: Since I had a pretty girl to impress.

I stared at my phone for at least a minute, telling myself that none of this was real. Even after everything he'd said last night, this felt too much like fiction.

JULIAN: I'll see you there at 8.

Sure, it's a date.

As soon as the text entered cyberspace, I cringed and began sending a follow-up message.

Well, not a *date* date. Just a planned time and date to meet you at Georgia's, of course.

JULIAN: Of course.

JULIAN: Our first date isn't going to be a rushed bakery visit that ends with eight hours in an office. I have better plans than that. For both the date and the after-party.

You do, huh?

JULIAN: Don't act surprised. You heard me last night.

JULIAN: See you soon, Juni.

See you soon.

Oh, and Julian?

JULIAN: Yes, Juniper?

The flattery is unnecessary. You don't have to do that.

JULIAN: Oh, it's necessary. Been holding my tongue for far too long.

This time when I turned my head into the pillow, I screamed.

And then I sprinted to my shower. I had less than an hour to figure out what I would wear, and I would need every minute of it.

I took the daily event of getting dressed very seriously. Working as a woman in a male-dominated field meant that presentation was as important as anything else. A staggering number of people in this world wouldn't listen to a word out of my mouth unless they liked the lipstick on it.

However, even though I knew I should dress a certain way to be taken seriously, I struggled to do it. Office attire for women—all those pantsuits and sharp blazers—seemed like another way to perpetuate the idea that professionalism was akin to masculinity. But I found that wearing dresses with soft lines did nothing to undermine my credibility as a lawyer. I was still damn good at my job.

Today was more than just dressing for the job, and scouring my closet for the right outfit had never been more important.

A race against the clock later, I walked into Georgia's wearing one of my favorite long-sleeved wrap dresses beneath my winter coat. Julian, who was already in line, smiled when he spotted me, and I stomped my feet a little on the inside mat to knock the snow and slush off my heeled boots.

Joining him in line, I returned his smile, feeling a little shy. I didn't know how to do this, how to be around this smiley version of Julian. But luckily, he took the lead, putting a hand on the small of my back and leaning down to murmur about the menu.

"I was thinking we should bring something in to share with our colleagues today. But I wanted your opinion on what would be best. Thoughts?"

He wanted...*what*?

When all Julian did was continue to give me his pleasant smile despite my confusion, I whispered in his ear. "You hate when I bring in treats."

Julian shook his head, his smile twisting. "I hate when I have to share your attention," he corrected. "I think it's adorable and generous that you like to buy treats for the office. Decide what you want to bring in today, and I'll get it."

My mouth opened and closed, unable to process what he was saying.

"Hurry up, love." Julian gave me a little nudge as we moved closer to the counter. "It's almost our turn."

"The turnovers," I blurted out. "I've always wanted to try those."

"So you'll have one, too? Right?" Julian asked.

"I—yes."

"Good. I want it to be something that you like as well."

Without another word, Julian stepped up to the counter and ordered more apple turnovers than anyone ever needed in one morning. And not only that, but he got the *big* ones. Not the small ones I'd been eying up, but the massive ones that no one could actually eat in one sitting. And then he ushered me up to the counter beside him and asked what I wanted to drink.

"Oh, I don't really like coffee," I assured him, trying to push the question aside.

"You don't like coffee?" He stared at me. "You get coffee for everyone all the time, and you don't even..." Sighing, he broke off and ordered me a hot chocolate.

We walked out of Georgia's a few minutes later with our hands full of pastries and hot beverages.

"How did you know I liked hot chocolate?"

He shrugged. "Doesn't everyone?"

"Maybe I would have preferred tea."

He raised a brow. "Would you have?"

"No," I mumbled, staring down at my hot chocolate nestled between my mittens. Out of the corner of my eye, I saw Julian smile. "You shouldn't have bought all that," I added.

"Why not?"

"It's too much, Julian." I sighed, suddenly feeling guilty as I remembered Noah's words from last night. "I know you're saving money for Gianna's tuition."

"I am," he agreed. "But you're just as important to me, and I thought you would like it. It's just breakfast. My finances are not something you need to worry about, Juni."

I ignored the swirling heat in my stomach.

Important to me. He said I was important to him. Just as much as Gianna? That couldn't be true.

"They're just pastries. They're not important."

"I didn't say the pastries were important. I said you were." He opened the front door to our office building, letting me walk inside first. "Now, why don't you go share them with people."

I had to push down the urge to continue arguing with him about it. This was silly, all of it. And yet, I smiled. Because I did love this part of the day, connecting with everyone before they got too caught up with the stress of the job. And if I were honest...the food? It was an excuse. I wasn't always the best at knowing how to start a conversation or meet new people. But "*Hey, I brought doughnuts. Do you want one?*" worked every time.

Sure, it was bribery. But it also made other people smile, and I liked that.

I liked making other people smile.

I liked that Julian was smiling.

We were quiet on the elevator ride up to our floor, and when a ding sounded to indicate we had reached it, I glanced over at Julian.

"This was nice of you," I said. "Thank you."

He nodded, a look of ease on his face. I couldn't remember the last time I'd seen Julian acting so relaxed. I could get used to it.

Pulling off my mittens, I shoved them in my coat pockets before stepping out of the elevator. Julian seemed to think my available hand was an invitation and grabbed it as we strode across the lobby. My mind began racing into overdrive as I over-analyzed that simple hand-grab. But there wasn't any time to make conclusions about it because Julian started to slow his steps as we approached Tyler at his reception desk.

Tyler gave us a wary look as we neared, and I had to swallow a laugh.

"Morning," I said cheerily, setting my hot chocolate down to open up the box from Georgia's on the counter. "Want a turnover?"

Tyler looked from me to the box to Julian and then back to the box again. "Sure," he said slowly. "Thanks, Juniper. They look delicious."

"They're actually from Julian," I said, flashing a grin up at him. He squeezed my hand back.

"Thanks, Julian," Tyler amended, his eyes darting between us again. Confusion was written all over his face, and honestly, I understood. I was still trying to catch up to what was going on, too.

"I'm going to find Cameron," I said once we walked away from reception. "Ever since I introduced him to their muffins, he loves Georgia's."

A bit of wariness entered Julian's gaze at the mention of Cameron, but he nodded. "Okay. You don't need to tell him they're from me, you know. That's not the point."

"I know." I shrugged. "But I think he'll get a kick out of it."

Julian rolled his eyes but didn't argue.

Later that day, there were two emails in my inbox that caught my attention. I had to blink twice to make sure I wasn't seeing things because the first one was from Greg Kennedy. How he'd gotten my work email, I had no idea. But it was a congratulations on my new job, which was a little strange considering I was already a few months into working here and Greg and I didn't have that kind of relationship.

I deleted the email and moved to the one I was more interested in—the one from Julian.

Because Julian and I had spent most of our time at Gardner working on different cases, we didn't often exchange emails. For the most part, that lack of interaction had been a saving grace. But now things were different.

I glanced over my shoulder to find Julian typing away on something else and wondered what the hell this was.

I barely got to the end of the first sentence of the email before I pushed all my snacks away so I could fully concentrate.

From: julianbriggs@gardnerlaw.com
To: juniperstjames@gardnerlaw.com
Subject: Draft for HR - Please Review

Juniper,

I've drafted this email for human resources. Please let me know if you find it satisfactory or if you would like me to make any changes. It will remain a draft until you want me to send it. If you ever want me to send it.

Yours, Julian

With my heart in my throat, I read the rest of his email, which detailed how Julian and I shared a relationship that we wished to disclose to HR. It was short and to the point, but it made my pulse race.

I spun around in my chair to face him. "Julian..."

I struggled to find the words. His movements were slow as his gaze met mine, simmering with something that made my insides melt.

"There's no pressure, Juniper," he said softly. "We don't need to send it. I just wanted you to see that I'd prepared it. That I'm so fucking serious about this."

He misinterpreted my speechlessness as concern, but before I could correct him, Julian switched the topic, pulling out a stack of papers from beneath his briefcase.

"We also need to talk about how we want to move forward with Grayson. After the information I've shared with him, he's interested in pursuing the case. And that means officially approaching Gardner Law about representing him. He wants us, specifically, to do it."

Oh, look. Another thing I didn't know how to respond to. Today seemed to be full of those.

"He's a celebrity," I said, saying the first words that came to mind. "It'll be high-profile. They're going to want one of the partners to represent him. Not...us."

Meaning not two associate attorneys fresh out of law school.

"They definitely will," Julian agreed. "But Grayson tends to get what he wants, so we should get our shit together just in case."

A bit of panic rose in my throat as I thought of just how much shit we needed to *get together* if we were going to do that. "Tonight, maybe?"

Julian and I hadn't looked at Grayson's case in a few weeks because we'd been, well, avoiding each other.

"Sure. How about we work at my place?" he asked casually. "I'll cook us dinner."

"You can cook?"

"Moderately." He chuckled. "I know what you like. I'm sure I can whip up something."

I shook my head in disbelief before Julian once again added to the whirlwind.

"Cameron and I were going to grab a drink at the Bellflower after work, though," he said. "If you want, I can cancel. Or I'd love it if you joined us before we head to my place."

I twisted to face him. He was relaxed in his chair, one leg crossed over the other as he pretended that what he'd said was no big deal. But just like all the other "little" things he'd done today, it definitely wasn't.

"I don't want to intrude," I said. I meant it, too. My intent had never been to burst my way into Cameron and Julian's relationship. I was more than aware that I didn't belong there, just like I didn't belong between Noah and Julian. I liked Cameron and Noah a lot, but mostly, I'd wanted to annoy Julian. Maybe get his attention. Just maybe.

Either way, that was no longer necessary.

"You wouldn't be."

"But Cameron—"

"Already asked if you would be joining."

"He did?"

Julian raised a brow as if to say, *Are you really that surprised?* But I was, I really was.

Julian didn't say anything else. His gaze started to trail down, lingering on the bit of cleavage I'd decided to show off with this dress today. When I cleared my throat, his eyes snapped up to mine. If he was embarrassed or ashamed that he was caught, he didn't show it.

No, he was too busy watching me hungrily. Barely concealed desire flashed behind his hazy gaze, and I tried not to let my thoughts get the best of me. I tried not to remember what he said last night or what we'd done in this office. Not right now, anyway.

"We'll meet up with him after work," he said, putting an end to the moment as he gave his attention back to his computer.

I put a hand to my chest, trying to suppress what was happening inside it. But it was no use.

The office was hot the rest of the afternoon, stiflingly so, and it was a relief to get outside at the end of the day. That silly little expression had returned to Julian's face, and it stayed even as we walked into the Bellflower, grabbed drinks at the bar, and found Cameron sitting in the back.

We sat, and Julian's hand slid onto my knee beneath the table. He squeezed it before running his fingers under the hem of my dress teasingly. His touch vanished a moment later, and my skin tingled. *I* tingled—everywhere.

"Well, would you look at that," Cameron said, his cheeky grin wide. "He's smiling."

"He's been doing it all day," I laughed, trying to sound normal after what Julian just did beneath the table.

When I'd brought Cameron an apple turnover this morning and told him that Julian and I had picked them up that morning *together*, he hadn't looked surprised. Well, maybe a little bit. But not nearly as much as I'd been expecting, considering how much of our arguing he'd listened to over the last few months.

Ignoring his friend, Julian sat back in his chair, his expression unwavering. I bit down on my lip while watching Julian take a sip of his cocktail. God, the relaxed confidence in every one of his movements made my insides scream. Julian had always been attractive, but this version of him was new. And I *liked* it.

His eyes flicked to mine, catching me staring. His lips curved even more.

"I wonder why," Cameron muttered into his own drink, pulling me out of my Julian-daze. "A good night last night, huh?"

I'd picked that inopportune moment to take a drink of my Aperol Spritz, and I nearly choked on it.

But Julian popped the cherry from his drink into his mouth and smoothly answered, "You could say that. The part of it at Juni's place, at least."

Cameron's eyes widened, and I smacked Julian in the chest for putting ideas in his friend's head.

"Not like that," I hurriedly added. "Not yet."

When Cameron's brows raised, I nearly bit my tongue off. *Shit.*

"Not yet?" Cameron repeated with a tilt to his lips. His reaction made it more than clear that he was enjoying this conversation a little too much. When I refused to open my mouth again, his attention shifted to Julian. And, of course, I took that as an opportunity to also look at Julian. I'd take any opportunity I could.

Julian smirked lazily back at Cameron as his tongue toyed with a cherry stem in the corner of his mouth. His eyes slid to me.

"Not yet."

Going to Julian's apartment with alcohol—even just one drink's worth of alcohol—coursing through my veins was likely a bad idea. But I was having a hard time tearing myself away from today. And we really *should* look at Grayson's case.

With one step through the door, I realized Julian had decorated since the last time I stood here. A few family portraits were on the wall and bits of simplistic art and nice cozy touches. A candle, a blanket, a few throw pillows. Nothing over-the-top and all very monotone as far as a color scheme, but it actually looked like an adult lived here.

Julian's eyes raked over me as I stood awkwardly in the entryway to his apartment. He took my coat from me without saying a word, hanging it up before stealing one more look and breaking the silence.

"I'll go find something more comfortable for you."

"Comfortable?" I called after him.

"Your clothes," came his muffled reply.

I didn't bother telling him that dresses were by far the most comfortable article of clothing that I owned.

Julian returned a moment later. I expected him to return with some of Gemma's clothes—like he did the night we went to the New England game. But the clothes he tossed at me when coming back into the room were distinctly *Julian*.

After sneaking into the bathroom to change out of my dress, I returned to the living room wearing sweatpants and one of his old high school football sweatshirts.

Julian did a double take.

"Damn," he muttered, rubbing his jaw as he took me in. "Looks good on you. I always knew it would."

"I can't believe you hung on to this sweatshirt," I said with a light laugh.

"You think I would have ditched it before getting to see you in it?" Julian shook his head. "Nah."

Laughing with unbidden glee, I did a little twirl for him in the middle of his apartment, showing off my new look.

"I could really get used to you doing that for me," he said, his voice lowering into something that felt intimate, that brushed against my skin. "You did it that night in the hotel, too. One of my favorite fucking moments."

"I still have your shirt," I admitted, ignoring how my racing heart kept trying to force its way into my throat. "From the wedding. When you let me sleep in it."

"Keep it," he insisted. "I like to imagine you wear it sometimes."

Refusing to admit that I'd definitely worn it to bed again since the wedding, I bit down on my grin.

"Do I get to keep these, too?" I asked teasingly, gesturing at my outfit.

"If you want," Julian answered, even though I wasn't at all serious. "You look damn good in my clothes."

I let the moment linger, sweet and perfect, before I cleared my throat.

"We should get to work."

He nodded, although I thought I saw a flash of disappointment. "Why don't you pull up our notes while I start dinner. Do you want a drink? Glass of wine?"

"Maybe just one," I agreed. "I already had that drink at the bar."

"Look who's suddenly being reasonable about their alcohol intake," Julian said with a chuckle.

I tried to tame the flash of embarrassment as memories of the wedding tried to take over. "Well, I still have to make it home."

Julian shrugged, walking into the open-concept kitchen to grab a wineglass from a bar cart in the corner. "Or you could stay."

"Stay?"

"Stay." His eyes rose slowly. The glasses clinked on the granite countertops as he set them down. His voice dropped again. "I want to be around you constantly, Juniper. You can have the bed to yourself, I don't care. Just...stay."

It was hard to say no to that.

It was hard to say no when he was showing me that he wanted me.

Morning.

Noon.

And night.

nine years ago

"Julian."

I froze when someone hissed my name, swinging my head toward the door leading to Gemma's room. It was a mistake moving that quickly. The hallway spun around me, but I could still make out her face.

It was my little flower bouquet. And she was scowling at me. It was a little bit cute. She looked at me that way a lot. Maybe that was why it felt so oddly comforting. I loved how her lips drew together like that, and her jaw ticked, and eyes narrowed.

But then her face shifted—contorted. Swam, too, as I watched her expression change. It blossomed in slow motion like a time lapse.

"Are you okay?" she asked.

"I'm great, Rosie. Especially now that you're here."

I was sure she thought I meant that sarcastically, but damn, she really was a sight for sore eyes. Even if I hated to admit it.

Juni stepped out of Gemma's room, closing the door behind her until it shut with a nearly inaudible click. "What are you doing in the hallway?"

I couldn't tell her I'd stumbled up the stairs, but I also couldn't find any other words. So I just shrugged.

Her lips quirked—I could tell even in the darkness.

I was very good at paying attention to the things that mouth of hers did.

"Was that loud thump I heard just now you falling over?"

"Absolutely not." I cleared my throat. "Have you seen my coordination, Daisy? It's superior."

"Superior is not how I would describe it," she said dryly. Her eyes rolled up, and I couldn't help but smirk.

"I'll have to prove you wrong about that."

Shit, did I say that part aloud? I couldn't tell, at least not by looking at Juni's expression. It was still poised on the precipice between amused and irritated. And maybe a touch—a tiny, itty-bitty touch—of concern.

Concern? No, that must be the alcohol talking.

"You're drunk. You're not gonna remember a lick of your eighteenth birthday, Julian."

A smile tugged at my lips as I glanced over at her again.

"You sure about that, Juniper?"

She froze, eyes widening.

My brows furrowed. "What?"

She licked her lips before talking. "You said my name."

My smile broadened annoyingly. I hated not being in control of my facial features like this.

"Don't get used to it. You'll always be Daisy to me."

CHAPTER TWENTY-NINE

JUNIPER MADE ME SLEEP on the couch.

I mean, she didn't *make* me. As much as I'd wanted to crawl in beside her last night, sleeping in the same bed as Juniper was a proven form of torture. Until she was convinced of every fucking thing I said recently, I didn't trust myself that close to her.

We shouldn't be doing any of this, but I no longer cared. As hard as I tried to reason, I couldn't push Juniper away like I did when we were younger. If the last few months had taught me anything, it was that. She was there, right fucking there, and unless I changed jobs and moved out of Boston, which I really didn't want to do, that wouldn't be changing.

From the minute she walked out of the office to go on a date with Noah, I knew I wouldn't be able to do it. I couldn't sit on the sidelines and watch her live life without me. Especially when she looked so goddamn unhappy about it. It would be different if I thought she wasn't hurt, if she didn't ache just as much.

All I could do was embrace it. I pushed down all those other thoughts that had been circulating in my brain for the last decade and embraced every ounce of emotion, all of it surrounding Juniper. *Juniper.* And I came to one conclusion.

She was fucking mine.

Juniper St. James was mine; there was no denying it any longer. She thought she was Noah's to take out on a date? Never, not ever. They were both fucking around with me, and I knew it, but that didn't stop me from spiraling until I had Juniper back in my arms again. She. Was. Mine. And now I just needed her to stick around long enough so I could prove it to her.

I'd never had a problem sharing.

But sharing Juniper St. James?

Not a chance in hell would I ever be good at that.

Closing my eyes to shield the sun coming through the windows of my living room, I wondered if I'd manage to get another twenty minutes of sleep when all I could think of was how Juni was in bed less than twenty feet away. My bed. She was in my bed. And I was out here, getting a crick in my neck.

Maybe I could climb in with her, just for a few minutes. Just to savor a bit of closeness before we went to work and spent the whole day pretending that we didn't want to jump each other's—

"How's my little sleeping beauty?"

Juniper's sugary voice broke through my daydreams of crawling beneath the covers to find her warm body, and I sighed with the realization that it wouldn't happen. Not today. She was already awake—*of course* she was already awake.

"Who the hell you calling *little*, Daisy?" I muttered. She'd be eating her words soon enough. Until then, I resigned myself to reality and opened my eyes. And then nearly fell off the couch. "Jesus fuck."

"Oh, you are awake." Her smile stretched wide as she walked into my kitchen to grab a glass of water. "I thought maybe I'd need to play Prince Charming and kiss you to get you up."

I groaned, running a hand over my face. Nothing sounded better than a good-morning kiss from Juni, but if she came over here dressed like that, we probably wouldn't make it to work at all.

"I peeked into your closet," she added cheekily as if it weren't already fucking obvious. She rounded the corner of my kitchen counter, leaning on the end of it so I could get a full view of her in my college football jersey. And nothing else. In a slow, torturous movement, she set her glass of water back onto the counter before spinning. *BRIGGS*, written across the back of the blue-and-gold jersey, flashed at me.

"I'm a little sad that I never got to see you play in college," she said before flicking her long, wavy hair over her shoulder. With the small *C* on the front of my jersey showing, she added, "*Captain*."

She was trying to fucking kill me.

"Juniper," I intoned—a warning.

"Julian," she said, her voice sultry and sweet. Her eyes landed on my bare chest, dropping until they hit the blanket around my waist, which was thankfully covering a painful case of morning wood. Today, it had nothing to do with it being morning and everything to do with Juniper standing in my kitchen half-naked.

I leaned forward, pinning her with a stare so she knew how goddamn serious my next words were.

"Unless you want to lose your virginity by getting bent over my kitchen table before work, I'd suggest you go back into my room right fucking now," I said, lowering my voice and making sure it dripped with intent.

Juniper worried her bottom lip between her teeth and cocked her head to the side in consideration, but she didn't leave. She returned my look, and hers simmered.

Unable to bear it, I flung myself back onto the couch, rubbing the heel of my hands over my eyes. "What are you doing to me, Juni?" I groaned.

"Does it bother you?" she whispered.

"Bother me?" I pinched the bridge of my nose. "When you tease the hell out of me? Yes, yes it—"

"No," she cut me off. "Not that."

Her voice didn't have that heat that I just saw in her gaze, and it forced me to open my eyes again.

"That I've never—" She glanced away.

"No." I shook my head as I understood, and then I kept shaking it, pushing myself up. "*Fuck* no."

Juniper still wasn't looking at me. So I ignored any sense of reasoning—a common trend these days—and rolled off the couch to close the distance between us.

"I'm obsessed," I emphasized, which got her attention. Her eyes snapped to me, widening when she realized I was walking toward her with clear intentions. I needed her body against mine, and then I got it. My fingers tangled into her hair at the nape of her neck, and I yanked down, forcing her to look up at me and listen to every word I was about to say. She gasped, and the heat was back. "I'm beyond obsessed with the idea that no one else has fucking touched you like I plan to."

Juniper's eyes did the talking as she searched my face for any indication that I was telling the truth. But all of it was so goddamn true. I still couldn't believe it, that she hadn't been with anyone else.

"I'm a selfish man, Juniper," I murmured, "and you made my goddamn year with that news."

She frowned. "You're not selfish."

"Oh, I am with you. Haven't you figured that out by now?" Giving in to temptation, I whispered a kiss over her forehead. "I get grumpy when I have to share you with others, and I've been doing it my whole life. So now..."

"So now?" Juni repeated when I didn't finish my sentence.

"Now I can't stop thinking about getting a part of you all to myself." I sighed, knowing I needed to stop this conversation before I got carried away. "But I know I won't get it this morning, so I need you to give me a goddamn break."

Juniper's lips curved, her expression now sparkling and satisfied. "Do you really think you deserve a break, Julian Briggs?"

Goddamn her. "I'm sure I don't."

She shrugged, and I released my hold on her hair, trailing my fingers down her neck in a soft caress. "Yesterday was a good day," she said, shivering a bit. "I'll give you that."

That was an understatement, in my opinion. Everything from the morning together to the drinks after work to us staying up late working on Grayson's case was good. *Great.* I wanted days like that every day now.

"But you don't have to do all that, you know," she added.

"All what?"

"The food, the drinks, the sweet talk, everything. I appreciate the effort, but I just want you for who you are, Julian."

"And you have me."

Her shine dulled just a bit when she looked up at me. Disbelief still touched her irises, making me want to punch something. Of course I knew it would take more than one day to erase years of being a shithead. Of course she thought I was acting yesterday when in reality, it felt freeing. But it still hurt to see.

"We need to get ready," I said, accepting that I wouldn't be able to change how Juni felt in the next ten minutes. "Go change, and we'll stop by your place on the way to work."

Juniper began walking backward toward my bedroom. Her sly grin reappeared. "You mean you don't think I should wear this to work?"

"It's up to you." I shrugged, returning her smirk. "It's your virginity at risk."

"You just really love football, don't you?" she said with a laugh. "It does it for you, huh?"

"It has nothing to do with football," I said, shoving my hands in the pockets of my sweatpants as I watched her dance away from me. "And everything to do with seeing you wear my name."

She paused by the bathroom door, seeming reluctant to step inside and separate again. She didn't want to admit how much she liked hearing me say shit like that, but she did—I could tell. It gave me hope, and I decided to capitalize on that.

"You're right that I never accepted you like the rest of my

family did," I said. "I never wanted to hurt you, Juniper. It's just that this...this was the only kind of Briggs I wanted you to be."

"And what kind is that?"

I swept my gaze up and down her body one last time, memorizing how she looked in my jersey.

"The kind that's mine."

TAKING JUNIPER'S FEEDBACK, I SPENT THE NEXT WEEK AND A HALF GIVING her as much genuine attention as I could. I didn't pile on the sweets or the sweet-talking, even though I would have been more than happy to do it, and instead focused on proving to her that we could more than just exist in our office together.

I worked on proving it to myself, too. I could do this; I could be an excellent employee while also giving my all to the pretty associate attorney sitting next to me. This would work. If growing up with so many sisters had taught me anything, it was how to efficiently divide my energy so everyone got the most out of me and I could be there for them all. This was basically the same, wasn't it? I could do it.

Part of the problem, of course, was that I didn't want to divide any of my time with Juniper. I'd much rather talk to her than discuss cases with my colleagues. I'd much rather talk to her than do just about anything. But actually working at work was somewhat unavoidable. Unfortunately.

I smiled, watching as Juniper chatted on the phone in Spanish with a client. Her voice was warm, and I just knew whoever she was talking to had to feel like they were in trustworthy, caring hands. Juniper wasn't just good at her job because she was smart and tactical about law; she was also incredibly good at building personal relationships. She was a whole goddamn treasure.

As soon as she hung up the phone, I seized the opportunity.

"Juni baby."

She froze. Her eyes flicked over her shoulder, flying to the door, which was open. And then a surprising scowl appeared as she turned to face me.

"Someone's going to hear you call me that," she hissed.

I took a sip of my coffee before grunting, "Good."

Everyone in this office loved Juniper. No surprise, honestly. But some people loved Juniper a little too much. And the faster they got the picture of what was going on, the better.

"Good?" Juniper repeated. "You haven't sent that HR email yet, Mr. Briggs."

"Just waiting for your approval, Ms. St. James."

"Well, it's not like we're dating," she said with a little sniff as she spun back toward her desk. "I can't help but notice that you haven't bothered to ask me out."

She always did know just how to test me.

"You haven't bothered to give me any indication if that's what you're ready for," I said, lowering my voice. "I figured you'd need a little time to decide if I'm even worth it after, you know, everything."

"Oh, is that what you're waiting for? An indication? Generally, if you want to know the answer to something, you ask." She started typing as if we weren't in the middle of a conversation that I considered extremely important. "It's called communication, Julian."

I shook my head as I tried not to glare at the back of hers. Half of Juni's hair was pinned up with one of her bows, but it was smaller than usual. I sort of missed the big ones. "I think you just like fucking with me, Juniper."

"No, that's not true."

"It's not?"

"No." She grinned over her shoulder, looking at me beneath sooty lashes. "I *love* fucking with you."

God, she drove me wild.

"Juni," I said, "are you ready for me to ask you out?"

Her fuck-me eyes vanished, and she lifted one shoulder with a shy expression instead. "I suppose it wouldn't hurt for you to ask, would it?"

I smiled. "I'll keep that in mind."

"But maybe we should focus on getting through this weekend first," she added. "Assuming you're okay with me coming."

My thoughts momentarily raced as I reentered reality and remembered I had more obligations in life than Juni and work.

Christmas. Our annual family Christmas party was this weekend, and wait, what did she just—

"Okay with you coming?" I frowned. "Juni, please don't say things like that. I want you there." When all she did was blink at me with those big, brown eyes, I sighed. "My sisters would kill me if you weren't there, but even more than that, I would miss you. A lot."

She nodded, but the hesitation couldn't have been clearer. "I'm sorry. It's just still a little hard for me to wrap my head around, I guess."

I should have known that no matter how many ways I showed her that I wanted to be around her, going back home would still cause feelings like this to pop up. I could prove to her that I wanted to share an office because we'd only existed in this space for a few months. But proving to her I wanted to share my childhood home after years of making her believe otherwise?

"Fuck." I started to push out of my chair and then stopped, remembering our office door was open. So I tried to touch her with my eyes instead. "Juni, I'm sorry I couldn't handle being around you and I made you think that was your fault. It was my fault. I took out the hate I had for myself on you. But you should know that you belong at my house on Christmas."

"Okay," she whispered. "Have you said anything to Gemma about...all of this?"

I shook my head. "I didn't want to bring anything up without your permission, but just say the word, and I'll tell her everything."

I wasn't looking forward to that conversation, but I knew it would have to happen at some point if I wanted to keep both of them—something I was determined to do, even though I was worried as all hell about it.

"Okay, Julian." She seemed more sure of herself, but not by much. "Maybe we should focus on getting through this weekend first," she repeated. "Before talking to Gemma."

"Sure."

I didn't mind that Juniper wanted to wait to say anything to Gemma. But this woman had slept in my bed more than once in the last couple of weeks. My bed smelled like flowers. *Flowers.* And I shamefully loved it. She walked around my apartment wearing nothing but my jersey to tease the hell out of me. She ate dinner on my couch before cuddling up next to me and asking to watch my old college football games.

And now I was supposed to spend Christmas pretending I didn't desperately want her.

How the fuck was I supposed to do that?

nine years ago

"So, did you get everything off your wish list?" I asked.

The living room was dark except for the twinkle of the Briggs' tree lights. I didn't expect anyone to be down here when I came to grab a glass of water.

But of course he was.

"Well," Julian drawled, "I haven't figured out a way to escape you yet, so..."

I rolled my eyes, trying to push aside his teasing.

"Just for that comment, I'll make sure to haunt you even once you leave for college."

He sighed, bright eyes flicking up to mine.

"I'm sure you will, Rosie."

CHAPTER THIRTY

juniper

GEMMA WALKED INTO MY apartment in a whirlwind, her red hair flying behind her as if caught in a breeze. She squealed when she saw me all packed and ready to go for the weekend, and I held out the sugared-up holiday drink I got for her at Georgia's after work.

"Julian isn't here yet, is he?" she asked, scoping out my apartment—which was definitely small enough to check with one quick look around.

Julian, Gemma, and I made plans to drive to Whitebridge together. They would drop me off at my parents' tonight so I could spend time with them, and then we had the Christmas party tomorrow. Since Julian and I both had to grab our bags from home after work and Gemma had skating practice, we decided to meet at my place before heading out.

"If Julian was here, he would already be pushing us out the door," I laughed, my stomach turning as I thought of times Julian *had* been here that Gemma didn't know about. Including when he'd trapped me against my kitchen counter and whispered toe-curling words I was still digesting.

Gemma nodded as if to acknowledge the truth of what I'd said before she dropped onto the barstool, leaning her elbows on my kitchen island. "Thank God. I feel like we haven't been able to catch up in so long. I want all the details of the wedding like *now*. Hurry, before he comes."

She was right. We hadn't been able to properly hang out for weeks, and a bit of guilt tinted my mood because I knew it was partly due to how consumed I'd been with work and Julian these last weeks. But it was also because Gemma was out of town for a week for a competition and then training really hard with her team when she was in town. Plus, when we saw each other at Thanksgiving, it had been hard to actually talk with the other Briggs sisters there.

"It was good," I said honestly. Considering everything that had happened since, the wedding seemed ages ago.

"Good?" Gemma repeated. "That's what you told me on the phone, but I thought there'd at least be *something* else to spill."

I laughed. "I don't know! Sofia was a gem. She was really sweet, and I'm glad I went so I could finally meet her. I feel like we come from different worlds, but maybe one day, we'll exist in the same one."

Gemma tipped her head to the side, sipping her drink while she thought. "I think you could," she said after a moment. "If that's what you want."

"It would be nice," I said quietly. "But for some reason, I thought I'd feel different after meeting her, and I don't, really."

I felt different since the wedding, but it didn't have anything to do with Sofia.

"And Julian?" Gemma probed, right on track with my thoughts.

"He was..." I cleared my throat. "He was surprisingly a gentleman."

"A gentleman?" Gemma repeated, clearly in disbelief. Her tone hinted at something else, too, but I couldn't place it.

I nodded, daring to smile a bit, even though it would confuse the hell out of Gemma. Oh, well. She should probably start getting used to it. Every day, I grew increasingly attached to the idea that Julian was real. *We* were real.

"Yeah," I said. "Don't tell him I admitted this, but he was really nice about the whole thing."

Gemma narrowed her eyes. "Nice?"

My grin widened. "Yeah. Nice."

The Briggs family always spent the week of Christmas on Cape Cod, where Gemma's grandparents lived. Aunts, uncles, cousins—they all joined in one hoopla of merriment.

The weekend *before* Christmas, they celebrated in Whitebridge. Jenny and John, Julian, Gemma, Janie, Josie, Gianna, Genevieve...and me, Juniper.

We called it a party because we made it one. We always dressed up, drank wine from the crystal glasses that only got used once a year, and sloppily sang Christmas carols while Josie played the piano. She wasn't very good, but then again, neither were we.

Christmas was the highlight of my year. Because after I celebrated with the Briggs family, I got to do it all over again with my own. A two-in-one special.

But while the Briggs family Christmas was an annual tradition, this one managed to hold a lot of firsts for me. The first time I was nervous about going to the Briggs' house. The first time I sat in my bedroom at my parents' house beforehand, obsessing over what to wear. The first time I felt guilty because of what I wasn't telling Gemma.

Janie and Gianna crowded me as soon as I walked through the door, followed by Genevieve and Josie, giving hugs and performing choruses of holiday greetings. But as happy as I was to see them, my eyes scanned the surroundings for one Briggs in particular.

Julian hung back, leaning with one shoulder against the wall in the foyer of their old Victorian home. A black sweater clung to his athletic frame, making his hair stand out in contrast even in the dim lighting, candlelight flicking up the walls.

His lips tilted up in a half-smile, but his eyes...God, his eyes watched my every movement as I shrugged off my coat. They appraised my velvety emerald-green dress and black, polka-dotted tights. They studied me over the rim of his glass as he sipped from what I could only assume was a beer, likely a cheap one.

Finally, Julian pushed off the wall, and all of his sisters' chattering voices muted, dying down until all I could hear was my heartbeat as Julian approached.

I didn't think I could do this. Who would have thought that pretending *not* to like Julian would be more challenging than pretending to like him had been at the wedding? Maybe it was because I hadn't needed to pretend much at all.

"Hey, Rosie," he said, sounding all beautifully gruff. "I can take your coat."

"Look at you being a gentleman," Gemma said, elbowing her brother as I tried to ignore how Julian's fingers brushed over mine when taking my coat from me.

Julian rolled his eyes up but otherwise ignored his sister before walking away with my coat. So I leaned in, grabbing Gemma's arm and muttering, "Told you."

"I've yelled at him a lot lately for acting like an ass toward you," she murmured back, walking us into the house. "Maybe some of it finally got through his thick skull."

"Maybe," I agreed. "I think he's trying harder now that we have to work together."

It wasn't a lie.

But it also wasn't the truth, and I hated not being completely honest with Gemma. Yesterday in the car, both Julian and I had been quiet, barely interacting. This was hard to navigate, and I didn't like it.

"I was hoping something like that might happen when you

both started at Gardner." Gemma glanced sideways at me. "Maybe now we can all coexist peacefully."

I gritted my teeth, wondering if Julian and I dating would help or hurt Gemma's dream of coexisting. Worry swirled in my gut.

It stayed there, in the pit of my stomach, all through dinner, causing my appetite to dwindle, even though the au gratin potatoes Jenny prepared looked amazing. I took small bites and pushed my food around on my plate until I felt a shiver run up my spine and glanced over to see Julian staring at me from the far end of the table.

"You okay?" he mouthed, his brows furrowed.

No, I wasn't okay. Everything was utterly the same yet completely different, and I didn't know what to think.

Around us, Josie explained her latest musical while everyone piped in with commentary about the plot, and suddenly, I understood. I understood why Julian was afraid to change the dynamic we had existed in for so long. This was his home, his family, where things had always been a certain way, reliable and consistent and wonderful.

But while I worked through that dawning sensation for the first time, Julian stared at me with such sureness. He wasn't paying attention to Josie or his mom asking for the dates of her opening night or Gianna's under-the-breath teasing of her sister's butchered audition for the main role that she didn't get.

He was waiting for me to answer him.

He was waiting.

For me.

Maybe changing the status quo wasn't so bad. Not when it meant feeling tingly in all of my limbs.

I nodded at Julian, giving him a slight smile, but he didn't look away. Even once I dropped my gaze and took a bite of my potatoes—a bigger bite this time—I felt his eyes on me. They didn't leave, not through all of dinner, and when everyone started clearing the plates, I brushed up against Julian as he stood from his spot.

"You have to stop looking at me," I hissed.

"How? I don't know how, Juni," he murmured before clearing his voice and talking normally as he took my plate from me. "Here, I'll clear that for you."

Unable to find any words, I let Julian take my dishes, noticing how he once again tried to prolong the minimal contact between our bodies when his fingers brushed mine.

God, I wasn't going to make it through tonight.

When we moved into the living room to huddle around a colorfully lit, eclectically decorated Christmas tree, I made damn sure to stay clear of Julian. He seemed to be of the same thinking, sitting in a lone armchair near the front picture window. Snow drifted down behind him, and the glow of the streetlamps outside gave him an angelic quality.

Not that I would ever describe Julian that way, although he *was* acting sweet tonight.

I curled up next to Gemma on the couch, watching the proceedings as Josie shoved a Santa hat on Genevieve's head so she could dole out the presents as she usually did. But not, of course, before she snapped a few pictures—some of her and Josie and then some of Gemma and me. Genevieve had always loved photography and photo editing, but lately, she seemed to be taking it seriously and producing amazing results.

A quick glance at Julian left me with a feeling of warmth as he smiled at his sisters. His mom walked over, perching herself on the arm of the chair he sat in. Jenny placed a hand on his shoulder, and he reached up to give it a squeeze before she drifted off to sit next to his dad on the love seat.

I felt that squeeze around my heart. This was *his* family, and maybe I was wrong not to give him and them more space growing up. For crying out loud, it was Christmas, and I knew every one of his family traditions. But Gemma had always insisted, and so did Jenny, John, and all the other girls. So I never stopped to consider how it was perfectly fair for Julian not to want me here. Except now I knew that wasn't entirely the truth, and if the way he kept looking at me meant anything, it definitely wasn't true tonight.

Any remaining doubts I had of that vanished when Gen's surprised and curious voice read, "To Juniper. From...Julian."

Sitting next to the tree, she stared at the present, a midsized box wrapped in candy-cane-striped paper, before lifting her head to look from me to Julian and back again.

"You bought Juniper a present?" she finally asked, staring straight at her brother.

Julian's response was cut off by the rest of his sisters chiming in.

"You never buy Juni a present." Gianna sounded just as confused as Genevieve.

"This better not be a prank gift, Julian."

That was Gemma.

"Oh my *God*, what is it?"

Josie pitched forward onto the balls of her feet, squatting on the opposite side of the couch so she could see over the rest of her family as Gen handed me the gift.

I stared at it, feeling like breaths were hard to take.

That sounded dramatic; it was just a gift on Christmas, a day when gifts were the norm, and it was probably a small one at that. But while his sisters always went in on a gift for me and his parents always gave me something small, Julian had never, ever put anything under the tree with my name on it. This candy-cane-striped package meant more than I knew how to put into words.

"It's not a prank, Gemma." Julian's drawl extended across the room. "It's just something I thought she would like."

Something I would like? I didn't know what it could be, but suddenly, I couldn't wait to find out. I ripped into the package with probably too much eagerness, letting the wrapping paper fall to the floor with the rest of the mess littering the hardwood.

After slicing through the tape on a slightly battered cardboard box, I opened it to find another box inside.

"I thought you needed better ones." The humor in Julian's voice made me crack, a slight laugh releasing from my own lips. There were headphones—the padded, nice kind that would actually keep my sound from leaking out when I was listening to things I probably shouldn't be listening to at work. "There's more," Julian added.

More?

Sure enough, when I looked back at the tissue-paper-filled box, a book stared up at me, and this time, I gasped.

"How did you get this?" I asked in awe, picking up the fifth and final book in a series I'd been reading. I turned it over to admire the cover art, front and back. "It was only just released, like, yesterday."

When Julian didn't reply right away, I glanced over at him. He was fighting a smile and eventually managed a slight shrug. "I preordered it."

"You preordered it," Gemma deadpanned next to me.

"Yes, I preordered it. I knew Juni was reading that series, and I preordered the next book so it would be here for Christmas," Julian replied, keeping his voice even.

When all his sisters stared at him silently for a few seconds, he threw his hands up in exasperation.

"It took three clicks on my phone. Stop looking at me like I flew across the country to hand-select it."

"Yeah, but—"

"Thank you," I said, cutting Gemma off. I crossed my legs, resisting the urge to fly to the other side of the room and kiss him in front of his entire family. "Thank you for this."

"You're welcome," Julian said with a simple nod.

There wasn't anything simple about the look on his face, though. He looked just as eager for that kiss as I was, making it much harder to stay put in my seat.

"Well." Genevieve cleared her throat. "On to the next present."

I sat, clasping my new book in my hands, as Gemma opened a

present from her parents. I tried to wipe the smile off my face, but it was really, really hard. In fact, it was *so* hard to act normal that when Gianna started unwrapping an odd-shaped package from Janie, I gave up and excused myself to use the bathroom.

I closed myself inside it, leaning against the door and letting my lips spread wide.

He meant it, didn't he? All of his words and promises and declarations. He's meant them. He wanted me here.

When there was a knock at the door, followed by Julian's low voice calling my name, my breath hitched. Before I could overthink it, I opened the door, grabbed him by the front of his black sweater, and hauled him into the bathroom. Julian gasped my name, but he didn't get any other words out before I shut him up with a kiss.

It was *my* turn for that, and I intended to do it even better than he had.

Julian melted beneath my mouth, molding to me as he groaned into the kiss, eager and desperate to return it. *God*, I'd missed this, missed feeling like we were both going to lose it unless we got another taste of each other.

I knocked Julian back into the closed bathroom door, wrapping my arms around his neck and letting my fingers sift into his gingery hair. Julian fumbled with the lock before his hands landed on the small of my back, holding me tight to his body.

We fit together so perfectly. Having him like this, feeling him everywhere, spurred me on. I knew I should stop, but I also knew I wouldn't be able to. Abandoning reason was the only option at this point.

I pressed my lips to his harder, coaxing them open so I could taste him. Julian's fingers dug into my back as our tongues twisted, and then his hands fell lower and lower, sneaking beneath my dress until he was cupping my ass. I suddenly wished I wasn't wearing tights, wanting to feel his hands on my skin. But even through the tights, Julian's touch set me on fire, and when he gave my rear a little squeeze, I groaned.

Julian mumbled for me to be quiet. He said it so sweetly, though, that it barely registered. And when he bit down on my lip, I gasped even louder.

"*Juniper.*"

The way he growled my name caused heady awareness to zip through me. *Right.* Right, we were in a bathroom. On Christmas. At his parents' house. Shit.

"Do you think they'll realize?" I muttered between kisses.

Julian shook his head and responded in short sentences while trying to keep his mouth on mine. "They were done with gifts. Everyone's cleaning up. No one noticed that I left."

"Good." I pressed my smile against Julian's mouth, and it seemed to transfer. I felt his lips curve beneath mine before he cupped my cheek and deepened the kiss again. His lips roved over mine, exploring.

"God, Juni." He breathed his words against my mouth while sliding his fingers down my jaw to grip my chin. "Please don't make me go that long without kissing you ever again."

"Ever again, huh?"

"Ever." He brushed his lips over mine once. "Again." And then once more before asking huskily, "Did you like your present?"

I would have thought that the answer to that was obvious, considering how wildly we were kissing, but I obliged him by nodding. "I loved my present. I wished I'd known you were doing that so I could have gotten you something, too."

His smile caressed mine as he replied. "There's only one thing on my wish list this year, and you can still give it to me."

Badly wanting to make Julian as happy as he made me, I perked up. He noticed, and a rough little laugh hit my lips before he pulled back, eyes wandering my face like he was memorizing the moment.

"Juni baby..." He paused, releasing his grip on my ass to reach up and touch something on the top of my head. It wasn't until I felt a little tug that I realized he was readjusting the bow in my hair. Then his gaze dropped to mine, and it shone with a thousand holiday lights. "Can I have a date for Christmas? I want to take you out."

On the inside, I squealed. But on the outside, I kissed him tenderly before whispering against his lips. "You can have as many dates as you like, Julian."

"Thank fucking God." Julian crashed his lips into mine, transitioning our kiss from sweet to passionate and needy. He cupped me in his hands again, lifting until nothing remained between us, and I felt everything. *Everything.* His erection pressed into my stomach, flooding me with forbidden desire.

This shouldn't be happening. Not when the only thing that separated us from the rest of the Briggs family was this bathroom door. But I couldn't stop. I couldn't pull away until I'd given him something. Something he could have *now.*

"But that won't be for a while, will it?" I breathed, kissing down Julian's neck. He tipped his head back, letting it hit the bathroom door with a light knock and a rumble from his throat. "Our date won't be until we get back to Boston. What about tonight?"

"Tonight?" he grumbled, no longer paying attention to what I was saying and focusing more on how I sucked that spot on his neck where I could feel his pulse beneath his hot skin. So I lowered slowly down his body, dragging my fingertips over his chest, wanting to clarify what I meant.

"Tonight, Julian." I hooked one finger into the waistband of his pants and used another to trace the outline of his growing erection. "I want to give you something tonight."

Although, it was for me just as much as him. He didn't let me last time, and I hadn't quite gotten over that rejection.

"Holy—" Julian looked down at me, clearly comprehending but glitching internally at what to do about it. "But you—I want—"

"I want to, tonight. Me first," I said, repeating my words from that night in our office. I was on my knees now, grateful for the fluffy bathroom mat beneath me as I tugged at Julian's belt because I knew we didn't have much time. "Please."

A smirk pulled slowly onto his expression. "Did I just hear that correctly?" His voice was husky and soft now, his eyes no longer blue and bright but midnight and deep. "Was that Juniper St. James begging for my cock?"

"I'm not begging." With Julian's belt undone, I hastily unbuttoned his pants and yanked down the zipper. "I'm asking nicely. That's what people do when they want something, remember?"

"You want it?" he asked, his bottom lip gliding through his teeth.

I stroked my fingers over the fabric of his briefs, harder this time. Julian shivered. "I want it, Julian."

"It's yours."

He spoke those words so firmly, so calmly, that my heart flipped. And then Julian kept talking in that low voice of his, and that tingling sensation in my chest spread to the rest of me.

"You know that sound you make when you nibble on the little treats you bring into work?" Julian watched as I pulled down his waistband, and then he grabbed his hard length himself, fisting it. He was...oh, *God.* "I want you to make that sound when I hit the back of your throat."

"Well, you *have* been a good boy lately. So I suppose..." I licked his tip as he held it out for me, not tearing my gaze from his face while I did.

I wanted to see his expression, and I wasn't disappointed. The muscles in his face ticked, and his breathing came faster as I wrapped my hand around his cock, taking his place so his hand could wind its way into my hair instead. I let Julian guide me, gradually taking in more and more of him until my mouth was stuffed full, and Julian's eyes were blazing hot as he watched.

And then I sucked, and Julian lost it. His eyes squeezed shut, jaw clenching, fist tightening around my hair. "Jesus fucking Christ, Juniper."

His reaction spurred me on, sliding my lips up and down his

length while twisting around his base with my hand. He was so hot and hard while his skin was so soft, and I moaned with the satisfaction of it all.

"That's it, love," Julian muttered, his lips twisting. He liked that, liked hearing me and feeling me around him. He let loose his own groan, one that I knew he'd been trying to hold in for the sake of being quiet. But he was struggling with any sort of control, and my pulse raced faster at seeing it.

I wanted to make Julian Briggs fall apart. I wanted to drive him past his breaking point. And he was close to it.

"I'm not gonna last," he grunted through heavy breaths. They were coming quicker and quicker as I sucked harder and faster. His voice remained quiet and hoarse. "Oh, *fuck*, Juni. I promise... when it's for you, I'll do better, longer. But you look so goddamn beautiful on your knees taking me like that. You don't even realize, do you? You don't even realize how impossible you make it for me. This whole night, I've been wondering why you have to be so fucking pretty."

His grip tightened on my hair, and I smiled around his cock, looking up at him through watery eyes and feeling more empowered than ever before despite being down on my knees.

My own body ached in ways I'd never experienced, but it wasn't like with other guys, like when I'd wanted this step to be over so it could be my turn for some sort of lackluster relief. No, this *was* the main event. This was all I wanted right now.

Julian's lips pressed together as he tried to contain himself, and I decided right then and there that nothing would ever be hotter than Julian trying to stay quiet while he neared climax. His eyes drilled into mine, never breaking as I licked the underside of his cock before sucking him as deep as I could manage, gagging slightly at how thick he was in the back of my throat.

That seemed to do it for Julian. He said my name in a clipped sort of way that I understood to be a warning I didn't care about or need, and then he shot his release down my throat, tipping his head back so I could watch the veins in his neck strain with the cry he was holding in.

I swallowed, licked my lips, and then stood before Julian had a chance to recover.

"Merry Christmas, Julian," I whispered, pressing a light kiss to his lips.

I tried to step away, conscious that we'd been in this bathroom too long. But Julian caught me around the waist before I could escape. He dropped his forehead to mine, still trying to slow his breathing.

"That was incredible. How about you accidentally fall asleep in the wrong bed again tonight?" I heard the smile in his voice. "I want to go down on you until you scream into my pillow to stay quiet."

As if I hadn't already been wildly aroused, now I could feel my heartbeat between my legs.

But I couldn't stay in his room tonight, and I couldn't stay in this bathroom a moment longer. Not if we didn't want to get caught.

"I'm going home soon," I whispered regretfully. "I wasn't planning on staying over. I shouldn't."

Julian grunted, not liking that answer. "Let me drive you home, then."

I shook my head. "How would you explain that to Gemma?"

"I already told her I'm trying to make up for Thanksgiving. That's how I explained the present."

"We shouldn't push it, Julian," I sighed.

"It might be too late for that," he muttered, reaching between us to readjust his pants.

I laughed, but Julian caught my laugh with a kiss. It was a short kiss, but when he broke away, his words were as soft and tender as a million kisses.

"Merry Christmas, Juniper."

And then he disappeared, shutting the door behind him

because we obviously didn't both want to leave at the same time. I took a moment to look at myself in the mirror while I waited, fixing my hair and the straps on my dress. Thinking that enough time had passed for it not to be suspicious, I went to open the door.

And a second later, I was face-to-face with John Briggs.

"Oh, Juniper." He cleared his throat. "I'm sorry, I thought I just saw Jul—"

He stopped, his brows furrowing, and I could practically see the gears grinding in his head. He looked over his shoulder, but I couldn't tell what at because most of his body blocked the view. John was a tall, broad guy—a bigger, huskier version of Julian.

When he faced me again, he sighed. But there was a slight smile in that sigh. "Christ, it's about goddamn time he got his head out of his ass."

My brows shot up. "I—"

"If he doesn't treat you like a fucking queen, you let me know," John cut in, his expression stern but his eyes soft. "And give him hell if he deserves it."

Feeling bewildered about this entire interaction, I could barely muster a nod. "I always do."

He chuckled at that. "I know. It's why you're perfect."

John moved to the side so I could slip past him, but as soon as I started moving, my senses returned to me. I looked up at the tallest Briggs. "Could you maybe not say anything to...anyone? We haven't exactly—"

Mr. Briggs put his hand up. "That's one thing your dad and I don't have in common, Juniper. I'm not one for gossip," he said before winking.

I gave him a grateful grin before making a quick exit, trying not to think about how Julian's dad damn near caught us hooking up in the bathroom. I couldn't decide if I was mortified or relieved. His reaction only reaffirmed what I'd thought this entire time: the Briggs family wouldn't care if I started dating Julian.

But I supposed we'd find out for sure soon. Although not soon enough for my liking. Julian and the rest of the family would leave tomorrow to visit their extended family, and I'd spend the rest of the holidays at home with mine. Which meant I had to wait over a week before I'd get to see him again.

I didn't like that.

I did like what I had to look forward to when we both returned to Boston, though.

A date.

CHAPTER THIRTY-ONE

julian

MY GRANDPARENTS LIVED ON Cape Cod, and spending the week of Christmas here every year was a tradition I'd always loved. There was just something about removing yourself from everything and everyone except for who and what really mattered.

But this year, there was someone I *didn't* want to be removed from, someone who *did* matter who wasn't here, and it wasn't hard to figure out why I felt so off.

I found a quiet spot to sit by the massive fir Christmas tree—the same one my mom had scolded her parents about as soon as we'd arrived. One of them would get hurt one of these days if they weren't careful. Which they weren't.

I stared at my phone, wondering what Juniper was doing. It felt wrong that she had to work without me. But besides spending Christmas Eve and Day with her parents, she'd never traveled much over the holidays. There was no real reason for her to take off the week between Christmas and New Year's. I probably shouldn't have taken off either; a mountain of work would be waiting for me when I got back. But I wanted to prioritize this time with my family.

Nothing felt right, though. This week, it hadn't felt right.

I was more than aware that Juniper was an intelligent, capable woman. However, that didn't mean I liked the idea of her walking around Boston by herself, especially at night. Before leaving Whitebridge, I gave her a set of my apartment keys while ignoring her arguments that I was skipping like ten relationship steps. My apartment was way closer to the office than hers was, but I worried she'd be too stubborn to actually stay there...until I got a text that she was tucked into my bed with a glass of wine and a book. Then she teased me about the things we could do in that bed if I were there, and just thinking about what she said caused me to groan and shift in my chair.

I shouldn't be thinking about Juniper right now. Mostly because I was sitting in my grandparents' living room, but I could also hear my sister laughing with my cousins in the kitchen, and here I was, thinking about how badly I wanted her best friend. Her best friend, who was *in my bed* at this very moment.

My sheets were going to smell like flowers when I got home, and I couldn't fucking wait.

My eyes fluttered shut as I tried to imagine anything that wasn't Juniper lying in my bed with her hands between her legs —like she'd hinted at in her texts. Or how fucking fantastic she'd looked with her lips wrapped around my cock.

When that was unsuccessful, I returned to my phone. I was addicted to talking to her.

Any big plans for New Year's Eve tonight?

DAISY: Excuse me, reading in bed with a glass of wine *is* a big plan.

I chuckled, but my smile immediately faded when Juni sent a follow-up text.

DAISY: But Greg Kennedy did text me to see if I wanted to get a drink. So I'm considering that.

No, you're not.

She was doing it again. She was messing with me and was *way* too good at it. I could practically feel my blood pressure rising even though I knew there was no way that comment was serious.

DAISY: I'm not. Considering it, that is. He did text me.

I gritted my teeth, wondering if I could telepathically break more of Kennedy's fingers so he couldn't text anyone ever again.

Block him. Right now, Juni.

DAISY: Hmm, I'll think about it.

Juniper.

DAISY: I already blocked him, Julian.

She followed that text up with a kissing emoji, and a rueful smile sprang to my lips.

A shuffling of feet on the opposite side of the room forced me to put my phone down, which was likely for the best, considering I wanted to throw it across the room at the thought of Greg Kennedy getting anywhere even close to Juniper.

A second later, my dad stood next to me, drinking out of a mug. I knew it was bold, black coffee even though it was early evening.

"Something on your mind?" I asked when he didn't say anything.

He chuckled. "I was going to ask you the same thing."

I shook my head, not able to divulge that information. My dad and I were close, but not close enough to share dirty secrets or murder plans.

"Something got you down?" he asked.

It was hard to say yes or no to that. I wasn't down, not really. I was with my family in one of my favorite places in the world. I had the career I'd always wanted. I had a date lined up with Juniper St. James. How could I be down about any of that? I was living the life that I'd spent years dreaming about. Some of it, I hadn't even *dared* to dream about.

"Not down, no," I said. "Just...off."

My dad nodded. "It's a weird feeling," he commented.

He was being really fucking vague, and yet it *was* a weird feeling, whatever I was going through.

"What is?"

Maybe he could clarify it for me.

"When that feeling of home transitions from a place to a person, and then they aren't there."

I reeled back, absorbing his words. And holy shit, they were true.

"I don't even know how this happened," I groaned. "It's ridiculous, Dad. I used to love coming here because she *wasn't* here and I could finally breathe. And now..."

Juni told me about her encounter with my dad at the Christmas party, so I knew he knew. But we hadn't actually talked about it. I'd hardly admitted any of this aloud to anyone. After all, I'd kept all my feelings about Juniper hidden for so long that I'd convinced myself they weren't real. But now, the truth was impossible to ignore, and I found it incredibly hard to keep to myself.

"It's not ridiculous." My dad shrugged, unfazed by my admittance. "I'm not sure why you're still here, to be honest."

"What?" I jerked my head back, looking up at him in confusion.

"Did you think your mom and I expected that all of you kids would be making these trips with us forever?" He grinned—well, it was a grin for him. It probably wouldn't seem like a smile to most people, but I knew better. "You've done a lot for this family, Julian. But your mom and I also want you to have your own, and you can't make that happen sitting around here with us. It's okay to live your life, too."

Speechless, I stared at my dad. And when I couldn't find any words, he sighed.

"I should have told you that sooner, years ago, and I'm sorry. But I worried you'd settle down with the wrong person if I said it at the wrong time. I needed to wait until you got your head out of your ass about Juniper." He stuck his hand into his pocket and produced a set of keys, which he held out to me. "Here, take the truck. The rest of us will fit in Mom's van, and we can swing by Boston to get the truck on our way home."

"You want me to..." I took the keys for him, unsure if I truly understood correctly.

"Go to Boston," my dad filled in, exasperated.

"Right now?"

"Yes, right now. Christ, Julian." My dad rolled his eyes. "Do you miss her or not?"

Yes. Yes, I missed her. I missed the hell out of Juniper, and the thought of getting her in my arms tonight was suddenly all-consuming. I jumped to my feet like there was fire under my ass, and my dad looked satisfied at my sudden action.

"I'll tell the others something came up at work," he said as I put on my coat.

"It's New Year's Eve, Dad."

He pursed his lips before shrugging. "I'll figure something out."

I doubted it would be believable, but I didn't even care. I pulled my dad in for a quick hug, and we shared a look that said a lot more than words could before I walked out the door. The cold air stung my face as I climbed into my dad's truck and pulled out my phone.

Don't get out of bed.

I'm coming home, Juni.

Home.

When I opened my apartment door, Juniper was once again standing in my kitchen, wearing nothing but my OSU football jersey. A smile lit up her face, and she bounced on her tiptoes when she saw me.

I leaned inside the doorway, soaking in the sight. This was one of my favorite moments. Ever. I loved this moment. I was in love with so many parts of it.

"You got out of bed." I raised a brow. "I told you not to."

Juni's lips curved higher. "And you're surprised that I didn't listen?"

I shook my head. "Not one bit."

Her smile turned knowing. "Disappointed?"

"Disappointed?" I stepped inside, shutting the door behind me. "To see you as soon as I walk in the door? Never."

Juniper watched me with smiling eyes as I kicked off my shoes. Her gaze followed my hands as I unzipped my coat and threw it on top of my bag on the floor. She seemed impatient. I was, too.

"Does you wearing that mean what I think it means?" I asked, dropping my voice as I crossed the apartment to reach her.

"Yeah," she admitted shyly, just as I scooped her into my arms and carried her to the couch, kissing every available inch of her that I could find. Her next words were muffled against my neck as I cradled her in my arms. "Yeah, it does."

I tried not to let my brain linger on that because I was going to explode if my thoughts even touched on what I told her I'd do if I saw her wearing that jersey again.

"You didn't come home because of what I said about Greg, did you?" she asked worriedly. "I was just fucking with you, Julian."

"I know." I dropped Juniper onto the couch so she was on her back while I hovered about her. "You're always fucking with me. This has nothing to do with Kennedy. Nothing at all."

Greg Kennedy definitely hadn't been the person on my mind as I raced back into the city.

Juni stared up at me. "But you left your grandparents', and it's late. The roads must have been icy. And your family—"

"I missed you," I said simply before closing in for a deep kiss. Heat blossomed in every inch of me, lighting me up as our lips reunited. Juni gasped as my tongue swept into her mouth, tangling with hers, and when we broke apart, we were both panting, breathless. "Everything felt wrong without you."

"Everything felt wrong without me," she mumbled, repeating the words to herself as a crease formed between her brows. "You missed me."

Disbelief lingered in her expression, so I said it more forcefully this time. "I missed you, Juniper."

The seconds the words left my mouth, something visibly clicked for Juni, and her lips spread into an earth-shattering smile. All I could think was how much I wanted to taste that smile, and I couldn't have been happier when she grabbed the front of my shirt to drag us together again.

Her kiss was just as eager as it had been at the Christmas party, and the memories of that night sent my pulse on a race. And it immediately became apparent what part of my brain would win tonight.

Juniper's legs wound around my waist, urging us closer. I could feel every fucking inch of her beneath me as she rocked her body up to meet mine in a dirty rhythm that was dangerous as all hell. Grinding my hips down, I soaked in the sound of her gasps. She whimpered into my mouth, breathing my name, and that was when I decided enough was enough. It was beyond time to give this needy, gorgeous girl what she wanted.

"I'm tired of waiting for my turn, Daisy."

"Your turn?"

I peppered kisses down her neck, sucking on the hollow near her collarbone until Juni writhed beneath me. Then I lowered myself down her body while pushing the jersey up and out of the way. "My fucking turn," I said, bending to nip at the waistband of her underwear. "I heard you were having to do all the work around here lately, and that's not what I want."

"What do you want, Julian?"

What did I want?

I wanted a lot. A fucking lot, and most of them involved the woman lying beneath me on my couch. But I settled on the most important thing at the moment.

"I want your pussy in my mouth, Juni baby." I hooked my fingers into her underwear, and she tipped her hips up so I could strip them off her. "Can I have it? I want to taste you again."

"You can have it," she breathed, tipping herself up like an offering.

It was an offering I would *gladly* accept after I took a moment to appreciate the sight—how she was spread out for me. Juni's hair fanned across the throw pillows on my couch, her eyes hooded as she watched me. My jersey drowned the top half of her, and she looked so perfect in it. So utterly mine. And her bottom half? A naked, glistening pussy between two beautifully thick thighs. Fuck, it was so pretty. She was so wet, and it was all for me.

Mine.

I wanted her to say it. Just like I made sure she knew I was all for her the other night, I wanted her to tell me now.

"Why can I have it?" Reaching out, I gripped Juni's chin and ran my thumb over her bottom lip as she watched me. "Why are you letting me have it, baby?"

Juniper's eyes darkened as understanding washed over her face. She knew what I wanted to hear, but she was purposefully holding her tongue because she was a little brat who loved to toy with me.

"Say it," I demanded.

"Because it's yours." Her voice dripped with the longing I felt in my bones, and something told me that I wasn't the only one here who was fulfilling a once-forbidden dream.

"Yes," I murmured while urging her legs to open wider for me. "That's right."

"Yours, Julian," she whined, rocking toward my mouth.

I blew over her clit, and she made a noise I'd never forget while bucking up to meet my mouth. As soon as my tongue made contact with her needy cunt, Juniper cried out—both in relief and ecstasy. I knew that feeling exactly, recalling it with painful accuracy from when she sucked my cock down her throat for the first time.

I pressed Juni down into my couch, wanting her to relax as I found my home between her legs. She tasted like a fucking dream, just how I remembered. As I licked and sucked, her unrestrained groans filled my living room, echoing in my ears. I fucking loved that sound. It belonged here, in my apartment. In my bed. With me.

"I'll take care of you now, Juni," I breathed, working a finger through her slick pussy until I could drive it into her. "I'll take care of you."

Juniper gasped something that sounded an awful lot like *yes*, and I suppressed a smile while burying my face deeper between her legs.

In some sliver of my vision, I saw Juni thrash her head to the side, unleashing a scream into a pillow. But that wasn't going to work for me. Not here where there was no reason to hide.

"Don't do that," I rasped, glancing up her jersey-clad body. "I need to hear you."

"And I need you to stop talking so you can focus," she snapped, eyes burning as she stared back at me.

I grinned.

So beautiful.

So alive.

I pumped my finger in and out of her. "I'm good at multitasking. How do you think I made it through law school, love?"

She flushed, but I wasn't sure if it was from how I started

swirling my tongue over her clit or from the term of endearment. But tenderness now existed in her gaze.

A moment later, it vanished when she smirked. "If you think I'm going to believe you without proof, then you should clearly go *back* to law school."

"You always want fucking proof." My expression shifted to match hers. "I'll give you proof."

Enough fucking around.

While keeping my pace with my finger, I flicked my tongue repeatedly over her pussy, making sure to only *graze* the spot where she really wanted it. Simultaneously, I brushed my fingertips over her stomach, raising goose bumps on her skin.

Juni tipped her head back with a satisfied groan. "Oh my God. I need—I need—"

More. She needed more.

I gave her the slightest taste of it, of the bliss. I pressed a bit harder with my tongue, with my fingers, and Juni started panting. Her back arched as she searched for something only I could give her.

I took all of her into my mouth, sucking and stroking. She rode up against my face, taking what she needed until she fell apart with a cry. Her body shook in jolts of pleasure that I basked in, and I only eased up on her when I felt her muscles begin to relax and melt beneath me.

My name flew from Juni's lips once, and then she repeated it like a nearly silent prayer.

I waited until she'd completely collapsed into the couch before I climbed up her body again. Juniper didn't waste any time grabbing my shirt and yanking me down for a kiss. She licked the taste of her off my lips before winding her tongue into my mouth.

Juni's body shook slightly, but then, so did mine. I was desperate to wrap myself in every sensation she could give me. I wanted to drown in her touch. I was convinced it wouldn't be enough until I was drowning.

Ignoring all attempts at logic, I began grinding my unbelievably hard cock between her legs while her lips took from mine, needing *something*. Juniper gasped into my mouth before wiggling up to feel more and more of me.

"Please, Julian," she cried, such a sweet, sweet sound. "Please fuck me."

Jesus Christ, what was she trying to do to me? I rocked into her with a groan, nearly coming from hearing those words alone.

"I was going to take you on a date first," I muttered, finding her ear and nibbling on it. "I was going to earn taking you to bed."

"You've earned it," she whispered.

"But—"

"Julian," she cut me off, and I pulled back to find her pretty eyes. They sparkled brighter than New Year's Eve sequins. "You said if I wanted someone to fuck me, you'd do it. And I'm tired of waiting. I've been waiting a long time, so don't make me wait any longer. Unless you'd rather I ask someone else—"

With a surge of possession, I snatched Juniper off the couch, flipping her over my shoulder to cart her off to my bedroom.

"No one else," I grunted, dropping her onto my bed with a tenderness that shocked even me, considering how my hands damn near shook. Desire surged through me, along with anticipation and all those feelings that come to life when dreams become reality.

Juniper stared up at me, all tangled in my bedsheets. Goddamn, she was a sight. Flushed cheeks and messy hair. Half-naked and so fucking radiant.

"No one else," she breathed.

No. One. Else.

There was no one else—just me and Juniper.

And tonight, my bed.

ten years ago

I hated that I was hiding from my ex-boyfriend at the Briggs' house on Valentine's Day.

And I hated that Julian finally realized why I was here.

"I didn't know he was bothering you again," he said through gritted teeth. Then he stood with a huff, stalking off to open the freezer. "Chocolate chip cookie dough or mint chocolate chip?" he asked over his shoulder.

He was offering me...ice cream? After trying to get rid of me for the last twenty minutes?

"Obviously, chocolate chip cookie dough."

Julian wordlessly brought the ice cream over to the table. He handed me a spoon, and I took it, though tentatively.

And then we started eating quietly, taking turns.

Back and forth.

Julian cleared his voice. "We almost always have cookie dough ice cream in the freezer, you know. It's usually behind the frozen fruit if you ever need to come over and...eat ice cream again."

CHAPTER THIRTY-TWO

"ARE YOU SURE ABOUT this?"

Julian stood at the end of his bed, looking down at me like he thought this was too good to be true. His room basked in the soft glow of the singular lamp on his bedside table. I'd made fun of his apartment the first time I saw it, but the more time I spent here, the more I loved it.

My apartment maintained a bright and chaotic vibe, slightly cluttered with my collection of books, clothes, and plants. Julian's place featured clean lines and a minimalist approach. Modern furniture filled the spaces, but little touches like soft lighting, comfy linens, and framed family pictures kept it from feeling cold.

And Julian, too. Warmth blossomed beneath my skin as he studied me. But while I could appreciate how he admired me, I was so over dragging this out. For fuck's sake, I'd been waiting for *so long*.

"I'm sure, Julian," I groaned. "Look, I know that it's my first time, and it probably won't be good—"

"Wait." Julian held out a hand. "Stop right there."

I struggled to withhold a smirk. I should have expected that response. Julian took a dramatically long moment to squeeze his eyes shut before piercing me with a glare of annoyance. "Why don't you think it's going to be good?"

I leveled him with a look. "I read books, Julian."

"So?"

"So...my expectations are unrealistic. And I'm aware of that."

Shouldn't this be self-explanatory? I wasn't expecting the fireworks that people write about in books, especially not for my first time. I wasn't naive, and I thought he'd be relieved to hear that, but that clearly wasn't the case.

Julian's lips twitched. His stare narrowed. "Is that so?"

"Yeah, I mean you're..." I waved a hand in his direction, trying to point out the obvious.

"I'm what?"

"You know..." I cleared my voice. "Not fictional."

Julian went from acting hurt and irritated to flashing me one of his brilliantly cocky smiles. "You need to be careful there, Juni, insulting me like this."

"It isn't insulting," I argued. "It's simply a fact. You *are* real, aren't you?"

Julian reached behind him, pulling his shirt over his head in a theatrical but incredibly attractive way. He shook out his hair before facing me again, now half-naked. His toned chest rippled as he moved, and the golden hue from the bedside lamp reflected off his broad shoulders as he leaned on the end of the bed.

"I'm more than real, Daisy." Mischief flashed across his features as he lowered his gaze over me in a way that chased away all my nerves. When he spoke, the husk in his voice was ironically unreal. "Tell me how a fictional man would fuck you, then."

"I—" My words got stuck on the tip of my tongue. That had been the last thing I'd expected him to say.

He crossed his arms over his chest, raising a brow. When I was too shocked to speak, he began offering suggestions. "Do you want me to make sure that you come first?"

"Yes." I pushed myself up onto my elbows to better meet his stare. "I mean, I guess you already did that."

Julian's grin turned crooked. "So I did."

"But that wasn't during sex," I pointed out—just in case he thought he might get away with not even *trying* to give me another one.

"I'll do it again, then." The offhanded comment wasn't boastful. He said it as an easy truth, and my breath hitched before he continued. "What else? Do you want me to talk dirty about what I plan to do to you?"

"Yes," I breathed. Because I did; I really did want to hear that.

"Easy." His eyes dragged over me, making me shiver, and then returned to meet my gaze. "Do you want me to be rough or gentle? You never did tell me what you like when I asked that day."

"Both." I didn't want him to treat me like I was glass, but I also wasn't sure what Julian's definition of *rough* was.

"I can do both." Julian's eyes softened, but his lips smirked. "Do you want me to use toys?"

"I—" I bit down on my lip, caught off guard but not opposed to the idea. "What kind?"

A flare crossed Julian's irises. "*God*, Juni."

Apparently, he'd expected a flat-out no.

"What kind, Julian?" I whispered.

He plowed his fingers through his hair, giving a tiny shake of disbelief. "I think we'll start with something you're probably familiar with. Okay?"

A flush crept up my neck. "Okay, but I didn't...like, bring anything."

Cheekiness lit up Julian's face. "It's time for you to see what's really in my bedside table, right next to my list of plant names."

A laugh rippled through me. "You told me that what was in your bedside table didn't concern me. And that you *didn't* have a list of plant names."

"I lied. Just like how you told me in New York that you lied to me all the time. But we're done with that, right?" I nodded wordlessly, and his gaze burned into mine as he stood at the end of the bed. "Good. Now, as much as I love that jersey on you, it's time to take it off."

My pulse sped up. I didn't know why I thought I could have sex with Julian without letting him see me naked, but I suddenly didn't feel prepared for this moment. How was that possible? After twenty-six years, how was I *still* not prepared?

Julian began unbuckling his belt as he watched me with heavy lids.

"Take it off, Juniper," he repeated, slower this time. "I know this will destroy me forever, but I'm already wrecked. So let me see you."

I pushed into a sitting position, unable to tear my eyes from his. He stared, taking me in as though this moment right here was the main event, and it gave me the confidence to slip the jersey over the top of my head. I threw it at his feet, but he didn't give another glance at the jersey after it came off. All his attention remained glued on me as I sank back into his bed again, my head hitting his pillows. He didn't move except his eyes, tracing my shape against the sheets.

The heat of his gaze licked my skin, and it was the only thing that helped me resist the urge to cover up again. That, and the way his jaw kept clenching with desire.

When Julian finally spoke, his voice descended into something deep and gravelly. "You look so fucking perfect in my bed."

"Julian..."

I didn't know what to say. But that was okay. Julian leaned forward with his pants half undone to skim his hands over my skin. And as soon as we touched, I knew there was no going back tonight. No going back, not ever.

It was that pull, that magnetism that coursed from my body to his. Everything in me strained toward his touch, feeding off it. I felt it in Julian, too. He climbed onto the bed over me, needing to touch more of my body than he could reach.

"*Fuck.* So beautiful." He cupped my breasts in his palms, squeezing experimentally. Like the rest of me, there was more than enough to grab. I'd always been self-conscious about it, but not right now. Not with how Julian curved his hands over me so reverently. "You are so beautiful."

The awe in Julian's expression was breathtaking. I never imagined he would look at me like this. His eyes didn't stray from my skin once. They blazed a trail of heat while he continued muttering breathy praises. The words made me hum in delight, but it was that gaze of his that made me believe them.

Julian lowered himself until his lips were poised to take mine. My breaths came in quick spurts while the anticipation of the kiss hung heavy and sweet in the air. One of his hands continued to explore my curves, smoothing over my hip. His pupils dilated while roaming my face.

"Do you have any idea how badly I want you?"

I lifted my hips so they grazed his. My bare skin against his unbuttoned pants, the fabric brushing roughly over delicate flesh. I inched higher, and Julian's hard cock pressed between my legs.

"I have a pretty good idea, yeah."

Julian growled, partly in frustration and partly in heady arousal, as he flung himself off me, landing on the side of the bed. He slipped his pants and underwear to the floor, stealing all my attention down south.

Now I had a *really* good idea of how badly Julian wanted me.

Noticing the direction of my attention, his gruff voice cut in before I could have any doubts. "It'll fit perfectly, baby. Just fucking perfectly."

I looked up at him from beneath my lashes. "Show me."

"God, Juniper. You do things to me," he groaned before pouncing back on the bed, pulling me under the covers as he kissed and dragged me close. "I can't wait to finally fuck your pretty little cunt."

My entire body hummed with awareness as Julian's bare skin skimmed mine. His lips captured mine repeatedly as the bed swallowed us whole. Only a dusky light surrounded us beneath his sheets as we tangled in limbs and kisses. Julian's fingers wove into my hair, desperately holding me to him.

I started bucking my hips against him shamelessly. The touches, the kisses, the press of his body against mine. It wasn't enough. I'd never felt this aching pressure before. An emptiness replaced the high he gave me on the couch, and I knew what I needed to fill it. Him. All of him.

I'd never needed someone to complete me like I needed him to. But right now, it felt like I wasn't enough on my own. I needed Julian. I needed Julian to feel whole.

Julian's lips began an exploration, sweeping away from my mouth to taste my neck and then my collarbone, and finally, my chest. His teeth scraped my skin as he began kissing the swell of my breasts. The feeling of his harsh breaths was my only warning before he sucked one nipple into his mouth, causing an eruption of heat. His tongue swirled over it, flicking, and the ache within me blossomed into something nearly unbearable.

Crying out, I arched my back, handing myself over to Julian.

"Fuck, Juni," he mumbled, and I wound my fingers into his hair. My other hand found his cock and wrapped around it, stroking slowly.

Julian's fingers gripped my wrist, stilling it as he cursed.

"Careful with that hand there, Lily," he grunted, still nestled in my tits, and I couldn't withhold my grin. "It feels too fucking good for you to be doing that right now."

Everything felt too fucking good, and I decided it was about time we did something about it. I needed him. I needed him so badly that my hands shook, a wild, frenzied feeling dancing in my veins.

Lacing both hands into his hair, I tugged Julian up until we were at eye level. And as soon as his hooded, hazy gaze met mine, he understood. He knew everything I wanted and needed. He grabbed my wrist to bring one of my hands between us and covered it with his own as he squeezed, calming the shakiness.

Glancing at our entwined hands, he noted how my body vibrated.

"Excited? Or nervous?"

He searched my face for the truth.

"Both," I admitted before biting down on a groan as Julian's bare chest brushed mine. The slight sensation against my already aroused nipples felt like torture.

Julian nodded, and then a seriousness set into his expression right before he took action.

Rolling over, Julian pulled open the top drawer on his bedside table, rummaging in it until he found what he was looking for. He immediately folded whatever it was—likely a condom—into his palm.

"I'm on birth control," I whispered, worrying my lip as I watched him. "Just so you know."

My ex, Evan, refused to use protection—one of the reasons I'd never slept with him. But Julian...I just wanted to live up to his every expectation, which I worried would be hard to do, considering I'd never done this before. *This* was one area I had control over, though.

"Good to know," Julian muttered, a slight smirk skewing his lips as he rolled back over, grabbed my hips, and tipped me up on top of him. "But I don't mind using protection if it makes you feel better."

I gasped as I straddled Julian, his erection rutting between my legs. I nodded, admittedly relieved that he'd said that.

Julian didn't seem to give a shit about the condom. He agreed absently, eyes darkening as he took me in. I was utterly exposed but surprisingly warm as I admired how he looked beneath me. His auburn hair was mussed against his pillow, and his lust-filled gaze roved over me. The moment of mutual appreciation stretched out between us until it turned heated, making me squirm.

Julian stroked his cock, running a knuckle over my clit. Meanwhile, he tore open the condom package with his teeth before rolling it over his length with his other hand. I watched, fascinated and painfully aroused.

"You ready to take me?" His voice grew thick as he watched and waited for my response.

"Me?" I repeated.

He was going to make *me* do it? He was the one who had done this before—not me.

"You," Julian confirmed, his breathing ragged as he plucked something from the sheets beside him. "I had an idea, and I bought something for you. Because it'll kill me if I cause you even a prick of pain. Do you trust me?"

"Yes," I said automatically. No need to even consider it.

At my answer, a buzzing filled the room, muffled slightly, and I realized it was coming from whatever was hidden in Julian's hand. I jolted as Julian pressed a vibrator to my stomach, dragging it down slowly while keeping my gaze, searching for any signs of discomfort.

But my only discomfort was how my body felt like it would burn up if he didn't touch me soon. And when Julian hesitated, teasing the vibrator right above where I wanted it most, I wiggled on his lap.

"Julian."

But he did the opposite of what I'd wanted. Instead of giving me relief, he dragged the toy up his length, releasing a little moan that I found unbearably hot. When he got to the tip, Julian spun the vibrator around in his hand, and that was when I realized it didn't look anything like the one I kept in my bedside table.

It circled his cock, hugging it. Two prongs formed a ring, branching out from where they met on either side to create a vibrating landing spot, the two little balls on the end buzzing as Julian held it in place around his tip.

"Come here," he breathed, and I obeyed without thinking, lining his erection up. And as soon as it was in position, Julian pressed the vibrator right into my clit, causing my cries to saturate the air.

"Feels good, doesn't it?"

I nodded, speechless. The vibrations hummed within me, and while I certainly wasn't a virgin to using a vibrator, this felt different. More intense, more all-consuming. My vision swam momentarily before I found Julian's heated stare again.

"Focus on that as you take me, baby."

Julian's attention flicked between my face and where we were joined as I slowly lowered onto him. He held the vibrator in place, letting pleasure racket through my body as I sank, losing the ability to breathe as he filled me. Finally. Oh, God, *finally*. This was what I'd been missing, this feeling of wholeness, of completion.

I barely felt the burn, only a slight stretching sensation when I sank fully onto him, whimpering Julian's name. It was too hard to feel anything but pleasure when the toy pulsed so intensely. Julian made a guttural noise, jaw clenching as he removed his hand, settling the vibrator in its spot. I experimented with rocking forward, grinding my clit over it. Oh, *hell*.

Meanwhile, Julian gripped my hips, fingertips digging in like he was trying to hold on to something. Control, likely. If his expression was any indication.

"See? Perfect. I've never felt anything this good in my entire fucking life, Juniper," he rasped. "So goddamn wet and warm. You're killing me here."

I couldn't help but smirk down at him. "Good."

Julian's lips quirked at that. At least until I lifted up and slid back down his length, causing a rough curse to explode from his lips. Oh, I loved that. I loved that I had that effect on him and could drive Julian this *wild*.

Every little movement sent me careening toward a spiral. Every roll of my hips resulted in cascading jolts of pleasure. Every rock caused the vibrator to rub over my clit while Julian stroked something deep inside me. My lips parted in awe, eyes rolling back. Unbelievable—it was unbelievable, and I was left eating every single one of my words from earlier.

Julian knew it, too. His eyes roamed my face as I experienced pure bliss for the first time, and satisfaction dripped into every one of his features.

"Ride that cock, love." His grip tightened on me as he helped me find my rhythm. "Just like that. You're doing so good."

His praise washed over me, empowering me to ride him harder. I thought I'd feel too exposed being on top like this, but I reveled in Julian's burning hot stare. His attention made me feel alive. More desired and beautiful than I ever thought possible. I ran my hands down my front, cupping my breasts and toying with my nipples until Julian groaned, his bottom lip sliding between his teeth.

"I'm never going to recover from this," he said, his husky voice nearly doing me in.

"Good," I repeated with a naughty grin.

It was all I could say, but it was the truth. I didn't want him to recover. I wanted to ruin him.

I leaned to sweep my lips over his, dragging them teasingly. With a growl, Julian grabbed me by the nape of my neck and pulled me lower so he could kiss me properly, and then he held me there while he pistoned his hips up into mine. I cried out from the intensity of the new, jaw-dropping position, and sparks of heat built one after another until I was burning all over.

I almost didn't recognize my orgasm. It certainly wasn't my first one, but it felt like it. Because this explosion, this free-falling, was all new. I gasped against Julian's lips, not even recognizing the sounds I was making as I clutched the pillow beside his head with a white-knuckle grip.

"Julian!" I shook, struggling to come down from my high when the vibrator still pulsed between us. "Oh my God, oh my God."

My vision was stilted, but I made out Julian's cocky grin as he gently urged me off him. His touch was tender, his fingertips gliding over my skin in reassuring caresses. But I frowned as he left my body. He was still hard. Really hard. And I didn't miss his muffled moans as he slipped the vibrator off his cock, clicking it off and tossing it aside.

He didn't finish.

But just as I was about to open my mouth to say something, Julian's large hands wound their way around my waist and flipped me onto my back. He climbed on top of me in a swift movement, clear intent in the tight lines of his face. It reignited my spent body in undeniable ways.

"I know you can handle more," he said gruffly before checking my reaction for confirmation. "Can't you, Juni baby?"

I nodded, still trying to catch my breath. He needed more, and I wanted to give it to him. Hell, *I* wanted more.

Julian caught my chin, forcing my lips to part with his thumb. "Say it."

"I can handle more," I said, my voice wispy as I ignored the burning between my legs.

My words washed over him, dousing him with the realization that he would get what he wanted, and he made another groan. "I know you can. Because you match me in every fucking way."

I reached up, dragging my fingers down his chest and making him shiver. "Give it to me, Jules."

His eyes rolled back momentarily at my words before they refocused on me.

"It's my turn now," he grunted, keeping his gaze steady while aligning himself between my legs again. He sat back on his haunches, allowing an unobstructed view of him entering me. "When you come this time, it will be because of my cock and my cock alone."

Before I could absorb his crude words, he thrust inside me with one swift stroke. I felt a slight twinge of pressure, but it was overpowered by the euphoric sensation of being filled again. I arched back, crying out his name.

A wickedness worked its way onto Julian's face as he retreated just enough to plunge into me harder. He repeated it again and again as I writhed up against him. His eyes dropped, studying how his cock slid in and out until he grabbed both of my legs and threw them around his waist as he leaned down to cover my body.

Julian caged me against the mattress as he sank deeper and deeper inside me. He stilled slightly, letting me adjust. His lips were reassuring against mine, breathing my name.

"Tell me again that you can handle it," he whispered.

"I can handle it," I assured him. "I want it."

Julian nodded, taking my breath away with his beautifully intense expression before driving into me again. My breasts rocked with every mind-numbing thrust, grazing Julian's broad chest. His hair hung over his face, all his features ticking as he continued to hold on to some sort of control.

Fuck control. I raked my fingers down his back, tipping my hips up to meet his, and Julian lost it.

"*Fuck*, you're so—" He released a low groan as he pounded into me, finding a filthy rhythm that filled the room with sounds of slapping skin. "You know this little virgin pussy belongs to me now, right? It's *mine*, Juniper."

"Yours, Julian," I gasped.

His eyes glazed over as he continued his punishing strokes. "No one else's."

"No one else's." An intelligible sound ripped from my throat between my quick pants. "There's never been anyone else."

"Oh, *baby*." Julian dropped his head to mine. Sweat dripped off his forehead, mixing with mine. But I didn't care. My entire body was slick, sliding against his as the world slipped away. It was only him and me. His rough gasps and my tiny whimpers. His hard body and my soft one. His racing heart and my full one. "Never anyone else," he breathed, almost like a question. Like he wanted more reassurance.

I shook my head. "Never."

"That's my girl." I felt the rumble of his voice everywhere. It rattled in my chest. "Now, come for me one more time, love."

"I don't—" I swallowed past the dryness in my throat. "I don't think I—"

"Yes, you can." Julian smacked his hips into mine harder as if to prove a point. "You told me you could handle it, Juni. Now, where's the fucking proof?"

Goddamn him.

I felt Julian smile when I wrapped my legs tighter around his waist, pulling us closer until it was impossible to decipher where I ended and he began. I was beyond powerless to the force that kept us together. I always had been, hadn't I?

A ball of heat settled deep inside me; every time he moved, it grew and grew. And it felt so good, so jaw-droppingly good.

I tucked my head into the crook of Julian's neck, my sharp breaths hitting his skin as he steadily slammed into me. His movements were sloppier, more desperate, and just as he growled my name as a warning, I found my release.

It was different. It was blindingly hot, blossoming from a part of me I didn't realize existed. As I screamed, it washed over me like a heat wave before settling in my bones. My body shook and shook with the intensity of it, pulsing with a beat that Julian controlled as he gave one final thrust. He cried out, body trembling, before finding my lips and kissing me through his climax.

This kiss was brutally rough at first, his teeth scraping over my lips, unrestrained. But it softened as we both melted into each other. Tenderness seeped into the moment, taking me by surprise.

"Good girl," he whispered, trailing his lips down. He pressed his mouth to every inch of skin he could find, kissing me into a blissful stupor. "You did so well, Juni."

I closed my eyes, basking in...him. His words, his touches. My limbs tingled. And they felt heavy. I couldn't move even if I wanted to. So I let Julian kiss me everywhere, moaning when his lips skirted between my legs.

Julian murmured that he would be right back, but I barely heard it. There was a faint buzzing in my ears, the echoes of our climax still vibrating in my head. I didn't realize that Julian had returned until something warm pressed between my legs, a soothing, damp heat. He murmured for me to keep it there as though I planned on moving anytime soon.

It was pleasant, so pleasant, and my lips curved in a sated smile. I felt a dip in the mattress before lips brushed my temple, and heat encased me again as Julian pulled me into his chest.

A comfortable silence settled between us as we breathed in each other's presence until Julian eventually broke it.

"I want to ask you something."

"Hm?"

It was the only answer I could muster.

"Why?"

"Why?" I opened one eye to see Julian watching me with a thoughtful expression. And then I opened the other, curious.

"Why did you decide not to have sex before?"

"How do you know it was my decision?"

"Because no one in their right mind would be dating you and *not* want to sleep with you."

I swallowed, trying to ignore what his words did to me. "It's hard for me to trust people sometimes. That they really want me. That they won't leave me. And I just couldn't get myself to sleep with any of my exes until I felt some sort of...reassurance. I figured if they cared about me at all, they would wait. They'd stay." I closed my eyes again. "They never did."

Julian's gentle touch urged me to open my eyes again. His blue eyes were so beautiful as they studied me that I almost had to look away. He seemed to be trying to find the right words, but he didn't have to. He didn't need to find any words. Not tonight.

"But I trust you, Julian," I whispered.

"I'm not going anywhere." He cleared what sounded like emotion from his throat. "I've always been here, and I always will be."

I snuggled deeper into him.

"I know."

A contented sigh breezed over the top of my head before Julian murmured in my ear.

"It's after midnight. We missed the countdown."

I smiled into his bare chest. "Well, I still got my kiss, and that's what really matters. Happy New Year, Julian Briggs."

"Happy New Year, Juniper St. James." He paused. "And excuse me, but you got *more* than just a kiss. I think that means it's going to be a good year."

Hugging him tighter, I nodded.

"I think that means it's going to be the best year."

CHAPTER THIRTY-THREE

FOR THE FOURTH TIME since starting my job at Gardner Law Firm, I woke up next to Juniper St. James. And this time, she was naked. More importantly, though, I was allowed to touch her.

I smoothed my hands up her sides, remembering how all these curves had looked when she was on top of me, how she'd felt herself up while riding my—

"Oh, really?" Juni's raspy morning voice broke through my recollections as she squirmed beneath my hands. "That's pretty, uh, unusual for him, isn't it?"

I lifted my head, and when I realized Juniper was on the phone, I scowled at her back.

"Hang up, Juni."

She whipped around, turning on her side to face me. "*No,*" she emphasized into the phone, her eyes widening as she spoke. "No, of course I'm not with a guy. That was just the TV. I should really *turn it down.*"

Those last words were definitely directions that I fully planned to ignore. Even when Juniper mouthed, "Gemma," at me.

Nope. Uh-uh. My sister didn't get to take this from me. I let her have Juni for years, and now she would have to share. But not right now. Right now, Juniper was naked in my bed for the first time, and we had plans that didn't involve my sister. Right now, she was mine.

"Hang up," I muttered, softer this time.

Juniper didn't hang up, telling Gemma she had stayed in last night.

Yeah, *stayed in* my bed.

Where we still were.

Had she forgotten?

Deciding she needed a reminder, I caught her lips with mine as soon as she'd finished her sentence. She sucked in with surprise as I tugged on her lower lip with my teeth. *Mine.* These lips were for me this morning. They weren't for talking to best friends.

I dipped my head to her neck, sucking lightly on her skin as she muttered something noncommittal into the phone. God, she smelled good. The floral bouquet was still there, but her usual perfume was mixed with the scent of sex and sweat. It was intoxicating. This was what being drunk first thing in the morning felt like, huh?

Juni's breath hitched, but it didn't keep her from answering Gemma's question about what book she had read last night. When she *stayed in.*

Sliding my palms up to her breasts, I cupped them and brushed my thumbs over her nipples. Juni's eyes closed as she pressed her lips together, holding in a sound that I desperately wanted to hear. When I took Juniper's nipple into my mouth, she gasped. Audibly, this time. She clapped a hand over her mouth, but it was too late. After a pause, she sighed.

"Yes, fine, I *am* with a guy," she admitted with a half groan. "And I have to go, but I'll call you later. Okay?"

Juni barely waited for a reply before ending the call and throwing her phone to the other side of the bed, letting loose a loud moan.

"You're the worst," she complained. "The absolute worst."

Even as she said it, she wound her fingers into my hair and held me against her chest. I smiled and flicked my tongue over her taut nipple.

"You like it," I shot back.

She didn't say yes, but she did whimper my name. I'd allow that. For now.

"Gemma was confused that you left without telling her last night," Juni explained between cute little attempts to catch her breath as I continued to work my mouth over her. "She thought I might know what happened because your dad said something came up at work."

"God, I told him that was a bad excuse," I muttered, moving to take her other nipple between my lips.

"Yeah, Gemma doesn't really believe it."

I shrugged, not caring. I couldn't remember a happier moment than when I'd walked through the door last night to find Juniper waiting for me. I couldn't remember feeling more at peace than when I was so deep inside her that I didn't know where I ended and she began.

Gemma could be suspicious; I didn't regret leaving last night. Not at all. How could I? Look where I was right now.

"We're done talking about my sister," I decided. "Actually, the fact that you're talking at all tells me I'm not doing my job well enough."

After that, I got to work.

And Juniper didn't say much else.

Except to scream my name, of course.

JUNI PEPPERED ME WITH QUESTIONS ABOUT MY PLANS FOR OUR FIRST date. First, over text message because she wanted to know what to wear, and then, as we drove through the city. But I wasn't sure why she thought she would get me to fold. I had *years* of experience holding myself back when it came to her, so I just smiled and kept my eyes on the road, which made her all the more furious.

My plan was a bit of a gamble, and I wasn't usually a betting man. But I was at the point where I'd risk it all to give Juniper even a slice of happiness.

My heart rate tripled when I led her into a small boutique in the heart of the Beacon Hill neighborhood. But with one step over the threshold and one look around, reassurance flooded through me. Because, just like I thought the first time I was here, this store *was* Juniper.

Colorful fabrics filled the racks lining the walls while the displays in the center of the store boasted more accessories than I'd ever seen. Jewelry, bows, and other hair contraptions I didn't understand sat in tiered arrangements. For being such a small shop filled with so much stuff, it didn't feel tacky or overdone in the slightest. The dresses were pressed and perfect on their hangers, the jewelry sparkled beneath soft lighting, and Juni fit right in.

Her little intake of breath told me she agreed. "Oh, this place is so cute."

She said the words in a hush under her breath, which I found adorable, considering there wasn't anyone around to overhear. Well, a middle-aged woman with long, black hair stood behind the register, but besides that, we were alone.

I stepped forward to greet her, but she beat me to it.

"Julian." A smile cracked on her face as she moved to look at Juni. "And Juniper. Here, let me take your coats."

Juni's eyes popped wider as she slipped out of her coat and handed it to the woman, and I didn't even bother trying to hide my smile.

"Charlotte." I passed her my coat with a nod. "Thank you again for having us."

"Of course."

She clapped her hands together, nearly as delighted as I was. And after giving me a wink, all her attention switched to Juniper.

"Let's get started, shall we? Julian told me a bit about your style, so I selected a few items and hung them on the rack by the dressing rooms." Charlotte pointed to the back of the store, and Juni's head turned on a swivel, her lips parted. "Of course, no pressure if none are quite right for your date," Charlotte continued with a wide grin. "And if you *happen* to see a bottle of bubbly around over there, feel free to pop it open while you shop. Any questions?"

Juniper looked like she had a lot of questions, but she shook her head absently.

"Excellent!" Charlotte exclaimed. "I'll be around if you need anything."

Juniper blinked twice at the beaming woman before saying thank you in a breathy, wispy voice. She flashed a soft grin, but I could tell she was a little lost. Planning to rectify that, I expressed my gratitude to Charlotte once more before whisking Juni to the side to murmur in her ear.

"This is why I told you not to worry about what to wear. I wanted to take you shopping for an outfit before dinner."

Her eyes lifted, stunned. "You—*what*?"

I smiled. "I just thought you'd like this place."

"You just..." Juniper's voice trailed off as she stared around the store again. "You just thought I'd like this place."

"Yeah." I shrugged, leading her slowly to the dressing rooms where the bottle of champagne was. I wanted to pour her a glass. "I came here because they had the sweater I got Janie for Christmas. And as soon as I walked in, I thought of you. Do you think you can find something?"

I hadn't just *thought* of Juniper. I hadn't been able to get her out of my head for a single goddamn second. It led me to ask Charlotte, who'd been working the register, if I could ever arrange something like this and how much it would cost. She was immediately tickled that I even asked—that much had been clear—but then I accidentally spilled how Juni was my sister's best friend and coworker, and then Charlotte wouldn't even answer my question about the cost until I told her the entire story. Or most of it, anyway.

Now, I was pretty sure that she was our biggest fan.

She didn't charge me a damn thing.

I'd make sure it was well worth her time to keep her doors open just for us, though.

"Do I think I can find something?" In a daze, Juni walked to the clothing rack with the dresses Charlotte had selected. She ran her fingers across the matching hangers before looking over her shoulder. "Do I think I can *find* something?"

"Okay, you gotta stop just repeating me, Juni baby." I held out a champagne flute, and she took it from me, her lips beginning to spread in the slowest, most pure smile I'd ever seen. "Answer the question."

"Is—are—do we have this whole place to ourselves?" she whispered, leaning in like it was a secret.

She didn't answer my question, but the shiny anticipation in her expression was enough for me.

I nodded, striding over to give her a little pat on her ass. "Now, get to shopping, will ya?"

"Okay," she squealed, the corners of her eyes crinkling now with excitement. "But you're not buying me anything. Just bringing me here was more than enough."

"Oh, *no*, you don't." With a little push, I buried us between the racks of clothes, caging Juni between my arms. "No more saying shit like that. If I want to buy you a dress, I'm gonna buy you a fucking dress, Juni."

She bit down on her lip while eyeing up the racks next to us. Specifically, the price tags.

"But it's—"

"I've worked hard for years," I muttered, cutting her off, "so I could take care and spoil the people I—"

Love.

"—care about."

Fuck.

She swallowed, her throat visibly bobbing. Her eyes dropped to my mouth, and my fingers curled desperately around the fabric fluffed up behind her. Sequins shimmered across her face, and the vision before me was so Juni-like.

And I...cared about Juni.

For so long, I was scared to admit that, but now it was impossible not to let it rule all my thoughts and actions. I *deeply* cared about Juni.

More than I should on our first date before we'd made anything official or talked about how serious this was. But I was in deep, so, so deep, and as far as I was concerned, this was as serious as it got. This was I'm-never-letting-you-go serious.

I slipped a finger beneath her chin, tipping it up so she'd look at my eyes, not my mouth. For my own sanity, of course. "Have I ever been irresponsible with my money? Do you think that's something I would ever risk?"

She shook her head mutely.

"Good, then we agree." Because I couldn't help it, I brushed my lips over hers. It sparked something I couldn't finish, not now, and I hated putting space between us again. "Now I desperately want to see you try on some dresses."

She nodded, that smile returning. And then it cocked to one side. "But you hate my dresses."

I stepped back, letting her slip by so she could start perusing the handfuls of outfits as beautiful as her. "No," I scoffed. "That's not true."

A raised brow told me she didn't believe me. "Is that so?"

"I never hated your dresses, Juniper." I kicked back on the velvety sofa arranged outside the fitting room. "I hated that you always looked so fucking pretty in them, and it only made it that much harder to resist you." I dropped my voice. "I hated how goddamn fuckable you looked in them."

My response made her cheeks flush, and I grinned with delight. She was going to pick out a pretty little dress, and then tonight, I was going to fuck her in it just like I'd imagined.

Never in my wildest dreams had I imagined I'd be excited about a fashion show.

But then again, never in my wildest dreams had I imagined I'd be taking Juniper St. James on a date.

And tonight was only the first of many, many of those.

CHAPTER THIRTY-FOUR

CONSIDERING JULIAN HAD FIVE sisters and years of experience buying them gifts and listening to their dating stories—likely with gritted teeth—I wasn't shocked that he knew what a girl might like on a first date. But this? This was more than that. This was specific to me. To what *I* liked.

Shocked was an understatement to how I felt when I looked at the collection Charlotte had picked out for me. Julian hadn't just taken me shopping at the most adorable boutique in Boston, but he'd also explained my style *perfectly* to the shop owner.

Taking two big gulps of champagne in the hopes it would settle me, I stared at all of my options, struggling to decide which to pick first.

"Put on the black one," Julian called through the dressing room curtain, surprising me with how closely he must have paid attention when I pulled dresses off the rack.

"I already have a lot of black dresses," I said while considering the dress in question, another one of my favorites from the selection.

"I know." Julian's voice had a hint of satin to it, sliding over my skin appreciatively. Whenever he admitted to knowing things about me, it made my heart skip a goddamn beat. "But you always look good in them."

I stuck my head out of the dressing room, using the curtain to shield the rest of my body. "I sometimes worry that they're too similar or boring."

Julian snorted. "Nothing about your style is boring, Juni. None of those dresses are *plain* black. They're all...you know, decorated."

I giggled. "Decorated?"

"Shut up," he grunted. "I'm not good at fashion. You know what I mean."

The best part about it was that I *did* know what he meant. I liked my dresses with a bit of bounce or flair or a subtle polka dot. But it was more fun watching Julian flounder.

Flashing a smile at his grumpy face, I ducked into the small changing room to put on the black dress, as requested by my date. And once I finally managed to squeeze into it, I stared at myself in the mirror.

The dress cinched around my waist with a tiny, tied bow while the bottom flowed loosely around my hips, exactly how I liked it. It only hit mid-thigh, shorter than I usually wore, and the bodice was a structured fit, nothing like anything else I owned. The off-shoulder neckline plunged between my breasts, and the deeply scooped design combined with the airtight fit meant more than a bit of cleavage was on display.

"Let's see it, Daisy," Julian called impatiently.

Something akin to anticipation thrummed in my veins. I wanted to show him this dress, to see his reaction, but the idea tripped my nerves, sending them haywire. I slipped into my heels and swept my hair off my shoulder for the full effect before nervously stepping out to show Julian.

"Holy fucking shit."

Julian's lips parted as he stared at me, seeming momentarily stunned. It reminded me of his expression when I'd shown him my dress at Sofia's wedding, forcing me to see that moment clearly for the first time. His shock was a good thing. In fact, I found that I *loved* making Julian speechless. Watching him grapple for words after so many years of verbal sparring? Incredibly gratifying.

Julian sat unmoving on the velvety couch, one arm resting over the top while his champagne flute dangled between his fingers in the other hand.

God, he was so unfairly handsome. I wasn't sure I'd ever been more attracted to him than now when he was surrounded by pink, plush, and sparkling things. His eyes lifted as he heard me come out of the dressing room, and they warmed while trailing over me.

I didn't need summers on the Cape. I just needed Julian's gaze to make me feel the sun, like a hot, shimmering spotlight.

After soaking in his heat for a moment, I cocked my head to the side and returned his look. "Do I look fuckable in this one?"

Julian's grip on his glass tightened, and he leaned forward, resting his elbows on his knees. "Why don't you come over here, and we can find out?"

"Julian," I hissed, and he lifted his hands up in defense before returning to his casually relaxed position on the sofa.

"We're getting that one," he said after clearing his throat.

I bit down on a secret smile. "What if I want another one?"

"I'll buy that one, too." He shrugged. "I'll buy all of them; I don't care. But this one is coming home with us."

"What if I *wore* it home?" I asked. Julian's eyes remained hot and attentive, sweeping over me in a continual appreciative assessment. I had to swallow before adding, "And on our date?"

"Please do." He took a sip of champagne, eyes glittering over the glass rim. "I know how to break bones if I need to."

I sighed, confident that wouldn't be necessary. But the way he looked at me still made my cheeks flush, and heat rippled through my body. "Well, I think you've answered my question."

"About what?"

Julian's eyes locked on mine, curiosity lingering in them. But I lowered my voice before responding, not wanting Charlotte to overhear. There was an entire wall of dresses between her and us, and I didn't see her anywhere in sight, but still.

"About whether or not I look fuckable," I said, my grin cocking to one side.

Julian pushed off the sofa, striding toward me. "I should hope you know the answer to that," he said, husky voice washing over me as he gripped my hip with his free hand and tugged me into him. Into his—*oh.* "And the only one fucking you tonight will be me, Juniper."

A zap of heat hurtled through me. It had been days since he'd proven me wrong and fucked me precisely like a fictional man would, and then he'd refused to do it again every night since. Apparently, I'd winced one too many times on New Year's Day, and now he kept spewing some bullshit about not wanting to hurt me. Although, he'd definitely made it up to me in other ways.

I felt like I was on cloud nine lately. The only time I got an inkling of unease was when Gemma texted me, digging for information about the mystery man I'd woken up with on New Year's Day. I was going to have to figure out how to tell her, but I might as well see if Julian and I could get through a date night without biting each other's heads off first.

I'd say it was looking promising so far.

I groaned as Julian tipped his hips into mine, grinding so I could feel how ready he was.

It was a promise for later. My stomach flipped just thinking about it, and I snatched Julian's glass of champagne out of his hand, needing something to wash the dryness from my throat before attempting to talk.

"You better," I finally muttered in response to his promise for later. He'd given me a taste of what he could do, and I wanted more.

"So greedy, aren't you?" Julian chuckled darkly. "Always wanting it."

I made an indecipherable noise, too distracted by how Julian's fingers had drifted beneath my dress, caressing my skin in tight, ascending circles. When he found my underwear, he traced the seam down until I had to bite my tongue to avoid making other sounds.

"I'm not—" I started to protest, but Julian swiped a finger beneath my underwear, toying directly with my clit, and my ability to talk vanished momentarily.

"Don't lie, Daisy." He whispered a kiss over my forehead, breathing his words softly.

And then Julian pulled away, leaving me to stand there breathless as he stalked back to the sofa. Once settled, he threw one arm up again, resting it along the top.

"Do I get to see the blue one?" he asked like the last minute hadn't happened, nodding his head to the row of dresses I still hadn't tried on in the fitting room.

I shook my head, struggling to withhold a smile of my own. "You're enjoying this, aren't you?"

"No, Juni." He shook his head. His grin grew, sly and charming, and it nearly took me out completely. "I'm *loving* this."

That was it. Those words right there. They were the best part about this entire evening so far.

Because I knew, without a single doubt, that they were true.

Julian didn't take me here out of a sense of obligation or duty. He didn't want to take me on a date simply to prove something or to fulfill his side of a deal. He asked me out because he wanted to.

And amazingly enough, he was loving it.

And so was I.

It was the first date I'd probably ever had that felt like the guy cared about what I might enjoy, but I wasn't surprised. When Julian said he knew me better than any other guy out there, he was right.

Meanwhile, Greg Kennedy had dropped into my DMs on social media at least three times this week, but I wasn't sure why he thought I'd ever respond when he'd treated each of our dates like an annoying prerequisite to getting sexual favors. But not enough sexual favors that he wouldn't cheat on me, of course.

When I couldn't seem to get my legs to move, Julian encouraged me.

"Come on, Rosie." His look was gentle as he urged me to get going. "As much as I love staring at you, we've still got a seven o'clock reservation to get to."

"Who needs dinner when you've got dresses?" I laughed.

"*You* need dinner," Julian said seriously before growing amused again and dropping his voice. "Think of it as fuel for later, love."

He winked, knowing what he was doing.

Meanwhile, I tried not to melt on my way back to the dressing room.

MUCH TO JULIAN'S SATISFACTION, I WAS STILL WEARING THE BLACK DRESS when we left the boutique. However, Charlotte also boxed up one other dress—a blue one—for me to pick up another day.

I tried not to feel guilty about how much Julian had insisted on buying. I really didn't want to argue with him, especially considering how strongly he reacted when I offered to pay the first time. But no one had ever spoiled me like this before. It felt...nice.

He settled his hand on my leg as we made the short drive to the restaurant where he'd made reservations. I squirmed beneath his fingertips, impatient for more of his touch with how he'd teased me in the boutique. Julian knew it, too. He tucked his fingers beneath the hem of my dress, tickling lightly as we pulled into a parking spot. He squeezed my thigh as he put the car into park, and I gasped.

"It must be a little uncomfortable, isn't it?" he asked, glancing over at me.

I cocked my head to the side. "What is?"

"Sitting there wearing underwear that's soaked for me."

A roll of my eyes was my only response because I didn't want him to get the satisfaction of knowing he was right. My whole body pulsed, needing him. I tried to look away from his knowing face before he could catch the truth in my eyes, but I was sure he still saw right through me.

Which was why it didn't surprise me when his lips spread in a cocky smirk.

"Take them off, Daisy."

My head whipped back around at that. "What?"

"I'm solving the problem." He held out his hand, palm up. "Take them off."

I stared at him with wide eyes. Besides the light filtering in from the streetlamp, the car was dark. But I saw the desire and mischief brewing in Julian's gaze all the same.

His demand was ridiculous, but I found myself *wanting* to obey. After all, it would drive Julian wild knowing I didn't have anything beneath this dress, and I loved driving Julian wild.

With slightly shaky hands, I pushed my dress up around my hips and hooked my fingers in my underwear to wiggle out of them. Julian's burning gaze traced my every movement as I snuck them off one foot and then the other before dropping the damp underwear in his outstretched palm.

He raised a brow. It was an *I-told-you-so* brow raise. Because he had been right; I'd been so disastrously wet for him. My lips pressed together, indenting with a slightly embarrassed smile in response to his expression.

He curled his fingers around my underwear, balling them into his pocket. "Good girl."

Indecision flashed in Julian's eyes, and I could tell he was debating skipping dinner altogether. But after a pause, he slipped out of the car and walked around to open my door for me.

"How are your feet holding up in those heels?" Both concern

and humor lingered in Julian's voice as we walked hand in hand across the street.

"Don't you worry about my feet," I said with a laugh. "I told you. There's a lot I can do in these things."

"Can't wait to find out," Julian murmured before swinging open the restaurant's front door for me.

My jaw dropped at the adorable sight that greeted us when we walked in. A feeling of warmth filled the tiny Italian eatery, likely from the fireplace that acted as a focal point on the back wall. A curved ceiling hosted twinkling lights, making the restaurant feel a bit cavernous. But in a secretive sort of way—like we'd just strode through a portal instead of a door.

Based on the presence of white tablecloths and perfectly uniformed waiters, I was glad to be wearing this dress as opposed to the one I had left the house in earlier. In his well-tailored suit, Julian fit right in as he walked to the stand to inquire about our reservation.

He flashed me a smile as the hostess gathered our menus, and I wished I could conjure up something to say. I was almost too blown away to speak. But mostly, I hoped Julian didn't think he had to spend money to impress me. That couldn't be further from the truth, but once again, I was hesitant to bring up the cost, not wanting to offend him.

So I settled on expressing my awe instead.

"This place is really nice," I said under my breath as I slid into our chairs across from each other. "Like really nice."

Julian appeared to find that comment amusing, his brow quirking.

"What's that look for?" I asked.

"It's just...did you think I was going to take you out for a cheap beer on our first date?"

"You do love cheap beer," I said in defense, even though I'd always known he would take tonight seriously.

Things felt serious.

But we'd never confirmed that, and tonight, that felt wrong. I wanted to know that this was precisely what it felt like.

"Julian..." I hesitated, trying to plan my words out. But a moment later, they just tumbled from my lips. "Exactly what kind of date is this?"

Julian cocked his head to the side but didn't miss a beat before answering. "The kind that's repeated."

I attempted to suppress my smile, but it was a useless effort. "We haven't even gotten drinks yet, and you already know you want a second date, huh?"

"Second date?" He chuckled. "No, Daisy. I want all the dates. Every date."

I swallowed, knowing I needed even more of an answer from him. Just to be sure. "And while we're going on all those dates, are we going on other dates?"

"Other dates?" Julian repeated. "You mean with other people?"

I nodded, quickly snatching the glass of water that a passing waiter had placed on our table.

"Fuck no." He leaned forward, resting both palms on the table's white linen. He hissed the next words beneath his breath, voice slithering down my spine. "Do I need to remind you of what I said the other night while you were getting your pretty pussy fucked for the first time?"

Suddenly, my lungs felt two sizes too small for my body, and the fireplace at my back sparked way too much heat. Sweat tickled the nape of my neck. I crossed my legs, but that only reminded me how Julian had my underwear in his pocket, and I was left feeling exposed and aching for him.

"I love making you blush," Julian commented with a light chuckle, the fire melting from his eyes again as he leaned back in his chair. His gaze plummeted to my bodice and then quickly back to my face. "I can't wait to see that color cover the rest of your body."

"So this is..." I started, bringing the topic back around before I lost the ability to breathe entirely. I wanted confirmation of what this was. I couldn't decide on the right words, though, so Julian filled in for me.

"This is dating, Juni." The smile he gave me was easy. Nothing between Julian and I had ever been easy, but ironically, this was. Julian spoke as though nothing had ever been easier than this conversation. "Not a date. Dating. How's that sound?"

Dating. Not a date, dating.

"That's acceptable, I suppose."

When Julian began to frown, I tossed him a wink. But that didn't stop him from having something to say. Of *course* it didn't.

"Acceptable?" He rolled his eyes in response, lips twitching. "Baby, I know you're used to mediocrity considering your previous boyfriends, but we don't do *acceptable* here. You deserve more than that."

I took a quick sip of my water, fumbling with the glass a little and spilling a splash on the table. Julian had just said the word *boyfriend*, and while I understood that was the entire concept of what he had been explaining with the whole exclusively dating thing, I hadn't expected to hear that word so soon. And I hadn't expected to feel so incredibly giddy about it.

"Okay, Juni?" Julian went on. "So either stop it with the lies or tell me what you want to change so that this isn't just...acceptable." He wrinkled his nose as he said the last word.

"I don't want to change anything," I said breathlessly. "I don't want to change anything at all."

It was still a little unbelievable to me that we were here, but I wouldn't want it any other way.

Julian nodded and tucked his sharp tongue away. For now. He reached across the table, sliding his hand over mine. I laced my fingers through his, my heart beating so loudly that I worried we'd drawn attention.

But we didn't. Because no one knew. No one knew who we were or what this simple touch meant. They didn't know that we were Juniper and Julian, two people who spent years being too confused and scared of their feelings that they latched onto playing a little game instead. A game that was predictable, as equally humorous as it was hurtful, but most importantly—fake.

I'd immediately known that taking Julian to Sofia's wedding would be disastrous because suddenly, it wasn't a game anymore, it ironically *wasn't* an act, and there wasn't a script. We'd flown too close to something too real, something bright and warm like the sun, and everyone always warned against that, didn't they?

But now we were here, and the sweat sprinkling my back from the heat was surprisingly comforting. And I liked that not knowing what to expect felt safe for the first time in a long time. There wasn't a script, but there were lines I'd always wanted to hear. And Julian Briggs was hitting all of them.

He looked down at the menu before him, still grasping my hand. And when he glanced up again, his expression was serious.

"I have to admit something, Juniper."

My forehead creased as my thoughts chased worries around in my brain.

But then Julian said, "I've never had gnocchi."

A smile broke out on my face so wide that I felt it crack. "How can you go twenty-seven years without experiencing gnocchi?"

"Closer to twenty-eight years," Julian muttered, though he was grinning back.

"That does *not* help your case," I said, laughter following my words.

Although, the reminder of Julian's upcoming birthday brought me back down to earth. We were living in a bubble where nothing existed except us and this date and heated glances. But next weekend, we would be going to Whitebridge to celebrate his birthday with his family, and other people were going to burst through that bubble.

Julian and I hadn't talked about work or family or breaking out of our bubble. We'd just wrapped it tighter around us. For the most part, I'd ignored Gemma, feigning a busy work schedule. But she would be there next weekend, and I didn't know what I'd say.

I was sleeping with my best friend's brother. Dating him. And obviously, I needed to come clean about that.

The rest of our meal was delightful. Julian tried the gnocchi and approved, although I doubted he would say anything even if he didn't. Meanwhile, I had a delicious plate of the world's cheesiest pasta. Julian smiled as he watched me eat the last noodle, feeling like I was about to explode but too happy to care. And unsurprisingly, we were able to make it through dinner without any broken bones.

Not that I thought that would be necessary. No man had ever looked at me like Julian seemed to think they would. Only him, and I was definitely okay with that.

As we slid into Julian's car at the end of our date, his hand returned to my thigh. His fingers traced my skin the entire way home, and all I could do was clench my legs tighter in response. The thrum of anticipation was heady in my veins as we pulled into the parking garage below his apartment building. It only increased as Julian led me to the elevator, every step making my body pulse with need.

As soon as the elevator doors closed, Julian's lips slammed onto mine.

Apparently, his restraint and control had been just as close to snapping.

"It was so hard," he rasped between hard kisses. "It was so hard not to touch you beneath the table at dinner. Knowing you are so wet and naked for me beneath that dress. I've been dying to get you alone all night."

"We are alone," I pointed out, my head beginning to spin from the tight space and the proximity of every part of Julian to every part of me.

"We are, huh?" Julian's hand slipped beneath my dress, his fingers crawling over my bare skin. "So if I made you scream right now, no one would notice?"

"Oh, I—"

Even if I had an answer, I wouldn't be able to talk. Julian's fingers were tickling the seam of my legs, caressing them apart. He wanted me to spread my legs for him, and I didn't know how to resist—not anymore.

"I've always wanted to be able to render you speechless," Julian murmured, brushing his lips over my jaw.

I let my body talk for me, shifting so Julian could drag his finger across my inner thigh, teasing my slit with the tip of his finger. And then I had to swallow a whimper, not wanting him to know how easily he could make a mess of my pussy. Except he already did know. Because a second later, he slipped his hand from beneath my skirt and brought his glistening finger—the one that swept between my legs—to his lips.

No sooner had his tongue wrapped around it, sucking off my arousal, than Julian dropped to the ground with a low groan. I gasped his name, unconsciously threading my fingers through his hair. His expression glowed, but I only got to enjoy it for a second before Julian dipped his head, kissing a path beneath my skirt.

"You're dripping down your thighs, and it's a bit of a mess," he mumbled, "but since it's my fault, I'll help clean you up."

I wanted to roll my eyes at the cockiness in his tone but threw my head back with a moan instead. Julian's tongue was lashing out, branding my skin with his hot attention. He licked and licked, ensuring that my thighs didn't have even a bit of wetness coating them.

My hips tipped forward of their own accord, straining for something more. I needed his tongue where it ached.

When he gave it to me, teasing my clit with the faintest brush, I nearly screamed. His fingers gripped my legs, urging them to spread wider so he could bury his face deeper between my thighs. He wasn't teasing my clit anymore; he was lapping at it steadily and with intent, his tongue driving me to my breaking point.

He was *trying* to make me scream, wasn't he?

"Julian, *please*," I begged, my hips writhing between the tight hold he had on them.

His eyes darted up, spearing me with their heat. "Please, what?"

No sooner had he asked the question than he continued his ministrations, his sinfully talented tongue dancing between my legs. Pleasure filled every inch of me, and even though I knew I should beg for him to stop so we weren't caught if the elevator stopped, I knew I wasn't going to. I was so damn weak when it came to him.

"Please...please make me come," I said through clenched teeth, feeling my knees begin to buckle and my limbs begin to shake.

Julian's lips curled; I felt it. I felt it, and I knew exactly what he was going to do.

He pulled away, standing instead as his wicked eyes trailed over me.

Goddamn him.

"Jul—" I gasped, but the faint chatter of people broke through my thoughts, and I realized the elevator door had opened behind Julian. He bracketed my body with his, shielding anyone from looking at me, but after quickly tugging down my dress, he stepped away.

"Come on," Julian murmured, giving me his hand. I took it, mostly because I was afraid I might fall if I didn't. My body felt like it was ready to break if I didn't get a release soon.

I followed Julian to his apartment door, where he stopped and looked over at me. He licked his lips while his eyes fell to my mouth, lingering on it before he finally spoke. He gripped my chin lightly before brushing his thumb over my lower lip. His voice dropped low enough that it made my knees even weaker. "I like this color on your lips," he breathed. "But I think it will look even better when it paints my cock later."

I flicked my eyes up to his. "Open the door and we can find out."

Julian's smirked wolfishly.

And then he opened the door.

ten years ago

Juni stood in my garage, wearing a dress.

It was white and flowy and annoyingly angelic. But most of all, it was short.

"What the hell are you wearing?"

"Happy birthday, Julian," Juni said, ignoring my question.

"It's January," I muttered, still stuck on her choice of attire.

"Yes, I'm aware. Your birthday has always been on January 8th. My birthday has always been on July 8th. It would be odd if they suddenly changed to different months."

"I don't understand why you're wearing that," I continued. "The heaters in here aren't very warm." She was going to catch a fucking cold.

"I told her she should wear it because she looks hot," Gemma cut in, handing a soda to Juni. "Don't you think, Jules?"

I frowned at my sister while refusing to look at her friend.

And refusing to answer that question.

CHAPTER THIRTY-FIVE

julian

"KEEP THE HEELS ON," I commanded as Juniper walked into my apartment. "I need to see what you can do in those."

Juniper listened, walking straight into my apartment with a slight sway to her hips. Her heels clicked as she walked across the living space and sat on the corner of my couch to wait for me. Butterflies—goddamn fucking butterflies—erupted in my chest when she lifted her sooty gaze to mine.

"Finally alone," I muttered, low enough that I didn't think she heard me.

But her legs clenched tighter, a telltale sign that she didn't just hear my words—she heard my intent.

Juniper tracked my movements without saying anything. I dropped my keys on the kitchen counter, and the gentle clinking reverberated through the quiet apartment, stirring up the tension. I swore I could hear her heartbeat. Or maybe it was just a feeling. I could *feel* her heartbeat.

I wondered if she could feel mine, which picked up as I crossed my apartment and sank onto the couch next to her.

"Hi, gorgeous," I said, immediately sliding my hand onto her thigh.

I was going to be the clingiest fucking boyfriend, and I didn't even care. I was obsessed.

"Hi, handsome," she replied, her body shifting toward me as her attention warmed me from the inside out. A pretty blush spread over Juni's cheeks, making me smile. If my simple compliment made her blush like that, I couldn't wait to see what would happen next.

I dropped my eyes, letting them trail over her outfit for the hundredth time tonight. "Look at you sitting here, waiting for me like a good girl."

Her eyes flicked up in a half roll, but her lips twitched in an attempt not to react. "Don't get used to it. Consider it an early birthday gift."

"Yeah?" I cocked a brow. "We'll see about that."

I was more than confident that she would want to replay tonight.

I drifted my palm up her thigh, squeezing slightly. Juni instinctually opened for me, gasping my name as her body betrayed her. With her legs parted, I snuck my hand under her dress for the third time tonight and wasn't disappointed with what I found. I was still a greedy asshole who wanted more, though.

But before I could continue touching her, Juniper moved. She shifted onto her knees, swinging one leg over my thighs to straddle me. And as soon as she sat her ass down on my lap, all I could think about was how fucking good her weight felt on top of me. Not to mention her tits were in my face, and *goddamn*. She could lean forward and suffocate me with them, and I would say thank you.

Juni placed both hands on my chest before sliding them beneath my suit jacket, forcing me to shrug it off my shoulders. Then she began unbuttoning my shirt, and every time her fingers brushed my skin, I had to suppress a shiver. She knew exactly what she was fucking doing to me, smirking as she ground her hips down, making my cock stiffen with every movement. I clenched my hands into fists, wanting to touch her but also not wanting to interrupt what she was doing.

Juniper's eyes flicked over my tense body.

"That control of yours won't last long, baby," she cooed after a long moment of pulsing silence.

I groaned. She was right; I wasn't going to last. Not when she called me baby, making me melt into the fucking ground.

"You forget something, Juni," I breathed, somehow rallying from the beautiful blow she'd dealt me.

"Hm?" Juniper hummed as she pulled the bottom of my shirt out from my pants, continuing to unbutton it.

"I have years of practice controlling myself around you," I replied before sucking in as she raked my bare chest with her long nails.

I might have controlled myself around Juniper over the years, but she wasn't sitting on my lap then, and she definitely didn't have her hands all over me. For that reason, I knew my argument could have been better, and Juniper saw right through my words.

She smiled, looking down at me with triumph in her gaze. "Is that so?"

God, she was about to do something utterly irresistible, wasn't she?

With my shirt draped open over my chest, Juniper slid down my front and then dismounted from my lap to lower herself to the floor. She kneeled before my feet, leaning back on her heels while still wearing those killer shoes.

I watched as she slid a finger into her cleavage, fishing out lipstick wedged in her bodice and reapplying it to her pretty lips. Her hooded gaze studied me steadily while the color on her lips deepened to a cherry red. Once she finished, her eyes dropped, skimming my body until they landed on the tent in my pants. She pressed her lips together, giving the lipstick a little smack of finality.

When she was done with that little show, Juniper flung the cosmetic tube to the floor and put both hands on her thighs.

Slowly, she rucked her dress up, causing all the air to vanish from my body as she stopped just before I had a full view.

The worst sort of cliffhanger.

Juniper looked up at me beneath her lashes, and there was a challenge in her gaze. But I didn't care about that. All I cared about was having more of her.

"Let me see you," I said, my words deadly soft.

"You're bossy when you're..." Her eyes flicked back to my erection. "Hungry."

At that, my mouth stretched wide in a smirk. "I told you to remember that."

"Believe me...I didn't forget." Juniper bit down on her bottom lip, sucking it between her teeth in such a tempting way. Her lips were so fucking kissable. "But I think I'll take matters into my own hands."

Before I could even absorb her words, Juniper dragged her dress up the rest of the way, letting me see her beautiful pussy. The visibility was low in the living room, with only a few lamps and the lights from the cityscape casting a glow over the space. But even through the dimness, she glistened for me.

I put both hands on my knees, gripping them tightly as though I could physically hold on to my control.

Her words finally caught up to me as she reached between her legs and swiped a finger through her pussy until she zeroed in on her clit, rubbing in tiny, circular movements. A moan left her lips and reached my dick, making it twitch in my pants.

She was making my high school wet dreams come true right now. I'd die a happy man, having seen the sight before me.

Juni met my gaze, beat for beat, and I had to clear my throat before I could speak.

"You can make yourself come, pretty girl, but it's not going to give you the relief you want." I leaned forward, bracing myself on my knees as I spoke in a slow, measured way. "You're not aching for an orgasm. You're aching for me. There's a difference."

A tiny, adorable growl ripped from Juni. It was soaked in frustration because she knew I was right. I was sure she was enjoying herself, but it wasn't satisfying in the way she wanted. The way she needed.

I thought she would give up, but she took it a step further instead, dipping her middle finger into her pussy, plunging it deep. I clenched my jaw as she groaned. As hot as this was, I was starting to feel impatient as all hell. I couldn't wait to elicit those noises myself.

I was so busy thinking about how I planned to make that pussy mine tonight that I barely noticed when Juni pushed up on her knees, not until she lifted her glistening finger, bringing it to my mouth.

"Suck," she demanded before brushing arousal across my lower lip.

Jesus Christ. She was playing with fire now, wasn't she?

I crushed her wrist in my grip, holding her hand there so I could do as she said, immediately parting my lips to let her finger slip into my mouth.

An opportunity to taste Juniper? I'd never pass that up. Not in a million years.

The familiar taste of her blossomed in my mouth as I sucked her finger past her knuckle, wrapping my tongue around her so I could get every last drop. And then I ripped her finger back out and pinned her with a heated look.

"Your turn, love."

She smiled, and I didn't even have to explain what I meant before Juniper was tearing at my belt buckle. In record time, she had my pants undone, hanging open as she paused to stroke my cock through my briefs, making me throw my head back with a groan.

I squeezed my eyes shut, trying to get the rampant desire under control as I felt Juni pull my waistband down, letting my erection spring free. A wet heat consumed me, and I opened my eyes again, needing to watch Juniper swallow my cock.

Fuck. Those red lips worked over my length, taking me deep

and then pulling back to kiss my tip. She was destroying me. This was completely destroying me. She dragged her tongue up the underside of my cock and then licked that spot right below my tip that really did me in. I knew she'd find it. She always did.

"I'm obsessed with the things your mouth can do," I rasped, threading my fingers through her hair to encourage her to pick up the pace slightly. I was so impatient after everything that had happened tonight. I needed to hit the back of her throat and then come down it.

I felt Juni's lips curve around my dick at the praise and decided she deserved more.

"I've never seen anything prettier than how you take my cock, Juni baby. Nothing is prettier than you."

She whimpered. I felt it around my length, and her sounds ricocheted inside me like a pinball. Meanwhile, I was lighting up like a winner, racking up pleasure, higher and higher, until I knew I wasn't going to last.

"It's too good. You're too good, Daisy. I'm going to—"

Juniper drew me to the back of her throat before looking at me with clear, hot intent. And there wasn't a chance in hell that I wasn't going to give her what she wanted.

My high took over while Juniper had me locked in a staring contest, flashing me those fuck-me eyes while she took every last drop of my cum. And then she made sure to drag her lips over my length, leaving a red lipstick stain before popping me out of her mouth. As soon as she swallowed, I tugged on her hair.

"Get up here," I gasped, but it was unnecessary. Juniper was already crawling into my lap, all but launching herself at me. I caught her, and within seconds, our mouths collided.

Juni, Juni, Juni. I'd never get tired of feeling her lips move beneath mine, of tasting her. She might feel like a goddess beneath my fingers, look like a princess, and smell like an entire bouquet of flowers...but Juniper tasted like sex.

No wonder I was fucked from the minute she kissed me in that hotel room.

No wonder I could feel myself growing hard again from how her tongue thrust into my mouth, coated with my taste.

"That was—*fuck*." I ripped my lips from hers to kiss her jaw, neck, and every inch of skin I could find. "But it's never enough, not with you."

Juniper took her turn exploring, kissing a path up my body until she had my earlobe between her teeth, grazing my skin. "If you want more, you'll have to come and get it," she whispered before springing off my lap.

I watched as she took off across my apartment, moving gracefully, still wearing those heels and that dress. I took off after her, catching Juni around the waist from behind as she was about to dive onto my bed and pulling her against me. And then it was my turn to find her ear and let my hot breath fan the shell of it, making her shiver.

"It's cute that you thought you could get away that easily. I'm going to catch you every single time, Daisy."

Her breaths were short, but I heard her smile between each one. "I'll catch you, too."

Pure appreciation swept through me for how she matched me in every single fucking way. She always had, and I wasn't sure why I didn't realize earlier that there would be no denying this. No denying us. There would never be anyone better for Juniper than me, and there would never, ever be anyone better for me than Juniper.

"You caught me a long fucking time ago, Juni. I never could escape you. I tried. God knows, I tried. I moved across the country for college because I thought it would help me forget you, but how could I ever forget someone as goddamn perfect as you?"

"Julian..." she moaned, but I was pretty sure it was more in response to how I encouraged her to bow down over the bed, giving me all the access I needed to tease her exposed, soaked pussy with the tip of my cock.

Stealing her underwear earlier was the best idea I'd ever had.

"You want it like this, don't you?" I smoothed a hand down

her back, appreciating her curves. My fingers itched to strip her, but I'd been thinking about fucking her in this dress all night long. "You want to be bent over and taken from behind like the dirty girl you are, huh?"

Juniper sucked in, and I knew I hit a bit of accuracy with my words. I let my smirk fly free, knowing she couldn't see how satisfying that knowledge was. Meanwhile, I wiped lipstick off my cock with the bottom of my shirt as I waited for her answer, wanting it to be ready to bury deep inside her.

"Yes, I want that," she admitted breathily, surprising me. "But I have a feeling you're not going to give me what I want."

I chuckled. She was right; as much as I wanted to sink inside her right this second, I wasn't going to fuck Juni from behind tonight. I needed to see her face light up as she found heaven.

"What's holding you back, baby?" Juniper looked over her shoulder at me, fluttering those lashes and speaking in a sinfully soft voice. "Do I get to see what else is in your bedside table?"

I swallowed a moan. If Juni realized that calling me baby was my weakness, she would use it on me all the time, and I'd be done for.

"Not tonight. I don't think you're ready for me to stretch your pretty ass." I drifted my hand over her backside, feeling her shivers explode beneath my palm. My fingers inched between her beautiful cheeks, giving her a small taste of pressure, and she gasped with appreciation. *Fuck*, this girl. I pressed my length between her legs, wanting her to feel what she did to me. "No, it's just that you've been driving me wild for years, and it's time you feel what it's like."

I flipped Juniper over so suddenly that her shriek filled my bedroom. But her lips stretched in a smile as she bounced back on the bed, staring up at me. That smile melted into an expression of surprise and arousal when I yanked down her bodice, desperate to see more of her, even though I was reluctant to take off her dress entirely.

This would do, though. This would definitely do.

My cock stiffened at the sight of her. Christ, every inch of her was beautiful, but those tits...*shit*, they were incredible. They heaved as Juni took deep breaths, and I brushed a finger over one nipple, teasing with a feathery light touch until it peaked for me.

"So beautiful," I murmured.

Juniper whimpered my name. She squeezed her eyes shut and arched into my hands as I moved from one breast to the other. I smiled, watching how she tried to get more from me as she squirmed.

She would get everything. But she was also going to use that sweet mouth of hers to beg for it.

"Yes, baby?" I prompted before brushing my lips over her collarbone, sucking lightly. "Is there something you want?"

Juni's quick intake of breath was her only response. She chose to writhe and twist instead, encouraging my lips to lower. I obeyed because I couldn't help it, roughing my lips over her breast before latching onto a nipple, enjoying how Juniper's back lifted off the bed in response.

She moaned loudly, tangling her fingers in my hair and holding me there so I wouldn't stop.

But I couldn't wait any longer. Juni's mind met mine in the same place because she immediately reached for my shirt, pushing it off. It fell to the floor, followed by my pants as Juniper tugged them down.

"I can't wait to be inside you again," I grunted, loving how frantic her movements were. It was exactly how I felt.

Once I was naked, Juniper fell back into the sheets again, and a surge of arousal attacked me when I watched her melt into the fabric, her tits rocking gloriously. She cocked a brow, surveying how I wasn't doing a damn thing, too stunned by how amazing she looked.

"Clearly, you can wait...otherwise, you'd be fucking me already."

I shook my head, my smile creeping out. "You're such a smart-ass."

Her expression matched mine. "You like it."

My grin grew wicked. "No, I *love* it."

I loved her sharp, talented mouth. I never dreamed I'd get to taste it so freely.

"Julian...please. Please fuck me," Juni whimpered, finally giving me what I wanted as she begged for it. Not that I would have been able to deny us much longer, anyway. No matter how badly I wanted to stretch this moment out forever, my restraint was nearly nonexistent. I started to pull away, reaching for my bedside table, but Juni stopped me.

"I don't want you to use a condom," she said, gasping for air. "I just want...*please*."

"You sure?" Even as I clarified, I eagerly returned to my spot between her legs and bunched her dress up around her waist. Her words were too good to be true, and my head spun.

She nodded, eyes wide and wanting. Her dark irises bloomed with desire—like the prettiest flower. "I told you. I'm on birth control, and I trust you. I'm yours, Julian."

Tonight was almost more than I could handle. *I'm yours, Julian*. Fuck, I wanted to make her scream those words until she came.

As for birth control, I didn't give a fuck about that. But I figured telling a girl that you wanted her to have your babies on the first date probably wasn't the way to go.

"You want it?" I rasped, trying not to let the emotion overcome my voice. I wrapped my cock in my fist, pressing the tip between her legs and taunting her with the pressure. And even though her hips lifted, asking for more, she shook her head. My lips curled at her continued smart-assery...that is, until her lashes fluttered, and her lips parted with a breathy sigh.

"No...Julian, I want *you*."

"Oh, baby," I groaned before any remaining shred of restraint dissolved, and I *sank*. Fell into her, deeper and deeper, as her hot, wet pussy stretched around me. Heat rippled up my body, and I wasn't sure how I'd manage to keep myself in check when she felt this fucking good. Perfect—Juniper Kate St. James was perfect.

She'd always been perfect. But I'd realized recently the only thing I ever wanted to change about her was her last name.

Her head tipped back, her mouth opening as a wordless cry poured out. Face flushed, eyes rolling, neck arched—Juniper was a vision. I stilled, buried to the hilt within her, and she finally blinked up at me, our eyes connected.

She was killing me. Fucking Juniper was one thing, but fucking Juniper bare was otherworldly. I felt like the luckiest man on Earth. Or off it. I was the luckiest man in the universe.

She started to make tiny rocking movements with her hips, rubbing against me, searching for that friction that I so desperately wanted to give her. I slipped my hand lower until it was wrapped around her throat. While squeezing slightly, I pulled my cock out and thrust back in again, making Juniper's eyes fly open. They were wide enough that I could see every dark, beautiful part of her.

"You have no idea how beautiful you are right now, do you? You told me that you're mine, but baby, I'm yours. I've always been yours. And I've never wanted *anything* as much as I want you. I will always want you." I closed my eyes, catching my breath and my control before I came too soon. When I opened them again, Juniper was staring straight into my soul. "I'm so fucking lucky, Juni," I whispered.

A spark ignited in her eyes, and without warning, she tipped her hips higher, wrapping her legs around my waist. I felt the scrape of her heels as they settled on my back, and a growl slipped through my lips at how much further inside her I could reach in this position.

Juniper's heels dug into my back, almost as though she was punishing me for the years we could have had this, and I deserved every mark undoubtedly left on my skin. Clenching my jaw, I lost it as waves of pain and pleasure rolled through me.

I repeatedly bucked into Juni's sopping wet heat, and my

name started rolling off her tongue with every unrelenting thrust. The way she chanted it felt like a promise, and *damn*, I wanted to be good enough to make her keep it. I dropped my head, nuzzling into the crook of her neck, where I knew all she could probably hear were my ragged moans, in time with the way our bodies moved together.

Her cries were rising in volume, but it wasn't quick enough. She felt too good, and I'd be damned if I came before she finished. With that singular thought in mind, I grabbed her legs and pried them from where they were currently locked around my waist.

Juniper scowled like she hated that tiny bit of separation I'd created. "What—what are you doing?"

I smirked. "I think these heels would look even better over my shoulders."

Juniper's breath released in a hiss as I flung her into that exact position, and I smirked while reaching between us to find her clit. Her body tightened as I increased the pace of my thrusts, now determined to see how quickly I could make her explode.

"That's it," I moaned. "You take me so good. It's so fucking amazing."

I watched the praise light her up, and her lips parted. She was holding her breath, and since I'd learned that meant she was close, I kept my pace steady. Seconds later, glorious satisfaction rolled through me as she fell apart, clenching sweetly around me. The points of her heels and the curves of her fingernails dug into my skin as I fucked her through her climax, wringing every last wave of pleasure from her body.

And then I followed her, coming so hard that the room flipped upside down and inside out. Juniper was the only one keeping me grounded, and I clutched her to me until every last aftershock faded. I felt my cum spill from her body, and filling her up was so fucking satisfying that my eyes momentarily rolled back.

"Juni..." I breathed, coming back down to Earth. "Juni, I—"

Speechless. I didn't have any more words. None that I could piece together at the moment, at least. So I forced myself to move instead, slowly pulling out and stripping Juni until she was finally naked in my arms, her dress discarded onto the floor.

I rolled her on top of me, not wanting to crush her. She rested her head on my chest, right above my heart, and I stroked my fingers through her hair leisurely.

"Julian?" she whispered.

"Yes, love?"

Her smile curved against me. I felt it, etching into my heart.

"Do you remember your eighteenth birthday?"

"Of course I remember."

"Of course?" She scoffed. "You were drunk off your ass."

I smiled. She wasn't wrong, but... "It snowed all night. It was cold as fuck in the garage, even with all the teenagers packed together and the heaters we pulled out. And you..." I sucked in at the memory. "You wore this shimmery, white dress like you wanted to outshine the snowstorm."

Juniper's breathing stuttered. "You hated that I wore that."

"Yeah, well, it was cold, and I was drunk. I didn't know how to keep you warm without offering to be the one to do it, and I was too scared to do that."

The moment stretched between us, quiet but peaceful, until Juni's sweet voice broke it.

"Julian?"

"Yes, love?"

"I'm cold."

My grin grew so wide that my lips cracked. I rolled Juni over, holding her against me until I'd wrestled the blankets over us.

"Can I be the one to keep you warm?" I murmured, leaning in to brush a kiss over her bare shoulder.

She giggled adorably.

"I thought you'd never ask."

CHAPTER THIRTY-SIX

I COULD REALLY GET used to waking up in Julian's bed. I could really get used to wake-up calls filled with kisses and slow, hot sex. I could get used to hearing his gravelly voice tell me how he'd wanted mornings like this from the first time we'd accidentally woken up in the same bed together.

I could get used to this—all of this. The mind-blowing orgasms, the sweet dates, and the attentiveness.

Everything was absolutely perfect. Everything except...

"Gemma texted me," I announced on Monday morning as I prepared for another week of work. "She wants to get together. She also asked if I ever learned if Noah is a good kisser."

Julian's eyes shot to mine, the fire in them bright until it clicked in his brain why she would ask me that. His irritation dimmed, but only slightly.

"Tell her you wouldn't know, and you never will."

Of course he would say something like that. Ignoring his bristly possessiveness that secretly made my insides turn to mush, I cleared my throat.

"I think I'll just ask Gemma if she wants to grab dinner this week, and then I can tell her everything."

Julian, who was in the middle of putting on his tie as we both got ready for work, stilled.

"I wouldn't tell her *everything*, Daisy."

He looked horrified at the idea that I would tell his sister how he'd eaten me out in an elevator after our first date.

"Of course I'm not going to tell her everything." I opened the drawer that Julian insisted on giving me in his dresser and grabbed a pair of tights. "Although, it's a little annoying that I can't."

Julian's brows furrowed as he continued getting dressed, his movements slow and measured like he was overthinking each step.

"What do you mean?"

"She's my best friend." I sat down on the edge of his bed to pull on my tights. Julian's eyes dropped to my legs, and his hands fell to the side, his tie forgotten. "I've always told her everything," I added. "Especially about the guys I've been with. She made me promise a long time ago that I would tell her about my first time. It's been weird staying quiet."

Julian's handsome face tightened, his lips pressing into a firm line. His silence was longer than I expected, but finally, he spoke, and his words surprised me.

"It's very important to me that your friendship with Gemma isn't affected by our relationship," he said, voice unyielding. "I never thought...This, what you're saying, isn't a problem that I even considered."

The way he was taking my offhand comment so seriously made my heart flutter. He was so cute, and he didn't even realize it.

"It isn't a *problem*," I assured him. "It's just something I have to get used to. Throughout the whole time we've been doing this...thing—"

"Dating, Juni," Julian amended. "We're dating."

"—the only person I've had to talk to about it all has been Noah, really."

"Noah?" he repeated, looking like he was about to choke on his own tongue.

"When he took me out for dinner," I explained, smoothing my tights up to my knees. "We talked about you almost the whole time, actually. He convinced me not to give up on you after you pushed me away."

Julian swore under his breath, mumbling about how he owed Noah more than he realized but sounding oddly pissed about it. His expression remained tense and irritated as he chewed on his bottom lip, thinking. Julian was a fixer, and this wasn't something he could fix.

"Well..." He cleared his throat, shrugging on his suit jacket. "You have my permission to tell Gemma whatever you're comfortable with." He paused again. "Do you want me to be there when you first explain about us?"

I looked up at him, pausing my struggle with my tights. "Do you want to be there?"

A shrug. "I want to be supportive if you want me there. But I have no problem letting you tell her alone if you think that's better. I can talk to her later."

"She's your sister," I pointed out.

"We both know she's practically yours, too." As soon as the words were out of his mouth, his nose scrunched, and his eyes shut tight. "Forget I said that. Delete that thought from existence, please."

I laughed, enjoying how mortified he was as he dragged a hand over his face. Poor guy had gone through a roller coaster of emotions in just a few minutes, and while a part of me still thoroughly enjoyed watching him struggle a bit, I also had this innate need to put him out of his misery.

"Relax, baby."

His body immediately melted at my words. He dropped his hands and sighed, leaning casually against the wall. To no one's surprise, he was completely ready for work, while I still had an entire laundry list I wanted to complete before we left his apartment.

He raised a brow, appraising my half-covered legs. "Need help with those?"

"No." A flush immediately rose to my face, and I internally begged it to go away. "It's just...putting tights on isn't exactly *cute*. Maybe you could give me some privacy for a minute."

A snort left Julian, pulling a scowl out of me. "Juniper, everything you do is cute."

"That is *not* true," I insisted, unsure if I should be placated or offended. I was a grown woman with a whole-ass law degree, after all.

"I get it." Julian heaved a dramatic sigh, but I saw a twinkle in his eye from whatever he was about to say. "You just want me to leave so you can sneak into my bedside table without me knowing. My girl's curious, isn't she?"

That definitely hadn't been on my mind, but now that he'd brought it up...

"Maybe your girl wouldn't have to be curious if you stopped treating her like she was too innocent for all your little sex toys."

Julian's brows skyrocketed, and then he walked toward me, and I felt my stomach drop. Tension balled in my gut as his heavy steps echoed in the otherwise still bedroom. His voice husked over my bare skin when he spoke.

"Turn over."

He was standing above me now, and I blinked up at him.

"What?"

"You want to be treated like you're not innocent? Turn over."

I balked at him momentarily, heat spreading through my body, and then I did as he commanded. Because, goddamnit, I *was* curious.

Flattening onto my stomach with my tights still wrapped around my knees and my dress barely covering my ass, I breathed into his bedsheets. Meanwhile, Julian's hands spread over my legs, pushing my dress up and out of the way, baring me. He massaged my ass in his palms before gripping my hips and yanking them up until I was on all fours.

"If you wanted it so badly, you should have just asked," Julian said, his soft drawl riddled with tension. I heard the sound of a drawer opening and closing, and my arms and legs shook from some sort of forbidden anticipation. "My goal will always be to give you what you want, baby."

"Julian..." I gasped. "We have...we have to go. We have that meeting..."

My words vanished as a finger drifted down the rim of my ass, moving my thong to the side until I was completely exposed to him.

"You're so pretty," Julian murmured soothingly. "This won't take long. Do you still want it?"

He brushed against me from behind, and I felt the clear outline of his arousal. He wanted it, that was for sure. And as for me... I wasn't even sure what *it* was, but based on how he was teasing a finger from my pussy to my ass, I had a reasonably good idea.

But what did he mean that it wouldn't take long?

"Juni..." Julian sang my name while teasing every inch of me that he could find. A second finger started swirling around my clit, making me groan into the sheets. I squirmed beneath his touch for only a second longer before giving in.

"Yes," I gasped. "Yes, Julian."

"Fuck," he grunted, pushing my shoulders down so my ass was propped up higher. "I can touch you here?"

I appreciated his clarification, but the sweet pressure building deep within me from how he worked his finger between my cheeks left me desperate for more. It was so foreign but so *good.* And I trusted Julian more than I knew how to put into words.

"You can touch me anywhere," I breathed.

My words caused an appreciative growl to rise from Julian. "Say that again."

"You can touch me anywhere, Julian. I'm yours, all yours."

"Fuck, this is going to be the best Monday ever," he replied thickly.

His response confused me slightly, but the sound of a cap clicking open distracted my thoughts. Julian's touch vanished, and when it returned, slick fingers circled around my entrance. My breathy pants grew more and more desperate, needing...God, I wasn't even sure what I needed.

But then a groan flew from my lips when Julian nudged inside, leaving me amazed at how full and perfect it felt. He settled there momentarily, toying. But then his touch was gone, leaving me with the urge to kick him.

"Julian," I hissed, and he chuckled.

"I'm here, love," he murmured, and then, true to his words, the bliss-filled pressure returned, making me melt into the bed from the satisfaction of it. He wasn't using his fingers this time; one of his secret toys hit me deeper, stretching my ass further—just how he'd threatened doing last night. I held my breath as one of Julian's hands caressed my hip in soothing circles before I felt him pull back completely.

Except the glorious pressure remained, even as he gently moved my underwear back in place.

"You wear your pretty little accessories so well, Juniper," he said, voice deep. "You always have. And now you'll wear this pretty reminder of my touch. Just in case you forget even for a second what it feels like to have me deep inside you."

"I—Jul—" My words stuck in my throat as I twisted to look at Julian, and tingling pleasure spread through me. And since speaking wasn't possible, I hoped my expression did the trick.

Julian's lips pulled in a smirk as he looked down at me. I wasn't sure if I had ever seen him looking so utterly satisfied with himself, not even in all the years that Julian had teased and taunted me.

"We should probably go, Daisy. Don't want to be late for that online meeting, especially because it's not even scheduled to go for long. I want to watch you try to make it through with that plug in your ass."

"I can't—" I gaped at him, still struggling to find words.

"Oh, you can. You took me beautifully this weekend. You can take this, too. It'll be less than an hour, honestly." When I continued to stare at him, he cocked his head to the side. "I picked the smallest one. Does it hurt?"

I shook my head slowly. No, it definitely didn't hurt. "It's not that. How am I supposed to—to work like this?"

"You're very good at your job," he said seriously, his praise making my cheeks heat. God, his validation shouldn't make me feel quite this good and especially not at a time like this. "I'm sure you'll figure it out."

With that, he started walking away, out of the bedroom. I could only stare after him until I finally came to my senses. Even as I scrambled to my feet, my insides felt confusingly good—like I was scratching the surface of an itch that I couldn't completely reach. I gasped, and when Julian just kept walking, I gritted my teeth with frustration.

"*Julian Briggs*!"

He was seriously going to simply *leave* after that?

"Yeah?" He stopped in the doorway and leaned against the frame as he looked me up and down. I swallowed, suddenly unable to talk. Again. Julian noticed. "Are you shocked at how good my last name just felt in your mouth, baby? There's a reason for that."

I balked at him, flustered for so many reasons. But Julian simply chuckled. It was warm, trickling down my spine. *He* was warm, and I was grateful that I'd get to bask in a bit of heat today, even though it was the dead of winter.

"I'm sorry we didn't have enough time to stop at Georgia's this morning, but I promise we can go tomorrow."

My brain was still trying to process that Julian had fulfilled his husky promise from last night, and meanwhile, he was over here talking about baked goods. But then his words caught up to me, and I was stuck looking at him with my mouth gaping open again.

"What?" He looked taken aback at my expression as the elevator doors closed, encasing us as we rode up to our office.

"*We*? *We* can go tomorrow?"

"Did you not want to go to Georgia's with me tomorrow? I thought it was your favorite."

"It is my favorite."

"So, what's the issue?"

"Are you going to meet me there like we did that one time or..." I stopped, mulling the scenario over in my head. "It doesn't make sense for you to pick me up. I could pick you up, though."

"I'm sorry..." The elevator doors opened, and Julian stuck his foot out to keep them from closing while staring at me, brows furrowed. "Are you trying to figure out how to not stay over at my place tonight and still get your muffins in the morning?"

"Do you want me to stay over?" I struggled to meet his brilliant blue gaze. "I just figured that after this weekend, you'd want some space."

"Space from you?" Julian scoffed, looking irritated at the idea. He gestured for me to leave the elevator. "Never."

This new version of Julian still threw me for a loop sometimes. It was so hard to get used to hearing him say things like that.

"Didn't get enough sex this weekend?" I joked, dropping my voice as we walked across the lobby. I could feel Tyler eyeing us as we moved past his desk.

Julian stopped at my words, turning to face me. "Don't do that. I know it's partly my fault that you have this narrative in your head, but I thought we were breaking it. I didn't get enough of *you* this weekend. Don't get it confused."

I gulped, feeling warmed by his words, even though what I had said was mostly meant in jest. Or a mechanism to protect myself, despite rationally not having any doubts that Julian wanted this relationship. Wanted me.

"Hey, St. James. Briggs."

Cameron's voice made me jump. And that jump made all my insides tumble and tighten...sweetly. Unbearably sweet. I stifled a groan as I looked anywhere but at Cameron's face. I just had this feeling that if I looked at him, he would know. He would know everything.

Out of the corner of my eye, I saw Julian's lips twitch.

"Hey, man," Julian said, barely skipping a beat.

"Morning, Cameron," I said, finally looking over at our coworker and friend. My voice sounded overly bright to my ears.

Cameron's brows furrowed as he looked between us, and then he shook his head, stepping through the glass doorway leading to our workspaces.

"You two are going to be so fucking ridiculous to work with, aren't you?"

"Haven't we always been?" I tried to joke.

Cameron shook his head, smiling as he decided not to answer that question. "Just remind me to never enter your office without knocking."

"Hey, Cameron," Julian teased. "Don't enter our office without knocking. Especially not today."

My eyes grew round at the promise in Julian's words.

CHAPTER THIRTY-SEVEN

JUNIPER AND I DIDN'T often attend meetings together. This was a special occasion. A *very* special occasion.

It was a virtual client meeting primarily run by Daphne. I did a lot of grunt work for her cases, which honestly didn't bother me in the slightest. It was the price to be paid until I moved up in seniority. And today, my role as notetaker granted me ample opportunity to admire my girlfriend, who was sitting behind me at her desk, providing translations for our client as needed.

Despite the irritation I used to feel that we were pursuing the same career, I've always thought that working in law was a good fit for Juniper, mostly because of her smart mouth and determination. But now that I'd uncovered the hidden parts of Juniper, I saw the makings of an *outstanding* attorney. She wanted to fight for people. She wanted to use her bilingualism to open more doors and reduce barriers. She wanted to be an adoption law advocate.

She was a better person than me on so many levels; I'd picked law as a career more for what it could do for my family and me than for what I could do for others. Not to say I wouldn't fight like hell for my clients or put my all into my cases, but Juniper had a passion that exceeded what I recognized in myself.

It was just another thing to love about her.

Juniper was passionate about the world, and I was passionate about her. Everything about her. Especially how she kept wiggling in her chair as another language flew from her lips.

Good fucking thing my camera was off because the number of times I'd looked away from my notes to study Juni's mannerisms, every little shift of her body, was sky-high. She'd dared to look back and glare at me at least once, but I wasn't exactly sure why. I hadn't *done* anything.

Well, I hadn't done anything *else*.

She was just mad that thoughts of having me deep inside her were creating a distraction.

I watched her gorgeous face flush brighter on my computer screen, almost like she could hear what was happening in my head.

"I hate you," Juniper snapped as soon as the meeting ended. She clicked her computer shut before spinning in her chair to attack me with her glare. But it immediately shifted into something different when she moved too quickly. Her lips zipped closed as she withheld a groan, and I felt my dick stir in my pants at even the slightest sound of her arousal.

"You did so well, baby," I said, ignoring her comment. She didn't hate me; she hated what I could do to her so easily. But moving forward, I vowed to only ever use that power to make her feel good, and she was about to find out. "I'm so proud of you."

"I—what?"

She hadn't been expecting that, and the fire drained away from her glare. I could almost see how she warmed from the inside out, melting beautifully at my praise.

"It used to irritate me so much, how perfect you are," I explained. "But that was only because I couldn't have you. So now I love that I can sit back and watch you be amazing while getting to appreciate it."

"Julian...I—appreciate?"

Her jumble of words was adorable, but I just nodded. And

when it was clear that Juni was still struggling to fully understand everything I was saying, I lowered my voice and continued.

"I appreciate every bit of you, Juniper."

My eyes stayed glued to hers, despite wanting to sweep them over the rest of her. Juni, on the other hand, let her gaze lower until I felt her stare acutely on my growing erection. And damn, did that ever bring out the smugness in her.

"Who would have *ever* thought that Julian Briggs likes telling me how good I am."

I leaned forward with a whisper. "And who would have *ever* thought that Juniper St. James likes hearing it so goddamn much."

She glanced away, all shy-like, and I knew we understood each other perfectly. But she was dead wrong if she thought we were done with this conversation. Standing, I locked our office door, thankful that there weren't any windows looking in. I strode to where Juni sat at her desk. When she kept her eyes averted, I slid my hand up her throat until my thumb landed on her jawline and had the power to turn her face back toward me.

"It's okay to admit to liking it, Juni. I have a lot of things that I could admit to."

That piqued her interest. "Such as?"

The tips of my fingers pressed right against Juni's pulse, and I felt it speed up as she waited for me to answer. I loved that, that reaction. I loved it so much that I couldn't help but draw out my response even more, watching the anticipation light a match in her waiting gaze.

I swiped my thumb up to her lip, tugging it down slowly. "When we started working together, sometimes you'd open this beautiful mouth and snap my name, and I wondered how many other ways I could get you to say it."

Her breath hitched. And then...a whisper. "Julian."

"Yeah, baby, like that. It sounds so good when you say my name." The corners of my lip curled up. "But it sounds even better when you scream it."

Her pulse was sprinting now, that little beat in her neck thrashing out of control. "What else? What else can you admit?"

I paused, thinking. There were so many things.

"I'd look for you in the stands at my football games in high school," I admitted, suddenly wanting to spill every little secret I possessed about her.

Juniper's eyes rounded, growing in size. "Really? I'd hide from you in the stands at your football games in high school."

"Why?"

"I didn't want you to know I cared about you."

"You cared about me?" The thought made *my* pulse pick up.

She nodded slowly, holding my gaze. "I'd have to disguise my worry every time you were tackled so Gemma wouldn't notice."

"I was tackled a lot. Our offensive line sucked."

"I was worried a lot."

She said it like it was simple. It was anything but.

"I worried about you all through college, too," she added. "I used to be embarrassed about how I cared, about how much I thought about you when I was so sure you never thought of me. I was..."

Her words drifted away, and I nearly toppled straight over, considering I'd been hanging onto every one of them for dear life. I wasn't sure anyone had been worried about me before. I was always the one doing the worrying.

"Finish the sentence, Juniper."

She steeled herself as though worried her vulnerability would have consequences. "I was happy when you decided not to go pro. I knew I'd probably obsess and worry over your games if you did."

God, every day. Every single day since starting this job, I had some sort of conversation with Juniper that made it hard to breathe for one reason or another.

Juniper's pulse hadn't slowed.

"Are you worried now?"

She shook her head.

My lips split into a wicked grin. "You should be. Because you know what else I can admit to?"

"What?"

I let my voice drop. "Thinking endlessly about what you'd look like bent over my desk."

Leaning down, I brushed my lips over hers right as she gasped at my words. I kept it light at first, kept my grip around her throat loose. But then Juni parted her lips, and I couldn't *not* taste her. I wrenched us closer together, plundering her mouth with my tongue. She strained toward me, and I felt her body shudder, needing more.

When she breathed my name against my lips, it felt like pulling away from her would destroy me, but somehow, I managed it.

"You feel it everywhere, don't you?" I let my voice scrape over her skin. "The way you need me."

She whimpered in response, gliding her teeth over her bottom lip as she blinked up at me.

"You did so good in that meeting, acting like you weren't getting wetter for me by the minute." I held her by the chin, not letting her look away. "I know what it's like to pretend you're not dying inside. I had to do it for so many years, Juni baby."

"Not anymore, though," she breathed. "So show me everything. Give me everything."

A smile spread slowly over my face. She would regret those last words, but I was more than happy to oblige in doing them.

As soon as I held out my hand, Juni took it. She let me lead her to my desk and position her in front of it. I wanted her to have as pretty of a view as I was about to have.

"You've always been such a fucking princess." I splayed my hand across her back, bending her over my desk precisely as I imagined. "And if you want everything, I'll give you everything."

Juni looked over her shoulder at me, a hot, simmering grin sliding into place. But then her eyes caught on something behind me, and uncertainty washed over her. She was staring at the door.

I knew she was. So I waited for her to tell me to stop, to emphasize how bad of an idea it was to fuck in the middle of the day at our office. But she couldn't find the words. We both knew she wanted it too fucking bad, and *I* knew that she had nothing to worry about. This wouldn't take long.

She didn't realize that, though. She didn't yet realize how fast I could make her come if I wanted. And I'd follow her instantly; that was how badly I ached for her. Watching her get more and more aroused during that meeting had been torture.

But I still wanted to ease her worries, so I left Juni bent over my desk to snatch the headphones off hers. The noise-canceling headphones I'd gotten her for Christmas, of course. Then I double-checked the door before grabbing her phone, holding it in front of Juni's pretty face to unlock it, and finding the exact thing I was looking for.

Of course Juniper had the audiobook version of my other Christmas gift on her phone. I would have expected nothing less. And I knew just what part to have her listen to.

When I placed one side of the headphones over her ear, she balked at me. I knew she could hear the audio, which just happened to be the dirtiest part of the book.

"How—"

"This book has been sitting around my apartment for the last week. Did you really think I wouldn't want to learn about my competition?"

"My books are not your *competition*, Julian."

"Yeah?" I smirked, ignoring her. "I think after you experience both in real time, you'll no doubt realize which is better."

I dropped the other side of the headphone over her ear before she could say anything more and got to work, shimmying Juni's dress over her hips like I did this morning. And also like this morning, I pulled down her tights and worked her underwear to the side to see how perfect she looked for me.

Fucking hell, I was dying. Absolutely dying at this point. I *needed* her, needed to finish what we had started in my apartment. Should I be doing this? No. Just because I'd sent that email to HR last week didn't mean we could fuck in our office whenever we wanted. But I also couldn't stop. I would have to figure out some sort of method for resisting Juniper during the workday, but I wasn't going to figure it out today. That was for damn sure.

Without warning, I drove my finger inside her slick pussy, enjoying how tightly she immediately clenched.

"Julian!" Though she whispered my name, hissing at me, I could hear the urgency in it, the desperation.

"See?" I chuckled to myself, knowing she couldn't even hear me. "My name sounds so good when you say it, love."

Juni's quiet cries continued as I worked my finger in and out faster. "Julian, I don't think...I can't. I can't. It feels too good. I won't be able to—"

I clapped my hand over her mouth and leaned down. After momentarily pushing the headphones out of the way, I breathed in her ear. "I know, Juni baby. I know. You're about to come harder than you ever thought possible, but you'll be a good girl and take it while staying quiet for me."

"Yes," Juni moaned softly into my hand, and I returned to her pussy, playing with her clit with one hand while unbuckling my belt with the other. By the time I had my cock ready at her entrance, Juni was a panting mess beneath my fingers. I replaced my hand over her mouth, knowing I'd need to stifle everything she was about to feel.

I watched Juni's eyes flutter shut, her lips drifting apart as she listened to something sinfully sweet. And then, in case she needed a reminder that I was still here, I applied the slightest bit of pressure to the...accessory still sitting snugly in her pretty ass.

Prepared, I caught her groan with my palm, and then before she could fully recover, I pushed my cock into her dripping wet pussy.

True to her word, Juniper swallowed those hot noises of hers, and I tried to do the same as I reacquainted myself with how goddamn good she felt. Thank fuck I wouldn't have to last long. I could already feel Juniper tightening around me, likely overstimulated with being filled in more than one way. Which was exactly what I had been banking on.

I pulled out slightly before ramming into her harder, rubbing her clit in time with my thrusts. Juniper's fingers curled into little fits as she took it, and I realized just how much I was getting off on watching her try to contain herself. Her muffled cries, her eyes squeezed shut, her pussy strangling me.

Only seconds later, she exploded around me, her entire body trembling and quaking beneath mine. It was perfect timing because I came moments after she did, filling her to the brim. Juni slumped to the desk immediately following her climax, and I tried to be as gentle as I could when I pulled out of her and removed the plug. Little whimpers were my only clue that she even noticed, and I bit down on a smile.

I didn't take the headphones off until I'd cleaned us both up as best I could, and then I prompted, "So?"

If she said the fireside fuck in the audiobook scene she was listening to was the best part of that, I wasn't quite sure what I'd do. Probably try again to convince her otherwise, not that I minded partaking in that. Maybe I'd have to recreate the scene for myself, rent a cozy place in Vermont for the weekend that had a massive fireplace to fuck in front of. Yeah, that sounded pretty nice.

Juni pretended to think hard, moving to stand slowly—almost as though it was now foreign *not* to have something inside her. She grinned, teasing me with how her lips curved as she crossed her arms over her chest. "I really can't say which is better, and if you loved me, you wouldn't make me pick between you and my books."

My smile grew as hers faded amidst the realization of what she'd just said. It was an offhand thing, I could tell. Brown eyes popped wide in instant anxiety.

"Julian, I didn't—"

I cut off her floundering with a hard kiss before moving

toward the door. The noises of people chatting and phones ringing went on outside the door, the rest of the office completely unaware of what had just happened inside our little space.

"What are you doing?" she hissed, looking bewildered.

"I'm not making you pick," I said with a grin. "Between me and the books." Juni's jaw dropped slightly, but figuring I'd already pushed her limits a few times today, I pointed her toward her desk and switched the topic. "Now, go sit down and cross your legs before you make a mess out of those tights with my cum."

Her jaw dropped further, but I didn't miss how she squeezed her legs together tighter as she stood there. It was then that I realized I'd just switched putting one thing inside Juni for another. And that thought would equally torture me the rest of the day.

Fuck.

I closed the door behind me when I left, still thinking it was the best Monday ever.

That is, until I returned from the bathroom and saw a text that ruined fucking everything.

> GRAYSON: Hey, man. Can we schedule a time to chat about Gabriel's case? There are a few things I wanted to talk about with you.

I SAT AT MY DESK, STARING AT GRAYSON'S TEXT AS THE CLOCK TICKED AND tocked behind me. Juni was somehow engrossed in her work, her keyboard clicking as she typed at a furious pace.

I didn't know how she did it, how she returned to her computer so easily. The only reason I wasn't still obsessing over what we'd just done was because of Grayson's text.

Gabriel's case.

I hadn't even thought about Gabriel's case since before

Christmas, when Juniper first stayed over. The last several weeks, I had been so wholly focused on Juniper that I'd forgotten entirely about the promise I'd made to Grayson to finalize our approach, discuss the case with Daphne, and actually take legal action.

I was a shitty friend.

I was a shitty friend *and* a shitty lawyer.

Christ, I'd just fucked Juni over my desk in the middle of the workday without pausing for even one second to think about the consequences. We'd only been dating for a couple of weeks, and already I was throwing away my rationality and commitment to my career.

To be honest, I knew this would happen. From the second her lips touched mine, I knew that if I let Juniper in, she would completely take over. It had been the whole reason I'd tried to push her away, even after making her come apart against our office door. I was obsessed with this woman to the point that I didn't know how to balance my life in a way where I had room for every part when Juni was *so many* parts of it.

I couldn't blame it on Juni. Considering how focused she was on her work right now, *she* wasn't the problem here. It was me.

What was I supposed to say to Gray? *Yeah, man, we can definitely talk about it. But I haven't done any of the things I said I would do the last time we talked because I've been too busy with my own life to care about yours?*

Was this who I was now? Someone who dropped the ball when their friend needed them? And not just *any* friend. This was Grayson. I was the best fucking man at his wedding. And Gabriel, who had a congenital *heart defect*, was my *godson*.

Shame crawled over me, coating my entire body with disgust. I was disgusted with myself. That glow that I'd felt when I walked away from Juni earlier had vanished, and now I only felt...dread.

I wasn't sure how much time had passed when I heard Juniper sigh behind me, pulling me out of the existential time warp I'd been stuck in.

"Do you want to grab some lunch?"

After swallowing past the dryness in my throat, I shook my head. "No, I should really keep working on..."

I drifted off when I realized I was so lost in my own brain about how I should be focused on my job that I wasn't even remotely focused on my job and had no idea what I should even be doing.

God, I was a mess.

"Okay," Juni said, sounding nonplussed about my refusal. "I'm just going to run across the street and get a sandwich. I'll bring you back something?"

"That would be great." I turned to look at her, withholding a groan when I saw how happy and pretty she was, especially today. Her hair was curled in loose waves, and her earrings sparkled in the sun when she cocked her head to the side with a grin. I wanted to scoop her up and bring her back home to our bubble. "Whatever you're getting would be perfect," I said. "Thanks, Daisy."

She nodded before grabbing her coat and walking from the room. I regretfully watched her disappear before returning to my computer with a heavy sigh.

Maybe now that she was gone, I could concentrate on doing *something* for my job.

But that thought only made a different type of guilt swell inside me.

On top of everything else, I was a shitty boyfriend, too. I should have offered to go with Juni. She was only running across the street, and it was so unlike Juniper to remember to eat during the day that I was sure she'd asked only to spend time together. And what were another few minutes off task in the grand scheme of things?

As if to belabor the point, I barely got through any of my notes before Juni waltzed back into our office. She set a to-go box on my desk before sliding both hands onto my shoulders and squeezing, massaging them.

Oh, *hell.* Did she not understand that even just a breeze

carrying the scent of her fucking perfume could turn me on? If she *touched* me, I was really done for.

"How's it going?"

Hearing her voice, sweet and tinted with concern, combined with her touch, which made my body heat from the inside out, nearly tipped me over the edge.

"I'm struggling to concentrate."

It was very much the truth, but the words sounded harsher coming out of my mouth than I'd meant for them to.

Juni's hands disappeared from my shoulder.

"I'll leave you alone, then."

Alone. Yeah, maybe I just needed a little time alone. I couldn't feel guilty about ignoring Juni if she wasn't in the same room as me, and I couldn't get distracted by how perfect she was if I couldn't see her, right?

Wrong.

Moving to work in the commons area for the rest of the afternoon definitely hadn't improved my mood. Since I texted Grayson back, saying I would call him later, I pushed all my other work around to focus on Gabriel's case.

But Gabriel's case reminded me of Juniper. She'd done most of the legwork with this; she deserved to help me finish it. That meant going back to our office, though. That meant risking another preoccupation.

So I stayed. I stayed at an uncomfortable table surrounded by the hustle and bustle of the rest of the office, trying to get anything done that I could without letting my thoughts drift back to the beautiful brunette sitting next to my desk—who only a few hours ago I had bent over *my* desk.

Impossible. Absolutely impossible.

I gave up a little after five o'clock. I'd managed to get something done, though it wasn't much. An afternoon free of meetings was so rare, and I wasted most of it. But I gave it my best. And now I'd get to spend the rest of the night with—

I spun in a circle like a dog chasing his tail, looking for Juniper inside our office. But she was gone. Her computer was gone, her coat was gone, she was gone.

How did I not see her leaving? How did she not see *me* and stop to say something?

More of the familiar dread sank low in my gut. After fumbling with my phone, I found Juniper's contact and hit Dial. And thank fucking God, she picked up on the second ring.

"Hello?"

"Juni baby," I said, my stomach tangling in knots. I'd fumbled everything this afternoon; I knew I did. Hurting her had never been my intention, but I was still so bad at this—so bad at juggling everyone who needed me. "Did you leave already?"

"Yeah," she replied, her voice sounding strangled.

There was a pause where the background noise seeped in through the speaker. She was definitely somewhere busy, somewhere crowded. Somewhere that had clinking glasses and loud laughter. But I tried to pay close attention to her voice, to the tone and her words. But they weren't at all the ones I had been expecting.

"Do you..." She took another brief pause. "Do you have any chocolate cookie dough ice cream in your freezer? I could use some right about now."

The question caught me off guard, and I froze, standing in the middle of our office, the phone smashed against my face as if I could somehow get closer to Juniper that way. And as soon as I ran her words back through my head, my entire body tensed even tighter.

Valentine's Day in high school. Juniper hiding at my house from Kennedy. Me telling her we always had ice cream if she ever needed to come over for some more, for if she ever needed to escape Kennedy again.

"Always, Juniper," I breathed, trying to keep the tension from my voice. "Where are you?"

"I'm getting a drink at—"

The line cut off right before the sentence finished, and a curse ripped from my lips.

What the *hell*?

I didn't understand how Juniper had gone from sitting next to me in our office to sitting somewhere with Greg Kennedy, but I was almost positive that was what she had just told me. Kennedy or some other ex or asshole bothering her. And she clearly didn't want to be obvious about it, otherwise she would have said it outright.

Fear swallowed my already tense body.

If *anyone* fucking touched her...

I wasn't planning on breaking more fingers tonight, but that didn't mean I wouldn't. Fuck, I should have done more about Greg a long time ago. How he showed up unannounced when Juniper was back at her parents and kept trying relentlessly to worm back into her life was a huge red flag that I should have taken more seriously.

My phone chimed, and hope rose back up until it was immediately crushed when I saw the text was from Gemma.

GEMS: Are you the reason Juni begged to get a drink after work? What the hell did you do this time?

I ignored the guilt and pang of annoyance at my sister for both assuming it was my fault and also being right about it. Instead, I focused on the first part of what she'd said.

Are you with her?

GEMS: No, I'm on my way to meet her.

Where is she?

Staring at my phone, I held my breath while waiting for a reply. But when Gemma didn't immediately answer, I gave up and called her.

"Are you calling to confess your wrongdoings?" she questioned as soon as she picked up.

"Where is she, Gemma?" I said lowly, cutting to the chase. Grabbing my wallet and keys, I left the rest of my stuff for tomorrow and headed toward the lobby doors. I had a feeling about where Juni was, but if Gemma could confirm it for me, that would be best. I didn't want to waste a single minute.

"Oh no, I'm not going to tell you so you can go make it worse."

"Gemma," I ground out through clenched teeth. "Tell me where the fuck she is. Now."

She snickered, and the fact that she thought this was funny made my blood boil. "Tell me what you did first."

"This isn't a game. Something's wrong, and if anything fucking happens to her, I swear to God—" Visions of Juniper hurt danced before my eyes, and I snapped. "*Goddamnit*, Gemma, please. I love her, okay? I fucking love her more than I even know how to comprehend, and I need you to tell me *where the hell she—*"

"She's at the Bellflower," Gemma cut in, sounding breathless. Shock ran through her words.

I sighed raggedly, relieved I was close and that my suspicion had been correct. I was already halfway there. Only a few more steps and I'd be striding into the bar. And then afterward, I could deal with what I'd just shouted at my sister.

"Gemma, I..."

"I know, Jules." Her voice was small, but I couldn't quite tell the other emotion swimming in it. "I've always known."

She'd always known.

Because I'd been in love with Juniper St. James since I was seventeen years old, standing in the hospital waiting room, waiting to see her with bated breath.

Before that, even.

Swallowing past the thickness in my throat, I shook my head. "I'm almost there," I said. "I have to go."

"I'll be there soon," Gemma replied, and we hung up.

Pushing all other thoughts aside, I entered the bar and immediately began searching for Juniper.

CHAPTER THIRTY-EIGHT

juniper

JULIAN BENT ME OVER his desk like nothing could stop him from having me, like he was a man *obsessed*, and then just like that, he forgot about me. He spent the morning reassuring me that he didn't want space and the afternoon proving that was *all* he wanted.

I could tell something was bothering him, and it took a lot of self-talk to convince myself that he wasn't trying to push me away again. The stress in his eyes had been apparent, so I tried to give him the distance he needed to work through whatever was going on. But when he went so far as to leave our office and shut me out for the entire afternoon, I cracked.

I wanted to help him, but he needed to trust me enough for that. He needed to care about me enough to communicate. And clearly, he didn't.

Refusing to stick around just to be ignored, I closed my laptop, called Gemma for an emergency drink, and made my way to the Bellflower. I didn't really want to mention how I was dating her brother when I was irritated with him and hurt by his actions, but it might come to that. Because today, I needed my best friend.

But the person sitting next to me now wasn't my best friend.

Not even close.

Greg scooted his chair closer to me at the bar, and I had to wring my hands together to keep from smacking him. I didn't like how his hot breath stuck to my skin. I didn't like how his eyes felt greedy while looking me up and down. I didn't like how he just *happened* to be here.

"I'm happy we ran into each other," he said as if he could read my mind, and the smile he flashed made me want to choke.

Ran into each other was one way of putting it.

"I've been wanting to talk to you," he continued, "but my texts won't deliver for some reason."

"I blocked you, Greg," I said bluntly.

It probably wasn't the smartest thing to admit. Greg's eyes hardened in a way that tripped warning bells in my brain. He'd already snatched my phone away from me when I'd tried to tell Julian where I was, and now I felt oddly trapped even though I was in the middle of a crowded bar.

"Is it because *Julian* told you to?" He spat Julian's name like he was the devil himself.

"Of course not."

Sure, Julian had told me to block Greg, but I'd already decided I was done entertaining my ex's faux niceness and attempts to "catch up."

He raised a brow, a hint of satisfaction in the slight movement. "I thought you guys were fucking."

Greg leaned in, making his curiosity about the question clear. He wrapped an arm around the back of my chair, and I felt slight brushes against my back that made me tense and want to bolt. But at least here we were in public, surrounded by onlookers. If I walked out of the bar now, Greg might follow me into the night.

Just the thought of that made my skin crawl.

When I didn't reply, Greg continued to probe.

"That didn't last long, huh?"

I couldn't decide if it would be wise to tell the truth or not, so I avoided answering. I just needed to buy time until Julian got here. I hadn't been able to say much on the phone, but I could tell he understood my ice cream comment. He remembered. He knew that I was with an ex, and he would likely deduce that it was Greg. And there was really only one place in the city where I went to get a drink, especially right after work.

Julian would be here. He might have acted grumpy and stand-offish earlier, but he'd been like that toward me for most of his life. And he always came. When I needed him, he was always there.

"Greg." I sighed heavily as I tried to inch away from him. He wasn't really letting me. "Why are you here?"

"You know..." He cocked his head to the side, eyes scrutinizing me. "I don't really get it. You went from hating Julian to sleeping with him. Tell me, how does that make sense?"

"You said yourself that I always used to talk about him when we were dating," I replied without meeting his eyes.

"*When we were dating*," he emphasized, making it obvious that I'd said the wrong thing. "*We* dated, yet you decided to let *him* fuck you and not me."

Oh my God. He was absolutely delusional, wasn't he?

"First of all, that was nearly a decade ago," I snapped. "You need to let it go, Greg. We never slept together because I never trusted you. And clearly, for good reason, considering you cheated on me. Second of all, Julian and I *are* dating. Third, aren't you engaged?"

Julian obviously had his faults, but he was the most loyal person I had ever met. He was endlessly selfless, and I trusted him with everything that I was. I always had, and I always would.

Greg's head jerked back at my admittance. "You're dating?"

I couldn't help but notice he didn't comment on the engaged part.

"Yes." My jaw was clenched now, knowing I only had so much restraint left in me. I didn't want to cause a scene, but I didn't want to keep having this conversation. "We're dating. So if you could *please* leave me the *fuck* alone, that would be great."

Greg swallowed. And then narrowed his eyes before saying the most ridiculous shit I'd ever heard.

"I think you owe me." His voice dropped to a level that made my hairs stand on end. "And I think golden boy needs to experience what it feels like to have everything fucking taken from him. When he kept me from finishing our senior season, he fucked up my entire goddamn life."

Just as I felt his grip twist around my arm, I caught sight of a tall, handsome man with auburn hair pushing his way through the crowd by the entrance to the bar. Pure, sweet relief swept through me.

I was positive Greg hadn't noticed him yet because he kept going on about how much he hated his life as if I would find sympathy for him. There was the possibility, I supposed, that if Julian hadn't broken Greg's fingers and ruined his football chances, he might not have this vindictive spirit in him, that he might have grown into someone who wasn't as much of an asshole as he was in high school. But somehow, I didn't think so.

Julian's eyes caught on mine, and I melted into them. He mouthed my name, his expression desperate. Knowing he was there, just feet away, was what I needed.

Without wasting another second, I jerked my elbow up, connecting it with Greg's nose. I didn't think it was hard enough to do any damage, but it definitely surprised him, and I used that to twist out of his grip.

Seconds later, Julian caught me, enveloping me in his arms. I wanted to hang on to him and never, ever let go, but before I could even say a word, Julian tucked me behind his body and advanced on Greg, who had a hand to his nose, glaring furiously.

"What are you doing here, Kennedy?"

To the casual onlooker, Julian might sound conversational. But I could hear how his words were strained, forced. A hum of barely concealed rage wrapped around how he said Greg's name.

Alarm sparked in Greg's eyes, but he shrugged. "Got a new job nearby. I heard this was the place to go after work."

Julian tensed at his clear implication. I could tell that he was fighting like hell to keep his temper under control, and honestly, I was impressed. But the reality was that there were countless eyes on us, and Julian was no longer a seventeen-year-old who could blame broken fingers on a football accident. The last thing I needed was for Greg to goad Julian into an assault and battery charge.

"Yeah?" Julian leaned in, clapping a heavy hand on Greg's shoulder—hard enough that he flinched. "And where'd you hear that?"

"Fuck off, Briggs." Greg tried to shrug off the hand, but Julian doubled down, fingers digging into Greg's crisp white dress shirt.

"I'd be happy to fuck off and never see your face again, Kennedy," Julian snarled, making my stomach somersault. "But that would mean you'd have to leave my girlfriend the hell alone. And since you can't seem to manage that, I hope your *new job nearby* is understanding when you get served with a restraining order in the middle of a nine o'clock meeting."

Greg's face paled slightly at that, and I realized he must not be lying about the new job. I didn't know how to feel about that, though. He seemed to care about keeping his job, which was good leverage, but I hated that he might live in Boston now.

Clearing my throat, I stepped up beside the fire-breathing dragon that was my boyfriend at the moment. "I think we know a few judges that could help with that. Don't we, Julian baby?"

I watched the red cloud dissipate from Julian's gaze as he blinked over at me, removing his hand from Kennedy's shoulder and readjusting to wrap his arm around my back, tugging me closer.

"We sure do," he said, his voice filled with grit and gravel. And also tenderness. Tenderness that I knew was for me.

I relaxed. It felt really good knowing that we got to shoulder our problems together from now on. Julian brushed his lips over my temple before turning back to Greg.

"Enjoy your first and last drink at the Bellflower, Kennedy.

Pretty soon, you won't be able to get within three city blocks of Juniper without being arrested, so don't *ever* fucking plan on coming back here."

Greg didn't reply. He simply glowered in Julian's direction, even though Julian didn't seem to care. Having said what he needed to say, he nudged me back a step, and I was more than happy to lead the way out of the bar.

As soon as I emerged onto the city street, I whirled around to face Julian. His clenched jaw softened as soon as our eyes met, and then he crushed us together, slipping his hand to the nape of my neck and using his grip to pull my face to his.

"Juni..." he breathed.

I loved it when he did that. When he seemed to say my name just because he liked the way it sounded coming from his lips.

"Yeah?" My voice was just a wisp on the wind.

"You scared the shit out of me," he groaned before slamming our lips together for a rough, bruising kiss. It only lasted a few moments, but I felt Julian everywhere—from the tips of my toes to the lips he was kissing.

That is, until we were interrupted by the clearing of a throat.

Realization slammed into me before I even pulled back from Julian. I knew exactly who that was. After all, I'd called her to meet me here. And now here she was. Standing in the middle of the sidewalk, with the wind blowing her gingery hair around her face, was my best friend.

And she'd just caught me kissing the life out of her brother.

CHAPTER THIRTY-NINE

MY FIRST INSTINCT WAS to push Julian away and pretend like we *hadn't* just been making out. But my boyfriend was a stage five clinger who simply drifted his hands to my waist and pulled me in closer when I'd turned to face his sister and attempted my escape.

So instead, I tried to make my case while still in Julian's arms.

"Gemma, I..."

The words weren't coming to me. All the things I'd planned to say to her seemed pointless now that she'd seen what she'd just seen. And I was also struggling to compute how Gemma was...smiling.

"I take it everything's okay?" she asked.

Around us, traffic whizzed by. Horns honked, and the wind howled, January air whipping my skin. The sun had lowered, creating a dusky hue in the sky. The streetlamps had just turned on, casting a glow over Gemma's head.

"I—what?"

"I was worried, you know," she went on. "When Julian called me screaming about how—"

"*Gemma*," Julian growled. It sounded like some kind of warning, which only made me frown in confusion.

"*—you were in trouble,*" Gemma emphasized, "I got here as quick as I could. But I knew Jules would be here. He always is."

Always.

"Everything's okay," I reassured. "Greg cornered me in the bar."

"Seriously?" Her smile momentarily vanished. "Oh my God, Junes."

"But Julian found me," I quickly added.

"Of course he did." Her expression grew playful again as her eyes shifted to her brother. "You know, Julian, when you said... what you said on the phone, I didn't *really* think you'd get the nerve up...for this." She gestured to Julian, still holding me in his arms, refusing to let go. "But now here we are, and I suppose you proved me wrong. About fucking time."

"I got the nerve up a while ago, Gems," Julian said dryly. "If we're being honest about it all."

"You didn't *even*," I scoffed, looking over my shoulder at him, "I kissed you first, remember?"

"You had liquid courage," he countered after a soft chuckle. "Doesn't count, especially since you tried to take it back with all that shit about getting swept up in our fake date."

"Fake date?" Gemma interrupted, brows furrowing. "Sofia's wedding? That was months ago."

Guilt crawled up to my face; I felt it burning. "I know, but we had some road bumps. We've only really been *officially* dating since..." I paused, trying to pinpoint when exactly it was.

But Julian filled in the blank for me. "New Year's."

That had been the wrong thing to say. Gemma's brows lifted higher and higher until they nearly disappeared, and then her eyes narrowed. "New Year's, huh?"

A flush worked over me, heating me from the inside out, and I chose not to confirm or deny what she was thinking. "I was going to tell you this week," I said, knowing I didn't sound super convincing with how my words squeaked out. "I promise, Gems."

She didn't seem mad or even surprised, but that didn't stop

my stomach from somersaulting. I tried to step forward, wanting to go to her, but Julian's arms tightened around me.

Gemma noticed, her eyes rolling up. "You know, I think Juni was right about you. You *are* a little...over-the-top sometimes."

I felt the rise and fall of Julian's shoulder as he shrugged. "You're just going to have to get used to sharing now, Gemma."

"Are you kidding me?" A disbelieving laugh burst from her lips. "I've been sharing Juni with you for *years*. You're welcome, by the way. I made sure, even when you had your head up your ass, that she was always there. For you. Because even though you were too thickheaded to admit it, I knew you wanted her at your games. I knew you wanted her at your birthday parties and Christmas and every holiday in between. And I knew she wanted to be there, too."

Her words bounced around in my head.

"You...knew?" I repeated, awe in my voice.

Gemma's smile broadened. "I knew. I've always known. And I knew if someone shoved you two into a room together, maybe you could finally realize it, too."

I was too stunned to speak, but Julian wasn't.

"Good thing Cameron got me my job, then, huh?" he said hoarsely.

"Mhm." Gemma lifted her hand and began inspecting her nails. "Good thing someone who knew both of you were starting on the same day suggested to him that you should share an office if he could convince someone to do it."

"You didn't," I breathed. "*Gemma*."

Gemma looked up, the warmth in her eyes trickling over at me. "You're welcome for that, too."

And because I couldn't find any words as Julian hugged me closer, I mouthed, "Thank you," at her.

To which she smiled in return. "Just do one thing for me, okay?"

I nodded. I'd do anything for her.

Her voice dropped to a stern tone.

"Next time you're in bed together, do *not* pick up the phone when I call."

"CAN I GET YOU ANYTHING?"

Julian's gaze was nervous as he took my coat from me in the entryway of his apartment. We parted ways with Gemma pretty quickly, not wanting to hang around in case Greg made another appearance. And while Julian said he would understand if I wanted to go home with Gemma instead, I knew I needed to talk to him about earlier. And I knew he would have been reluctant to actually let me go.

"Maybe a glass of water," I said, realizing how dry my throat was. "I want to change into something comfortable, too."

Julian nodded before taking off for the kitchen. A few minutes later, I was curled up on his couch with a glass of water, wearing one of Julian's old sweatshirts. He was so tense that even though I saw his gaze warm when he saw me walk out in his clothes, he didn't say anything. Instead, Julian sat stiffly beside me, turning his body to face mine before resting his elbows on his knees.

"Juni..." He paused to run a hand down his face. "I—I need you to tell me what happened with Kennedy before I arrived."

I nodded. I'd been prepared to talk about what happened at work, but I wasn't surprised that Julian needed to get this out of the way first.

"He—" I hesitated, knowing how Julian would respond to my next words. "I think he threatened me. And you."

Julian grew even more rigid as he studied me closely. "What did he say?"

I curled into a tighter ball, wrapping Julian's sweatshirt around me. "He didn't like that we're dating. He said I *owe* him and that you need to experience what it feels like to have everything taken from you. He's still mad about football, I think."

Julian balled his hands into fists, his eyes squeezing closed as if he could shut out Greg Kennedy from his life.

"Fuck, I regret not kicking his ass now," Julian said brusquely, opening his eyes again. They blazed bright blue.

"No," I argued. "You made the right choice."

Julian's jaw clenched as he remained quiet, clearly not agreeing with me. Reaching out, I sifted my fingers through his hair, and he relaxed slightly at my touch. "Julian..." I whispered, wishing I could take all the tension, the worry, the responsibility from his shoulders.

As soon as his name left my lips, Julian scooped me up and pulled me onto his lap. He tucked his head close to mine, his lips grazing my ear. "He doesn't get to do that," he said, a soft growl. "He doesn't get to threaten taking you away. Because when he says he'll take everything, he's talking about you. That's what you are to me, Juni. You're everything, absolutely everything."

It was my turn to close my eyes, basking in Julian's fierce grip and those words that sounded an awful lot like a promise. I should feel nervous or scared at what Greg had said, but when I was wrapped up in Julian, I couldn't feel anything but safety and security.

"We're getting that restraining order," he added. "That kind of threat combined with his stalking tendencies should be enough to convince a judge."

"Okay," I agreed. "If that makes you feel better."

I just wanted Julian to feel better.

"It does," he grunted before burrowing his face deeper into the crook of my neck. "Does it make you feel better?"

I nodded, mostly to appease him. But I did like the sound of not having to worry about a repeat of what had just happened.

He squeezed me harder before mumbling the softest "I'm sorry. I'm so sorry. You wouldn't have been there, wouldn't have called Gemma to get a drink if I hadn't been such an utter asshole today."

The desperation in his voice made my chest feel like it was

cracking. I had to catch my breath before words were able to come out. The last thing I wanted was for him to feel worse, but I knew I had to be honest about how he'd made *me* feel.

"It felt like you were pushing me away, and it hurt. It hurt, Julian."

With a deep sigh, he pulled back to look at me properly. His eyes were sad and resigned, as though he already knew what I was saying was true.

"I'm so sorry," he repeated. "I'm struggling to...find a balance. I got a text from Grayson—oh, *fuck*."

He extracted his arm from where it was wrapped around my middle, checking his watch. And whatever he saw wasn't good.

"Shit, I told him I'd call a half hour ago."

"You can call him now." I started to move off Julian's lap, but he quickly replaced his arm around me.

"No, I'll call Grayson later. I need this, *you*, right now."

"You don't need to pick between me and your friends, Julian." I sighed. "I just need you to communicate. And I...I should have talked to you before leaving, too."

He groaned inwardly. "I know. I know I do. I'm so sorry, baby. I fucked up. Grayson texted me this morning that he wanted to discuss the case."

My stomach dropped, and I immediately knew everything Julian was about to say. Because he didn't just fuck up; *we* fucked up. And Julian's commitment to his friends and family meant everything to him.

"The case..." I breathed. "We forgot about the case, and then you shut yourself away to keep working on it so you wouldn't let Grayson down."

Julian's expression was strained as he nodded. "*I* forgot about the case."

"No, *we* forgot about the case," I repeated. "We were working on it together, Julian."

"He's my best friend. Gabriel's my godson. It shouldn't have been up to you to remember."

"We're dating, aren't we?" I whispered, brushing my lips over his cheek. "We're colleagues, right? We're a team in every sense of the word. You should have told me."

"Dating. Colleagues." He scoffed. "You're right. I should have told you. But those words don't feel like they even touch on what we are."

"What are we, then?"

"We're...so much more." He rubbed a hand over his jaw and the five-o'clock shadow growing there as he found his words. And then his gaze found mine. "You've always been there, and you're part of me in a way that no one else in this world is. I don't know how to explain it, but you're...you're the person I think of when I think of home."

"Julian..." Tears stung the back of my eyes as he said the words I'd always wanted to hear. For more than a decade, I wanted Julian to admit that I was something, *anything* to him, and he'd gone and admitted even more than that. Home. We were home together. But a question still lingered in the back of my head. "What did...what did you say exactly to Gemma? On the phone?"

His hand dropped, and he pressed his lips together momentarily. "She wouldn't tell me where you were, and I...I lost it. I told her if anything ever happened to you..." He shook his head. "I just lost it, Juni."

I snuggled closer to him, a shiver running through me despite his embrace and the oversized sweatshirt. "Nothing is going to happen to me."

He nodded, his shoulders dipping as though he needed to hear me say that. "Are you cold?" he murmured, and I realized my little shiver had become shakes. I didn't feel cold, but deep exhaustion had settled in my bones.

Julian rose from the couch before I could answer, carrying me across his living room and padding through the hallway. He finally let me slide to my feet in the bathroom and nodded at the pearly white free-standing tub I'd always admired. "What about a bath?"

I agreed wordlessly. That sounded heavenly.

Julian took action as he turned the knobs on the tub to find the right water temperature. Once he was satisfied, he pointed at the cabinet beneath his sink. "I'll be right back, but I think some Epsom salts are under there if you want to check."

I raised a brow, surprised to learn that Julian was a bath guy. "Epsom salts?"

He rolled his eyes. "They're good for achy muscles after working out."

Laughing lightly, I moved toward the sink while Julian ducked back into the hallway. But when I opened the cabinet door, I froze.

"Julian!" My voice was shrill as it echoed in the bathroom.

"What?" His footsteps quickened as he raced through the apartment, and I managed to unstick my feet and meet him in the hallway. He stopped short at the end of it.

Both of us were breathless, staring at each other. Julian's expression was riddled with concern as his gaze flicked over me, undoubtedly assessing my well-being. But all I could do was look back at him, slack-jawed.

"Under your sink..." I started.

A bit of understanding dawned on his face. But he remained quiet, tense...waiting for me.

"There's got to be at least a dozen bottles of my perfume under your sink, Julian," I gasped, still struggling to comprehend what I'd just seen.

He nodded wordlessly. Because *of course* he knew that there were that many bottles of perfume under his bathroom sink. He raked a hand through his hair before correcting me. "It might be closer to two dozen."

I swallowed. "Why do you have that many bottles of my perfume under your sink?"

"I told you I would buy out the entire stock." He lifted one shoulder. "I'm sure I could get more, but that was as many as they had available at the store."

"So I can't torture you with it anymore?"

He grimaced at hearing his words repeated. "So you can't ever run out, Juniper."

"Why?" I breathed again.

"Juni..." I realized for the first time that Julian was holding a glass of wine. But then it disappeared as he shockingly tossed it back and retreated into the kitchen to set the glass down. Afterward, he turned and stalked toward me. His steps were slow and measured, and his voice was even more careful. "Do you want to know what I really told Gemma when I lost it earlier?"

"Yes." Of course I wanted to know.

My feet wanted to move, to walk toward him, meet him halfway. But his eyes, all dazzling and sharp, held me captive. I'd seen Julian on his worst and best days, but I'd never seen him look anything like he did now. Like he didn't give a damn what kind of day he had...as long as I was in it.

"I told her I'm in love with you," he confessed with bone-aching clarity. "I told her I love you more than I even know how to comprehend." He shoved his hands in his pockets, still taking slow, even strides toward me, not breaking eye contact. "I'm in love with you, Juniper St. James. I know a lot of things have changed between us recently, but the one thing that has never changed is how much I love you. I have always...loved you."

I didn't realize I was crying until I opened my mouth and tasted salt on my tongue as I licked my lips.

Julian was only two steps away now. And then one. And then his hands were sliding onto my face, cupping my cheeks, wiping the tears away. His lips took over for his hands next, and he chased tears away with kisses. A light one brushed over my lips, and I held on to it, prolonged it, turned a little something perfectly sweet into something wild.

This man drove me wild, and I was so profoundly in love with him.

"I love you," Julian gasped again between rough kisses and exchanges of heavy breaths and longing sighs. "I love the way you smell and the way you smile. I love your laugh and your lies. So many, many lies we've told, Juni."

I pulled back slightly with a nod, both elated and heartbroken simultaneously. "I know. I know, Julian. I'm sorry. I'm so sorry."

He shook his head, nose brushing over mine. "Don't apologize, baby. Just tell me the truth now. Just one single truth."

"I love you." The words fell out on a sigh. "I love you, Julian. I—"

The rest of my declaration was cut off with a kiss as Julian dragged us back together.

"Do you need proof?" I asked when I had the chance to get a breath in. "I'll give it to you. Anything."

"I don't *need* anything but you," Julian replied forcefully, leaning back to look down at me. "But I *want* to take you home and tell the rest of my family that you're mine. I *want* to officially make you into a Briggs one day. I *want* to make more Briggs with you. I *want* to sell your goddamn apartment, Juni, because I don't want any fucking space." He took a steadying breath. "But we've only been dating for two weeks, and I don't need you to do any of those things. I don't need proof, Juniper."

His words shattered every hurtful thing that had happened between us in the past and made room for a future that I could hardly even wait to have. I loved him. God, I loved him and the picture he was painting.

"My apartment is leased." I spit the words out, knowing they were the right ones. "The lease is up in two months."

"Two months...I can do two months." Julian smiled as he traced his thumb over my lips, his eyes dropping to watch my mouth. "Say it again."

"My lease is up in two months."

"No, the other thing."

My lips spread into a grin. "I love you."

Julian's gaze burned as he absorbed my words. "I love you, too, Daisy."

We stood there, basking in the glow of the moment. It felt like nothing could break it, break us, but then I heard the trickling of water on tiles.

"I think the bathtub is overflowing."

Julian laughed before reluctantly releasing me and urging me toward the bathroom again. "Then you'd better get in it."

"Will you join me?" I looked hopefully over my shoulder and held out a hand. "I don't want space from you, Julian."

He took my hand, following me into the steamy bathroom. He stripped my sweatshirt over my head and tugged my pants off before beginning to shed his own clothes. And once we were finally settled beneath the suds of the water, he breathed, "I don't want space from you, either."

I settled back, leaning against his chest with the warm water swirling around me. Meanwhile, I stared straight ahead at the blank, white wall.

"Will you let me decorate?"

"It's a requirement, actually." Julian's deep voice rumbled through my body. "I'll need help picking out houseplants, too."

My smile stretched painfully wide. "I'm going to fill your living room with moonflowers."

"*Our* living room, Juni baby." He kissed the top of my head, his hands stroking up my naked sides. "You're going to fill *our* living room with moonflowers, and I can't wait."

I couldn't wait, either.

CHAPTER FORTY

"HEY, GRAY."

Grayson picked up his phone on the first ring, and I could practically hear the guilt in my voice when I greeted him. I stood at the far end of my apartment, looking out over the cityscape of Boston from the floor-to-ceiling window I had in the corner of my living room. Juni had fallen asleep about thirty minutes ago, and I finally convinced myself to leave her side to make this call.

"Hey, man. Everything okay?"

I wondered if Grayson could tell my mood from those two words alone or if my uncharacteristic lateness gave it away. I never let my friends down. If I told him I'd call him at six, I'd call him at six.

Except I didn't, and he must have realized something was off.

"Yeah. At least now it is." I cleared my throat. "Something came up with Juni after work, and I just...forgot about everything else."

"Fuck, what happened?" Grayson's voice tensed, and I heard a door click shut from his end of the phone.

"She called me from the bar where her ex had cornered her."

"The one from high school? Please tell me you kicked his ass."

"I've *matured,* Grayson." I paused. "I threatened him with a restraining order. Which I fully intend to help Juni carry through with."

"Good."

"I'm sorry I didn't call earlier, man." A heavy sigh. "I'm really, really sorry."

"You definitely don't need to apologize, Jules." Grayson's voice filled with exasperation. "I should hope that Juniper is your first priority these days...right?"

He was fishing for some sort of confirmation, and I was all too happy to give it to him.

"She is," I said firmly. "I'm guessing Noah filled you in on what happened after we came back from the wedding since you two are like gossiping children."

Grayson chuckled, unfazed. "He might have mentioned that he took Juniper out to dinner and that your reaction was a bit... caveman-esque. We both assumed—or hoped—that the rest was history."

"You'd be right about that. Juniper won't be having dinner dates with anyone but me from now on." I frowned as my thoughts drifted to Noah. I probably owed him a phone call, too. "He never had a football thing the weekend of the wedding, did he?"

"Noah?"

"Yeah."

"Definitely not," Grayson confirmed. "He told me it isn't any fun taking out girls who are already hopelessly in love with other people."

I rolled my eyes, ignoring how my heart tripped over itself while trying to maintain a steady rhythm at the reminder that Juniper loved me. Those words right there made me feel like I was fucking flying.

"So he's still trying to do that thing where he tries to hide that he's a good friend by exaggerating the whole playboy thing, huh?"

"Pretty much." Grayson sighed into the phone, and it reminded me how late it was.

"We're getting sidetracked. I'm sure you're busy, and I should have called earlier."

"It's okay," Gray insisted. "You were focused on Juniper. You think I don't understand that? If Nessa called me because of that asshat ex of hers, I'd stop fucking everything I was doing. I could be about to win the Super Bowl, and I'd walk off the field."

I closed my eyes, nodding. I knew that was true. For the last several years, I'd watched Grayson put his family first in every move he made. Of course he would understand.

That was the whole reason that all of this started. So I could help Grayson fight for his family.

"I'm struggling to find a balance," I admitted for the second time today. "I want to give her everything—all my time and attention. But I know that's obviously not possible. I don't know how you do it. How do you be the perfect husband, dad, son, friend, and professional fucking football player all at once?"

At that, Grayson started laughing. Meanwhile, I frowned because here I thought we were having a serious conversation.

"What?"

"Bro, I'm not perfect. I'm far from fucking perfect, and it's not easy. I have to make sacrifices all the time to keep all the balls in the air, but here's the good thing."

I waited, wondering where he was going with this. I hoped he'd just give me the magic answer, but that seemed far from happening.

"Juniper doesn't expect you to be perfect, Jules," he said after a dramatic pause. "Not any more than you expect *her* to be perfect."

Goddamn him. "I've fucked up with her...in the past. A lot. I want to make it right, make it up to her. I *want* to be perfect."

"Then just be there. It doesn't need to be all the time or every moment of every day. But be there when it matters. Be there for the best parts of her day and the worst. And then—this part is even harder—let her be there for you."

"Why are you saying that like it's an accusation?" I scoffed. "*I'm* not the one who didn't tell his girlfriend that he had a congenital heart defect. I can't remember...who, exactly, had to tell your future wife about that after you had a stroke and fell into a coma?"

Grayson started grumbling into the phone at that, and I laughed. "You," he grunted. "Which is exactly why you should learn from me."

"You're right," I agreed.

"I know I am."

I snorted. Grayson would always be a cocky fucker, but he'd also always be one of the best guys around.

"So...the case," I prompted.

"Yeah...about that."

My stomach twisted at the odd note in his voice. He was pissed. He was pissed that I hadn't taken care of what I'd said I would. *Shit.*

"Listen, Gray. I just wanted to say—"

"We decided not to go through with it."

I froze, my mouth still gaping as I waited for Gray to say more. And I couldn't believe what he said when he did.

"Look, I know you put a lot of work into compiling a case, and I feel like such a complete ass telling you this, but...Nessa wants to let it go, and I do, too. I thought going after this lawsuit would make me feel like I was *doing* something about what happened, but the reality is, it won't change the past."

I nodded, even though he couldn't see me. All I could see was my reflection in the window, intent on catching every word of Grayson's.

"I realized it just isn't where I want to put my priorities right now," he continued. "It's like we were talking—I don't want to sacrifice the energy meant for my wife and kids to chase after this. And Nessa agrees. We'd rather focus all our energy on Gabe and Gracie."

"Gracie?" I choked.

"It's a girl," he whispered. "We're having a girl."

"Fuck," I breathed. "Congratulations, Gray. Gabriel's going to be such a good big brother."

"Yeah, although I don't know much about being a good sibling." Gray exhaled, sounding wistful. Like Juniper, he grew up as an only child. "I guess Gabe will have to rely on his godfather to teach him all about being the best older brother."

My throat squeezed tight, and I wished to hell that Grayson and his family didn't live on the other side of the country so I could see them all more.

"I'll teach him everything I know," I said, my voice catching.

"Thanks, man." Grayson's voice remained soft. "I'm really sorry—"

"It's my turn to tell you to stop apologizing," I interrupted. "Let's face it. It would have been a really fucking hard case to win."

He chuckled. "You could have done it."

I shrugged. "Maybe. I was hopeful."

"I know you worked hard on it," he acknowledged. "I wish I had reached this conclusion earlier so I hadn't wasted your time."

I thought about working on the case with Juniper, all the nights we'd stayed late, all the dinners we ate together, all the little moments when I started to feel more alive.

"You didn't waste my time at all," I said finally and with complete confidence.

"You sure?"

"Yeah, I'm sure." I smiled to myself. "That case was the best thing that ever happened to me."

"You're lying."

Janie, my mini-me, was staring at me. She hadn't said anything since I'd announced that I was dating Juniper, but Gianna, on the other hand, kept insisting that I was fucking with them.

"This is absolutely a prank."

"Gi, it's not a prank," I said calmly. "Juniper and I are dating. I am dating Juniper. She is dating me. We're together. Are you going to help me out here, Gems?"

Gemma shrugged. "I think you're doing just fine on your own."

"Don't think I don't see that little smirk on your face, Julian," Gianna continued. "You're pulling something, and I'm not buying it."

"It's not a smirk. It's a smile," I laughed.

The accusation didn't leave her eyes. "I think *both* prove that you're up to something."

"Or maybe I'm just *happy*."

"Wouldn't that be something," Genevieve muttered.

I couldn't even get myself to glare in response to Gen. She was right. I'd spent far too much of my life being miserable without Juni, but I wouldn't ever be going back to that.

"Look, you can find out for yourself in a few minutes. She's on her way over."

"Really?" Josie perked up. And damn, I loved how excited she was to see Juni. I loved how perfectly Juni fit into my life, but I hated that I never saw that it could be like this before.

"Really."

For the next approximately three minutes and twenty-six seconds, my sisters volleyed questions at me while waiting in the living room at my parents' house. After every question, they stared between me and the front entryway, waiting anxiously for someone to ring the doorbell.

Juni and I had come home for the weekend to celebrate my birthday with my family. *Our* families. Juni's parents would be coming over later, and even Sofia and Marc planned to swing by.

That was sort of a happy coincidence; Sofia had reached out that she was going to be in the Boston area this weekend, and Juni was really bummed to have to tell her that she was going to be in Whitebridge. So I told Juni to invite Sofia tonight, too, and Juni was so adorably excited that Sofia said she'd love to join for a bit.

When the doorbell finally rang, I walked to the door, feeling irrationally giddy at knowing Juni was behind it. I could feel the eyes on my back, but I ignored them and focused on greeting my girlfriend.

I opened the door to a tentatively smiling Juni and raised a brow.

"I'm a little nervous," she explained under her breath, understanding my look perfectly.

"Don't be," I chuckled, sweeping her into the house. I shielded her from my sisters, wanting a moment with just the two of us before I lost her attention to them.

She'd walked through those doors thousands of times, but I hoped it felt different today. I hoped she felt the shift in the air that I was experiencing. Just to be sure she understood exactly why that was, I cupped her face between my hands, tipped it back until I saw the sparkle in her eyes, and leaned to kiss her soundly.

Juniper's lips parted with a gasp, and I took that opportunity to taste her, sweeping my tongue in to stroke hers. Juni responded with the tiniest, sweetest moan that made it clear I needed to pull back before losing it.

"Julian..." she muttered against my lips as they broke from hers. She said my name with a slight admonishment, but it didn't sound serious. She couldn't even *try* to make herself sound serious when she reprimanded me these days.

"Oh. My. God."

I couldn't tell which one of my sisters that was. Actually, it might have been two of them talking in unison. They did that sometimes.

"Again?" Juniper kept her eyes on me, sounding panicked. "We have to find a better way to announce this than just kissing in front of people," she hissed.

I laughed, pulling away. "I already told them, baby." I turned to see my four slack-jawed sisters. They were all perched on the edge of their seats in various states of shock. "They just wouldn't believe me."

Gianna glanced sideways at the other three and whispered, "Did he just call her *baby*?"

"Oh my God," Janie choked. "He was telling the truth."

"No shit, he was telling the truth." Genevieve laughed. "I'm pretty sure Juni would have already smacked him for that kiss if he weren't."

"Juniper," Josie said, beaming at my girlfriend. "We're so, so happy that you aren't smacking Julian, even though I'm sure he probably deserves it."

Juni cleared her voice, shifting as she smiled back at Josie. She wound her arm beneath my back, sliding into my side, and I couldn't contain my excitement at the simple gesture.

"Don't worry." Juni's voice was so fucking sweet. "I make sure Julian gets exactly what he deserves."

She winked at me, and then, as if on cue, my four youngest sisters all jumped out of their spots simultaneously, squealing as they ran straight past me to Juniper. Unsurprisingly, they stole my goddamn girlfriend from me, dragging her into the living room in a fit of screaming and laughing. A look of slight bewilderment danced across Juni's face, but she was smiling. She was smiling so incredibly wide.

Meanwhile, Gemma sat on the couch, watching the chaos. She wore a grin nearly as wide as Juni.

"Julian!" Janie screamed as if finally remembering that I was also there. "Why the hell did it take you so long to come to your senses?"

"We've been waiting for *so long*," Gen added dramatically.

Of course. Of course they only acknowledged me just to yell at me.

I rolled my eyes. "You'll all be happy to know I'm done wasting time, then. Juniper's moving in with me by the end of next month."

She was already starting to bring her stuff over gradually, and my apartment was becoming more and more Juni-like by the minute. I was obsessed with it.

"Oh, thank *God*," said another dramatic sister. I honestly didn't catch who because my eyes were currently trapped in Juni's brown gaze.

But then, movement to her left caught my attention, and I blinked away to realize that Janie was walking toward me. My mini-me slipped under my arm, hugging me.

"I'm happy for you," she whispered.

I looked down at her. "You've known forever, too, huh?"

She shrugged. "We all suspected and hoped it would happen eventually. And we thought it might be soon, considering how you acted at Christmas...but I'm mostly happy because you *seem* happy."

I glanced up to find Juniper still watching me, her eyes growing glassy.

"I'm so happy, Janie," I said quietly, as though it was a secret between the two of us. In reality, it was plain as day for anyone to see.

"Is Juniper staying over tonight?" she asked, eyes flicking between Juni and me as she slowly released me from her tight hug. "After the party?"

Not liking the distance between Juniper and me, I strode back into the living room, directing all my attention toward her. "Do you want to stay the night?" I asked.

"Depends..." Juni cocked her head to the side. "Are you going to get mad if I miscount the doors in the hallway when I'm finding a place to sleep tonight?"

"Only if you end up somewhere that isn't next to me."

"Okay, okay," Gianna broke in. "That is *enough* cute stuff for now. You're going to make me wish you'd go back to arguing."

I stifled my next words, chuckling as I pulled out my phone to text them to Juni instead. Her cheeks were pink as my sisters enveloped her in their conversation, and I couldn't wait to make them even pinker.

> JULIAN: Cute is not how I would describe what I plan to do to you tonight.

I could tell when Juniper felt her phone go off because her eyes immediately darted to me. I restrained a laugh as she struggled to resist the temptation of checking her phone when she knew all my sisters' eyes were on her.

But eventually, there was a lull in the conversation, and she gave in. Her cheeks dimpled as she read it, and her eyes shone as she rolled them at me.

My parents arrived home with pizza shortly after the big reveal to my sisters, and I didn't even have to say a word to my mom. She looked at me and then at Juniper, who had crossed the living room to snuggle on my lap, and simply passed me a quiet smile.

My dad must have already told her, but I loved that my mom would never be one to give me the kind of grief that everyone else did. She didn't know how to do anything but show her love for her kids, and I would forever appreciate that about her. Especially because I knew she'd always loved Juni in the same way.

Katherine and Brooks St. James arrived next. Juniper immediately popped up from her spot and pulled her parents aside. They formed a little huddle in the front entryway, and her dad leaned in conspiratorially, always eager to hear the gossip.

The gossip was about me; that much was easy to tell. I debated whether I should go over there but decided to let Juni have this moment with her parents. Their expressions told me that while they weren't expecting the news of their daughter dating the guy she'd always claimed to hate, they definitely weren't shocked. More so surprised that they hadn't sniffed it out sooner—especially on Brooks' part.

Katherine gave Juniper a wide, knowing smile before pulling her into a hug, and Brooks' head swiveled to find me. After giving Juni's shoulder a squeeze, he sauntered my way, shucking his hands in his pockets.

"I'd give you the talk, but..." He laughed softly. "I know you've been looking out for her for nearly as long as I have."

"I'll always look out for Juniper," I said, meeting his gaze so he knew it was true.

But he already did. "I know. But now I need you to make her happy, too."

"I'm trying my best," I said honestly.

"And he's doing a very good job," Juni cut in, slipping back onto my lap. I wrapped a possessive arm around her. I probably should keep my hands to myself, considering how her dad flashed me a critical eye, but I didn't care enough to let her go.

Luckily, Sofia and Marc's arrival cut our conversation short, and Juniper once again hopped off my lap. This time, I followed her to the front door, wanting to greet the couple whose wedding invitation had helped me realize that being Juniper's boyfriend was a role I never wanted to give up.

Sofia, as bright and cheery as ever, pulled both Juni and me into a hug before turning and doing the same to Juniper's parents. I watched Juni as she introduced them, catching every bit of her reaction. Her misty eyes and fidgeting hands, which I enveloped in mine. Her smile—such a big, beautiful smile. I regretted all the years and all the things I did that made it disappear.

Juni directed Sofia, Marc, and her parents further into the house, where most of my sisters were huddled around the food. I hung back, watching as Juniper played hostess in a house that I realized was every bit hers as it was mine. I was too in my head as a kid to realize that by constantly reminding Juniper she didn't belong here, that she wasn't a part of this family because we didn't share DNA...it only reinforced that she was alone. Because she didn't know anyone who shared her DNA.

But now all I saw was family. This was her family—our family. And she belonged here, always had.

"And finally, everything was right in the world." A voice sighed, and I knew who it was.

"I'm sorry it took me so long to make it right, Gems," I said without looking away from Juniper. She had a plate full of pizza, laughing as she chatted with Sofia and Marc.

"As long as you don't fuck it up, I forgive you."

"I won't."

"It's funny..." Gemma started, her tone of voice making me look at her. Gemma's eyes shifted to mine before she shrugged and left her thought incomplete.

"What?" If it concerned Juni, I needed to know.

"Oh, I just hardly ever see Juni eat in social situations like this."

"And why's that?" I jumped on the opportunity to ask the very thing I'd wanted to know for months.

Gemma bit down on her lip, debating whether or not to tell me. But after a few seconds, she gave in. "It's mostly anxiety, nerves. Makes her lose her appetite. I think she gets so in her head about not fitting in or being wanted, about people not liking her..."

Her words drifted away, letting me figure out the rest on my own. And I did, my thoughts chasing down memories of all the times I'd urged Juni to eat something. At the football game when I'd introduced her to Noah, on the way to Sofia's wedding, at Sofia's wedding...

The early days in the office with me.

I made her nervous. Sharing an office with me made her nervous because she thought I hated it, hated being around her.

But I only hated it because I knew I wouldn't fucking survive being that close to Juniper day in and day out. I knew all our walls would come crumbling down, and they had been the only thing keeping the status quo intact.

"I thought she'd be really nervous about Sofia coming or about the relationship reveal," Gemma mused. "But I guess not."

"I guess not," I muttered, my eyes tracking Juniper's movements and her bright smile again.

Later, after dinner and drinks and a round of long-winded goodbyes, I had to snatch Juniper from the upstairs hallway. She kept hovering in the doorway to Josie and Gianna's room, chatting endlessly with them, and I was tired of waiting.

"Say goodnight," I whispered in her ear before barely giving her a chance to do it and whisking her away.

Juni protested weakly as I brought her into my childhood bedroom, leading her to my bed. She wore the same pajamas that she'd packed when we went to New York for the wedding, and the memories...well, they were good memories.

"It was nice of Sofia to come," I said, wanting to hear more of Juniper's thoughts about the night.

"It was."

I scanned Juniper's face, hoping to glean more from her expression. But it was neutral. Calm.

"Would you ever want to reach out to your birth mom?" I asked. "Maybe if she came with Sofia sometime?"

Juniper sucked her bottom lip between her teeth, thinking before she shook her head.

"I don't think that's something I need. I think I remind her of something painful, of my birth dad, maybe. I don't know exactly, but it's okay. She has her family, and I have mine. It's been so nice getting to know Sofia, to finally have a sister of my own, but earlier today, my mom reminded me that blood only counts for so much. And I have more than a few people in my life who would consider me their sister."

"Yes, you do," I agreed. "A lot of them are in this house." And in case there was any confusion, I added, "I'm not one of them, though."

Juniper laughed. It sounded lyrical, magical. "What do you consider me, then, Julian?"

"You're the love of my life, Juniper," I answered without thinking twice. "And you are a part of this family, *my* family. You always have been, and you always will be."

I didn't miss the shine in her eyes as she crawled across the bed, cupped my face, and kissed me. She kissed me, and it wasn't gentle or sweet. She might have smelled like roses and tasted like tears, but there was a fierceness to Juniper that I adored. She would love me as fiercely as she kissed me, and I knew that to be the absolute truth.

"I have to grab something," she murmured against my lips once her kisses had grown soft.

Before I could protest, Juniper jumped off the bed and crossed the room to rummage in her overnight bag. She pulled out an envelope, bringing it over to me.

"What's this?" I asked, taking it from her.

She shrugged. "For your birthday."

"You didn't need to do this," I sighed. This was already the best birthday I'd ever had, simply because I had her.

"You don't even know what it is yet," she argued with a smile.

"I know it's something you didn't need to do," I said before pulling out the card inside. A folded sheet of paper fell out, and I went for it first, opening it only to realize what she'd given me. Plane tickets. Plane tickets to...

"Grayson told me there's an alumni game in September," she said tentatively. "I know I'll never be able to go back in time and watch you play in college, but I thought maybe you'd be willing to play for me now. Plus, Nessa will have had the baby by then, so I thought you'd probably want to go and visit them, and—"

I cut her off with a kiss because I didn't have any words. Juniper giggled against my mouth as I whispered thank you between kisses. My thoughtful girl.

"There's nothing more I'd love than to play for you," I said honestly. Just thinking about seeing Juniper in those stands, wearing my jersey, had my heart beating faster. "And share my friends with you."

Juni pulled back, her gaze roaming my face to judge whether or not I was being serious.

"I don't want to share you, but I'll share them," I clarified with a grin, brushing a piece of hair out of her face.

She rolled her eyes before leaning in for another kiss. "You said you weren't going to be cute," she murmured.

"This isn't what I had planned," I said honestly, taking that moment to sweep Juniper's body beneath mine, pinning her to the bed.

"What did you have planned?" she asked, all breathless and pretty.

My lips pulled sideways in a smirk as I looked down at her. "Now that you're finally in this bed, and we've established that it is *exactly* where you are supposed to be, I fully plan on going down on you until you need to scream into my pillow to stay quiet."

"*Julian*," she gasped before giving my shoulder a little push.

I didn't budge. "That was a pretty weak protest, love."

"Who said it was a protest?" she said hotly. Juniper rolled her body beneath mine, reminding me of that morning I'd woken up to find her tangled in the sheets with me.

I grabbed the hand that half attempted to push me away and threaded my fingers through hers. Then I used my grip to anchor that hand and the other above her head.

"You're so needy for me, and I love it," I said, lowering my voice to a husky pitch.

She raised her hips, rocking against the obvious bulge in my pants. "Look who's talking, baby."

"You're right." No point in arguing the truth. "Fuck, I've definitely imagined you in my bed like this before."

One of her brows lifted. "Is reality meeting your expectations?"

"Exceeding." I dropped to kiss her exposed neck. "Definitely exceeding."

Juniper sighed as I continued to kiss across her soft skin, lowering until I had the swell of her breasts beneath my mouth. But apparently, I wasn't moving fast enough.

"I want your mouth on me, Julian," Juniper groaned, wiggling against my body.

"My mouth *is* on you," I pointed out.

"That's not what I meant," she said through clenched teeth.

"Oh, really?" I smiled, releasing her hands as I inched down the bed, slowly taking her pajama bottoms with me. Then I dropped my face between her legs, nipping at her inner thighs. "Think you can stay quiet?"

She sucked in as I grazed my tongue over her underwear, precisely where I knew her clit was hiding beneath. "I'll do my best."

"That's my girl," I murmured, and I caught a glimpse of her smile growing out of the corner of my eye. It bloomed, spreading over her face.

"What?" I paused because I needed to know exactly what caused that expression to come over her.

"I just like that," she said with a shrug. "I like being your girl. I've always wanted to be your girl."

That was the best answer she could have ever given. My heart soared as I let my own smile blossom. "You always have been mine, Daisy. And you always will be."

Her eyes flashed, sparkling with the Juni-like wonder I knew —and loved—all too well.

"Say it," I prompted, knowing she had something on the tip of her tongue.

She shook her head. "I don't need to anymore. I know you're telling the truth."

"Say it anyway."

"Fine."

Juniper's eyes rolled up, but then they returned to mine, and I felt sucked in—trapped by the magnetism between us. When she spoke, it was in a sultry, toe-curling whisper.

"Prove it."

So I did.

epilogue

"I'M NERVOUS."

At my words, Julian instantly spun in his desk chair. When he saw me standing at the door to our office, a slow smile spread over his face. Such a one-eighty from a year and a half ago when I first showed my face to Julian outside our office.

Usually, I would welcome his smile. But right now, it was annoying me. He *had* heard me, hadn't he?

"Did you hear me? I said I was ner-vous."

I pronounced my words extra clearly for him this time.

Julian still ignored them, sweeping his eyes over my black dress and the blazer I had in my hand, ready to go for court. I'd paired it with an impressive pair of heels, and after fussing over my hair this morning for over half an hour, I gave up and let Julian curl it. It fell in loose waves around my shoulders.

Why was he looking at me like that? His eyes were taking me in like it was the first time he'd seen me in years...when in reality, we got ready for work and walked into the office together.

"I heard you," he acknowledged. "You're just very pretty. And I can't wait to see you walk out onto the courtroom floor looking like the pretty badass you are. I know you're nervous, but you're going to do amazing."

I sagged against the doorframe, exhausted even though the day had only begun. "Honestly...where does your confidence come from?"

"My confidence in you?" He grinned wider. "It comes from knowing you for over half my life. And from working with you for over the past year. You're very good at your job."

I sighed, all my annoyance in him washing away. It was odd when he did this—this role reversal. There he was, acting all perky as he gathered his things up on his desk, packing them into his briefcase while I brooded in the doorway, trying to shake the rest of my nerves.

I had confidence in myself, but this was the first case I had taken over at Gardner Law. It was a big deal. When Julian told me how Grayson had decided not to pursue the malpractice case, I understood. We both did. Taking any kind of legal action was time-consuming and energy-sucking, but it would be even more extreme for the Elez-Everetts on account of their high profile. Plus, they had spent so much of last year worrying about Gracie and if she would also have the same congenital heart defect.

Thankfully, Gracie Everett was a healthy baby girl, and Gabriel Everett was a healthy big brother who cared greatly for his little sister. But regardless of their happy outcome, I couldn't shake the feeling that we had unfinished business. So when Grayson told us that he knew of another family experiencing negligence at the same clinic where Gabe had been born, I told him to have them reach out to me.

They did, and now, today was the day we would finish settling this in court.

Julian wanted me to have the case. It was unrealistic for us to work it together instead of with Daphne or one of the other partners, and Julian encouraged me to go ahead with it without him. I wanted very badly to win this case. It had been a long process, and we were very close to the end. And if all went to plan, there would be a verdict by nightfall.

And then Julian had a *surprise* for me.

"This is the best day ever," he said, grabbing my coat and holding it out for me to slip into.

"I don't know about that."

"I do," he said, still giddy and confident. "I get to watch my girlfriend kick ass in court, and then I get to celebrate with her all weekend. Just her."

"But what if we don't pull it off today? Won't it ruin the weekend?"

Julian shook his head and started buttoning my coat for me. He'd kept his promise to take care of me, and I had to admit it felt nice. The case consumed my brain, making all the other little things feel like big things. Julian seemed to know; he took care of all of them before I could even ask.

"Nothing could ruin this weekend," he said, again showing off his confidence.

"Are you going to tell me where we're going?"

"Nope. You'll just have to wait and see."

God, he was annoying.

But I was also so deeply in love with him.

I COULD FEEL JULIAN'S BRIGHT EYES ON ME WHILE I DELIVERED THE closing arguments to the courtroom. And when I finished, I caught his beaming expression from across the gallery. And after the jury deliberated and announced the verdict, he was the first person by my side.

We won. We did it. We got justice for Gabriel and Jude, the other little boy affected by the clinic's medical malpractice. It felt liberating and settling.

Julian didn't say much when we were still at the courthouse. I could tell he wanted to, but he was playing the role of supportive colleague—not boyfriend. It took us a few months to navigate that, to figure out how to work together while being so utterly obsessed with each other, but we'd finally found a balance.

Julian was a professional through and through.

But as soon as we were alone...

"Fuck, I'm so turned on."

Julian rammed his head back against his seat as he got behind the wheel. He didn't move to turn on the car, didn't check his rearview mirrors for pedestrians crossing the street, didn't do anything but squeeze his eyes shut.

"I'm regretting my life decisions," he mumbled before I could ask him what he was doing—besides trying to rein in his obvious arousal.

"Why's that?" I beamed; I couldn't help it. I loved toying with Julian, and I loved that we'd won the case. It was just too much goodness all at once.

Julian opened his eyes again. They darted to me, dark and wanting. "I have to wait three hours before I can fuck you in that hot little dress you just strutted around the courtroom in."

"Why that long?"

"Because that's how long it will take to get to your surprise."

"I think this will be good for you," I said with a smirk. Although secretly, I wished we were going home before heading straight out of town. Because I didn't exactly want to wait, either. Julian looked too damn good in that suit.

"Good for me?" he scoffed.

"I miss watching you work for it a little bit, you know?" I crossed one leg over the other leisurely, making sure a bit of skin was showing. "I make it far too easy for you to get what you want."

Julian's eyes narrowed as they flicked over me. "That's because you want the same fucking thing, Juniper."

Julian's voice was low, a warning I couldn't help but be intrigued by. Maybe it was the adrenaline of winning the case, but power drugged my veins. I could easily get swept away in it.

When I didn't say anything in response, Julian cocked a brow.

"You're fucking drenched between those beautiful thighs." His throat worked as he swallowed. "You know it, and I know it."

"Maybe I am." I shrugged. "Maybe I'm not."

"Oh, Juni," he murmured, and the sudden amusement in his voice felt like velvet on my senses. "You're good. But I'm better."

"What is that supposed—"

Julian interrupted my question by pressing Play on his phone, and the sensual voice of one of my favorite fictional characters began filtering through the car speakers.

"The glow of the fire illuminated her expression as she spread out for me on the blanket, letting me see every inch of her naked body. The winter wind howled outside the chalet, but I barely heard it. All I could hear was the rush of blood in my ears as I bent down and—"

I snatched the dial and twisted the volume down, feeling my cheeks flush.

"What?" Julian peeked over while maneuvering out of our parking spot with only one hand. "The memories too much for you to handle?"

Goddamn him.

The heat dispersed throughout my body as I thought about that day in the office when Julian had placed my headphones on my ears and bent me over his desk.

This was the scene. It was the scene that I'd listened to while getting absolutely railed in our office in the middle of the workday.

I sank lower in the seat of the car, crossing my legs. Tightly.

"Point taken, Julian." My voice was scratchy, parched. "You can turn it off now."

"Oh, I'm not turning it off."

Julian didn't take his eyes off the road as he merged onto a highway going north. I wasn't sure where he was taking me, but I knew it wasn't in the city, based on what he suggested I pack for the weekend.

True to his word, Julian did *not* turn off the audiobook. No. He reached out and turned the volume back up. "It's really a shame I didn't start giving you books earlier," he said over the dialogue. "Think of all the inspiration I missed out on."

"Inspiration?" I questioned. "How so?"

The bit of mischief I'd recognized bloomed into something much more obvious.

"You'll see."

Julian stopped replying to my questions after that. Every time I tried to talk, he jokingly shushed me so that he could hear the audiobook better. And because it was the final act of the book, it was filled with dirty, hot sex of the couple who had held out for the first two-thirds of the story.

I was a clammy mess by the time Julian pulled into the driveway of a gleaming timber-frame lodge. Somewhere along the way, we'd passed over the state line into Vermont, and now I was gaping at snowy paradise. Dusted evergreen trees framed the chalet, and I stared at it with wonder.

"That's beautiful," I breathed.

"That's where we're staying," Julian replied. "Seem familiar?"

I shook my head with a frown. "I've never been to this part of Vermont before—"

Something about how Julian was smiling at me made me pause. And then I backtracked. Vermont. A snow-covered lodge. A weekend getaway. And what I could only assume was a fireplace inside...

"Is this...?" I broke off with a gasp, pointing at his car display, where it showed the audiobook on pause. "Are you recreating the scene? From the book? From *this* book?"

Julian's lips broadened, his smile dazzling at this point. "One time, you told me that if I loved you, I wouldn't make you pick between me and your books. And I do love you. I love you a lot. So I wanted to make sure you knew that you could have both. You can have it all. But I will say...I put my own twist on the scene."

Julian's smile faded slightly as his eyes wandered my face. His amusement dipped into something more simmering, hiding just behind the surface, threatening to bubble over. And fuck, it made my whole body tremble. I knew that look.

"What's your twist?" I prompted unsteadily when he didn't say anything.

His lips twitched as he continued to look at me, memorizing my face. He didn't answer for a long time, but when he did, his voice was thick with emotion and need.

He held out a single house key. "Why don't you go find out, love."

My heart skipped a beat at the words, but I couldn't pinpoint why. They felt monumental, but I didn't care to consider the reason. Instead, I took the key and stepped out of the car on shaky feet, wrapping my coat around me as I made my way up the sidewalk. I heard Julian get out of the car, too. He followed slowly, meandering like he wanted to watch the scene from afar.

I fumbled with the lock before pushing the door open to...

Flowers.

Bouquets and bouquets of flowers filled a cozy living room with tall, expansive windows and even taller ceilings. My eyes caught on the stone fireplace, but only for a second because I was too overwhelmed with the...flowers. White flowers. Lilies. Roses. Daisies.

Lilies. Roses. Daisies.

"Lily."

Julian's voice scraped my soul. I twisted, looking over my shoulder to see Julian reading from a paper pad. A notebook of sorts.

He closed the front door behind him and stepped forward, his eyes still trained on the paper between his hands.

"Rosie."

Another slow step.

"Poppy. Iris. Ivy. Violet. Holly. Willow. Olive. Magnolia. Dahlia. Hazel."

For every word he had said, Julian took a step. Which led him straight to me, and only when he was within reach did he look up and whisper, "Daisy baby."

His arm dropped, the pad of paper forgotten onto the floor. I stared at him, not sure what was happening but knowing I didn't want to miss a second of it. He brushed my coat off my shoulders, leaving me in only my black dress again. His eyes raked over it while my jacket fell to the floor beside his notebook with an echoing thud.

"Julian," I breathed, wishing I had a million names to rattle off in return but knowing I only needed to say his once for him to understand everything I was feeling. "There was a list?"

His smile was gentle as he lifted a hand to my face. "There was a list. I told you."

I thought it was a joke, something we just teased. But before I could clarify, Julian went on.

"I grew up in a big family, baby." He put his other hand to my face, cupping it. "I should have been good at sharing, but the one thing I hated sharing was you. Even with my siblings, my parents. I hated that since you showed up on my doorstep and became theirs...that you could never become mine. Everyone called you Juni, but I didn't want the Juniper that everyone else had."

My lips parted as shock ran through my system. For over a year, Julian had reinforced how much he loved me. But these words...these words were new.

The corner of his mouth tipped up. "See, I told you I'm selfish," he said.

"You've never been selfish, Julian," I choked out. "Never. Not one day in your whole life."

Julian smiled softly, smoothing my hair behind my ear before returning to cup my face. "The first time I called you Rosie, it was Christmas," he went on. "You had just come inside from the snow, and your cheeks were flushed. You thought I was making fun of you, and I realized I had to return to the drawing board."

He looked pointedly at the notebook on the floor.

"So I kept trying new nicknames that reminded me of you,

hoping one would be perfect. For just us. So at least I could have one thing that was mine. But...I realized you were more than just a single flower, a single name." Julian's fingers traced my jaw to my chin, tipping it up until I was staring into his sharp gaze. "You were a whole goddamn bouquet, baby."

"My nicknames *do* belong to you, Julian. But so does my heart. And a whole lot more."

"I'm glad to hear you say that," he said, grin growing. "Because I was wondering if I could add another name to the list. One that means...a whole lot more."

Julian's grip slid down my sides until he had my hands in both of his. He held my fingers tightly as he dropped to the ground. Onto one knee.

"How does Mrs. Briggs sound?" he asked, eyes shining as he looked up at me like I was the only star in the sky. My hands shook in his, and he gripped them harder, refusing to let go. "Should I add it to my notebook?"

A disbelieving laugh broke through my lips. "But it isn't a plant."

"Yeah..." Julian winced, but there was humor in it. His eyes twinkled. "I was hoping you'd make an exception. Just this once."

"You were, huh?"

"Yeah, I was." Julian let go of one of my hands to reach into his pocket, producing a small velvet box. He popped it open, and I felt my knees buckle. "I even brought this ring along for the occasion."

My lips parted with a silent scream, and I slapped a hand over my mouth. A larger-than-life diamond sparkled up at me, but that wasn't what blurred my vision. Tears welled in my lash line, threatening to fall.

But then Julian kept talking, and there was no holding them back.

"I love you, Juniper," he whispered. Simple words that I had heard so many times before at this point. But they carried the weight of my heart. "I'm in love with you, and I know I can't live without you. I tried. I tried, and I was miserable. You aren't just the love of my life. You're the joy of it. You're my everything. And I'm hoping you'll let me marry you."

I blinked through the tears, trying to find my voice. "You want to marry me, huh?"

I couldn't seem to figure out how to do anything but repeat him.

"Desperately." Julian nodded. Aggressively nodded. "Can I?"

There was a time, back in high school, when I had made it my mission to always have a comeback for the words Julian Briggs said. But I never imagined, not in my wildest dreams, that I would have to come up with an answer for this. And even though the answer was obvious, all I could do was smile down at him, my lips stretched so wide they hurt.

"If you need the proof, it's right there," he teased, nodding to the ring in his hand. He was waiting...eagerly waiting for me to answer so he could slide it onto *my* hand.

"No." I shook my head, and Julian's eyes grew wide. "No, that's not the proof," I amended with a ridiculous, giddy laugh. "The proof isn't the ring. It's you, Julian. It's you and everything you've done for me. It's you and everything you are to me. I love you. And I very, very much want to add Mrs. Briggs to the list."

Julian tugged on my hand at that, and I came crashing down into his arms. Laughter continued to spill out of me, the happiest of sounds. Julian's lips found mine, and then he breathed against them.

"Say the word." His forehead tipped into mine, pressing us together. "Please."

"Yes." I brushed the word he wanted to hear over his lips. "Yes, yes, yes, yes, ye—"

Julian caught the last yes with his mouth, absorbing it with a soul-searching kiss. The way he kissed consumed me, and I almost cried out in protest when his lips eventually left mine. But then I realized it was only because he wanted to slip my new ring onto my finger. It distracted me, dazzling there, and when I looked up again, I realized Julian had left my side and was weaving through the forest of flowers. He stopped before the fireplace, slipping off his suit jacket and beginning to roll up his sleeves.

I stared, unashamed of how ridiculously attracted I was to him. I always had been, and now he was mine. Really, really mine.

This man. He loved so fiercely. I'd always known that, but to now be the center of that love was unbelievable. I admired him endlessly for the person he was, for the selflessness in his heart, and for how much he cared for others. I couldn't wait to return that care for the rest of our lives. He deserved more than anyone to be taken care of in just the way that he took care of everyone else.

Once his forearms were bare, Julian went to work making a fire. And unsurprisingly, it didn't take him long. Although, I wouldn't have even minded waiting. Despite being eager to have his lips and body back on mine, the moment couldn't have been more perfect. I liked watching him work. Even though he sat behind a desk most days, he was still someone who worked well with his hands. And who looked good while doing it.

"Come here."

Julian's soft voice called to me, and I crossed the room to crash back into his arms. Julian caught me, and then we crumpled back to the floor—as though the weight of our desire was simply too much to stay standing. Soft, plush carpeting cushioned my body as Julian's deliciously hard figure covered me from above. His lips found mine again, and then I was lost.

I wasn't sure if I had ever felt the frantic need that I did right now. It could have been the long ride here or the proposal or just the fact that my fiancé was fucking hot as he shed his clothes and then mine, but I was dying. And Julian was loving it. My hips rocked up, begging for him.

"God, you're beautiful," he breathed as he positioned himself over me again. His words were soft, but his touch was demanding as he encouraged my legs to wrap around his waist before driving into me with a single thrust.

"*Yes.*"

Nothing had ever felt better than this. Nothing had ever been better than Julian and me together.

"Say it again," Julian demanded, his voice strained as he pulled out and rocked into me again.

"Yes," I groaned, tightening my legs around him. Closer. I needed us even closer.

Julian reached for my hand—the one with the ring—and threaded our fingers together. His thumb brushed over the delicate jewelry before he anchored our hands above my head and continued fucking me with rough thrusts.

I gasped, unsure if I could manage much longer. He was destroying me—every movement was unraveling me from the inside out.

"Oh my God, *Julian.*" I tipped my hips, meeting him thrust for thrust. "I—I can't."

"Take it, Juniper," he demanded, his voice low and gravelly in my ear. "Be my good, gorgeous girl and take it."

My release didn't just wash over me at his words; it broke like a dam, flooding every sense and nerve ending. I held on tight to Julian while it overpowered me, and he didn't dare let go. Crying my name, he followed me, and pleasure dragged both of us under until we were a sweaty mess on the floor.

We didn't talk.

The fire crackled, and our heavy breaths mingled, but we didn't talk. I wasn't sure I'd be able to talk, honestly.

Julian eventually shifted so he wasn't crushing me. Although, the weight felt soothing in a way. He gently stripped the rest of my clothes from my body, and then I did the same to him. Somewhere amidst the forest of flowers, he found a pile of blankets and used them to create a soft cocoon in front of the fire, where we curled up together.

"This is better," I said definitively once I was nestled into Julian's arms.

"Hm?" He shifted closer before brushing his lips over my temple.

"This is better," I repeated. "I know I said I couldn't pick between you and my books, but that was a lie. This is better. *You* are better."

Julian chuckled. "I knew I could get you to admit it if I just gave you a side-by-side opportunity to compare."

"I'm so happy," I mumbled, feeling my eyelids droop.

Julian was right: this was the best day ever.

"Tired, love?" Julian's fingers began sifting through my hair.

I nodded absently, feeling drugged by the moment.

"It's not even that late," he teased. "What happened to my little night owl?"

Twisting in Julian's arms, I found his blue gaze, which burned bright in the reflection of the fire. "I used to stay up late because the freedom of nights made me think they were the best part of living."

"But now?" Julian prompted, seeming eager for the rest of my words.

"But now I get to wake up next to you. And I know the things that happen at night will still feel real in the morning. I'm not afraid of that anymore."

"That ring will still be on your finger when you wake up," Julian murmured, noting where my attention was. "I will still be here. And you will still be my fiancée."

I tucked my hand back into my chest, cherishing the thought.

"Then I can't wait."

extended epilogue

"I LOOK SO PREGNANT in this dress."

I couldn't turn my head very far because of the hot curling iron that had a hold on my hair, but I glanced sideways at Gemma. Her flowery bridesmaid dress draped over her baby bump, and even though she kept assessing herself from different angles, the bump was hard to miss.

"Gems, honey, you *are* pregnant."

She sighed, flopping down onto the bed in the bridal suite.

"I would be concerned if you didn't look pregnant," I added. "Besides, you're beautiful and glowing."

"Oh, shush." Gemma tucked a hair behind her ear, looking at herself with uncertainty.

"Pretty sure Noah would agree with me," I said softly. "Maybe I should text him to come up here to get his opinion."

Gemma's eyes flicked up, wide. "Don't you dare do that."

I laughed, but the noise was drowned by the sound of all the other Briggs sisters who were getting their make-up done in the ensuite bathroom, along with Nessa and Sofia. Gemma was the only one who was all ready for the wedding because she was the one who volunteered to get up early and take the first hair and make-up spots so the rest of us could sleep in a little longer.

"Hmmm," I continued. "I bet he can be pretty convincing with things like that when he wants to be."

Gemma turned a shade of deep red, nearly the color of her hair, and I had to bite down on my smile as I went on.

"I bet he's grumpy that he doesn't get to walk you down the aisle and that Grayson's doing it instead."

I was pretty sure the wedding party line-up, with Gemma and Grayson leading the way, was the only reason Noah cared that he wasn't the best man and Grayson was.

"Would you stop it?" Gemma rolled her eyes. "Noah does *not* care that I'm walking down the aisle with Grayson."

I shrugged but decided not to continue to push her buttons... even if I knew I was right. Noah might not be as bad as Julian when it came to being a touch possessive, but he was close. I could tell, even if Gemma refused to admit it. She'd refused to admit a lot of things in the last year, but I let go of any feelings I had about that. After all, she was growing a whole human inside her.

Gemma rubbed her belly while deep in thought.

"You know what's amazing?" I said, trying to pull her out of whatever she was thinking.

"Hm?" She glanced over at me.

"We're about to be sisters," I whispered.

Gemma's eyes rounded with emotion. "You've always been my sister, Junes."

"I know," I acknowledged. "But it's just so surreal. Our kids will be cousins. And not like pretend cousins, but actual cousins."

That got a smile out of her as she pointed at my stomach. "You have some catching up to do, then."

"Julian will be more than happy to help me with that," I laughed.

She wrinkled her nose. "Ew. I think I changed my mind."

"What?"

"Maybe you shouldn't get pregnant. It will be like a daily reminder that you've had sex with my brother."

The hairdresser snorted behind me, and I laughed harder.

"Gemma, it might be time to get over that. I've had sex with your brother *a lot*."

"*Juniper*." The door from the ensuite bathroom took that inopportune moment to fly open. "*Gross*."

"La-la-la-la-la-la-la." Gianna walked into the room with her fingers plugging her ears. "I can't hear you."

"As far as I'm concerned," Janie said dryly, "you and Julian don't even kiss."

"You've *seen* us kiss," I laughed.

"Shhhhh." Janie put her fingers to her lips while dramatically shushing me.

"Fine." I pretended to pout. "I'll talk to Nessa and Sofia about my sex life then."

Nessa laughed as she leaned in the doorway to the bathroom, and I saw Sofia smile in the bathroom mirror as she applied mascara.

"There's no way that Julian makes it until tonight without stealing you away for a quickie. That man is obsessed," Nessa said, and there was a collective groan from the other half of the room where all the Briggs sisters were.

"You can talk to Nessa and Sofia about your sex life all you want, but can you at least wait until we're out of the room?"

Ignoring them, I replied to Nessa. "And what about your wedding? Did Grayson make it to the end?"

Nessa grinned wickedly. "Oh, I made a no-sex rule for the ten days leading up to our wedding, and Grayson just about died. He nearly ended the entire reception early just because he'd had enough waiting."

"But you made him wait until the end, didn't you?" I asked, wishing I'd been there to witness Grayson's desperation. It would have made for an entertaining show.

Nessa nodded, a shine of mischief in her eyes.

"I can't wait to watch Julian struggle as soon as he sees you,"

Sofia snickered as she walked out of the bathroom. "I'm sure he'll be looking at you just like he did at *my* wedding."

She exchanged a look with Nessa since they'd both been there to witness the beginning of Julian and me.

Or rather, the *new* beginning.

The real beginning was years and years ago, on a sunny fall day in the Briggs' backyard in Whitebridge, Massachusetts—the day I met my new best friend's brother and then struggled every day after to get him out of my head.

"He was *acting* at your wedding," I emphasized to Sofia, who now knew the truth about my wedding date that weekend.

Her laugh rang around the hotel room, bouncing off the luxury linens and beautiful arrangements of flowers that Julian had placed around the space.

"He was *not* acting," she insisted. "He was the most convincing fake boyfriend *I've* ever seen. Please, I was just waiting for the two of you to disappear from the reception to release some of that tension. *Whew*."

Sofia fanned her face dramatically, Nessa's grin turned smug, and I felt a flush work its way up my neck.

"Well, I did end up kissing him that night," I admitted, "but then—"

"Okay, okay," Gemma interrupted. "We get it. You have the hots for our brother."

"I was *going* to say nothing happened because Julian decided I was too drunk."

"He's too responsible for his own good sometimes," Janie muttered.

"I thought so, too, but then that side of Julian vanished when—"

I cut myself off when I saw Gemma's bug-eyed face. Okay, maybe I didn't need to relay the details of how Julian both fingered and fucked me in our office.

"Don't stop there!" Nessa exclaimed, followed by the disagreement of all my future sisters-in-law.

I just shook my head with a laugh. I'd tell her the gist of it later. But keep the dirty details to myself, of course. I liked that I could hold onto those secrets and have them be just for Julian and me. There was something beautiful about the weeks when it had just been the two of us, but I also wouldn't trade getting to share it for the world.

A knock on the door saved me from having to explain myself too much. Gianna rushed forward to let one of our photographers into the suite, who then led all the bridesmaids to the adjoining living area to take some getting-ready photos as they got into their dresses. Only Gemma stayed behind to keep me company while my hairdresser started pinning my hair this way and that.

When someone knocked on the door again, Gemma crossed the room, cracked open the door, and promptly slammed it shut again before screaming, "Go away, Julian!"

He knocked on the door harder, and I couldn't help but smile. It had only been a few hours, but I missed him and was aching to see him.

"Open the door, Gemma!"

She glared at the closed door in response. "Why?"

"Because I want to see my wife," he replied, and my stomach erupted into a million butterflies.

"She's not your wife yet," Gemma pointed out, which I knew Julian would hate. My smile grew.

"Just open the fucking door, Gemma," Julian groaned.

"No, she's still getting ready." Gemma cracked the door again, peering around it to glare at her brother. "You can see her at the first look."

"I'm impatient," he grunted, giving the door a little push that had Gemma taking a quick step backward.

"Careful!" I called. "You're going to hurt the maid of honor if you're not careful, Jules."

"I don't care if it's your wedding day," another low, male voice cut in, "if you knock over your pregnant sister, I will kick your ass."

Gemma stilled by the door while I beamed broadly. "Noah, come in here! I need to talk to you."

"You're going to let him in and not me?" Julian growled on the other side of the door while Gemma crossed the room to close the adjoining door behind which the other girls were finishing getting into their dresses.

"Yep, that would be correct."

Julian cursed under his breath, but a second later, Gemma raced back to let Noah in. Only Noah. I tried to catch a glimpse of my fiancé, but it was futile. Gemma carefully controlled the door's angle so that neither of us could see the other and had to grab Noah by the tie to yank him in quick before Julian barged in afterward.

Noah's eyes immediately swept toward Gemma, and the room filled with a hot tension that should have probably been my clue to look away. But I was too intrigued for my own good and watched as Noah shoved his hands into the pockets of his dress pants while dropping his gaze over Gemma, memorizing every inch of my best friend while she shifted on her feet, growing rosy in the cheeks.

Once Noah had his fill of Gemma, he turned toward me. "What's up?"

"I was wondering if you could do me a huge favor. I left Julian's present in my car, and—"

A knock at the door once again interrupted.

I sighed. "Gemma, can you go keep Julian company so he doesn't cause damage to the property?"

Gemma shook her head with a small smile but went into the hallway all the same. Before long, I heard the two siblings pick up their banter where they left off. Knowing I didn't have much time, I turned to Noah.

"Look, I can tell Gemma isn't feeling great today."

He blanched, and I realized I could have phrased my words better. "What do you mean? What's wrong? Is it the baby? Do I need to take her to the—"

"No, no." I waved his worries away. "She's fine. She's totally fine. Just feeling a little uncomfortable in her skin, I think. I can only imagine carrying another life inside you would do that."

"I think she looks beautiful." Worry still threaded in his expression, he glanced toward the door where Gemma had just stood. "I think she looks beautiful carrying that little life, I only wish—"

Noah broke off, seeming to realize that he was about to admit something he hadn't even fully admitted to himself.

I lowered my voice. "You might not biologically be that baby's father, but you've supported Gemma in a hundred ways that he hasn't. Thank you for that."

His eyes shuttered as they slowly moved back to me. He gave a brief nod to acknowledge what I'd said, but I knew he needed to hear more.

So, I told him.

I told him exactly what he needed to know if he wanted to have Gemma in the way I suspected he craved. And then when I finally saw understanding and determination shine in his eyes, I waved him off. He had things to take care of. But not before I gave in and said, "Can you let Julian in when you leave?"

Noah lifted a brow. "You sure?"

"Yeah." I grinned. "I'm sure."

I wasn't in my wedding dress yet, and there was something I really wanted him to do. Noah nodded, and as he walked away, I turned to my hairdresser and explained what I was thinking, which she enthusiastically agreed to. By the time I looked toward the door again, Julian was standing there, looking frightfully handsome in his tux.

"Hey, Juni baby," he said, the soft side of Julian fully on display. His eyes were bright as they looked over me.

"Hey baby," I breathed in return. "Can you help me with something?"

"Anything."

I grabbed the lacy, white bow from the top of the dresser and lifted it up for him to see.

"Can you pin this in my hair for me?"

Julian's gaze glossed over at the sight of the bow, and he quickly crossed the room toward me. "I'd love to, Daisy."

He took the bow from me and pinned it into my hair with the same love and care he had that night in a New York hotel. Because Nessa and Sofia were right: he hadn't been pretending. Julian had been caring for me for so long, even if he didn't always show it in the best of ways.

And I'd loved him for just as long.

Thankfully, tonight I got to marry him.

THE END

acknowledgments

IT FEELS VERY SURREAL to be here, and to be writing this. But I wouldn't be here if it were not for the help and support of so many. I am so grateful to be surrounded by a community of people who have encouraged me to chase this dream.

Thank you, first and foremost, to my readers. To those who have been here since the beginning as well as those who are new to my author journey. Thank you for believing in me and thank you for being here. I wouldn't be anywhere without you.

To Nate, thank you for never diminishing my love of writing and for believing in me from the very beginning. Thank you for always getting me an extra cup of coffee when I need it to get things done.

Caitlin, thank you for wearing all the hats—from cover designer to beta reader to idea bouncer to swag creator to, of course, best friend. Thank you for putting up with how much I've talked about this for so many months.

To the best group of beta readers I could possibly ask for, thank you for your invaluable feedback. Thank you for helping to shape this book into what it is today by providing me with your knowledgeable and unique perspectives.

Jessica and Alwyn, thank you for being such wonderful critique partners and for taking the time to provide me with thoughtful and meaningful insights that were integral to my editing process.

Sandra, thank you for your editing expertise and for helping to polish this draft into what it is today.

To the online writing community and my talented author friends, thank you for the collective support and for being there to answer my many questions. I'm so grateful to know you all.

To the brat pack, thank you for reading my first inkling of a story back in ninth grade and sticking with me until we made it here.

Lastly, thank you to my family. You might not have been very good at keeping this a secret, but your enthusiasm and excitement for me makes up for it. I am so lucky to have you.

about the author

AMELIE RHYS is a romance author with a love for writing swoony stories packed with tension and heat. When she's not daydreaming about fictional characters, Amelie loves to travel new places (so she can write about them) and find new coffee shops and bookstores (so she can curl up and read in them). Amelie also likes spending time at the lake with her family. She lives in Minnesota with her husband and two rescue dogs.